Godfrey's Bookshop

~

**Doctor Godfrey Warlock,
purveyor
of rare and unusual books**

~

**Be warned, step into his bookshop
at your peril**

~

Alan Brookes

Published by New Generation Publishing in 2022

Copyright © Alan Brookes 2022

First Edition

ISBN
Paperback   978-1-80369-423-8
Hardback   978-1-80369-424-5

www.newgeneration-publishing.com

 New Generation Publishing

To readers of my book, the following quotes from esteemed citizens of the world may become useful in understanding where the initiations and conclusions of the story originate.

If you're a sleeping dreamer, come in.
If you're a daydreamer, a wisher, a liar, a hoper, a pray-er, a magic bean buyer, come in.
If you're a pretender, come sit by my fire, for we have some flaxen golden tales to spin.

Shel Silverstein, Philosopher 1923

Imagination is stronger than knowledge. Myth is more potent than history.
Dreams are more powerful than facts. Hope always triumphs over experience.
Laughter is the only cure for grief. Love is stronger than death.

Robert Fulghum, Psychologist 1976

I am enough of an artist to draw freely upon my imagination. Imagination is more important than knowledge. Knowledge is limited. It's imagination that encircles the world.

Albert Einstein, Scientist 1929

Imagination will often carry us to worlds that never were, but without it, we go nowhere.

Carl Sagan, Cosmologist at NASA 1969

A well-composed book is a magic carpet on which we are wafted to a world that we cannot enter in any other way.

Caroline Gordon, Author 1988

Reality leaves a lot to the imagination.

John Lennon. Musician 1979

Trust that little voice in your head that says, 'Wouldn't it be interesting if…; and then do it.'

Duane Michals, Philosopher

Satan isn't as black as he's painted.
In fact, he's more like us
than we care to admit.

Sir Alfred Hitchcock 1899-1980
English film director

Preface

Readers of modern fiction books seek escapism with stories describing adventures and situations out of reach of an ordinary person. However, contemporary authors create a plethora of imaginary crime, sex, and violence; the subject of such tawdry novels, to appease the insatiable pastime of such aficionados. The prime motive for most of these fashionable authors is profit rather than creating a literary masterpiece. The more renowned bookshops encourage and fulfil the public's desire for such melodrama by packing their bookshelves with the habit-forming fictional digests. The following week, the readers sequester most of the books to an idle bookshelf or recycle them at a charity shop. An analogy to this repetitive procedure is buying a newspaper eager to read its sensational headlines, only to use the same newspaper in which to wrap next week's fish and chips.

Doctor Godfrey Warlock offers discerning bibliophiles the opportunity to break free from such mundane fiction. His new bookshop caters for the more educated reader, who wants quality writing, symptomatic of the eighteenth and nineteenth-century's classic authors. Whatever the individual taste of the reader, Godfrey is guaranteed to supply a suitable book for them. Casual passers-by are at once attracted to his atmospheric, dusty, olde-worlde bookshop and by the hedonistic signboard hanging on squeaking, swinging chains above his low-hanging door. Be warned, step into his bookshop at your peril.

Doctor Godfrey Warlock,

Purveyor of rare and

unusual books

1

Prologue

Detective Inspector Donald Lawrence unashamedly muttered to himself as he ventured across Cannock Chase, a few short miles from where he lives with his growing family.

The virginal morning frost creates a stillness in the air that any church would be difficult to equal. He smiled at the reluctant thawing hoarfrost, stubbornly clinging to spiky yew tree fronds.

The winter sun was still slumbering behind the dense, grey sky and, as he walked, a cloud of his breath emerged into the mawkish air. At least, he convinced himself it was breath and not a ghoulish apparition. It's challenging not to let imagination overcome sensible reason when you're walking to one of the most haunted places in England.

Gazing south from Castle Ring, sandwiched between Gentleshaw and Upper Slaughter villages, stands Beaudesert Woodland on the garish valley's eastern slopes. Believed to date back to 8000 BC, this abandoned ten-acre forest on the southern edge of Cannock Chase has grown unregulated from human intervention thanks to the large, moss-covered boulders that line the forest floor. Because of unfettered growth, the dwarf oak trees, averaging six metres tall, have become gnarled with their finger-like branches contorting around one another, resembling a scene from a Grimm Brothers fairy tale.

Given its unearthly appearance, it's little wonder neighbouring inhabitants have attached many supernatural tales to the woodland. The early eighteenth-century writings of the local historian, Edwin Baxter, suggest the Druids conducted human sacrifices in the wood twelve centuries ago; Cannock Chase folklore claims the devil and his hell hounds, with blood-red eyes and awesome distorted fangs, rove the land looking for errant travellers.

As Donald set off from The Red Lion Hotel and walked along the unkempt bridleway towards the woodland, it hitherto was inconceivable to equate the stories with what he could see and hear. It was peaceful. Songbirds circled above, their voices resonating up and down the scales like an orchestra trying to reverberate in tune. The river washed through the lowlands. Black Aberdeen Angus cows and fleece-laden, pregnant Merino sheep grazed on either side of the water, greedily guzzling the ochre-coloured grass.

In springtime and summer, wildflowers clung to each rock, erupting into colour. But in the winter, the view is of bracken and gorse. They pop out of the earth in every direction, dropping over the valley as if in mourning of lost loved family. Donald passed a traditional stone farmhouse with white smoke cheerfully puffing from its blackened chimney, and followed the footpath alongside the cottage's dry-stone garden wall until he came to a sign engulfed in such thick moss it resembled a salvaged piece of a sunken ship shrouded in barnacles and coral.

After thirty minutes of walking, he caught his first glimpse of Beaudesert woodland on the other side of the valley. It looked dark and haunted: the oak tree's crooked branches created an oppressive canopy that caused the forest to appear reminiscent of an overturned bird's nest.

At that point, he realised his hiking boots were essential, as the footpath ended, and he crossed the open moorland and its sodden soil until he reached a stone wall.

It was at this moment that the paranormal stories of the ancient forest made sense. The dry, sandstone barrier felt like a partition between human life and the mystical world of the forest. Behind him, birds circled the sky, and the river meandered through the valley. But in front, all he could see were granite boulders with no discernible pattern, jutting out of the earth all the way towards the intriguing opening into the woodland.

At first glance, the convex stone slabs set along the entrance and the woodland floor looked identical, but they're not. According to Baxter, the Druids conducted pagan rituals within the woodland. They carved spirals and symbols into the moss and lichen that is still visible today, most clearly in an enormous boulder known as 'The Druid's Stone' or 'The Bull's Rock'.

However, the spirits of Druids and their victims aren't the only beings to wander the wood. Local legend retells the mythical tale that, come nightfall, the woodland becomes the kennels of Warlocks' hounds; dogs with huge fangs and a bone-chilling howl, who hunt across the bracken and moss-strewn moors for lost travellers. It's ancient but pervasive folklore, with locals still reluctant to venture to the woods once the sun goes below the horizon. As if responding to a director's cue, far off in the distance, he heard a dog barking. The yapping echoed around the woodland as clearly as a sound repeats itself in an enclosed building such as a cathedral dome, or buried cellar.

Thanks to its bloody history, the local vicar in 1791 declared that 'It's hardly possible to conceive anything of the sort so grotesque as this woodland appears.'

As Donald reached the wood and gazed at the twisted and gnarled branches of the stunted oak trees, grotesque wasn't the first word that came to mind. A convoluted maze seemed more apt, replicating twisted bonsai trees in a Japanese walled Zen garden.

It was strange looking, though. The trees bizarrely contort themselves around one another, with the last of their silvery leaves clinging onto them, before dropping to the forest carpet. Boulders stick out of the ground akin to remnants of an pre-historic asteroid shower, the stone colour long lost underneath blankets of slippery, fuzzy green mosses. Slimy lichens adorn the aged branches, hanging down and swaying in the wind like layers of straggly witches' hair. Pungent bilberries grow on the rocky floor, and ferns extend out of the trunks, silently observing anyone who enters the woodland, not unlike a security guard at a rarely used provincial museum.

Donald clambered through, from time to time losing his footing on the slimy moss, trying to find a boulder with enough stone remaining so he could stop and absorb the tastes, sounds, and aromas of the surroundings. The vivid odour of earth and age engulfed the woodland. As he sat on a pitted boulder on the edge of the forest, Donald watched the water trickle down the Redmoor stream, perpetually carving its passageway back towards the Red Lion Hotel, where he'd started the walk. Further down the valley, he watched a silhouetted figure of a bearded, stooped man emerge from the forest with his lively German shepherd dog bounding in front of him. 'One day, I'll return with Janet to order an Abbot cider and an Upper Slaughter cream tea. It would make for a rewarding tonic after a time exploring the mysterious Beaudesert woodlands,' he thought, inhaling the aromatic scent of feral wild garlic, infused with sweet hyacinth.

One

The ordinary brick-built semi-detached house at number nine Laburnum Avenue in Cannock Chase, England, didn't look any different from the other twenty-seven homes in the quiet suburban neighbourhood. When the local council built the houses, elaborate architecturally designed features were not a primary consideration. The tenants were equally as indifferent about such matters; they were satisfied simply to have a home in which to live with their families. Times were hard, and society classed most residents in this area of South Staffordshire as impoverished, with many of them subsisting on state-subsidised welfare benefits. Harry and Maria Bailey lived a happy life with their six-year-old daughter, Mary. However, their life was irrevocably transformed when Harry developed a newfound interest in literature that turned his focus away from everyday life and providing for his family.

'I don't know what's the matter with you these days, Harry. You don't speak to me, or anyone else anymore. I found little Mary crying the other night. When I asked her what was the matter, she told me you frighten her. What sort of father are you to create such fear in an innocent young mind? You sit here all day reading your ridiculous books. I know you've lost your job because we've no money in this house. Goodness knows how we're going to pay all the bills mounting up. Harry! Are you listening to me? Talk to me, for God's sake!'

Harry wasn't listening. Absorbed within his own private, inanimate world, his sole concentration focussed on the words in his book. Except for his forefinger turning the next page, his solitary physical movements were the iris of his eyes moving across the pages.

Maria busied herself in their meagre kitchen, preparing a vegetable stew from the few scraps she'd salvaged from the rubbish bins at the rear of the local supermarket. Harry came sauntering into the kitchen. 'Oh, so you've got up off your fat, idle arse, have you…?' Maria couldn't finish reproaching her husband. His powerful hands encircled her neck in a vice-like grip. She dropped the potato peeler she was holding and managed a few spittle laden gurgles before, wide-eyed, she slumped lifeless to the floor. As if in a hypnotic state, Harry reached into the cutlery drawer for the razor-sharp, serrated bread knife. With no hesitancy, he drew the blade across his unshaven neck and looked to the ceiling with a smile as his fresh, steaming blood trickled to the floor.

Two

Donald was born in Swanscombe on the River Thames' mud-spattered shoreline in Kent. The landscape of his suburban beginnings could never enthral his senses in the same way as his ethereal stroll over the moorlands and through the woodlands of Cannock Chase. Returning to his busy office at Cannock's police station, he felt rejuvenated and more competent to deal with the myriad of different incidents requiring his attention. Assimilating the qualities of the natural ecological environment gave him a more balanced perspective on life.

Detective Constable James Garbett, the newly appointed police officer, quickly brought him down to earth. 'Gov,' he called, 'can you come here, please?' Donald sauntered over to James's desk in the main office.

'What's the problem?' Donald slurped his mug of tea as he looked at James, anxiously holding his telephone.

'There's a paramedic on the phone. They've been called to a house in Laburnum Avenue. It sounds like there's been a murder, gov ...'

'... Get the address and we'll go there now!' Donald barked, with urgency. He slammed the hot, porcelain mug down on James's desk, causing the tea to slop across the polished surface. 'Damn it!' he yelled. He looked appealingly across at Veronica, his secretary.

''Leave it! Don't worry, I'll clean it up,' she replied, with a frustrated expression. 'Men!' she exclaimed, as Donald and James rushed out of the office.

'What motive possesses a bloke to wake up suddenly one morning, decide to strangle his wife and then commit suicide?' Donald muttered to James. They eyed with distaste the sight of Harry and Maria Bailey lying dead on their kitchen floor in a massive pool of Harry's congealed blood. James, the recruit, was keen to impress his gov and offered a motive. 'Perhaps they'd had a row. He strangled her and then couldn't face what he'd done?'

Donald nodded. 'In the absence of any other scenario, a domestic is the only reason we can assume for now. Good thinking, James, but let's keep an open mind. Usually, when couples have a blazing row, accompanied by violence, they leave behind evidence of upset furniture, or other damage. There's not a thing out of place. Look how tidy the house is.'

Paramedics had been called to Laburnum Avenue having been contacted by Maria Bailey's neighbour, aware of little Mary's constant screaming. Sitting in his office at the Cannock town centre's police station, Donald had been enjoying a rare quiet interval. It seemed residents had turned over a new leaf and now lived more peaceable lives. The phone call they'd received from the paramedics at once shattered the unusual calm. As he investigated the tragic murder and suicide, the more he would question how he viewed humanity's sanity and how he would conduct the rest of his life.

After leaving the kitchen's place of death to the Scene of Crime Officers, Donald and James began a routine search of the house. They found nothing untoward or out of order. Only when Donald casually looked at the opened book on the living room table did his usual unflappable demeanour change. His keen eyes noticed a few key words, encouraging further interest in the book. He read the words, '*strangled his wife.*' While James busied himself searching upstairs wardrobes, Donald drew a chair from under the table and read a further paragraph.

'*To gain respect and entry into God's immortal kingdom, it's necessary to perform deeds considered worthy of merit and courage. Taking the life of a close family member and then joining them in death is one such way of gaining God's recognition.*'

'What the devil does this mean?' Donald asked aloud.

'Are you alright, gov?' James called from upstairs. Donald didn't reply as he immersed himself in profound, troubling thoughts. He surmised Harry Bailey had committed precisely the same vile acts of murder and suicide described in the book.

Had Donald examined the hardback more closely, he would have noticed the stamp of indelible red ink on its flysheet.

'***This book is the property of Doctor Godfrey Warlock, Purveyor of rare and unusual books.***'

Instead, Donald closed the book and left number nine, Laburnum Avenue, with the book tucked under his arm. Back at his office, in Wolverhampton Road, he routinely placed the book on his bookshelf among many others. The constraints of being a Detective Inspector police officer dictated his forthcoming tasks of completing endless paperwork to enable post mortems and other statutory responsibilities to take place.

Three

The following morning, Donald's workload ballooned when he took a National Health Service paramedic's phone call. 'Inspector Lawrence, this is Chief Paramedic Jules Askham here. I'm attending a fatality and supervising another patient's treatment at number six, Hornbeam Avenue, Cannock. There are things here leading me to think this death is suspicious, which is why I'm contacting you.'

Closing his mobile phone, Donald shouted to Constable Garbett. 'James, drop what you're doing; we have another fatality. Meet me in the car park. Chop, chop, the sooner we're on the scene, the more chance we have of securing evidence.'

'Hello, Inspector Lawrence, you may not remember me. You gave me your card at an earlier incident. I'm Chief Paramedic Askham ...'

'... Yes, I remember you, Jules. We met at the Heath Hayes road rage fatality. What do you have for me? Oh, this is my colleague, Detective Constable Garbett.' Jules mundanely shook hands with James as he led Donald towards the stairway.

'Upstairs. There's a young woman drowned in the bath. In the front room is a distressed elderly lady who called for help.' Climbing the stairs three steps at a time, they reached the bathroom. In a side bedroom, Donald noticed a naked man being treated on a stretcher. He had an oxygen mask over his face and two drips into his arm.

'What's the situation with this guy, Jules?'

'We found him unconscious, lying on the bathroom floor. Because of a deep wound on the side of his skull and the amount of blood on the toilet pedestal, we think he must have slipped and hit his head...'

'... is he...?'

'... No! The bloke should be okay; we're about to take him to casualty. It's the woman in the bath I'm more concerned about...'

'... I thought you said the woman's deceased?'

'Yes, she is...'

'... well, she's beyond all our concern now, isn't she?'

'What I meant to say is I think she's been murdered.'

'With due respect, Jules, it's for my colleague and me to determine whether a crime has been committed.'

'Yes, of course, I meant no disrespect, but I'm sure you'll come to the same conclusion.'

From a first glance at the dead woman, Donald immediately agreed with the paramedic's assumption.

'Well, Inspector?'

'Well, Jules, it looks as if you're right.' They both looked round when the other paramedic spoke.

'Boss Askham, I think we need to move this guy now; he needs urgent treatment in hospital.'

'Yeah, okay, I'm coming.' He looked at Donald. 'I'll be off then, Inspector...'

'Thanks, Jules; keep me informed about this guy, please. I obviously want to interview him when he comes round. Which hospital are you taking him to...?'

'Stafford General Infirmary.'

Donald and James turned to the dead woman. 'Do we know who she is, James?'

'I think so, gov; I've found some correspondence in a bedroom. A Mrs Carole Beecham. There are also letters addressed to a Mr Jack Beecham, so I assume he's the injured chap.' They stared at Mrs Beecham.

'What do you think, James?'

'It looks to me as if she's been strangled, gov, and then held under the water.'

'Yes, I agree. Look at the red and bluish marks around her neck. With her eyes and mouth being open, drowned while being strangled is my opinion. We'll wait until the Scene of Crime Officers give their official verdict and after a post mortem before we act on an assumption.'

'Okay, gov. I suppose the next question is, who did it, but I'm thinking we look no further than her husband?'

'Other than the elderly lady downstairs who rang 999, we have to consider the obvious. I'd guess Jack Beecham strangled his wife and then slipped on the ceramic tiled floor and hit his head on the toilet pedestal. Look at all the water on the floor. I'd suggest the woman struggled, splashing water all over the floor, causing him to slip. Have you spoken to the other woman, yet?' James shook his head. Donald verified the ceramic tiles were slippery by sliding his rubber-soled shoes across the surface.

'Go downstairs and interview her. She's bound to be distressed, be sympathetic and caring.'

'Okay, gov.' On the stairway, James passed the Scene of Crime Officers. Donald moved out of the small bathroom to give them access. He looked in each of the three bedrooms on the first floor. The Beechams used the smaller bedroom as a storeroom. Another bedroom was in use as a study.

Donald focussed his attention on the Beecham's bedroom. The bed was tidy, with only the top cover being slightly crumpled, suggesting someone had laid on top of the bedclothes. He sat on the bed and gazed at each bedside table. There were books stacked on each table, suggesting the Beechams were avid readers. On the left-hand table lay unopened books on fictional romance. 'So, Mrs Beecham lay this side.' Donald assumed. He peered more closely at the right-hand table, 'by elimination must be the husband's side,' Donald's thoughts extended to what he was reading. 'The usual wartime adventure stories, Tom Clancy's, and Alistair MacLean's. Oh, what's this?' He picked up the topmost book with a bookmark inserted, entitled *The Path to Glory.* Holding the book in his hand, it fell open at the leather bookmark. He read a few words.

'The pathway to perpetual life is guaranteed when the tunnel by which we must all pass is enabled underwater. If you have a loved one in your life who is suffering illness and disease, the kinder path to take is set them on the watery trail to Glory.'

Donald read in silence, and his assumptions on Mrs Beecham's death remained silent. 'It appears the husband has deliberately drowned his wife. Perhaps she's been poorly, and he's seen himself as an angel of mercy and saved her from further suffering? It suggests a mercy killing.' Donald closed the book and put it back on the bedside table as James entered the room.

'Gov, the elderly woman downstairs is Mrs Beecham's mother. She's eighty-five years old and suffering from severe rheumatoid arthritis. She phoned 999 when she heard the bumping and banging coming from the bathroom. Because of her condition, she couldn't climb the stairs. She has a granny flat downstairs where she sleeps.'

'Is she aware her daughter is dead?'

'Yes, but she's bewildered. I'd say she has a touch of dementia, too?'

'Okay, James. I think we've done all we can here for the time being. We need to chat to Mr Beecham as soon he becomes conscious.' They left the bedroom, James walking down the stairs first. Halfway down, Donald paused. He thought of the words in the book, *The Path to Glory*. 'I know it's a ridiculous coincidence, but this is the second death in two days where a novel has suggested the method for a subsequent death.' He remembered what his old colleague, Tom Cropper, used to tell him when he was a junior Detective Constable in the Metropolitan Police.

'However improbable, it's folly to disregard any fact pointing the way to the perpetrator of a crime.'

Donald turned and recovered the book. Once back at his office, he placed it on his bookshelf next to the book he'd retrieved from Laburnum Avenue. Donald was an excellent detective. Although totally unaware at this early stage of the investigation, he was already in possession of vital clues and evidence pointing to some sort of explanation for both deaths. Stamped in indelible red ink on its flysheet was: -

'This book is the property of Doctor Godfrey Warlock, Purveyor of rare and unusual books.'

Four

Detective Inspector Donald Lawrence had been in his post at Cannock Police Station for four months. He and his wife, Detective Sergeant Janet Lawrence, moved to Staffordshire from London following Donald's promotion to Inspector in the Staffordshire Constabulary.

For many years they had been colleagues in the Metropolitan Police at Scotland Yard, where they had been involved in a number of infamous and gruesome murder cases. With a six-month-old baby boy, Zak, to care for, Janet was now content to put her police career on hold. They relied upon her husband's income as the primary provider for their young family. Janet's absence from regular policing didn't diminish her enthusiasm and interest in Donald's cases and workload. It was usually while sitting at their dining table, consuming their evening meal, where Donald divulged information on his daily investigations.

'These two fatalities are very upsetting, aren't they, darling?' Janet expressed, remorsefully, as she reached for a spoonful of tartar sauce to supplement the fish and chips they were eating. 'Especially in a small town like Cannock, where such unpleasant things rarely happen. We're not in London anymore, where murders and suspicious deaths are a daily occurrence.'

Donald merely nodded as he was deep in thought about the tragic circumstances of each death.

Janet eyed his seriousness and clear melancholy and decided not to expand upon the matter. 'How's the new detective constable coming along? What's his name again, I've forgotten?'

'Oh, you mean, James Garbett? He's okay. Hard-working and has an enquiring mind. As you're aware, excellent qualities in an aspiring detective.'

'... I meant to tell you; I received a call from Lucy the other day. Zak has kept me busy with his tummy upset and extra dirty nappies. It slipped my mind to say.'

Donald looked at her, askance, noticing the absence of any changed intonation or inflexion in his wife's voice before taking soiled plates to the kitchen from where he called out. 'Oh, is she okay? Still keeping busy in the Fraud Squad, is she?'

'She's fine. She asked about you and Zak.' Janet raised her voice in response. 'Oh, and I asked Lucy to call as she's passing Cannock on the M6 motorway in a couple of weeks. She's driving up to the Manchester Constabulary concerning a suspect she's tracking in a fraud case.'

Donald returned with dishes holding two fruit salads. He smiled at Janet. 'I'm sure you'll have a pleasant day.'

Janet quickly added. '... I also asked her to stay a night with us. It's a long drive from London to Manchester and back. You don't mind, do you, darling?' She looked expectantly at her husband.

With no change in his demeanour, he answered between mouthfuls of fruit salad, 'No problem at all, darling.' Janet contentedly ate the rest of her dessert, knowing their friend, Lucy, no longer posed any threat to their marriage. Donald and Lucy had once been engaged to each other. Although Janet had suspected her husband and Lucy had become involved in a brief affair during the early days of their marriage, neither Donald nor Lucy had ever confessed to an affair, and Janet had never asked. Sharing blissful happiness with her husband and their son, Zak, made such reminiscences of the past forgotten and unnecessary.

Later in the evening, sitting around the cosy fireside in the lounge, Donald watched his wife breastfeeding Zak. 'Are you doing anything tomorrow, darling? I'm attending the Coroner's Court in Stafford...'

'Why will you need to be in court, darling?'

'The Baileys. Harry and Maria.'

'You're not expecting any unforeseen verdict, are you?'

'No, it seems like a straightforward murder and suicide.' He watched Janet tease Zak's mouth with her breast as their son slumbered. '... and you, darling?'

'... sorry?'

'... are you doing anything tomorrow?'

'Only going to the supermarket. The weather has promised a fine day, so I'll put Zak in the pushchair. Ooh, you little monster...' Janet cried out. 'He's bitten me.' She shared a laugh with Donald. 'Like father, like son,' Janet offered with a huge smirk. 'Oh, and I thought

I'd call in at the new bookshop in High Green, the modern designer precinct in the town centre.'

'New bookshop...?' Donald questioned.

'Yes. *Godfrey's Bookshop*. It's receiving rave reviews in the local Chronicle.'

Donald returned to the kitchen to place the used plates and dishes in the dishwasher. Janet poked her head through the door, 'Oh, and don't forget tomorrow evening, darling...'

He turned and gazed at her. His facial expression told her he'd forgotten what was happening. 'Remind me please, darling.'

'The Prince of Wales Theatre. We're attending a brass band concert tomorrow evening. Don't you remember the band's musical director gave you complimentary tickets when we visited the church fete?'

Five

Cannock Chase is the smallest 'Area of Outstanding Natural Beauty' in mainland Great Britain extending to fifty square miles of rolling hills and forests. Notwithstanding its size, the area possesses idyllic settings laden with leisurely walks with which to immerse yourself in the former Royal forest. The infamous King Henry VIII regularly hunted wild boar and deer among the purple heather and perpetually flowering yellow gorse.

The Reverend John Spencer, the incumbent vicar at Saint Botolph's evangelist church at Hedgefield, a suburb of Cannock Chase, resolutely climbed the few steps to his pulpit. His mind had become apathetic to the unspoiled, picturesque scenery that surrounded his church. He cared not for the royal patronage that former Kings of England bestowed upon his parish. His resolute mind focussed upon a momentous defining time in his incumbency of the little church. He opened the book he carried and cried out to his Sunday congregation, 'In my eulogy today, I will at last confess to you, my trusted disciples, precisely who I am.'

Several parishioners, sitting in the dour wooden pews, stared at their immediate neighbour with widened eyes, wondering what their vicar meant, before gazing up at Reverend Spencer.

'Yes, I can see the puzzled looks in your eyes, and I will explain. I've been your servant in our beloved church for the past four years, but the time has come for me to leave you...'

'... What?' Dorothy Whitehouse, sitting in the third row, involuntarily called, 'No, reverend, please don't move to another parish, you've become our friend...'

'... bless you, my child, I won't preside at another house of worship, but my Father has called me to join him at his right hand...' Dorothy held her hand to her face.

A collective sigh emitted from the thirty-two loyal churchgoers. Derek Broadbent, a retired plumber, sitting in the front row, asked the immediate question on most people's mind.

'Are you poorly, then, Reverend? Has the doctor given you a terminal prognosis?'

'... and bless you, my child, yes, I have a diagnosis, but not one given to me by an earthly doctor. My Father has called me, so shortly I will ascend to join him in heaven.' The Reverend John Spencer gazed upwards to the timber criss-cross vaulted roof structure and raised his arms aloft.

Agnes Harper whispered to the woman seated next to her in the second row. 'Oh, sweet Jesus, it appears the vicar is going to die. At least he has his faith to comfort him.'

The reverend heard Agnes' comments. 'Ah, Mrs Harper, are you the only one amongst us who knows who I am?' John stared accusingly at Agnes, flustered as she received the stares from others in the congregation.

'... er! Ahem! Um! Reverend. I don't know what you mean?' Agnes stumbled through her question.

'I think you do, my child. I am your Lord. Your Lord Jesus Christ. Your saviour. Returned to earth for the widely proclaimed second coming.' Again he raised his arms aloft and started mumbling.

'Poor bloke,' muttered old Jake Prosser, sitting on the back row, who wasn't a regular parishioner. He'd only entered the church to get out of the rain and pass the time until the pub opened at lunchtime. 'He's lost his marbles. He thinks he's Jesus. Bloody hell, I get more sense out of my drinking mates after they've had a few pints of ale. Wait until I tell them later what's been going on in here.'

Dorothy Whitehouse turned around to peer at the old man before turning to her husband seated next to her. 'I don't know who the man is, but I think he's right, Albert. It seems John is having delusions about being Jesus Christ.' Before Albert could answer, the reverend called out.

The entire wide-eyed congregation watched him closely, unsure what was to come next.

'My confirmed flock, we cannot do everything we want to do, but we should do everything God wants us to do. He's called me to tell you these things.' He raised his arms as if to embrace everybody, but then pointed to the side.

'Matthew, Mark, Luke and John, my trusted disciples, I thank you for your love and devotion. My trusted biographers, who through your writing will spread the word of the Lord.' The Reverend Spencer turned and stared at four church vergers sitting in the choir pews. One embarrassed man pulled his starched collar away from his flinching neck in acute discomfort, as his rising blood pressure caused him to sweat profusely. Another man looked to the mass of confused churchgoers, his eyes searching for his wife. He saw her beckoning to him from the side nave. Without uttering a sound, he squeezed past the other choir members and walked down the aisle. His wife joined him, and they left the church, arm in arm, passing Jake Prosser, who laughed.

'Aren't you stopping for the wine, then?' he joked. 'Jesus is going to change the water into wine soon. Perhaps I won't go to the pub; I can get a free drink in here.' His bubbling laughter echoed around the austere whitewashed walls, causing the reverend to gaze at where the jocularity was coming from. He slowly descended from the pulpit steps and sauntered down the aisle.

'We have a disbeliever amongst us, my children. Blessed are those who repent their sins and enter God's kingdom.' The congregation watched the reverend with morbid curiosity. He reached Jake Prosser and laid both his hands on his greasy head. 'Barabbas, repent your sins and join me in the kingdom of heaven. The Roman soldiers will crucify us together, and we'll enter my Father's house together, hand in hand...'

'Saints preserve us,' whispered Agnes Harper. John thinks the man is Barabbas, the thief who died with our saviour at Calvary.

'... No, you bloody well don't. You're off your head. You need certifying as insane. You're a bloody danger. No one's going to crucify me. I'm out of 'ere.' Jake prised himself from the reverend's grasp and banged the church door behind him. The reverend turned and ambled back to the altar.

'Come and join me in the last supper, my children, my flock, my disciples, for tomorrow I have a pre-ordained rendezvous at Calvary. Come! Come! Everyone except you, Judas Iscariot.' The reverend suddenly turned and pointed at a small, plump, inconsequential, balding man who sat quietly with his equally bemused wife.

'Me?... but reverend, I'm not Judas...'

'... you betrayed me for thirty pieces of silver...'

'... but reverend, enough of this play-acting nonsense. You haven't given your sermon yet....'

'... and don't think I've overlooked you, Peter. Before tomorrow morning, before the cock crows at dawn, you will deny me thrice.' He turned towards a tall, moustachioed, elderly grey-haired man, who returned the accusation with a wide-eyed stare. Before he could answer, the reverend once more raised his arms aloft and shouted. 'Who has the crown of thorns? Who has the nails? Forgive them Father, for they know not what they do.' He started mumbling before it turned into a giggle. Then, laughing hysterically, he ran to the side door in the nave and left the bewildered congregation. The church immediately burst into loud chatter, with everyone talking to their neighbour in the pews. The unanimous verdict of everyone concluded the Reverend John Spencer had lost his mind and possessed a fixation assuming the persona of Jesus Christ. Gradually the people left the church, confused and chattering to each other. A senior verger, Jacob Simpson, noticed the reverend had left behind an open book on the lectern in the pulpit. He walked up the few steps to retrieve the gold embossed ledger. When closing the book, he read the title with mounting inquisitiveness. *'Jesus Christ and the second coming.'* What he didn't read was the indelible red ink stamp on the inside of the rear cover.

'This book is the property of Doctor Godfrey Warlock, Purveyor of rare and unusual books.'

David and Margaret Shaw were the last parishioners to leave the church. They were as perplexed as everyone else with the Reverend Spencer's behaviour. In their early thirties, they had only lived in Cannock for six months. David was a signal operator with British Rail and had accepted a new post with the company, moving from Crewe in Cheshire. Since leaving school at fifteen years of age, David had always wanted to be a signalman on the railways. Crewe is a significant hub in the United Kingdom rail network. He relished the romance and importance of his job. Daily David directed goods and passenger trains on the busy London-West Coast routes. In the early days of his career, he enjoyed physically moving the levers that worked the points, diverting trains from one track to another. In the modern digital age, computers now controlled a substantial part of his daily tasks. He was now, effectively, an administrative minion who constantly kept a check on the large screen digital displays showing where one train's position was in relation to the next arrival. David became bored and dissatisfied with his inconsequential life. When a post at Cannock in Staffordshire became available, advertised in *The Railwayman,* a journal published by his trade union, he applied at once. Albert and Margaret lived in the middle of a tawdry row of Crewe's Victorian hovels. They had been frugal and researched that they could afford a new detached house on Cannock's fashionable Hawks Green estate. In his new job as Controller of rail traffic, he had oversight of goods and passenger traffic on the active West Midland Railway.

For a while, David savoured the relative importance and new status in his life. However, he came to realise he was still an insignificant fish in a larger pond. He looked outwards to the exciting events that seemed to happen all around him, leaving him as a mere onlooker, incapable of influencing society. However, David's introverted view of the world changed the day he walked into *Godfrey's bookshop*. The book that Doctor Godfrey Warlock gave him to read made him realise the power he had within himself. He was now an essential member of society, capable of creating events and irrevocably changing Cannock and the surrounding areas. He foresaw the future where his name, David Shaw, would be in bold headlines on all the news bulletins and newspaper articles. Television networks would crave for an interview. Movie companies sought scriptwriters to portray his life story. He held his head high as he ambled from Saint Botolph's church with his wife, Margaret. He knew his destiny and appointed place in history would soon come to fruition.

Six

'I'll go, darling.' Donald whispered to Janet as Zak's crying had woken him. He noticed the red diodes on the digital clock displayed 06:45 and heard his wife's continual heavy breathing. Donald smiled, realising she was still sleeping. To avoid disturbing her, he tiptoed from the bedroom without switching on the light. Janet had prepared a bottle of milk the night before for their son, so Donald only had to re-heat the bottle in the kitchen. For the next thirty minutes he sat holding Zak, feeding the milk to him, while gazing outside at the approaching dawn lighting up the forests and moorland of Cannock Chase. His thoughts went to the busy day he had before him.

Donald gave his evidence at Stafford Coroner's Court at 10:30 that morning, describing how he and his junior colleague had discovered and investigated the scene of Harry and Maria Bailey's bodies. At 11:05, the coroner routinely gave his verdict to the sparsely attended court. 'While the balance of his mind was disturbed, Mr Harry Bailey strangled his wife before committing suicide. No other persons were involved, and there were no unusual circumstances.'

Outside the court, Constable James Garbett approached Donald. 'Well, the proceedings went as we expected, gov.' Donald nodded. 'Have a look at my mobile phone.' James showed him the text message on the screen. 'I've received this from Jules Askham, the paramedic. He says Jack Beecham has regained consciousness in Stafford Hospital.'

'Ah! So, while we're in Stafford, we may as well visit the hospital now, but we'll have a cup of coffee first.'

Donald and James showed their identification badges to the officious ward sister, Joan Harrison. She forcefully remonstrated with the police officers. 'Mr Beecham is extremely poorly and under sedation with morphine. I can only allow you to speak to him for a few moments, Inspector. It would be best if you made an appointment next time you wish to visit him.'

'I hear what you are saying, madam, and I know you are only doing your job, but I am doing mine too. Mr Beecham is the prime suspect in the murder of his wife,' Donald handed his card to her. '... Rather than make an appointment to visit here again, I'd be grateful if you would ring me when Mr Beecham is well enough to be interviewed. Where is he...?' Donald held out his arms to reinforce his question.

'Staff!' The sister called as she looked at Donald's card. A red-faced staff nurse came to their side.

'Yes, sister?'

'Staff Nurse Thompson, show these two police officers to Mr Beecham's side ward, please. Good day, gentlemen!'

Donald and James didn't return the ward sister's comments and followed the junior staff nurse who walked down the ward, closely followed by James. Rather than watching where they were going, he stared at the straight seam of the Staff Nurse's tights adorning her shapely legs. He nearly bumped into her as she stopped suddenly and pointed. 'This is Mr Beecham's ward, gentlemen.' She returned James's stare and smiles before walking away. His gaze followed her, and she didn't hear Donald's voice.

'I'm Detective Inspector Donald Lawrence of the Staffordshire Constabulary. I'm here to ask you about your wife, Mrs Carole Beecham...'

'... go away...'

'... do you understand what I'm asking you, Mr Beecham?'

'Yes, but I don't want to talk about it.'

'Why...?'

'... because she's dead.' Jack raised his voice as sweat appeared on his brow, and his eyes started darting from side to side. 'Leave me alone!' he shouted.

A figure in the doorway temporarily blocked the light into the ward. From the imposing silhouette of Sister Harrison, her icy voice barked at Donald.

'I've already told you, Inspector. You've had a few moments with my patient. I'm asking you to leave now. Can't you see how much distress you've already caused him?'

Donald turned to Constable Garbett. 'Come on, James, we must do a more in-depth interview with Mr Beecham another time.' Despite the sister glaring at Donald, he never made eye contact with her as he left the ward.

About the same time as Donald and James were leaving the Coroner's Court, Janet, dressed in a loose, flowery dress, strolled into Cannock's bustling Market Street. Pushing Zak in his pushchair, she chatted cheerfully to passers-by, gazing into various shop windows as she ambled along. She shielded her eyes from the dazzling sun and pulled down the pushchair's hood to create some shade for Zak, who dozed contentedly. A neighbour, adorned with a scarf wrapped around her head like a turban, stopped and made pleasant conversation with Janet but turned when they heard someone shouting. They looked up when other loud voices disturbed the earlier tranquil location.

'What's going on?' Janet's neighbour, Barbara Williams, asked. 'The general election is only a few months away. I bet it's politicians canvassing for people's votes.'

'The voices sounded quite offensive, Mrs Williams. I don't think they'll win the sympathy of many voters, and certainly not mine....' They heard laughter intermingling with the shouts. Mrs Williams and Janet stretched their necks to see what was happening.

'Why, that looks like a tree trunk or a beam of wood moving in the crowd. Over there, Janet, look!' The sound of people shouting and laughing grew closer. Zak suddenly awoke and started crying, adding to the mounting confusion.

'Oh, my God, there's blood...' Mrs Williams shouted to Janet, but she had bent down to console Zak. She put a dummy in his mouth, and he started dozing again.

'... blood?' Janet asked as she gazed at where the escalating commotion was taking place. Through a gap in the ever-increasing throng of people, Janet glimpsed a scene from a biblical film epic. A man covered in blood with a crown of thorns pressed into his head was labouring with a large wooden cross across his shoulders. Splattered in blood, his long white surplice trailed behind in the dust.

'May God and all the saints preserve us...' Mrs Williams uttered, holding her hand across her mouth. 'It's the Reverend John Spencer from Saint Botolph's Church...'

'Saint Botolph's? Where's that?' Janet asked, wide-eyed at the gruesome spectacle.

'... in Hedgefield, three miles from Cannock. Whatever is he doing replicating Jesus's march to being crucified at Calvary...?' Her voice became drowned out by the mounting derision and laughter from the people who followed and mocked the Reverend Spencer.

'Oh, my God, some youngsters are throwing things at him...' Janet uttered as they then heard a police siren. A few seconds later, three junior constables, whom Janet recognised as Donald's colleagues, raced past them. The din and confusion abated. Gazing over the tops of people's heads, they saw the wooden cross lowered and two constables support Reverend Spencer as he slumped between them in near exhaustion.

'Out of the way, thank you. Make room, please,' the third constable shouted to people gathered around, as his flustered colleagues dragged Reverend Spencer away. Janet and Mrs Williams eyed each other in disbelief at what they had seen.

'Well, I never did...!' Mrs Williams exclaimed. 'The things you see these days, it beats anything happening on television.' Janet's neighbour aimed her comments more to herself. She continued her shopping, leaving Janet to comfort Zak, who had burst out crying again. By the time Zak had ceased crying, the crowd had dispersed, and Janet continued her stroll, content that her baby son was sleeping soundly. Turning the corner from Market Street into High Green, she saw the Reverend Spencer being transferred on a stretcher into an ambulance parked next to two police cars. A creaking noise emphasised the intense contrast in ambience and noise from the tumultuous racket in Market Street to the sedate and peaceful High Green. She gazed upwards to see a signboard hanging by chains gradually swinging in the gentle breeze. She read the calligraphy style writing:

Doctor Godfrey Warlock, Purveyor of rare and unusual books.

'Oh, this is the bookshop mentioned in The Chronicle.' Janet applied the brake on the pushchair and peered into the large, dimpled, glazed panels fronting the shop. She had difficulty seeing anything, not even any books. Janet wondered if the windows were backed with a non-transparent material and cupped her eyes with her hand to blank out the light. What she saw made her jump backwards in fright. A grimacing, grey-haired man with piercing eyes had his face pressed against the window, staring directly at her.

'What!' Janet shouted and gazed at Zak who, thankfully, hadn't moved. Standing back from the window, she returned her gaze to the window to see the man now smiling at her.

'Phew!' She smiled back at him and put her hand across her heart, demonstrating that he had frightened her.

'I'm sorry,' Janet saw him mime. Bending over, he pointed at a mini signboard at the bottom of the window, replicating the prominent billboard swinging above her. The man mimed again. 'I'm Godfrey Warlock. This is me.' Pointing at his name. Janet noticed his unusual features. Spiky, grey hair topped his ruddy, clean-shaven complexion, giving way to a small, black goatee beard. Standing upright again, she noticed how tall he was. Godfrey sported a dark, old-fashioned waistcoat contrasting with a flamboyant, yellow, polka-dot bowtie.

'Ah! I see.' Janet joined in the miming interchange. He waved at her, beckoning her to enter his shop. She walked a few paces towards the shop door. A bell hanging above the door dinged as Godfrey held the door open for her. Before Janet had poked the front wheels of the pushchair across the threshold, Zak suddenly started wailing and screaming in obvious distress. His arms and legs thrashed from side to side, kicking and banging the sides of the pushchair. He was trembling and shaking. Janet pulled the pushchair back onto the pavement and lifted Zak into her arms to comfort him. Godfrey closed the door and returned to the window, watching her. Janet gently bounced up and down, clutching Zak, who struggled and whimpered on her breast as if he were in pain. A woman walking past looked across, alarmed at the baby's intense crying disturbing the quiet precinct.

'There, there, darling. What on earth's the matter?' Janet's soothing words caused Zak's sudden outburst to stop. With tearful, reddened eyes, he looked upwards at his mother as if pleading with her not to upset him again. A movement from the window diverted her attention. Godfrey held a book against the glass, so Janet could read the title. '*How to control unruly children.*' Janet smiled and shook her head. She mimed at Godfrey. 'Thank you, anyway,' and walked away. The rest of her eventful shopping day went ahead without incident. She only thought about the earlier unpleasant event when she walked through a trail of Reverend Spencer's blood.

Seven

As the grandfather clock in the hall chimed seven o'clock, the long entrance room echoed to a sharp rap on the door. DC James Garbett had answered his superior's request to babysit, while he and Janet attended the brass band concert. The world famous Black Dyke Mills Band from Queensbury, Yorkshire, was to perform a gala concert in the new Prince of Wales Theatre in Church Street, next to Saint Luke's Church. Dressed in a bright blue silk blouse and pleated skirt, Janet opened the door to him. 'Come in, James. I have everything ready in the kitchen.' James followed her, where she pointed out two ready-made bottles of milk, a bottle of gripe water and some tea and sandwiches for him.

'Thanks for coming, James. I'd forgotten all about this concert, that's why I only asked you this morning. I'm sorry for the short notice,' Donald said as he entered the kitchen. 'Are you ready, darling?'

'Almost. I've put the tickets on the hall table.' Janet turned to James. 'I hope this hasn't inconvenienced your plans, James? Do you have a girlfriend? If so, I hope she understands.'

Before James could answer, Donald commented, 'If he has, she's got serious competition. Isn't that right, James?' Donald arched his eyebrows at James.

'I don't know what you mean, gov?'

'I think you do. Staff Nurse Thompson, wasn't it?' James blushed slightly as he exchanged glances with Janet.

'Have a good time,' he called as he closed the front door behind them.

Once in the auditorium, they made their way to their splendid seats in the third row's centre. 'Oh, these seats are perfect, we have a superb view, and we should receive outstanding acoustics from here.' There wasn't a spare seat in the theatre as they made themselves comfortable. The first renderings of the musical ensemble confirmed Janet's expectations.

Major Peter Parkes, the Musical Director, announced their next piece of music was by Ludwig Van Beethoven. Spontaneous applause erupted when he announced it was the composer's esteemed ninth and final symphony.

After the sonorous opening, the band came to a quieter, more sedate section. Fifteen bars before the conductor extended his arms for the chorus *Ode to Joy,* a noise behind Donald and Janet disturbed their concentration. Sir Peter Parkes also heard the noise, but he didn't deviate from the score, testament to his professionalism.

'Sh!' Janet heard various people calling to where the noise had originated.

'I don't care.' A man's voice became more explicit.

'For goodness' sake, man, can't you keep quiet?' A woman sitting nearer the elevated stage turned and remonstrated with the middle-aged man who'd started waving his arms.

Major Parkes half turned to look at the woman, but turned further around to stare at the man waving his arms. He turned back to the band. 'Keep your concentration, band, ignore the disturbance...' Major Parkes eyed the score, knowing '*Ode to Joy*' was imminent.

There were still two bars of the sedate, pianissimo passage left when the man, dressed in an evening suit and black bow tie, stood, shouted, and walked towards the stage. Everyone glared at him, including some musicians, consequently allowing their concentration to waver.

'That's not how I composed the music. How dare you submit these poor, uneducated people to such a false, incomplete rendering of my symphony?' The moustachioed man finally had Major Parkes' full attention, and he turned to confront him. Dropping his arms, the band ceased playing. Donald and Janet turned to look at the man, wondering what was happening. The auditorium went silent.

In a stern, militaristic voice, the irate conductor asked. 'What seems to be the problem, sir? You are ruining the performance...'

'... me? Me! You, sir, are the problem. It's you who've ruined the performance. You, sir, are an infidel, an upstart. How dare you conduct my music like that? The *andante* section should be played in a more *cantabile* manner. What gave you the impertinence to begin my symphony at such an inflated tempo...?'

Major Parkes noticed two theatre security guards walking down the aisle. '... Your music? You say you wrote the score? May I remind you, sir, whoever you are, and before you get ejected from the theatre, it was Ludwig Van Beethoven who wrote the music in 1824...'

As the security guards reached the man, he shouted. '... and who do you think I am? It's me. I **am** Ludwig Van Beethoven...!'

'... Come with us, please.' As the guards tugged the man by his shoulders, the heels of his boots snagged on the carpet, causing it to tear.

'... And another thing, you are conducting the 12/8 rhythm all wrong. What sort of musician are you?' Everyone watched the man eventually leave the auditorium, and the audience's attention re-focussed upon the stage.

'Ladies and Gentlemen, because of this unprecedented disturbance, it's prudent to have a brief interval. We'll recommence the concert at 8:30.' Major Parkes gazed at his watch to verify the time before turning back to the band. 'Okay, fellows, let's leave the stage. I don't think we'll forget this evening,' and forged a tiny laugh that rippled through the ranks of musicians.

The audience erupted into multiple conversations as the theatre lights illuminated the auditorium. 'What the hell is wrong with people in Cannock, darling?' Janet raised her voice to Donald so he could hear her above the din. 'I haven't got around to telling you about a vicar in the town centre today imitating Jesus Christ by carrying a cross through the streets, and now this. A deranged man thinking he's Beethoven. Perhaps we should avoid drinking the water for the next few days, eh?' She exchanged a laugh with Donald. 'Oh, and I visited that bookshop, you know the one I told you about...'

'... did you buy anything?'

'No. Before I could enter, Zak started screaming. It's as if he didn't want to go in?'

'And?'

'Well, it seems as if there's one strange occurrence after the other. And you have two murders to investigate. Whatever happened to the calm, unruffled town we fell in love with?'

'I don't know, darling. It seems to me, judging from the general behaviour we see in this world, hell must be experiencing a population explosion.'

David and Margaret Shaw were having a quieter evening in their house at Hawks Green. Both sat in fireside chairs reading. Margaret was relaxing with a new cookery book that suggested alternative ways of spicing up traditional, bland dishes. David's reading, however, was concerned with his work. He regularly read details of the contracts that his employer, West Midlands Rail, were involved with. Most of the company's income derived from goods traffic and particularly with multinational companies. For some time, he'd been aware of the company's substantial involvement with British Nuclear Fuels. During the first few weeks in his new job, it horrified him to learn that massive, disused railway sidings on the district's edge were used to store nuclear waste. West Midlands Rail transported atomic waste from power stations around the United Kingdom to the storage site near Cannock. They even handled imported waste from France and other countries. He commented to Margaret of his disgust that a benign, peaceful town such as Cannock was blighted and used as a repository for such dangerous material. 'I'd wager my salary that few people living in this area are aware of this hazardous stuff being stored on their doorstep,' he remarked. As the months had progressed, he'd formulated a plan that would ensure his notoriety. Doctor Warlock's book had emboldened him. The new confident persona he portrayed made him realise such complicated matters were an opportunity rather than a problem.

Eight

The following morning, Donald woke to another bright and cheerful skyline over Cannock Chase. Showered, groomed, and ready to face another busy day, he went downstairs to find Janet seated at the breakfast bar waiting for him. 'Good morning, darling,' she offered chirpily as she fed Zak with a bottle of milk. He kissed her cheek. 'I woke early and saw how soundly you were sleeping.' He looked at his watch. 'Don't worry, I wouldn't have let you be late for work; after all, you were busy during the night, I'm pleased to say. You obviously needed your rest.' With an arched eyebrow, Donald eyed her shapely figure protruding through her skimpy lace nightie. He returned her suggestive smirk.

'They call this sort of diaphanous nightie, semi-shufty in Cannock. I know now what they mean.'

Picking up the local morning newspaper, Donald read the headlines describing Reverend John Spencer's sensational actions through the town centre streets. He was about to comment to Janet about the previous evening's events, but the doorbell rang. Donald looked over the top of the newspaper and caught Janet's eye. He knew from her reluctant expression that she wanted him to answer the door. He got up and pecked her on the cheek again as he walked past her. Entering the hall, he looked back. Despite his wife still wearing her nightie, silhouetted against the backdrop of light entering the kitchen window, she appeared naked. Donald wolf whistled.

'Phew! A sexy woman, or what? Whoever's at the door, I think I'd better keep them in the hall.'

Janet pouted her lips seductively and smiled before pulling her nightie down a little, revealing her breasts. Donald paused and ogled her shapely figure before closing the kitchen door.

'Sorry to disturb you at home so early, gov.'

'Oh, it's you, James. Good morning. It's a beautiful morning, isn't it? What's so urgent that it can't wait until I reach the office?'

'There's been another fatality, gov. I went into the office at 07:00. I've had a phone call from Constable Derek Richmond...'

'... do we know him? Is he from the Cannock station? His name sounds familiar.' Donald's question interrupted what James was about to tell him regarding the murder, and he paused before answering.

'... he's stationed at Heath Hayes. He lives in a police house there ...'

'... oh yes, I remember now. PC Richmond used to be stationed at Cannock ...'

Donald's attempt at ordinary conversation frustrated James. ... 'Gov, didn't you hear what I said? There's been another murder. Constable Richmond was dragged out of bed at 5:00 this morning by a neighbour. It sounds gruesome, gov. I thought I'd better come straight here and pick you up, especially as you live closer to Heath Hayes than the office.'

'Yes, quite right, James. I won't be a minute.' James took a few steps back and waited.

Returning to the kitchen, Donald found Janet completely naked. She was loading the washing machine with dirty linen. 'I hope you've left your dirty clothes in the washing basket, darling '... have you ...?'

She didn't finish speaking as Donald's grasp around her waist caught her breath. He whispered as he nuzzled into her neck. 'It's James at the door, darling. I have to go out on an urgent matter, so I'll skip breakfast. What I *can* say is that if James hadn't called, seeing you like this, I'd have taken the morning off.' Watched by Zak, sitting in his high chair, she turned, and they held a long, sensuous kiss. Unknown to Donald and Janet, their son wasn't the only voyeur. James wasn't watching anything in particular as he waited outside. His thoughts were on another potential murder case. A dazzling beam of sunlight shining through separating branches of a chestnut tree fluttering in the breeze, illuminated the kitchen. Through the window, James had a complete view of the rear of Janet's naked torso as she snuggled into Donald's erotic embrace. Focussing upon Janet's long bare thighs, his thoughts at once strayed to the straight seams of Staff Nurse Thompson's tights at Stafford Hospital, before he looked away in embarrassment.

'Right then, James!' Donald exclaimed as he joined him in the shiny, black Ford Focus. 'You said it was gruesome ...?'

James could sense that Donald wasn't entirely concentrating. He looked across from the driver's seat to see a quirky smile across his gov's face. From what he had seen, he understood why. James cleared his throat with a loud 'ahem!' and kept his eyes on the road ahead.

'... yes, gov. Mr Keith Newsome of Bradbury Road keeps pigs ...'

'... pigs?'

'Yes, gov; pigs, in a sty in his garden. Anyway, Mr Newsome's neighbour, Mrs Johnson, took her six-year-old daughter yesterday evening to look at the pigs and bring them some bread. The pigs are an attraction in the locality. The Tamworth Old Spot breed is quite a rarity ...'

'... Yes, James. Get on with it. I don't want an exposé on the genetics of pig breeding.'

'No, of course not. Sorry, gov. What Mrs Johnson and her daughter saw is why we've been called ...' James paused and thumped the steering wheel in frustration. 'Oh, sod it, gov, I've left my notebook on my office desk. I won't be able to ...'

Donald looked across at James in frustration and sighed. 'DC Garbett. James, forget the notebook! Why have we been called?'

'Because the pigs were eating Mrs Newsome, or what bits were left of her!'

Donald and James ducked under the blue and white plastic tape hung across the entrance to number ten, Bradbury Road. Constable Richmond had sealed the address as a crime scene. The tape forbade entry to unauthorised personnel. As the front door was ajar, Donald led James into the hall. A scruffy and unshaven, Mr Keith Newsome, sat at a table in the kitchen drinking a mug of tea. Another uniformed constable stood to attention in the corner of the room. Through the window that looked onto the rear garden, Donald saw Constable Richmond standing by a wooden shed.

'Here's my notebook, James. Have a brief chat with Mr Newsome, confirm his identity and get some basic facts. I'm going to have a chat with Constable Richmond.'

'Hello, Derek, nice to see you again ...'

'... and you, gov.'

'What do you have for me?'

'It's a nasty business. Mrs Mabel Johnson lives three doors away at number sixteen.' He pointed across the interwoven wooden fence to a row of houses. 'She visited here last evening with her seven-year-old daughter, Sophie, to feed these pigs.' He nodded to four enormous pigs that grunted and rummaged in the mud and soiled straw. Donald peered over the low wall at the pink-coloured animals that sported a huge dark brown spot on their shoulders. He looked back to PC Richmond as he carried on. 'Sophie threw some slices of bread into the enclosure and was disappointed that the pigs ignored the bread. Then Mrs Johnson saw the reason. One of the larger pigs was chewing Mrs. Newsome's severed head. The others were chewing her limbs.'

'... what did she do then?'

'She fainted!'

'Understandable, in the circumstances.'

'Sophie ran back home to tell her father. He came and picked up his wife and took her home. It was only later in the early hours that she could explain to her husband ...' The constable opened his notebook, '... a Mr Mark Johnson, what she had seen. He later came to my house at five o'clock this morning and explained the events. I called your offices straight away.'

'Excellent work, Derek, especially sealing off the premises. We don't need anybody else, neighbours, or the press involved at this stage. Have you spoken to Mr Newsome?'

'Only briefly, gov. I asked him where his wife is, and he refused to answer.'

'What do you know about him?'

'Mr Keith Newsome, fifty-six years of age. He and his wife, Glenda, have been married for thirty-five years. They have a married son, Michael, who lives in Cannock. Mr Newsome is unemployed, having been dismissed from his job with an engineering company about a month ago. As far as I know, the only misdemeanour he's committed is a speeding endorsement on his driving licence.' Constable Richmond paused as the pigs started squabbling and squealing. They gazed over the wall to see the pigs' sharp, fang-like teeth gnawing at each other's faces.

'Bloody hell, constable. I never realised pigs could be so vicious. It's easy to imagine a human body not lasting in one piece for exceptionally long, isn't it?' Constable Richmond grimaced at the bickering pigs.

'You've done well, Derek. I'll have a chat with Mr Newsome. In the meantime, can you keep the premises sealed?' The constable nodded.

'Has he spoken, James?' Donald asked as he entered the kitchen and sat down opposite Keith Newsome.

'Not a dickybird, gov. He's been like this for the entire time we've been here.'

'Mr Newsome. I'm Detective Donald Lawrence from Cannock police. Can you tell me where your wife is?' Keith remained impassive, hanging his head. Donald looked up at James, who remained standing. 'I've been looking at your pigs.'

'... keep away from my pigs.' Keith blurted out with saliva bubbles issuing from the corners of his mouth. He stared at Donald with a threatening gesture.

'Why should I keep away from them?'

'Because they are my pets, and they don't like strangers.'

'Does your wife, Glenda, like them?'

'No!'

'Where is your wife, Keith?' He lowered his head once more.

'Keith?'

Donald looked at James again. 'Have a look around the house, James.'

'Your pigs are the Tamworth Old Spot variety, I understand ...'

'... prized examples of a rare breed in this country.' James' impassioned shout cut short Keith's reply.

'Gov! Gov! Come up here ... I'm in the bathroom. Oh, may the saints preserve us?'

Donald got up. 'Keep an eye on him, constable.' Donald started walking up the stairs but paused when he saw James retching and vomiting onto the landing carpet. Donald eased past him, reached for a towel hanging on a rack by the door and gave it to him. He paused before fully entering the bathroom, wondering what had caused his constable's distress. The overwhelming stench gave him the expectation of what he'd find. Donald had often witnessed post mortems, dissected bodies, and various body parts in his career. He was familiar with the smell of death associated with a human body. What he saw in the white enamelled bath exceeded anything he'd previously encountered in his career. He didn't get as far as James. At once, he retched directly into the basin before turning on the taps to wash the vomit away. He then realised he was standing on a blood-soaked carpet. His shoes left footprints in the squelching material. As he heard James stumbling down the stairs, he dared to peer once more into the bath. It was two-thirds full of human organs, masses of intestines, human hair and faeces floating in blood. He turned to leave the bathroom, and his shoes kicked various spattered knives, hacksaws, and tree-lopping clippers. Pieces of intestines lodged in the cutting blades of the clippers. He pursued James down the stairs and out into the sunshine and fresh air, where he found him holding his feet under a garden tap, washing away the blood from his shoes.

Donald did the same before holding his head under the flowing cold water. He cupped his hands and took a long drink. Peering into the bright sunlight, his befuddled brain wondered about the vision of hell he'd witnessed in the bathroom of the Newsome household.

'Are you okay, James?' he called to his distressed constable, sitting on the front low garden wall with his head in his hands. Donald saw him shake his head.

'No, I'm not alright. Correct me if I'm wrong, gov. You have more experience than me, but if this is what's involved in being a detective, I must tell you I can't handle it. I'm not cut out for this shit. Is the ... mess ... in ... there ... all that's left of Mrs Newsome?' James didn't wait for his gov's reply as he bent double and vomited into the grass. Donald didn't hear his junior colleague's retching. He returned to the kitchen to confront Keith Newsome. More horror and catastrophe met him, and he questioned his own sanity. Slumped in a blood-stained heap in the corner was the headless body of the uniformed constable. Keith Newsome's unseeing eyes stared at the constable's head resting on the kitchen table alongside the unfinished mug of tea. Keith was also dead. The long, serrated bread knife he'd used to sever the policeman's head and cut his own throat was still embedded in his neck. Gurgling blood gushed over the knife's blade and handle like white water rapids in a river tumbling over rocks. Instead of cold white water, this was red hot human blood running down his body, forming an ever-increasing pool around his feet. Donald ran outside and pressed 999 on his phone's keypad.

'This is Detective Inspector Donald Lawrence of the Cannock constabulary here. I'm at number ten, Bradbury Road, Heath Hayes. I have multiple fatalities. I need help here, please!'

Donald walked over to James, still sitting on the wall. 'James, go home. Take the rest of the day off. I've telephoned for backup. I can handle things here. Take tomorrow morning off too. This awful thing here will take some coming to terms with.'

'Are you sure, gov?'

'Yes. I'll see you at the office tomorrow afternoon.'

As James drove his car unsteadily along Bradbury Road, two police cars and an ambulance, all with their sirens blaring and blue lights flashing, raced past him.

Superintendent Ernest Woodhouse, Donald's immediate superior, got out of the first car and approached Donald and Constable Richmond sitting on the same wall James had occupied. 'What's happened here, Donald?' the superintendent questioned, seeing Donald's uncharacteristically sallow complexion.

'Look in the kitchen and then the bathroom on the first floor, Super. Then we'll have a chat.' As the superintendent went into the house, Donald watched paramedics and the scene of crime officers stride purposefully through the front door. The last officer, carrying a camera and tripod, was almost knocked over by the superintendent rushing out of the house before he heaved and vomited over the concrete paving. Wiping the bile from around his mouth, he looked towards Donald.

'Christ Almighty in heaven, Donald, where do we start on this one?'

'It starts and ends with Keith Newsome, the bloke with the knife still embedded in his neck. The mess in the bath is all that's left of Mrs Newsome. The rest of her body has been fed to the pigs in the back garden.'

'Who's the dead constable?'

'Constable Richmond informs me, it's his colleague, Joe Swales, married with two kids ...'

'Oh God, Donald, this gets worse and worse at every turn.'

'...why?' The superintendent shook his head.

'Why a law-abiding, ordinary married man would turn into a maniac and do this is beyond me? Further, these types of incidents are mounting up, gov. Recently I've investigated two other such murders.'

'If you need more help, Donald, I've an experienced sergeant at HQ that I can spare ...'

'Thanks, gov. Can I take you up on that offer? I only have Constable James Garbett to call on, so another pair of hands would help with the increasing workload. Incidentally, it was James who picked me up this morning to come here. He discovered the mess in the bathroom. He's only young and reacted badly, as we all have, so I've given him the rest of the day and tomorrow morning off.' The superintendent nodded his agreement.

'What's the name of this sergeant, so I can look out for him?'

'Her! Detective Sergeant Nicola Bains. She's only recently received her stripes. Currently stationed at the county HQ. She's a promising copper, not frightened of hard work or getting her hands dirty.'

'She sounds exactly what I need right now. Thanks, gov.'

Superintendent Woodhouse eyed Donald, askance. 'I won't delegate a most unpleasant task ... I think you know to what I'm referring ...?'

'... Visiting Constable Swale's widow?'

'If you think I should carry it out, I'd be willing ...'

'Thanks, Donald. Once back at HQ, I'll retrieve his details from personnel records and arrange a woman PC to attend with me. What will you be doing?'

'Well, for a start, there're mountains of paperwork to begin on all of this. I also need to interview the neighbours who first alerted Constable Richmond.'

'Neighbours? What did they see? I'm assuming they witnessed nothing in the house.'

'No, not in the house.' Pointing along the street, Donald explained. 'Mrs. Mabel Johnson, who lives three doors away at number 16, regularly comes here with her seven-year-old daughter, Sophie, to feed the Newsome's pigs. Last evening, they came with some stale loaves of bread as usual, but the pigs were feeding on something more substantial, Mrs Newsome's head, arms and legs.'

Superintendent Woodhouse grimaced. He turned, donned his peaked cap, and waved for his driver to get ready to transport him back to County HQ.

As the superintendent left, Donald once more ventured tentatively into the house. He avoided the kitchen and bathroom and went into the lounge. He sat on a settee and looked around the room. It was ordinary, with everything in its appointed place. He was looking for clues that would suggest a reason, a motive, for why Keith Newsome should commit such atrocities.

On a glass-topped coffee table in front of him, there was a red coloured book with the title in embossed gold leaf. He picked up the book and, with a shaky voice, read the title aloud. '*Basic Pig Husbandry.*'

'Of course, it has to be, doesn't it?' he thought. 'His pigs, it's what he lived for.' He read the preface. *... summarises basic pig husbandry, covering boars, gilts and sows, the litter, weaners and grower herds.* He was going to place the book back on the coffee table, but he suddenly didn't want to stay in the house a moment longer. Carrying the book, he strode determinedly outside and asked a constable to drive him back to Cannock police station. Such was his temporary cerebral detachment from ordinary life. It was only when sitting in the car he realised he was still holding the book. Once in his office, the book joined others he'd retrieved at the other murder cases. Had he been in a more receptive mood, he may have eventually read the book's added appendix, dealing with a modern concept on a pig's diet. The hypothesis suggested wild pigs were rampant carnivores. In medieval times, evidence exists that the animals regularly attacked and ate unsuspecting humans. The appendix suggested this swine/human relationship should be revived. If Donald had read this appendix, he would also have seen the stamp of indelible red ink on its flysheet.

'This book is the property of Doctor Godfrey Warlock, Purveyor of rare and unusual books.'

Nine

Donald completed statutory initial forms and other paperwork on the Newsome case and left the office early at 16:30. It was a pleasant afternoon, so he walked the two and a half-mile distance back home. He needed to clear his head, breathe some fresh air, and attempt to feel normal again. Negotiating the shoppers in the pedestrianised town centre, he noticed the sandwich board outside the newsagent. The local evening newspaper, The Express and Star, already displayed lurid headlines. '*Butchery at Heath Hayes.*' On a second panel he read, '*Husband feeds wife to his pigs.*' 'Bloody hell, it's everywhere; I can't escape it!' he exclaimed.

Further along the town centre in High Green, Doctor Godfrey Warlock had already received his newspaper copy. With semi-circular reading glasses perched precariously on the end of his nose, he read the front page article, and smiled. The smile extended to a broad grin, followed by disturbed customers at the rear of the shop turning to see where raucous laughter was coming from.

Godfrey roared his delight. His body doubled in ecstasy as his spectacles fell to the floor, together with several pages of The Express and Star.

Janet eagerly awaited Donald's return. He'd already telephoned her to say he was walking home. When Donald had left home in the morning, he'd made it clear to her where his thoughts were. Zak had been fed and was sleeping contentedly in his cot. She'd prepared Donald's favourite dinner of paprika flavoured roast chicken with a side salad. A bottle of Rioja stood on the dining table, ready for him to open. She'd showered and applied a generous spray of the perfume he'd bought for her birthday, Chanel No 5. Standing in the kitchen, wearing the nightie she'd worn when he left, she put the finishing touches to their meal. With mounting anticipation, she heard his key in the front door. She didn't turn around when she heard the kitchen door open, expecting him to embrace her. Instead, he pulled a chair from under the dining table and sat down.

'Have you had a good day, darling?' she asked joyfully.

Her cheerful voice made him look towards her. 'Oh, you look lovely, darling.'

Accepting Donald's compliment, she turned in optimism. Her previous expectation of a romantic evening was immediately dashed. His eyes seemed sunken, his complexion sallow, his usual smart, combed hair was dishevelled. Despite his attempt at a smile, she saw the sadness in his face. 'Oh, darling, what is it? What's happened?' She stood by him, holding his head against her lace nightie. Donald smelled Janet's sweetness as he buried his face against her stomach. Stroking his head, she whispered. 'I can see you've had a hard day.' He nodded and felt tears stinging his eyes. He had experienced the worst of humanity in the outside world but, comforting him, he realised how exceptional Janet is. At that moment, nothing else mattered but returning the love she was showing him.

'Oh, darling, you smell so lovely ...'

'.... what would you like ... at this moment?' She felt him trembling.

He gazed up at her beauty and longed to snuggle up close to her in bed, to feel safe and loved and insulated from whatever the world could throw their way. He was about to explain how he felt, but she spoke.

'I bet you'd like a cup of tea before dinner, wouldn't you?' He nodded and sat at the table.

'The dinner smells good too ...'

'... are you...?'

'... if I told you, apart from a drink of water, I haven't eaten or drunk anything else today, you'll perhaps realise how hungry I am.'

Within a minute, he was holding his hands around a warming mug of tea, and he watched his gorgeous wife serve their steaming chicken paprika on the table. As she sat opposite, he'd already opened the bottle of Rioja. He filled two glasses, lifted his own, and offered a toast as Janet raised her glass towards him.

'To us, darling. Please know at this moment I love you more than ever.'

'I love you too, Donald.' Even though her earlier hopes for a romantic evening had been quashed, she relished the knowledge that the forthcoming evening would be a special one.

Ten

Detective Constable James Garbett's methodical work ethic did him credit. Although Inspector Lawrence had given him the morning off, he still rose to his digital alarm ringing at 07:00. He spent a leisurely hour in his flat before deciding to venture into the town centre.

The lovely spell of benign warm weather continued. It was market day, so with his coat across his arm and shirt sleeves rolled up, he took a stroll through the pedestrian area, peeping at the various market stalls. He heard Saint Luke's church bell strike eleven o'clock as he passed an open-air café next to the town's white marble war memorial. He sat down next to a colourful bed of petunias and salvias, as an elderly waitress came to ask for his order.

'A large cappuccino, please.' He gazed idly across the square at people coming and going, carrying empty and full shopping bags. A few more elderly shoppers dragged wheeled shopping trolleys behind them. The waitress brought his coffee. He took a sip and saw a pretty young woman, two tables away, looking at him. Displaying mutual awkwardness, they both looked out to the pedestrian square. Donald turned and took another sip of coffee and peeked at the attractive woman. Fresh-faced with a naturally rosy complexion, she had short, slightly curly hair that framed her face, and a small upturned nose. She lifted her eyes from her own cup of coffee, so he was aware of her ice-blue eyes studying him. This time they didn't turn away but smiled at each other. He felt a tingle of emotion running down his spine and acknowledged his luck. 'Bloody hell, the fates are kind to me today; since when did such a lovely girl even look in my direction, let alone smile?' he thought. Displaying uncharacteristic boldness, he picked up his mug of coffee and approached her table.

'Excuse me, Miss. I rarely present myself so confidently to any young lady I see. In fact, I'm quite shy. Still, it's such a lovely day, and you seem to be by yourself ... oh, I'm sorry, are you by yourself? Perhaps your boyfriend is coming to join you? Oh dear, I'm making a mess of this; what I mean to say is ...' The young woman giggled.

'Please sit down.' She opened her hand, gesturing to the chair opposite her. '... and yes, I am by myself, and no, I don't have a boyfriend joining me.'

He placed his coffee next to hers and sat down. 'Oh, good! No, what I meant to say ... I'm James, James Garbett ...' He offered her his hand.

'... and my name is Nicola Bains, but everyone except my Mom calls me Nicky.' It was fingers touching rather than a full handshake. He immediately thought how soft and sensuous her touch felt.

'Hello, Nicky. It's a gorgeous day, isn't it?'

'Yes, it is, and this is a lovely place to watch the world go by.'

'I haven't seen you before. Do you visit the market often?'

'Apart from visiting a bank in town a few months ago, this is my first time in Cannock. I live in Stafford. How about you?'

'Me? Oh, I live in Cannock. I have an apartment in the lower part of town.'

'What do you do for a living?' James asked.

Nicky didn't want to divulge her vocation as a police sergeant and answered vaguely. 'Nothing much, this and that.' She hunched her shoulders. And you?'

James felt the same. He didn't want her to know he was a detective. 'Oh, the same as you. This and that.'

A pregnant pause developed as they drank some of their coffee, peering at each other.

'The market looks interesting ...' Nicky said, as James spoke simultaneously.

'Would you like a wander around the market?' Their words overrode each other, and they laughed.

'Yes, let's.' Nicky offered. James left some money on the table for both coffees, and they got up to leave.

They strolled around the market stalls before extending their walk into High Green. 'This looks an exciting bookshop,' Nicky commented, looking upward at the swinging sign. *Godfrey's Bookshop.* 'Have you been in here before?'

'No, I haven't. It looks spooky to me.' James held his hand against the window. 'I can't see inside ...' He turned to Nicky. 'Do you read much?'

'Not much, but if I get into an excellent book, I can't put it down ...'

They turned when a bell sounded above the opening door. An emaciated elderly man came out carrying a large red book. They peered into the shop and saw multiple rows of floor to ceiling bookshelves brim-full of books. Further down the shop, they saw men and women sitting at a table, reading.

'Come in, come in, young people. I will not eat you,' a man's weak voice called to them.

Nicky and James stepped gingerly into the dark, fusty atmosphere and at once noticed the symptomatic smell that only an old book shop could create. It felt comforting and intriguing in one intermingled emotion. They both felt the urge to explore and walked further along the rows of books. Then they were startled by a tall man standing behind the counter. He seemed to emerge from the shadows. Tall and gaunt with piercing black eyes, he made their flesh tingle when he asked, in a trembling voice, 'What sort of books are you interested in? There are all sorts here that will enhance your view of life. That's what makes books so intriguing, don't you think? In our short time here on earth, they have helped us to progress to the momentous watershed moments we all have to face.' The old man's flowery rhetoric mesmerised them. He intimidated them with a menacing glare before raising his voice even louder and pointing at them. 'From then on, what is the correct decision and what is the appropriate path to take? Eh? My books can help you do that. So, what is it to be, my young people? What books are you looking for?'

James and Nicky looked at each other before Nicky attempted a reply, but her mouth was dry. 'Ahem!' She cleared her throat. 'Nothing really. We are strolling around the town, and your bookshop looked interesting. We aren't looking for any book in particular.'

'I see, young lady. Well, a lot of my devoted customers say that at first. Like your good selves, they've also come here, intrigued by my premises, but now they are regulars, my converts. I've changed their lives with my special, rare books.' Behind James's back, he felt Nicky's arm seeking his fingers. They held hands as if comforting each other. When they first walked into the shop, she had relished the welcoming ambience. Now, she felt a sudden urge to leave the cloying environment that had developed into a sinister mood. She looked towards the window and saw the buoyant sunshine illuminating the pavements.

'Perhaps we'll come again?' she added, nervously.

'Yes. See you another time, maybe? Mr ...?' James prompted.

'Doctor Warlock is my name. Doctor Godfrey Warlock, purveyor of rare and unusual books.'

When they'd entered the shop, they hadn't noticed they'd walked down a step. Hand in hand, in the dimness, they now didn't see the step, and Nicky tumbled forward. If they hadn't been holding hands, she would have fallen headlong.

'Careful, young lady. I can't be held responsible for anyone on whom misfortune befalls in my shop.' They heard the old man cackling, but by then the bell hanging above the door jingled loudly as James vigorously pulled the door open. With a massive mutual sigh of relief, they blinked in the bright sunshine and breathed the fresh air.

'Wow! You were right, James. That was spooky in there. I'm glad we're outside, aren't you?'

'Wow! Yes, I am. It feels like we've attended a sermon in church or been lectured to by an ominous teacher at school ...'

'... I felt I was being brainwashed.' Nicky laughed nervously. 'Do you have any more attractions like *Godfrey's Bookshop* in Cannock, then?'

It was only then they realised they were still holding hands, and they pulled them apart.

'None that I can think of, but ...' He looked at his wristwatch. 'I wish we could spend some more time together, but I have to get to work soon ...'

Nicky opened her mobile and checked the time. 'Oh, my goodness, yes. I have to go too.'

'It's been lovely meeting you, Nicky. Is there any chance? ... or perhaps? ... not as I'm presuming anything. ... but ... maybe ...?'

'Have you got a mobile?' Nicky asked bluntly.

James reached into his pocket and showed her his phone. 'What's your number, James?'

'...er! Oh, yes. 07089235766' Nicky keyed the number into her phone, created the contact in her address book list, and then pressed his number. His phone vibrated and rang.

'Oh, blast! Excuse me, Nicky, that's my phone ...' He put the phone to his ear and turned away. She laughed.

'It's me, silly. I've rung you. Now you have my number. We have each other's number.'

He turned back to face her, looked at his phone and pressed the red icon to stop the ringing. 'I'm a prize git, aren't I? That's great!' They both laughed.

'Well, which way are you going?' he asked, putting his phone back in his pocket.

'Wolverhampton Road, wherever that is ...'

'Wow! I'm going that way. I'll show you; we can walk together.'

'Well, what do you think of our little town?' he asked, as they strolled jauntily back through the market stalls. James's question was to stifle any silence between them and help to quell his own nervousness. They had only met an hour ago, but he already sensed his growing attachment to her and felt a reluctance that they'd soon be parting company.

'Apart from the bookshop, it's lovely. I love this street market and open-air cafes.'

They were already in Wolverhampton Road. He expected her to cross the road but was pleasantly surprised when they carried on walking together. They came to a blue and white enamelled triangular sign, standing on a stainless-steel post in front of a four-storey imposing building. The bold, black, acid-etched font on the signboard informed them it was the Cannock Police Headquarters. Nicky nervously cleared her throat, before adding. 'Well, here I am. Goodbye James. Give me a ring sometime, and we'll have another coffee ...'

'... but! ... but!' His attention was diverted when someone called him from across the street.

'James! James, can I have a word with you?'

'Oh, it's my mom.' He turned back to Nicky, but she had already climbed the few steps and was inside the circular revolving door. He turned and crossed the road to chat with his mom.

'Hello, I'm Detective Sergeant Nicola Bains, from the County HQ. I have an appointment with Inspector Lawrence,' she announced confidently to the receptionist sitting behind a glass shield.

'Yes, the Inspector is expecting you. His office is number 123 on the first floor. There's a lift, or the stairs are ...'

'... I'll take the stairs. Thank you.' Nicky marched assertively to the swing fire doors marked with a stairway symbol. She knocked on door number 123. There was no answer so she walked into the empty office containing several desks. She noticed one desk marked

'Reception.' She pressed the bell on the desk. A door opened, and Donald appeared.

'Hello, I'm Detective Inspector Donald Lawrence. I'm sorry, my secretary isn't back from lunch yet. Can I help you?' Nicky introduced herself. As she sat down in Donald's office, she looked through the window and noticed James, still chatting to his mother on the pavement opposite the police building.

After chatting for five minutes, Donald heard his secretary return. Two coffees please, Veronica, he called.

'Now, Sergeant Bains ...'

'... everybody except my mother calls me Nicky, Inspector.'

Donald smiled. 'Superintendent Woodhouse has told me of great expectations for your career. ... oh, and please call me, gov. That's the normal precedent for addressing a superior officer, isn't it?'

Nicky blushed. 'I've only recently received a promotion to sergeant ... gov. I suppose I've had a sheltered career to date, mainly dealing with company fraud and drug cases ...'

'... well, that will soon change. Of late, we've experienced some alarming cases in Cannock, murders and suicides and people having delusions.' Veronica interrupted him by bringing in two coffees.

'Has Constable Garbett come in yet?' he asked.

'Yes, he's sitting at his desk ...'

'... Ask him to step in here, please, Veronica.'

Donald and Nicky's laughter met James as he entered the office. He stared in surprise at her.

Nicky remained seated and smiled. 'James, this is our new colleague....'

'... Nicky, what are you doing here?'

'James, didn't you hear me? It's obvious that you two have met before, but....'

'... I'm sorry, gov. Yes, I heard you,' James commented and continued to stare at Nicky. She continued her enigmatic smile.

'I think I'm playing gooseberry here.' Donald sighed and took a huge slurp of coffee.

'Gov.' Nicky spoke. 'Yes, we have met before. Over a cup of coffee in the town, just now, but we haven't been properly introduced.'

'Well, even if you two have met before, let me formally introduce you. James, this is Detective Sergeant Nicola Bains. Nicky, this is Detective Constable James Garbett.'

Nicky stood and offered her hand to James. 'I'm pleased to meet you.'

James held out his hand and was at once pleased to feel her touch again so soon. '... Sergeant, eh?' That was all he could say.

'Nicky is transferring here from the county HQ. I was going to say that I hope you two can gel into a cooperative unit. We have some unpleasant cases too... but I can see my comments are already redundant.'

Nicky and James hadn't heard Donald's last few words. 'I didn't want you to know what I did for a living when we met.'

'... neither did I,' Nicky replied. Neither heard Donald as he shouted.

'Veronica, here please.' His secretary pushed open the door.

'Yes, Inspector?'

'Veronica, this is our new colleague, Detective Sergeant Nicola Bains. Can you arrange for all the passes and codes she will need to access our computer systems, please?'

An hour later, Donald ventured into the outer office, pleased to see Nicky sitting at her new desk in the corner of the large open-plan office. He went directly to her.

'Nicky, you may as well experience an immediate baptism into the unpleasant case at Heath Hayes James and I attended yesterday. Can you come with me?'

'Of course, gov.' She pulled her over jacket across her shoulders and reached for her notebook.

'We're going to interview the Newsome's neighbour... er.'

'.... Mrs Johnson.' James prompted.

'Yes. Can you finish some forms on my desk, please, James? Also, can you chase up that old maid of a ward sister at Stafford General Hospital? She hasn't been in touch with us. I'm sure Jack Beecham is fit enough to be interviewed by now. Here's the autopsy report on Carole Beecham. It makes interesting reading. Her cause of death is by strangulation.' Donald turned to a page he'd previously marked. 'Here it is. *No ingested water was discovered in her lungs.* So, she didn't drown.' Donald flipped the pages to another marked section. '... I remember reading a passage from a book Jack Beecham had on his bedside table. A section where the pages were open suggested mercy killing methods if you had a loved one who was terminal and suffering. According to this section of the autopsy report, Mrs Beecham had a small tumour in her stomach. It wasn't serious or life-threatening in any way. So, if her husband thought he was mercy killing, he wasn't. He committed murder with no extenuating circumstances. See what you can get out of him, James.'

'Will do, gov.'

As Donald drove his car towards Heath Hayes, he explained what had happened at the Newsome house. As the police car pulled to a halt outside number six, Bradbury Road, Nicky was already feeling nauseous listening to Donald's gruesome description of events.

Mr Mark Johnson answered Donald's knock on the door. 'If you are more reporters, you can sod off and leave us in peace....'

'... No. We're not from the press, Mr Johnson. Hello, I'm Detective Inspector Donald Lawrence from Cannock police station. This is my colleague, Sergeant Bains....'

'... I'm sorry, Inspector. These damned reporters. They're from the national and local newspapers. They don't care what time of day it is. We've even had a television journalist standing in front of our house being filmed by a camera crew today. If they don't stop, your next call at my house will be for me. For sure, if they carry on, I swear I'll take a cricket bat to their heads.'

'I'm sorry you're having your privacy violated. Please try not to resort to violence, sir'

Donald held out his warrant card for inspection. Without looking at it, Mr Johnson waved for them to enter. 'How's your wife?' Donald asked as they walked through the hall to the lounge.

'See for yourself,' Mr Johnson said and offered them a seat on a settee opposite where Mabel Johnson sat in a low fireside chair.

'The Inspector has asked me how you are, Mabel?' Donald looked towards Mrs Johnson and could see how shaken she still was.

'Hello, Mrs Johnson. I was hoping you could explain what you saw when you took your daughter to feed Mr Newsome's pigs. Sheila's her name, isn't it...?'

'... no, Inspector. My daughter's name is Sophie.' Donald was pleased to see that Nicky was already taking notes of the conversation.

'Sophie, of course. Events happened so fast yesterday, it wasn't possible to get all the facts. I can see you're still upset. We can come back another day if you wish?'

'No, that's alright, Inspector. It was so horrible; I don't think I'll ever forget it. So, today, next week, next year will make no difference.'

'You take stale bread loaves to the Newsome's pigs, I understand?'

'Yes, twice a week when we have some left-over bread. Sophie likes the pigs and the grunting and squealing noises they make. She thinks they're talking to her. Do you have children, Inspector? My Sophie is a fan of Peppa Pig. She's even christened some of Mr Newsome's pigs the same names as the characters in the TV programme.'

'I have a little boy, Zak. He's only six months old, so he's not into stuff like that yet.'

'Well, despite Sophie's attraction to Mr Newsome's pigs, I can tell you, Inspector, they're like something out of a medieval horror story. They're carnivorous monsters. I don't think I can ever eat a pork chop again. I saw nothing out of the ordinary at first. The pigs always seem to chomp in the straw.' Mrs Johnson reached for the handkerchief lodged in her cardigan's sleeve. She snuffled and blew her nose before carrying on. 'Poor Glenda, she was my best friend,' Mabel blew her nose again as her eyes reddened.

'Can't you see how distressed my wife is, Inspector? Surely this can wait for another day?'

Donald got up from the settee. 'Yes, of course, Mr Johnson, I understand.'

'... No! It's quite alright, Mark. I'd sooner get this over and done with.' Mabel composed herself and looked towards Donald again as he retook his seat.

'Glenda had lovely blonde, curly hair. We used to do each other's hair, you know, to save on hairdresser's costs. The two hairdressers in the village here have a monopoly. We can't afford their prices. Anyway, it was because of her lovely hair that I knew it was Glenda. The last time I did her hair, I put on a yellow, plastic, sprung clasp to keep her long pieces in a bun. Watching the pigs with Sophie, I heard a snap and watched one pig spit some yellow plastic bits out of its jaws. Then a louder snap, much the same as what an empty tin can sounds like when you stamp on it. Like an echoed, dull sound. I think that was Glenda's skull being crushed because the next thing I saw will live in my memory forever.'

'Oh, my God!' Nicky exclaimed. Mrs Johnson momentarily looked at her before carrying on.

'I thought the pig was foaming at the mouth. Then I realised it wasn't foam or spittle but pieces of Glenda's brain. Many pieces of white tissue fell into the straw along with one of Glenda's eyes.' Mrs Johnson only hesitated slightly as Nicky dropped her pencil. 'The pieces were only there a second before the ravenous beast sucked them up from the straw. Then the pig sounded as if it was choking. It was having trouble swallowing all of Glenda's head, and it started regurgitating her hair. Her lovely blonde hair!' Mabel started crying and, using her handkerchief, mopped the tears running down her face onto the white apron on her lap. Regaining her poise, she continued. 'Glenda's hair stuck in the pig's teeth, but another pig soon helped by licking the hair and then pulling. Can you imagine the horror from the hell of that scene, Inspector? Two massive pigs squabbling and squealing over what they left of poor Glenda. Carrying out a tug-of-war with…' She held her hand to her mouth as if she were going to vomit. 'I heard another louder snapping sound and watched a smaller pig snapping her legs' bones into several pieces. All the pigs were busy eating and took no notice of the loaves of bread my Sophie threw in for them, I can only assume they were all eating some part of Glenda….'

'… did your daughter, Sophie, know what….'

'No, Inspector. Thank goodness she didn't; I wouldn't want her to go through life recalling such horrors. I turned her head away when I realised what was happening. I'm thankful for small mercies that she went to school this morning as happy and optimistic as ever' She blew her nose again.

'Then I must have passed out because the next thing I remember was Mark,' She reached for his hand. '… Mark pressing a wet towel on my forehead in our kitchen.'

Mr Johnson took up his wife's harrowing narrative. 'The first thing I knew something was happening was when I heard Sophie calling and crying at the back door. She was crying, Mommy, Mommy, come quickly, Daddy. Mommy is poorly. I knew they'd only just gone to feed the pigs, so I dashed straight round there.'

'Did you have to knock on the Newsome's door…?'

'No, thank goodness. If I knew then what I do now, I'd have done Keith some harm. No, there's a pathway at the side of their house leading down to the rear garden. Well before I actually went down the garden, I could see Mabel slumped in the mud at the door to the sty.' He looked at his wife. 'I haven't previously told you this bit, darling.' He looked back to the two incredulous looking police officers. 'Protruding halfway over the low wooden gateway to the sty, a massive pig was leaning over. I swear it was trying to get at you, darling.' He went to his wife and placed his arms around her shoulders. Mabel's eyes widened in horror.

'Oh, my God!' she gasped.

Nicky suddenly got up from the settee, interrupting Donald's concentration as he imagined the dreadful scene. He heard the back door slam as she left the house. He guessed she had the same reaction that James, the superintendent, and he had experienced.

Mark Johnson watched Nicky leave the room before carrying on. 'There's not much more to tell, Inspector. I picked Mabel up in my arms and brought her back here. I couldn't believe what she told me when she came round. We discussed what we should do about it. Police Constable Derek Richmond lives down the street, so I went to his house and told him what Mabel had seen. I think you know the rest.'

'Thank you, Mr and Mrs Johnson. Thank goodness something like this only happens once in a lifetime....'

'Yes, thank goodness, but why me, why us, why our lifetimes. How can we ever forget this?'

'I'll repeat what I said to you earlier, Inspector Lawrence. If that bastard, Keith Newsome, hadn't committed hari-kari, I swear to God, I'd have stuck a knife in him. He used to be a pleasant, ordinary bloke; a pal, even. A month ago, he changed. He became inhuman. All he cared about was his pigs. Many nights we used to listen to poor Glenda's screams as we lay in bed, and we live three doors away, so you can tell how loud their arguments were....'

'... Inspector, what happens next in all this?' Donald hunched his shoulders at her.

'The only reason I'm asking is... please do something about those pigs. They're still in the Newsome's garden. Most of last night and this morning, they were grunting and squealing. Sophie heard them and asked me if she could see them again before she went to school. There's no way any of us are going there again. I can't bear to think that the remains of poor Glenda are still there. Can you do something... contact a veterinary organisation or an abattoir to come and take them away, please? If you don't, there's nobody that will look after them anymore. They will starve and become desperate for food. Just imagine if they got out of their sty. They could attack anybody.'

She turned to her husband. 'Mark, think of the neighbourhood kids playing in the street. They'd be the first target. It's too horrible to think about.'

'My wife's right, Inspector; you have to do something.'

'Yes, of course, I will. Rest assured, it will be my first action when I get back to my office.'

Outside, he found Nicky sitting on a low wall similar to where he and James had rested outside the Newsome residence. He saw how shaken she was, wiping away vomit from the corners of her mouth.

'I'm sorry, gov.'

'... no apologies needed, Nicky. This is worse than a nightmare; James and I reacted just the same yesterday.'

'You missed the last bit of Mr Johnson's narrative in there. When we return to the office, I want you to contact the County Veterinary Department. Those pigs are still at number ten. I want them removing and destroying as soon as possible.'

Eleven

It was 16:30 before Donald and Nicky arrived back at Cannock Police Station. Nicky at once looked up the telephone number for the County Veterinary Department. Donald's attention focussed on a handwritten note on his desk. It was from James. He'd gone to Stafford General Hospital, having verified that he could interview Jack Beecham.

'Hello, Sister, do you remember me? I'm Detective Constable Garbett'

'... I remember you, Constable. If you come with me, I'll take you to Mr Beecham. He's in another private ward but, after your interview, I'll transfer him into the general men's ward along with fifteen other patients.'

'How is he?'

'He's recovered well. When you were here before, he had a concussion and a severe head wound. We've since confirmed that he has a slight hairline fracture of his skull. His prognosis is good and will only need moderate sedation and rest. I'll leave you alone with the patient then, Constable. If you need help, there's a bell above the bed; do you see it, marked with a red bell symbol?' James looked to where she pointed and nodded. He drew up a chair to the patient's bedside; seeing that his eyes were closed, James gave a gentle cough.

'Mr Beecham, I'm Detective Constable Garbett from Cannock Police.' Jack Beecham opened his eyes, turned, and nodded.

'I'm here to question you about your wife, Carole Beecham....'

'... she's dead!'

'Why did you kill her?'

'I haven't killed her.'

'We have the results from your wife's autopsy. The findings are conclusive....'

'... I don't care what some fancy report says. How do these so-called experts know what was happening in our lives? How do you know? How does anybody know? They don't! Only Carole and I knew.'

'Knew what, Mr Beecham?'

'That my wife was dying. Can you imagine the misery and agony we were both going through?'

'What was she suffering from? Was she receiving treatment from the hospital...?'

'... she had incurable stomach cancer. She was already suffering terrible pain... there was no need to go to the hospital. What could they have done, anyway? All they do is dole out that useless chemotherapy and prolong the suffering....'

'... Mr Beecham, what you are telling me is not true....'

'... are you a doctor?'

'No, I'm not.'

'... then you don't know what you're talking about. You're giving me a headache.'

'The results of the autopsy also show that your wife only had a small tumour in her stomach. It was benign and not causing her distress or pain. The report says that the small lump wasn't life-threatening in any way.'

'... my wife was dying....'

'... how do you know that?'

'... I knew it; that's all my conscience needs.'

'... so, you killed her. You strangled her.'

'... in the most humane way, I eased her pathway to eternal life....'

'... how is strangulation humane, Mr Beecham?'

'... Water guarantees the pathway to perpetual life when the tunnel by which we must all pass is enabled underwater. If you have a loved one in your life who is suffering illness and disease, it sets the kinder path to take them on the watery trail to glory.'

'I don't know where you get such fanciful thoughts from, but the fact remains you strangled your wife. Drowning wasn't her cause of death. She was dead before you held her under the bathwater.'

'... you're wrong. I must have drowned Carole. That's the only way she could get access to glory.'

'Mr Jack Beecham, I'm formally charging you with the murder of your wife. You do not have to say anything, but it may harm your defence if you do not mention, when questioned, something which you later rely on in court. Anything you do say may be given in evidence.'

'... just empty words,'

'I'm going to put a guard on your presence here in the hospital. After you're discharged you'll be taken into police custody. Do you understand, Mr Beecham?'

'... but the book says my wife is now in a perpetual state of peace, in glory. Nothing can hurt her now.'

'What book is that?'

'Doctor Warlock's book.'

'Do you mean Doctor Godfrey Warlock...?'

'... yes. *Godfrey's Bookshop* in Cannock.'

James walked out of the side ward and rang Donald. 'Gov, I'm still at the hospital. Jack Beecham has admitted killing his wife. I've formally charged him. I suggest we put a guard on his ward. The sister says he'll be released soon.'

'... Excellent work, James, I'll organise it. Inform the sister what we are doing.'

Twelve

The reception area felt different. The stairway had a feel-good ambience. Well before he reached the office door, James realised what it was. Nicky's perfume. 'I remember it from yesterday,' he thought. 'Good morning, Nicky. You're in the office bright and early,' James offered, cheerfully. 'I knew you were here; I could smell your lovely perfume. What sort is it?'

'Hello, James. My perfume? It's called *Knowing* by Estée Lauder.' She had entered a number into her mobile phone and held it to her ear.

'I'll remember, for a future present for her,' he thought.

'Oh, blast! It's engaged!' Nicky commented and pressed the ring back option.

'We had an eventful day yesterday, didn't we? How did you get on at the Newsome's house?'

'I've never heard anything so horrible in my life.' Nicky related what Mrs Mabel Johnson had told her and Donald. 'That's why I'm in the office early. The gov asked me to arrange for an abattoir to collect the Newsome's pigs and destroy them' Her telephone started ringing. James listened to her voice.

'Oh, hello, thank you for ringing me back. It's Detective Sergeant Nicky Bains here from Cannock Police. Oh, was it you I spoke to last evening?' Nicky listened and saw James watching her. Her brief smile faded when she answered. 'So, you're sure you've destroyed the pigs?' She listened again. '... and what's happened to them?' James turned away as he saw a frown crossing her forehead. 'In the circumstances, I think the meat from such animals wouldn't be fit for human consumption, don't you?' she added forcefully, before listening again. 'Okay, Mr Robinson, I have to accept what you are saying. I disagree with you, but as long as you can assure me those pigs are dead, that's all I wish to know.' She listened again. 'Okay, thank you, goodbye.'

'So, the pigs are dead?' James asked.

'Yes, thank goodness for that, but do you know what the boss of the abattoir, a Clement Robinson, told me?' James looked in anticipation. 'He couldn't guarantee that the meat, the pork chops and sausages wouldn't be fit for human consumption. He said there are plenty of communities in the United Kingdom that would gladly accept such meat.'

'Our foreign friends, especially from the African communities, I suppose?'

'Exactly. They regularly eat bush meat. He pointed out that being a carnivore doesn't exclude an animal from being eaten....'

'... but surely, in this case, the carnivore, the pigs, have eaten human flesh.'

'He said that wouldn't put him off eating the meat, nor would it deter our African friends.'

James's desk telephone started ringing. 'Hello, James Garbett here.' He listened, and it was Nicky's turn to watch him speak. 'Oh, no, that's all we need.'

Donald walked into the office, heard James's words, stopped, and listened. 'Good morning,' he mimed to Nicky. She smiled.

James turned to face Donald as he continued to listen on the telephone. 'Okay, Constable, thanks for letting me know. Get that head wound attended to.' He put the phone down. 'Morning, gov. That was Constable Davidson from Stafford Hospital.'

'That's the officer assigned to watch over Jack Beecham. Superintendent Woodhouse from Stafford HQ took him off his regular duties last evening.'

'Well, it seems that Beecham has escaped from the hospital. The sister found Constable Davidson at 5:30 this morning when she started her work. He's got a concussion and a head wound from being hit with a metal bedpan. Of course, there's no sign of Beecham. His bed's empty, and his pyjamas were on the floor.'

'... so, he's at large, dressed in his own clothes.'

James nodded. 'You don't think he'd be so stupid as to return to his home, would you, gov?'

'That's a possibility, James. Can both of you go there now and check it out? Can you remember the address?'

'Number six Hornbeam Avenue.'

'Well remembered, James.' He turned to Nicky. 'How did you get on with the abattoir?'

She related her earlier telephone conversation. 'Outstanding work, Nicky. I think I must agree with Mrs Johnson. It'll be a long time before I eat pork again.' She nodded, picked up her notebook and mobile phone and joined James waiting by the door.

'See you later, you two.' Donald went to his office, thinking of how fast events were happening before he'd even sat down at his desk.

James stopped the car directly outside the Beecham's house. The front door of the townhouse opened directly onto the pavement. Nicky tried the door and found it locked. 'Is there any other access?' she asked.

'Only by walking to the end of the row, and then there's a rear alleyway going the entire length of the row of houses. You stay here, and I'll go to the rear.'

'Yes, Constable. Shouldn't I be taking the lead here?'

'Oh, sorry, Nicky. Yes, Sergeant, what do you want me to do?'

'You go to the rear, and I'll stay here.' She laughed.

A quick glance at the rear of the house confirmed James's fears. He noticed the broken glass in the kitchen window and the rear door open. Tiptoeing carefully, he entered the kitchen, treading on the splintered glass from the window. He moved into the hall and saw Nicky's shadow through the diffused glazing in the front door. He slid the deadlock latch and let her in. 'It looks as if he's already been here. The rear door was wide open.'

After searching the house and securing the rear door, they returned to the office. James went to the kitchenette to make a cup of coffee for them both. Nicky had only taken one slurp when James's phone rang. He listened, closed the phone, and called to her. 'Forget the coffee; it seems there's a public disturbance at High Green. PC Bellamy, the beat copper, has phoned me. Come on, we can dash there in two minutes.'

'Oh, for goodness' sake, what's going on?' Nicky gasped as they saw the small crowd of people gathered. They heard a man shouting and a dog barking. As they got closer, they saw PC Bellamy holding the people back. Pushing their way through, they saw the reason for the commotion. It was Jack Beecham.

'Hi, PC Bellamy, what's going on?'

'Thank goodness you've come, James. This bloke here has been going berserk. Threatening people and creating a disturbance.'

'Thanks for calling me. This man is a fugitive from the law. He's wanted for murder and escaped police custody at Stafford Hospital.

Hang on.' James reached for his phone and rang Donald. 'Gov, it's James. Can you send some back up to High Green, outside *Godfrey's Bookshop?* It's Jack Beecham creating a disturbance, and I think he's holding a knife. No, it looks like a scalpel. He probably took it from the hospital....'

'... I'll send a couple of constables straight away. Beecham is obviously dangerous. Be careful, James.' James closed the phone and went to PC Bellamy. 'The gov is sending some more reinforcements. What's Beecham doing here, do you know?'

'As far as I can make out, he shouted out that he wants to see Godfrey Warlock, the proprietor of the bookshop. As you can see, the shop is closed, with blinds drawn across the windows.' They'd heard the dog barking earlier, but now they were closer to it, they could see its frantic owner was straining to hold the brindled Staffordshire pit bull terrier from dashing towards the shop and Jack. Nicky winced, watching saliva run from its open mouth displaying sharp teeth.

'Sir?' She approached the middle-aged man. 'Can you take your dog away, please? Its threatening behaviour is not helping the situation here.'

'Who the fuck are you? I'll do whatever I like. This is not communist Russia.' Nicky stifled any further vulgar language from the man by holding out her police badge and warrant card. 'Ah! You're a police officer.'

'Yes, and furthermore, if you don't move, I'll arrest you for having a dangerous dog without a muzzle.' The man slunk away to the rear of the crowd, and the dog became silent.

James recalled the conversation he'd had with Jack Beecham in the hospital. 'I wonder if that's why he's here?' he thought. 'I remember him saying something about a book he'd read from the bookshop.'

'Jack Beecham!' James called to him. 'You're under arrest, Jack. Why don't you come quietly?'

'Go away, Constable. I want to speak with Doctor Godfrey....'

'... well, as we can all see, his shop is closed.'

'No, that's where you're wrong. He's in there; I know he is.'

'This isn't helping anybody, Jack.'

'Doctor Godfrey!' Jack shouted. Everybody watched as Jack started banging and kicking the shop door. 'Let me in!'

Two uniformed police officers came and stood next to James and Nicky. 'He's armed with a knife,' James offered. 'We need to tread carefully. He knows I've charged him with murder, and he's obviously unstable.' Jack's continuous ranting drowned out James's voice.

'Doctor, you told me my wife would enter the path to glory, but how do I know that? You told me what to do, and now you won't speak to me. Why are you doing this? You said you'd help me! Doctor Godfrey!' Jack kicked the door again. 'The police are here to take me away. Unless I know my beloved Carole is in glory, I won't be able to rest. I will not spend the rest of my life in jail, Doctor.'

James could see Jack's actions were getting more frantic. He whispered to the police officers. 'I think we need to step in now. When he next gets preoccupied with banging and kicking the door, we'll jump him. Get ready.'

'You heard me, Doctor. Be it on your conscience.'

James heard Nicky shout. 'Oh, my God!'

James turned to see what had caused her alarm and looked towards the shop window. In a sweeping arc like a rainbow, bright red blood sprayed the individual framed panels. Jack had slit his throat with the scalpel. He slumped against the shop door, and the rest of his spurting blood formed a layer that ran down the door and across the concrete step. In a few seconds, the blood started flowing across the sloping block paving of the pedestrian area. Jack and Nicky rushed forward and prevented him from falling backwards. Jack's eyes were wide open; they knew he was already dead. Jack called to the three police officers. 'Clear the area and then set up some tape to isolate the shop front.' Nicky took off her overcoat and laid it over Jack Beecham's lifeless form. James reached for his phone. 'Gov, I think you'd better come round here. We're outside *Godfrey's Bookshop*. Jack Beecham has cut his own throat. He's dead' James heard the line go dead. Donald was already on his way without uttering a word into his phone.

'What a mess!' Donald looked down at Jack Beecham. The crowd had dispersed, and the scene of crime officers were taking photographs and measurements. Within a few minutes, two orderlies dressed in white overalls brought a body bag and laid it next to Jack. They were about to lift his body when everybody turned. They heard the blinds of the bookshop being raised. Nicky was standing in the doorway and jumped backwards when she listened to the doorbell jangle. The door opened and Doctor Godfrey Warlock stood on the threshold, looking at the bloody scene.

'Are you the proprietor of the bookshop, sir? Can you explain any of this?' Donald asked him and mentally noted the sinister, almost threatening presence of the man.

'Yes. I'm the proprietor. Doctor Godfrey Warlock at your service.' He looked down at Jack Beecham. 'What a muddle. All this blood over the front of my shop. I assume the police or the council will clean all this away?' He waved his arm dismissively at the blood still seeping over the concrete paving blocks.

'Doctor Warlock, I'm Detective Constable James Garbett; do you remember me? I came in here yesterday with my colleague, Sergeant Bains.'

Doctor Warlock's piercing black eyes became slits as he peered towards James.

Godfrey held the lapels of his coat with both hands. His unruly grey hair looked like a wig worn by a judge. He wore a long, flowing, black silk gown that nearly covered his shoes. James pictured a similarity to a barrister addressing jurors in a courtroom. 'I don't remember you, young man....'

'... it was only yesterday....'

'... yesterday? What is yesterday? What is today? What is tomorrow? They are mere human terms to describe the passing of time. At the end of the day, after another sunset has occurred, they are only checkpoints along the world's inevitable path of destiny. We are all inconsequential pinpricks, a full stop on a page.' He cleared his throat with a sharp 'Ahem!' and carried on. He knew he had a captive audience and looked around at the crowd of people who had gathered. 'The yesterday you mention, Constable, means the same to me as the events at Auschwitz, Treblinka and Belsen, and so many more. So many people left this earthly toil yesterday. So, what are you fussing about? What is one man's passing in relation to all those tortured souls?'

'Sir, I'd be grateful if you'd answer my question...?'

'... I see so many people during the long day at my shop. I can't remember everyone.'

'It doesn't matter, Doctor Warlock. Yesterday I had a conversation with the deceased man, Jack Beecham....'

'... Is that who this man was? I say was because he is dead, isn't he? I know death when I see it? Do you know what death looks like, young police officer from Cannock?'

James ignored his rhetoric. 'Don't you recognise him? He said he knew you well and was one of your customers.'

'As I said to you, young man, I can't remember people from one day to the next. Anyone who comes into my shop is only a customer. I never form a personal relationship with a customer. It's not good business practice....'

'... Doctor Warlock, Jack Beecham told me he bought one of your books and that you told him to murder his wife.'

'Do you realise, young man, how ridiculous that sounds?'

'I'm only repeating what he told me in hospital.'

'This man was in the hospital, was he? Well, there you have the answer to your question, policeman. They administer drugs in a hospital, so I've been told. I've never frequented such a place. It's obvious to me this man must have taken drugs for whatever physical or mental complaint he suffered from. From what I saw from within my shop, it's understandable he was still under the influence of narcotics when he decided to leave his miserable earthly existence and seek solace elsewhere.' The doctor looked down at Jack Beecham's body. 'He looks peaceful, doesn't he? Perhaps he's found his utopia now? I always think a dead body displays a certain calmness and evidence of a life well lived, don't you, young man?'

'*Did* you know Jack Beecham?'

'... No, I didn't! I can't be responsible for every maniac that enters my premises. You can see how deranged this man's mind was for him to sever his own throat. The only unfortunate aspect for me is it's so messy. If only he could have selected a less dramatic way? Ah well, every person is unique in how they leave. At least he had a choice. Those lost souls in the death camps didn't have such luxury.'

Donald admired the way James interrogated Doctor Warlock, but intervened. 'Doctor, I'm Detective Inspector Donald Lawrence from Cannock Police. Constable Garbett is my colleague.'

'Another police officer, is this a police convention?' Godfrey sneered. 'Shouldn't you all be investigating misdemeanours that are occurring elsewhere in your territory instead of congregating here? It's obvious to me there's no crime here.'

'We're looking for answers here, Doctor. It's puzzling why a normal, working-class man living in leafy Cannock should suddenly change his behaviour and act as he has?'

'As I said to your constable, this has nothing to do with me, so I'm equally perplexed why you're interviewing me.'

'This is not an interview, Doctor; we're merely asking some questions.'

'That's all I'm going to say on this matter. I'm wasting my valuable time, and all this is not good for business. So be good little people, do your jobs and make sure all this gets cleared away.' The doorbell jangled as he closed the door behind him. The sound made Nicky jump, involuntarily. She'd heard the bell a few times now, and it was signifying alarm and sadness in her mind. She stepped back further and held her hand to her mouth as she saw Doctor Godfrey Warlock standing within the dimness of his shop, howling with laughter.

Thirteen

'Well, he's a cool customer; make no mistake about that.' Donald offered to Nicky and James as they sat in the office, sharing a cup of coffee.

'He gives me the shudders,' Nicky added. 'I don't think any of you saw what I did when we dispersed from High Green.'

'What did you see?' James asked.

'Doctor Warlock, standing inside his shop laughing hysterically.'

'I think he's a farthing short of a shilling. Did you hear him ranting about death camps in the second world war? What's that got to with the death of Jack Beecham?'

'The entire experience of meeting him makes me uneasy,' Donald added. 'Unfortunately, he's right on one point; there's been no crime committed that directly involves him. Nevertheless, it's worth noting what sort of man he is for future reference. For now, we're far too busy with other matters.' Nicky collected their coffee cups, took them to the kitchenette, and returned to find Donald and James discussing a funeral. Donald looked towards Nicky.

'We're talking about tomorrow morning's funeral for Constable Joe Swales.'

'Poor man,' she added, deep in thought. 'His family must be devastated.'

'Another occasion when we're reminded of how we put our lives at risk, all for being a police officer and dedicating ourselves to serving the public. We're all aware of the possibilities when we take the oath. Still, tomorrow morning will be a sombre, harrowing occasion, as they always are. In my brief career, I've attended three police fatalities, all in London.'

'What should we wear, gov?'

'Police uniforms as befits your rank, James. We'll mingle with every other copper from the Staffordshire Constabulary and form a guard of honour for Joe and his bereaved family for them to pass through. The funeral cortege will pull up outside the southern lych-gate of Saint Luke's Church. Have you been to the church, either of you?' They shook their heads. 'Perhaps you should take a walk and familiarise yourselves with the environment before the funeral? Anyway, back to work.'

Donald went to his office. James looked at Nicky, 'How about we have a walk to Saint Luke's Church at lunchtime? We could eat some sandwiches there in the gardens.'

Nicky smiled and nodded, 'Okay, I'll see you at the southern lych-gate at one o'clock.'

Fourteen

Janet needed to replace the dress over her breasts. She'd been feeding Zak, but a sharp knock on the front door disturbed her. Through the glass panels, she could see who the visitor was and burst into a radiant smile. 'Lucy, come in, come in. I'm so glad to see you. Wow! Kiddo, thank you for coming; it's been too long.'

Lucy held an overnight case in her hand that she dropped and returned Janet's eager embrace. 'Oh, Janet, you look so well and happy' Zak's cries interrupted their greeting. They walked into the lounge.

'There are only a few peaceful moments when you have a baby. Detective Sergeant Lucy Barnes, may I present Zak Lawrence.' Zak ceased crying when Janet picked him up and passed him to Lucy. Janet smiled because it was at once apparent that Lucy had no experience with babies. She seemed awkward and didn't know how to hold him properly. Zak started struggling, so Lucy quickly returned him to his mother. 'Make yourself comfortable, kiddo. I was in the middle of feeding Zak. Give me a minute, and then I can put him in his cot for his afternoon sleep.' With mounting intrigue, Lucy watched Janet resume breastfeeding. Her first sense of unease gave way to envy and admiration for her friend. She didn't need reminding that Zak was Donald's child. Had their engagement progressed to marriage, it could be her sitting in a cosy fireside lounge feeding their baby. Since her engagement to Donald had ended, she hadn't formed a deep, loving relationship with another man, despite a few minor interactions.

'So, how is life at the Met these days?' Janet asked as she realised Zak had gone to sleep.

'Oh, you know, the same as always, struggling to keep one step ahead of the villains.' Janet retook her seat by the fireside. 'Oh, and before I forget, Chief Superintendent Jack Croaker asked me to pass on his regards. I told him I was visiting you.'

'Ah! That's nice. We think of Jack often and our former life at the Met. Jack is Chief Superintendent now. We always said he'll become Chief Constable one day, didn't we? He's well on the way to doing that now. Would you like a cup of coffee? I'm due for one about now. I always like to give myself fifteen minutes of rest after feeding Zak. The little beast, he bites me,' She rubbed her breast. 'He has two front teeth showing through, and where does he want to teethe, on my nipples.' They laughed. Janet thought of repeating what she'd said to Donald about - *'like father, like son,'* but decided against it. Lucy, however, had envisioned the same erotic thought. She remembered with tenderness how Donald used to enjoy nuzzling into her breasts during intercourse.

'I have your bedroom all ready for you upstairs, and we're having your favourite chicken fajita for dinner, washed down with a bottle of chianti.'

'It will be like the old days.' Lucy sighed.

'Unfortunately, we have a sad occasion tomorrow morning. An officer, a colleague of Donald's, Constable Joe Swales, lost his life. It's his funeral tomorrow, perhaps you'd...?'

'... of course, kiddo. I always carry my uniform when I go away. You never know when it's needed. Tomorrow morning will be the saddest reason for me wearing it again.'

Janet passed her a mug of coffee, and they retook their seats in the lounge.

'Do you enjoy living in Cannock? I remember how much a shock it was to all of us at the Met when you and Donald left to come here.'

'It's vastly different to living in London but, after all, it was because of Donald's promotion to Inspector....'

'... Yes. Inspector Lawrence, eh? It only seems five minutes since we were all constables together investigating that horrible case on the south bank of the Thames.'

'Do you remember when we investigated those prostitutes in Deptford, and Donald nearly got compromised?' Janet laughed. They looked affectionately at each other and smiled.

'Janet, there's something I wanted to ask you. Why Cannock, why Staffordshire? Did you come here because of the case you stumbled on during your honeymoon at The Crucified Abbot? That's only a few miles from here, isn't it?'

'No, not really. Although we both love Cannock Chase. The scenery around here is spectacular. I don't know if you knew when we were at the Met together, but I originate from around here, anyway. I lived in a tiny village called Great Wyrley, a suburb about three miles to the south.'

'I didn't know that. So, for you, it's like coming home.'

'Partly. The major reason is Donald's promotion to Inspector came with the posting here in Cannock. The two are indivisible. A loving wife goes with her husband. I miss my career and the hands-on approach of being an active sergeant in the force but along came Zak, and that was that. Circumstances mean I'm now a wife and mother and thrilled and content, actually.'

'I'm delighted how things have worked out for you, kiddo.'

The black wrought-iron minute hand clicked onto the roman numeral XII on the town's war memorial clock tower. It coincided with a single bell being rung in Saint Luke's Church belfry. It was one o'clock. James stood under the south lych-gate, watching Nicky walking through the pedestrianised town centre towards him. Her attractive feminine form pleased him. She had a shapely figure, evident not only to him, but he noticed other macho heads turning towards her as she passed them. 'Are you going somewhere nice, Detective Sergeant?' James greeted her, flippantly.

'Well, to any casual onlooker, it probably looks like we're meeting on a date, but....'

'... on a date. Are we on a date?'

'James! Of course, we aren't. We only met the other day, and can work colleagues have a date? Let's have a look at this lovely church.'

They read an enormous, enamelled signboard. 'Wow! It says here Saint Luke's is over nine hundred years old.' James said. They turned to look up the long sloping pathway that led from the lych-gate to the main door in the church's nave. 'I suppose this is where we'll be standing forming the guard of honour tomorrow morning,' he mused.

Nicky was reading another enamelled sign. *'Saint Luke's is a Grade II* listed building. It occupies a prime location at the heart of the town centre. It's surrounded by well-maintained grassed areas to the north and south with a good range of mature trees, making a beautiful oasis in the middle of our town.'*

'What a contrast this is with the top end of town at High Green?' Nicky commented pointing at the sign.

'... meaning?' he asked.

'How peaceful, compared to the spooky building, misery, and tragedy we saw this morning outside *Godfrey's Bookshop.'*

'Yes. It's like one is God's building, the other is the Devil's,' James commented glibly. The irony resonated with Nicky and she gazed at his face, wondering how appropriate his comments seemed.

Donald made his way home, looking forward to a cosy evening with his wife. He relished temporarily being insulated from the crazy events that seemed to mount up day by day in his job. He opened the door and smelled the delicious aromas coming from the kitchen. He called for Janet to let her know he was home, but she was in the garage arranging some food in the freezer. Looking in the lounge, he saw Zak asleep in his carrycot. Donald heard water splashing in the bathroom and assumed Janet was taking a bath. He quickly poured a couple of glasses of rioja, slipped off his coat, and climbed the stairs. He smelled the feminine perfume that seemed to drift down the stairs. The further he went, the more pungent the smell. The bathroom door was ajar, and Donald slowly entered. He wanted to surprise his wife. At that moment, Lucy immersed herself under the soothing water, rinsing the shampoo out of her long blonde hair. With her eyes closed, she wasn't aware Donald had entered the bathroom. Without looking at her, he sat on the toilet seat holding the two glasses of wine. When Donald raised his eyes, he gazed longingly on Lucy's naked form. He thought he was dreaming, when she slowly raised her head and opened her ice-blue eyes.

Any other situation where a friend would inadvertently invade another's intimate privacy by seeing them naked would invoke an exclamation of horror or an embarrassing cry. Lucy merely whispered, 'Hello, Donald, how nice to see you again,' She smirked as Donald held an immobile stance, still holding the rioja. 'Oh, thank you for the wine.' She reached for one glass, allowing him a clearer view of her ample breasts. He passed her the wine, still too shocked to comment. 'I take it you weren't expecting to see me in your bath?' He shook his head. 'Ah well, it's like old times, isn't it? I don't think we'd better tell Janet, do you? I don't want my stay at your home to get off on the wrong foot. You'd better go before Janet comes out of the garage.' Donald got up to leave, but turned. He leaned forward and tenderly kissed Lucy on her lips.

'It's great to see you again, Lucy. All of you! Wow! You're as beautiful as ever,' he whispered, and left the bathroom.

Lucy lay back in the water, slurping the wine. 'Well! Well! That's was completely unexpected.' She'd wondered if Donald had any romantic feelings left for her considering all they'd gone through in the past. Now she knew he had.

Donald put his glass of wine back in the kitchen and approached the garage. 'Oh, there you are, darling,' he called, and they kissed.

'You're home! You'll never guess who's arrived. Its Lucy. She's upstairs having a bath, I think.'

Donald gulped, 'Really, darling? That's wonderful.'

Over dinner later that evening, they shared many laughs and reminiscences of the past. Janet had no knowledge that they'd met earlier in the bathroom. Despite trying not to gaze at Lucy with full eye contact, their knowing stare at each other only happened occasionally.

Fifteen

After introducing Lucy to his team, she took her place in line with the other seventy-two police officers. One other unexpected, uniformed police officer standing in line was Donald's wife, Janet. She had arranged for a neighbour to look after Zak for a couple of hours. The vast array of police officers had congregated on Saint Luke's Church, Cannock, from all over the County of Staffordshire to pay their respects to a fallen colleague. Television journalists and camera operators maintained a respectful distance from the solemn proceedings. The campanologists' captain selected the lowest diatonic tone of one of the eight Saint Luke's bells to toll for Joe Swales from the church tower. Six of Constable Swale's closest friends bore his pine coffin on their shoulders and trudged up the long avenue to the doorway of Saint Luke's nave. Joe's coffin lay before the altar as the officers filed, one by one, into the red sandstone Norman church. The nave door closed, excluding the outside world to the unique and personal service.

After the service, the police officers reformed the honour guard down the pathway leading to the southern lych-gate. Then the funeral hearse, followed by several other polished black limousines, drove away. Serving police officers dispersed back to their various police stations and workplaces. Janet and Lucy stood under the ancient curved oak timbers of the lych-gate. 'What happens now, kiddo?' Lucy asked.

'What would you like to do?'

'Well, I've never been to Cannock before, how about showing me this town of yours?' Janet smiled.

'Other than the funeral, it's a nice day to see Cannock. The open-air market is in the upper part of the town, and we can sit in the sunshine and have a coffee. Oh, and I know you like a good read. There's a fascinating, spooky bookshop in High Green I've been dying to visit. Perhaps you could pick up a delightful book to take back to London?'

'It sounds good to me....'

'... Hang on a second, Lucy. I'll check with my neighbour, Jenny Coleman, to see if Zak is okay, then we'll have a stroll.'

After wandering through the market, they sat opposite each other in the same seats that James and Nicky had occupied a week earlier. They realised they were conspicuous. People were staring at them. Their dark blue police uniforms contrasted markedly with the casual, and sometimes scruffy, clothes of other coffee drinkers. 'I suppose it's unusual in these parts to see two women police sergeants,' Lucy commented, before smiling and acknowledging a handsome man who offered a polite 'hello' to her as he strolled by.

'Here, Lucy, I have a fold-up bag; it's a beautiful day, let's put our heavy uniform coats in the bag. I'm sure we'll be better without them.' They retook their seats in their white short-sleeved blouses. '... and our checked ties. They're a sure giveaway that we're police officers.' They smiled at each other as wolf whistles came their way from a group of passing youths, seeing them discard their coats and ties. Janet realised the whistles were for Lucy, noticing that her thin blouse was almost translucent, revealing her black bra and generous breasts.

'Cheers,' they offered to each other, soaking up the sunshine and breathing in the heady scent of flowering shrubs in the municipal flower beds.

'I get it, Janet.'

'Get what?'

'The attraction of living in a small provincial town rather than being a perpetual stranger in an anonymous multinational conglomerate like London.'

'Donald likes it here too. In Cannock, he's the highest-ranking officer at the town's nick. People know him and like him. I know he already feels a sense of belonging here that the Metropolitan Police's vastness could never provide. In mitigation of defending their own positions, I suppose some Met officers would say he's a big fish in a little pond, but ...'

'... I'm surprised there's a but?'

'Well, until a few weeks ago, hardly anything ever happened here. The most traumatic cases Donald had to deal with was a traffic fatality caused by dangerous drink driving and catching a habitual burglar red-handed. Now, in a brief space of time, there have been three gruesome murders and suicides. A local vicar has gone bonkers imagining he's Jesus Christ, and a bloke at a music concert believed he was Ludwig Van Beethoven reincarnated. I wonder what's coming next?'

'I suppose, in our line of work, it must be better than being bored with nothing to do?'

'Yes, I guess. I feel for Donald, though. I see how tired he is, and sometimes when he comes home from the office - disturbed, almost. The murders have been horrible. In the last one, a man fed his wife to his pigs.'

Lucy's expression turned to a grimace. 'You say he's disturbed by these horrible cases, but we know we've all seen humanity at its worst when we dealt with the multiple murders in south London.'

'Yes, I know, and I don't think Donald fears that aspect of these cases. I'm sure it's because he's now in charge. It's his responsibility.'

'Who's the superintendent over Donald?'

'That's the point. There isn't one. Donald's immediate superior is Superintendent Woodhouse from Staffordshire County Constabulary, ensconced in his ivory tower in Stafford. Donald rarely sees him. He only contacts Donald by phone when he needs clarification on the weekly statistic reports.'

'It makes you realise, looking back, how much we came to depend on our gov, Jack Croaker, at the Met.' Janet nodded in agreement.

They finished their coffees, while watching people amble by and listening to a dishevelled, bearded street busker strumming his guitar and trying to sing.

Lucy put her finger in her ear and smirked. 'Where's this bookshop you mentioned?'

'Around the corner in High Green. Shall we go?'

Lucy gazed up at the swinging sign making squeaking noises as it swayed in the gentle breeze, coinciding with an isolated cloud temporarily blotting out the bright sunshine. Lucy developed goose pimples on her arms. 'Ooh, it's a cool breeze when the sun goes in.'

'*'Godfrey's Bookshop'* eh? I see what you mean; it sure does look spooky.' Lucy also read the signboard in the shop window. '*Doctor Godfrey Warlock, Purveyor of rare and unusual books.'* 'Ah, this looks a fascinating place. Do you remember that bookshop in Pimlico we found when we were on a drug case? It looks as mysterious as that one.'

'If I remember correctly, that bookshop turned out to be the hideout of the lynchpin of the drug gang boss.'

'Oh, yes, I'd forgotten.'

'Thank goodness we don't have a drug culture here in Cannock,' Janet added as she peered into the shop's dimness.

'You asked what's coming next? I'm hoping it's not drugs for yours and Donald's sake. As you know, it changes everything and nothing for the better.'

Lucy pushed the arched chromium handle and looked up at the jangling brass bell swaying on a rolled-up sheet of metal spring. Peering into the dim shop, she inhaled the fusty, old-fashioned smell of books. Lucy turned to Janet and missed the step, 'This place is a gem. Look at all the books; I could spend hours browsing in here'. Her voice checked as she regained her poise. 'Lookout, kiddo, there's a step here.'

'Mind the step, ladies. Welcome to my humble bookshop emporium. As my signboard explains, I specialise in rare and unusual books.' They turned to their left to see a tall, gaunt man appear from the shadows behind a counter.

'Oh, it's you, kind lady. You came to my bookshop the other day, didn't you? I remember your baby was crying, so I didn't get to introduce myself properly. I'm the proprietor, Doctor Godfrey Warlock, at your service.'

'Yes, I remember. My son, Zak, disturbed the peace a little, didn't he...?'

'... It was as if your son didn't want to come to my shop ... I trust Zak is alright now...?'

'... oh, yes, he's fine. In fact, only a minute after pushing him away from your shop, he was fine for the rest of the day.'

'That *is* good. Now, could I ask who your charming companion is?' He turned to Lucy. 'Please pardon my bluntness, but I don't recall seeing you around the town before. I have a knack for remembering faces, and I'm sure I wouldn't have forgotten such a beautiful one as yours.' He reached for Lucy's hand and kissed the back of it. As he bent forward, she noticed his spiky grey hair that seemed to sprout between rows of baldness across his scalp. She at once retracted her hand when she felt his trim, black goatee beard tickling her fingers. Whether or not it was her police training, but her senses reeled as if reminding herself not to divulge her name or any personal information. Lucy immediately noticed how receptive to human emotion he was. She saw the slight change in his demeanour as frown lines crossed his forehead. She sensed he knew his blatant flattery and attempted charm offensive hadn't deceived her.

Godfrey transferred his attention to Janet. She looked at him and remembered he wore the same flamboyant yellow polka-dot bowtie as the last time she was here. 'Are you looking for any particular sort of book today?' he asked with a leering smile. The display of spaced, blackened, and misshapen teeth that lined his mouth slightly repulsed both women.

'We'd just like to browse, if that's okay?' Lucy asked.

'Of course you can. I assemble my books into anthologies depending on their subject, shown by a sign above each aisle. Travel, culinary, engineering, quantum physics, and lots more ad infinitum. There's a large section dedicated to fiction and the classics. I'm sure you'll have no problem finding what interests you. If you wish to inspect a book more closely, I have a reading room at the bottom of my shop.' He pointed to rows of tables and chairs better illuminated than where they presently stood. Lucy and Janet turned to see several people sitting reading under low hanging lamps. As if they knew Godfrey had referred to them, they turned and offered their greeting. One man doffed his hat. 'I'll leave you to browse now. Please call me if you need help, won't you?'

Godfrey seemed to melt back into the shadows with no further comment, and Lucy and Janet were alone. They walked a few steps to stand under an enamelled sign that they had trouble deciphering. Still, both read aloud '*Fiction*' in the elaborate calligraphic font.

'Phew, kiddo, as soon as you walk into this eerie place, Godfrey is the sort of proprietor you almost expect to meet, isn't he! It's as though the shop couldn't exist without him and vice versa.'

'He sure is a character....'

'... yes, he is, but not one that I'd like to be part of my regular acquaintances,' Lucy added. They looked at several nondescript books that didn't take their interest. Then, with her forefinger in the spine's top, she prised a thick sepia-coloured tome from a middle shelf. 'Oh, look here, Janet. I haven't read this book since I was at school.'

'... The Kama Sutra, is it?' Janet laughed.

'Ha-ha, only for reference.' She feigned a laugh. '... but I'm laughing on the other side of my face. Look at this.'

Janet read aloud, *'The Posthumous Papers of the Pickwick Club.'* 'Isn't that 'The Pickwick Papers' by Charles Dickens?'

'Yes, it is, but as far as I know, they only used the longer title on the original cover when first published in 1836. It was his first novel, of course. Oh, my good Lord, Janet, look at the scribbling signature above the title.'

Janet peered at the faded writing. 'It's so sprawling and difficult to read; it's obviously handwritten in black ink, but all one word.'

'Yes, one word - Charles Dickens.'

'Lucy, are you suggesting that this is Charles Dickens' actual signature?'

'I'm no expert, but it looks that way to me. If it is, this is worth a fortune. I doubt if Godfrey knows what he has here. I wonder how much this copy is to buy?'

'Don't underestimate him, Lucy. He's the proprietor of a bookshop; I bet he knows every book on these shelves.'

Lucy thumbed through the book. 'Look, Janet, even the binding is all hand stitched. Full mass-produced machine book-stitching didn't happen until the end of the eighteenth century. See the edges of each page, sepia discolouration. You only find this in genuine old books where the page edges have been exposed to the light.'

'Ah, you like my copy of *The Pickwick Papers?*' Godfrey came and stood by them. 'Dear old Charlie, he was a dear man who always made the most of his talents. I say *old* because even as a young man, he always portrayed someone of much greater age.'

Lucy and Janet looked aghast from each other and then to Godfrey, wondering about his seriousness and sanity. This increased alarmingly when he carried on.

'Like the readers there, Charlie used to be a customer of mine and received a lot of background research material for his later books from me. He even used my feather tipped writing pen to sign this copy for me. I always think an author should sign a copy of his own work, don't you? It adds a certain authenticity to a book ...'

'... Doctor Godfrey. They published this book in 1836.'

'... you are such a knowledgeable young lady,' he complimented Lucy. '... 19th March 1836, if I remember correctly. The date is fixed in my mind. Considering it was early springtime, uncharacteristically, late snow covered the ground and Charlie was especially cold.' It was as if Godfrey's staring eyes transfixed at an infinite point out in space. He smiled, displaying his rotten teeth. '... you should have seen the steam rising from his baggy pantaloons as he stood next to my fireplace after he came in from the frosty air. Later that day, when he met his publisher, he changed into his usual long coat-tails and breeches. If you're interested, young lady, somewhere on the same shelf, I have a copy of his last novel, *The Mystery of Edwin Drood'*. Of course, I'm sure I don't need to tell someone as educated as you, Charlie never finished the novel. He gave his unedited papers to me as he exhaled his last breath and entered another realm. Ah! It was a sad day for the members of my book club he'd befriended, and his large family. It was a beautiful, warm, sunny day in Gad's Hill, Chatham. The 9th of June 1870 in the year of our Lord. That phraseology always puzzles me. Does it you too? By *our Lord*, I suppose they refer to the carpenter from Nazareth. He only managed to eke out thirty-three years scratching in the dust of that filthy little town, whereas that was two thousand years ago. Where was I? Oh yes, Charlie bequeathed to me everything he'd written about Edwin Drood and some earlier books too. I like to think he based the eponymous character on me, but he never got around to admitting that. You need some air in your lungs to be able to speak, don't you? Perhaps one day, he will. I must have another chat with him sometime about that. I can always re-inflate him by blowing a few puffs of air up his backside.'

Lucy slowly replaced the old tome back on the bookshelf. She nervously grasped Janet's hand and edged slowly back towards the front door. They left Godfrey still staring into space. Even when they pulled the door open and the bell jangled, Godfrey still stood where they'd left him. Closing the door behind them, hand in hand, Lucy and Janet sauntered across the pedestrian area to a wooden bench and sat down.

Janet gaped at Lucy. 'What do you make of all that, kiddo?'

'Never in all my life have I heard such a diatribe of nonsensical ranting.'

'... but Lucy, he worries me. He's so convincing. How would he know it was snowing on the 9th of March 1836? How could he know what Charles Dickens wore on that morning...?'

'... Janet, the man is as nutty as a fruit cake. Anyone could do some research and find out the weather on a particular day in history. Everyone knows what men wore in the early 19th century, pantaloons and breeches.'

'... but the book? Even you think the book is an original....'

'... yes, I must admit, it certainly looked legitimate. Think about it, Janet, for a moment; consider it may be genuine. What's it doing in a mysterious bookshop here in this small town one hundred miles from London, and why hasn't anybody discovered it before now? No, it must be a forgery. One point you could give him credit for, he's a convincing sales agent.'

Lucy looked back to the bookshop and held her hand to her mouth. 'Kiddo, don't look now but the old goat is watching us with his face pressed up against his shop window. Uh! Oh! He's now laughing.'

Janet got up and pulled Lucy's hand. 'Come on, we need another cup of coffee.'

Sitting back in the open-air café, they considered their experience in *Godfrey's Bookshop*.

'Janet, we both know he's off the wall. You told me earlier that other people in Cannock were having delusions. This is obviously another instance.' A screeching sound cut her words short. They heard the siren of a fire engine blaring in a Doppler effect, speeding somewhere across town.

'... but who do you think he was pretending to be?'

'... I don't know. Methuselah, perhaps? According to The Bible's old testament, didn't he live to be two hundred years old? Godfrey must think he's of a similar age, at least if he was present when Charles Dickens published his first novel in 1836.'

'I don't know whether to laugh or be afraid. It sounds so ridiculous.'

'Yes, I agree with you, Janet, but think of this, that book seemed to be the real thing. A signed first edition, Charles Dickens. Our police salary and pensions are pennies on a hoop-la stall at a fairground compared to what it's worth.' She turned and looked back up High Green.

'What are you saying, Lucy? Don't you dare tell me you're thinking of going back there?'

'Consider the facts. It's obvious to a blind man and his dog that Godfrey Warlock is a loony. He shouldn't be out in society, let alone be running a bookshop. Because he's deranged, I don't believe for a second he can know the book's true value. Obviously, no one else but you, I, and Doctor Godfrey know that book is there, or someone else would have snapped it up by now.'

'Well?'

'Well, I'm going to ask him how much he wants for it.'

'Oh, Lucy, you saw how menacing he can be.'

'I don't think he'll be intimidating if he thinks he can make a sale. Isn't that what he's in business for?'

'Lucy, I left Zak with Jenny, my neighbour.'

'Yes, of course, you get back and look after Zak. Go ahead, I'll catch up with you in a little while. It's okay if I stay another night with you, isn't it? I don't have to be back at the Met until after lunch tomorrow.'

'We'd be delighted if you stayed another night. I'll get back and prepare another lovely meal. Please be careful, Lucy. You have mine and Donald's mobile numbers if you need help...?'

'... I'll be fine. Don't worry. I want to satisfy my curiosity about that book. The thought of driving back down the motorway to London not having had an opportunity to buy it would send me to distraction. If he *does* know the book's true provenance, he'll obviously want thousands of pounds for it. That will count me out of the running, but at least I'll know.'

Sixteen

'Hello, my dear, I knew you'd be returning to my humble bookshop.' Godfrey was standing on the threshold of his premises with the door already open. 'It's Lucy, isn't it? I heard your charming friend call you by that name. Come in! Come in!' Lucy stepped into the gloom. '... and you know there is a step, so please take care.'

Godfrey ambled down the aisles to where Lucy had replaced *The Pickwick Papers*. With a bony index finger, that Lucy thought resembled a vulture's hooked talon, he prised the tome from the shelf and passed it to her. 'This is what you came back for, isn't it?'

'Yes, it is. I'm interested in buying this book. How much do you want for it?'

'Oh, my dear Lucy, not so fast. Don't you want to have a closer look at the book to be sure you know what you're buying?'

'Yes, okay.'

'Did you enjoy the funeral?' Lucy stared at him in surprise.

'Yes, I know you are a police officer. You stood with your friend in the honour guard for that tragic constable, Joe Swales. The man that beheaded that poor police officer was one of my best customers, Mr Keith Newsome. He was an expert at rearing pigs. Keith used to come to my reading room to study about them. We'll all miss him very much here at *Godfrey's Bookshop*. Ah well....' Godfrey temporarily went into one of his robotic trances, staring into space before addressing Lucy again. 'It's a wonder you didn't see me this morning. I was standing a few yards from you on the pavement and didn't come any closer to the church. They are such cold, damp places, aren't they? I prefer not to frequent such old buildings. You never know what ills may befall you there. From time to time, I've met a few Christians; in my experience, they give the impression they were baptised in vinegar. However, it was a wonderful turnout for that decapitated policeman, wasn't it? I always say, live your life, so when death comes the mourners will outnumber the cheerers.'

Godfrey turned towards the rear room where other people were still reading. 'I'm sorry to interrupt your concentration, my good friends. I have a new convert here. Her name is Lucy.'

She gazed at the ten or twelve men and women she estimated were sitting around the tables. 'Hello, Lucy, welcome to *Godfrey's Bookshop,'* they offered en masse with a dull monotone.

'Hello, everybody.'

'Move along, please, Jeremy. Make room for Lucy,' Godfrey asked, politely. He turned to her. 'Jeremy is studying *The Chemistry of Poisons,* aren't you, my dear chap?' Jeremy smiled, nodded, and returned to his book. 'Over there by the window is my excellent friend Griselda Craven; she's studying to be a mortician, you know. She teaches herself how to embalm dead bodies and other such morbid delicacies that the human world gets itself involved with these days.' Griselda heard her name being mentioned and looked across. Godfrey returned her wave. 'Keep up the wonderful work, darling,' he called before lowering his voice to a hoarse whisper. 'Do you know, Lucy, that Griselda is nearly seventy years old? She doesn't look a day over twenty-five, does she? We're all of the same opinion here. We think that instead of all those fancy face creams you ladies use, she applies some of that embalming fluid stuff to prolong her youthful looks. Still, whatever makes her happy, eh?'

Lucy sat down and looked more closely at the book. Lucy felt Godfrey's scrawny hand gripping her shoulder. 'I'll leave you alone for a while, so please relax and have a real close look at the book.' She looked up and once again recoiled at the sight of his unpleasant teeth. Her phone started ringing, disturbing the quiet ambience of the bookshop. She pressed the green acceptance icon and listened. 'Lucy, it's me, Janet. I'm checking that you're alright?'

Lucy murmured into the phone, aware some of the readers had looked up at the noise disturbing their concentration. 'Hi, Janet, thanks for thinking of me. I'm fine. I'll see you soon.' She closed her phone and was about to put it into her trouser pocket but thought again. She took several photographs of the book's cover and several important pages inside before putting it away. After closer examination, she was more convinced than ever that the book was a genuine first edition, Charles Dickens. The ultimate piece of evidence convincing her of its authenticity was the quality of the paper. In the early nineteenth century, there was only one writing paper type in everyday use, rag paper; cloth rags, mainly cotton, but sometimes flax would be used. The mill workers beat the slurry to a pulp using a pestle and mortar, on an industrial scale. The resulting mash was rolled and dried. This gave the finished paper a unique, coarse feel. The pages of this Dickens' book yielded the same texture that Lucy had felt on archive paperwork from nineteenth-century police files. She rose from the table and strolled down the fusty shop to the counter where Godfrey stood waiting for her.

'There's a stool there, Lucy. Please take the weight off your feet. I'll make myself comfortable on this side, and we can talk.' Lucy placed the book on the wooden counter and eased onto a high, three-legged stool. She peered through the panelled windows and contrasted the bright sunshine with the gloom of the bookshop.

'How much do you want for the book?' Lucy repeated her earlier question.

'Before we get around to discussing the price, can I ask why you want the book?'

Lucy hesitated and wondered why he was asking. 'Why do you want to know that...?'

'... well, my dear, Lucy, if you merely want the book to sell and make a quick profit, then the book is not for sale. I'm sure you're aware of the true value of the book, as I am.'

'If we're both aware of this book's value, then I have to tell you that I can't afford the price you'll be asking. So, it looks as if I'm wasting my time and yours.' She eased her body off the stool and turned towards the door.

'Not so fast. Please sit down again, my dear Lucy. I'm sure we can come to some arrangement. Correct me if I'm wrong, but you really would like this book, wouldn't you?'

'Yes, I would. To own a unique historical literary work such as this would give me immense satisfaction. Not to display to friends or colleagues or brag to people to inflate my ego, but simply to have it in my possession. I love every piece of writing that Charles Dickens ever produced. I'd never part with it.'

'... Charlie *was* a veritable genius and still is, as far as I'm aware.' Lucy was getting used to his fanciful ramblings and ignored him.

'... but, alas, I'm a realist. I know this is a pipedream for the likes of me. You should offer it to wealthy millionaires or, better still, the British Museum and let them have it to preserve the nation's heritage. So, when you talk of an arrangement between us, there's nothing I can give you in collateral for the true value of the book....'

'... quid pro quo! My dear Lucy.' He looked askance at her and arched his eyebrow.

'What...?'

'You help me, and I'll help you.'

'Help me? How?'

'I'll let you have the book for gratuit, gratis, gratuito, kostenlos, in any language you prefer, but in plain English - for free.'

'Hang on here, I don't like the sound of this. If you think I can enter some fraudulent illegality, you're mistaken. I'm a serving police officer.' Lucy eased off the stool again.

'I wouldn't insult your obvious intelligence by suggesting anything that has such petty monetary connotations.'

'I don't understand.' She picked up the book again and sensed the unique history in her grasp.

Godfrey knew he had her hooked. 'I know you're not from around these parts, but don't tell me, let me guess, I'm good with people's accents. From down south, London perhaps?' Lucy arched her eyebrow in acceptance of his worldliness. 'I think I can narrow that down further. Perhaps your home was in Essex? I also detect an inflexion of a foreign language. Hmm! Italian maybe? Am I right, my dear?'

'Maybe?' Lucy was defensive and becoming anaesthetised by Godfrey's persistent, almost hypnotic interrogation.

'Let me see?' Godfrey studied her face meticulously, making Lucy feel uncomfortable. 'You were born in Italy but emigrated here to England early in your childhood. One of your parents must have been Italian? Yes, I have it. Your mother is Italian.'

'Are you equally good at self-analysis as you are with assessing other people's characteristics?'

'Ooh! What a witty riposte, cleverly turning from a defensive posture into an attack. Still, being a police officer, you're rigorous training ensures you are adept in interviewing people in awkward situations, aren't you?'

'I'd sooner talk about why I'm in your shop.'

'Yes, of course, the book. *The Posthumous Papers of the Pickwick Club,* and a fine book it is. However, one matter needs clarifying; how, as a police officer, you could help me in return for you possessing such a fine book.'

'... a Detective Sergeant.' Lucy corrected him.

'... quite so, my dear. Even better concerning the matter of aiding our situation. As you're from London, I assume The Metropolitan Police are your employers....'

'... maybe?'

'... and at New Scotland Yard?' Lucy was now putty in his hands, and all he needed to do was apply a few finishing touches to her becoming one of his converts. Pulling a polishing cloth from under the counter, he reached for the book. He affectionately stroked it as if it were a revered possession or a hard-earned sports trophy. Lucy was almost salivating at the thought of becoming its owner.

'As you know all about me, how can I help you?' Lucy now didn't seem to mind his leering smile, revealing again his blackened and crooked teeth. Even his earlier odious breath became unnoticeable. He brought his face closer to hers and their eyes locked. He focused on her icy blue irises; his infinite black eyes beguiled her. He looked furtively from side to side as if verifying no one could hear them. Considering they were by themselves, it was a token gesture purely for effect.

'You may not be aware, but some of your colleagues in the Fraud Squad have arrested two colleagues of mine, friends even. That's where you work, isn't it, in the Fraud Squad?' Lucy nodded, not caring anymore how much he knew about her.

'It's so unfortunate. My two friends do such a lot of good charity work in the East End of London for the less privileged in our unforgiving society.'

'What are their names?' Lucy reached in her bag for her notebook.

'Dariusz and Vlad Krueger are two brothers whose parents settled in London in the late sixties, immigrants from Lithuania. According to their solicitor, Matthias Abramowitz, another respectable acquaintance of mine, the Fraud Squad's evidence against my two friends seems insurmountable. So, their subsequent convictions seem inevitable and will mean long custodial sentences for each of them. We can't let that happen, can we, Lucy?' He watched her write down their names.

'I can't promise anything.'

'... I don't need your promise, my dear. I *know* in my soul you will bring about their release I'm content you'll be looking into the fictitious lies your unscrupulous colleagues have concocted against them. In complicated police work, I appreciate evidence comes and goes like confetti blowing over a blissfully wedded couple in springtime.'

Lucy looked at him from under her meticulously mascaraed eyelashes. '... and in return, I get to keep the book?'

'Of course, my dear Lucy. That's what you came here for, wasn't it.'? She eyed him again and nodded as he passed her the book. 'I think that concludes our business for today. I have another appointment soon. An unfortunate young woman who is a virulent arsonist. Using my books, I'm doing my best to convert her to a straight and narrow path.' Lucy turned to go, gleefully clasping the book to her chest. Godfrey called to her as she had one foot on the step and was about to reach for the door handle.

'People like you are so special, Lucy. Most folks around here behave like they're brainwashed; they can't think for themselves.' He came closer to her. 'I went for a walk around the town the other day. I saw a woman walking with one foot on the pavement and the other in the gutter. I asked her why she was walking like that. She said, Oh, am I? I thought I was lame. That is the calibre of most citizens of this town. They must be reminded how to walk and breathe; they make such wonderful customers. You are in a higher category, my dear, you have an independent mind.' Lucy tried to imagine the scenario he had described.

'Please remember, Lucy, I know where you are. After releasing Dariusz and Vlad, there will be other work you could help me with. You want to *keep* the book, don't you?' She looked back at Godfrey. The earlier infinite blackness of his eyes now looked like piss holes in the snow.

In her excitement, Lucy didn't recognise Godfrey's implied threats. As the doorbell jangled and she left the shop, her phone rang again. 'Oh, hello, Janet. I'm on my way back.' Godfrey heard her upbeat tone as she jauntily walked away.

Seventeen

After the funeral, Donald, Nicky, and James sauntered back to the office. With little enthusiasm for work, they sat at their desks. They couldn't get the sad sight of Joe Swales' inconsolable widow, kneeling before his coffin, out of their thoughts. Even as Donald called Veronica to bring him a coffee, his phone rang. It was the commander at Cannock Fire Station. 'Hello, Donald, it's Lucas here from Cannock Fire Station....'

'... hello, Lucas, it's been a while since we last spoke. It can't be good news, or you wouldn't be ringing me,' Donald added sarcastically.

'On my command, I've dispatched three units to blazing residential apartments down by the railway station. From the initial feedback I've received, we suspect arson. It's bad, Donald. We already know there are fatalities. I'm on my way there now.'

'Okay, Lucas, thank you for ringing me. I'll be there in five minutes.' He reached for his coat and passed his secretary preparing the coffee. 'Forget the coffee, Veronica.' He looked at the office. 'James, Nicky, come with me; there's suspected arson at blazing apartments next to the railway station.'

Driving his car, all Donald had to do was follow the smoke trail. The strong wind blowing from the east kept the toxic black smouldering fumes high in the sky and ensured it didn't descend on the town centre. It also fanned the flames and made the inferno more intense. Donald parked a few streets away to the east, and the three officers walked the short distance to where the fire engines were working. Firemen connected the hose reels to the water hydrants, which soon became fully bloated. Firefighters wearing oxygen breathing equipment were running around in front of the four-storey burning building. Standing behind Donald and James, Nicky held a handkerchief to her face as a shield against the searing heat. 'I wouldn't get too close, Inspector,' Commander Lucas Sedgewick offered as he hurried towards them. They took a few steps backwards.

'How many people live in these flats?' Donald shouted to him.

'There are twenty apartments. From the information given by the council, sixty-three people live here.' He opened a folded sheet of paper. 'Forty-nine adults, of which twenty-eight are pensioners. The other fourteen are children aged from one to fifteen. Unfortunately, there are already seven people dead. Some garages to the left around the corner are a temporary store for the body bags.' He pointed to the extended ladders leaning against the eaves of the flat roof. 'From those ladders, my men have already rescued fourteen residents. Another thirty escaped via the fire escape stairway before the fire got too severe. That leaves another twelve people unaccounted for. Of course, we don't know how many residents were in the building. Obviously, some would be out, workers, and shoppers. My men are currently combing every room for anyone left in there. You can see the ambulances lined up. They're treating people for smoke inhalation.'

'Let's hope that none of those twelve are still in there? This is tragic, Lucas. How has it started?'

'Can't you smell what started it, Donald? To my men who are used to visiting many fires, the smell of gasoline, petrol to you and me is prevalent. Also, there have been two explosions that we think are bottles of liquid propane being consumed by the flames.'

'So, you consider it is arson.'

'It's almost certain. The smell of gasoline is unmistakable throughout the entire length of the building and on every floor. So, that discounts there being an accidental fuel spill. Still, I can't give you an official verdict until we've carried out a full investigation.' They stood helpless, watching the fire raging through the apartments. 'It's times like this that I loathe my job, Donald. Evil deeds, like arson, can be hidden for a short time – but the smoke can't.'

'Lucas, are those your men over there taking photographs?'

'Yes, they are. My officers are taking videos and still photographs. When we consider arsonists have caused a fire, we know the pleasure the criminals derive from their illegal actions. The more destruction there is, the more their pleasure. Three of the photographers concentrate on the crowds standing around, including those standing over there on the railway station platform. Can you see them? One of them has binoculars to his face. That strikes me straight away as questionable. How many people do you know that are waiting for a train also happen to have some binoculars with them?'

The three police officers looked upward to the station platform. 'James, can you get up there? It may be nothing, but whoever he is, it seems suspicious.' James left at once and didn't see some firefighters carefully carrying a blackened body down one ladder.

'That still leaves eleven.' Nicky thought.

James reached the platform after climbing the long sloping pathway. The first thing he noticed was the flashing red lights. They had suspended trains until the fire was under control, and the smoke passing overhead had ceased. Standing further along the platform, about a dozen people were ogling the burning apartments. One man, wearing a knitted bobble hat who James guessed was in his thirties, was looking through binoculars. It wasn't until he got closer that he could see that it was a woman. Her expression alarmed him. She was smiling gleefully. 'Hey, you!' he called. She either hadn't heard James, or she took no notice. He approached and tugged her jacket.

She turned aggressively. 'Don't you touch me! Who do you think you are, you pervert? I'll have the law on you!'

'I am the law, I called out to you, but you ignored me....'

'... how do I know you're the police? You're all alike, you degenerates are...?'

'James reached for his warrant card and held it before her face.'

'So what? So, you are a policeman. How dare you touch me...?' She studied James' card. 'I'll remember you, Detective Constable Garbett, number 23768. Your supervisor needs to know about miscreants like you. Is that what you joined the police force for, so you can touch women indiscriminately and get away with it?'

James ignored her threats. 'Madam, could I ask why you are watching the fire through binoculars?'

'This bloody country! What is it with Mr Plods like you? It's a free democratic country. At least it was the last time I voted.'

'You haven't answered my question. What's your name?'

'Eliza Doolittle.'

'Madam, you either take my questions seriously, or I must take you to the police station for questioning.'

'Fine, I'll go to the station with you. Maybe I'll get a cup of tea?' She folded her binoculars away. 'You do have a car, don't you? I'm not bloody walking. The newspapers will think it's their birthday when I tell them about this.' James took her arm and led her back across the platform, leaving the other people with gaping expressions.

Another explosion from the burning apartment block took their attention back to the fire and black smoke.

At Cannock Police Station, the woman sat patiently in a small interview room. The door opened, and a uniformed constable placed a cup of tea on the table for her. She'd taken off her hat, revealing, short brunette hair. She'd draped her brown oil-skinned leather jacket over the back of her chair, revealing her black leather trousers and high boots. Her skimpy tee-shirt highlighted her flat chest. 'I can see why you initially mistook her for a man, James,' Donald commented as he, Nicky and James watched her from the small one-way mirror. 'Come on, let's see what she has to say for herself. Nicky, you stay here and watch. I'd like your opinion afterwards.' Donald's phone rang, and he listened before answering. 'Oh, thank goodness for small mercies, Lucas. Thanks for letting me know.' He turned, 'That was Lucas; he says all the other unaccounted people weren't in the flats at the time of the fire....'

'... but that still leaves eight dead.' Nicky sighed.

'Yes. Seven pensioners and a young baby, all with smoke inhalation. The fire is under control now.' He and James entered the room. Donald pressed the recording machine and told the woman their conversation was being taped.

'Now, can you tell me your name and if you try to be flippant as you were to my colleague, I'll charge you with wasting police time.' She looked daggers at James; she sighed before answering.

'My name is Christine Follows; I live at twenty-one Fremantle Avenue, Cannock.'

'What were you doing watching the fire using binoculars and, according to my officer, enjoying the spectacle?'

'Can't a girl smile these days without being arrested for it? He touched me.' She stared at James.

'I won't repeat what I said earlier, Miss Foll....'

'... Mrs Follows. I live alone; my husband left me three months ago.'

'I ain't surprised,' James thought.

'Okay, Mrs Follows. You either cooperate, or I'll charge you, no messing about. I haven't got time.' Donald took a hard line with the brazen, confident woman.

'I'm a naturalist' Donald and James couldn't help looking at her figure and imagining her naked. She saw their eyes ogling her figure.

'Oh, for the love of money. Bloody men! Not that sort of naturalist. I watch birds. In case you didn't know, there's a nature reserve and pond across from the railway station. Mill Green reservoir it's called.' Donald and James looked at each other. 'I am talking to idiot Mr Plods, aren't I? Or have you only just arrived in this country from a banana republic?' She took a slurp of her tea.

'So, you were watching birds at the nature reserve?'

'Oh, my Lord, he's got it; I actually think he's got it!' She looked to the ceiling, in exasperation.

Donald felt uncomfortable by the woman's bravado.

'I was sitting in the hide with my binoculars–do I have to explain what a hide is? No? Good! Then I heard an explosion and saw the smoke. The station platform overlooks the flats, so I went to get a better view. I've committed no crime, have I?' Donald raised his eyebrows at James and turned to Mrs Follows.

'Okay. Thanks for coming in and explaining. You're free to go.'

Mrs Follows mumbled obscenities, got up and left the room. Nicky, watching from the adjoining room, saw her leave and went to join Donald and James.

'Well, she seemed genuine, gov; I apologise if I've been too cavalier in bringing her in.'

'... there's no apology needed. We're only doing our job and have to follow any and every lead.' Nicky joined them. 'What did you think, Nicky?'

'She's a noticeably confident and brash woman, and perhaps she's entirely genuine? However, in my dealings with fraud cases at County HQ, I've met other such brash suspects, who later proved to be as guilty as sin. Their bravado had been an attempt to divert attention elsewhere, away from what was really occurring. Mrs Follows may be telling the truth, but I think we should be wary and don't just file this interview away when we're considering suspects for the fire. I'll always remember what my first gov at Stafford police station told me, an arrogant person and a liar are first cousins.'

'Well said! I agree.' They collected various papers into a file and went back to their own desks. Five minutes later, Donald walked through the office. 'Well, that's been another interesting full-on day. I don't know about you two, but I'm looking forward to a quiet evening. See you tomorrow.' Left alone, James asked Nicky what she was going to do that evening.

'Nothing particular, having a bath, washing my hair, then watching a good movie... why?'

'... oh, it doesn't matter. I wondered if you fancied having a bite to eat together.'

'Yes, I'd like that.'

James looked across, expressing his surprise and pleasure. 'Where and what time?'

'I'll meet you at the new Chinese restaurant on Stafford High Street, 'The Intimate Wok', it's called. You do like Chinese...?'

'... yes, but it wouldn't matter if I didn't.'

Eighteen

'Ah, that dinner smells wonderful!' Lucy exclaimed as she breezed into the house.

'I'm so glad you're back; I was getting worried,' Janet breathed a sigh of relief. 'How did you get on at the bookshop?' Before Lucy could answer, they heard the front door; it was Donald.

'Hello,' he called.

'We're in here,' Janet called back.

'Where's here?'

'The kitchen!'

'What are you cooking, darling? It smells delicious. Hello, you two, how has your afternoon gone? Better than mine, I hope?' He went to put his briefcase in his study.

'See what I meant earlier, Lucy. He looks tired, doesn't he?' She nodded.

Lucy poured three glasses of wine, handed one to Lucy and one to Donald as he returned. He went to give Janet a peck on her cheek before taking a sip. 'Cheers,' he offered.

'Cheers,' they both returned. Lucy swallowed the wine also swallowing her jealousy, wishing she was welcoming him home as his wife.

Sitting at the kitchen table, Janet asked him about his afternoon. He explained about the fire and the harrowing sight of blackened bodies.

'Ah, don't you remember, Janet? When we were sitting in the town square, we heard a fire engine's siren.'

Janet nodded. '... and this was an arsonist at work? It's terrible. Whoever it is has committed eight counts of murder.'

'Any suspects?' Lucy asked.

'No, the fire officers have taken videos of the on-looking crowds. They reckon the arsonist usually watches the results of his work. Lucas, the boss of the fire service, is letting me have a copy tomorrow. We'll examine it to see if there's anybody we recognise. We interviewed a young woman that James apprehended. She was watching the fire through binoculars, but we had to let her go.'

'You said he, Donald. Why couldn't it be a woman?' Janet asked.

'Did I? It's a slip of the tongue. Can you imagine a woman causing such carnage?'

Lucy appeared pensive and looked to the floor. Donald noticed.

'Are you okay, Lucy?'

'Yes, I'm fine. I remember something Godfrey Warlock said to me earlier.'

'Godfrey Warlock, you went to visit that fruitcake?'

'Both of us went to see if we could find a book. I left Lucy there while I came back to check on Zak. Lucy only arrived back home a few minutes before you, so she hasn't told me how she got on.'

'I'll tell you in a moment, but Godfrey said something to me about an arsonist.'

Donald looked with interest... 'and.'

'... I'm trying to remember his exact words ... oh yes. He had an appointment after me. *An unfortunate young woman who is a virulent arsonist,* he called her.'

'What! A woman, eh? Perhaps James' instinct may have been spot on after all?'

'... Godfrey said something else about her, but I can't think....'

'... her name would be good....'

'... I remember. *Using my books, I'm doing my best to convert her to a straight and narrow path'.'*

'It sounds to me as if this Godfrey Warlock has some questions to answer. Thanks, Lucy. First thing tomorrow morning, I'll have a closer look at this bookshop myself.'

'Now, how did you get on about the book, kiddo?'

'You went for a particular book?' Donald enquired.

'Yes, she did, darling. *'The Posthumous Papers of the Pickwick Club.'*'

'I've never heard of it.'

'Yes, you have. It's more commonly known by its later title, *The Pickwick Papers,* by....'

'... by Charles Dickens. Yes, of course, but I've never read it. Forgive me, Lucy, I'm not a fan of the classics.'

'... but it goes much further than that, doesn't it, Lucy?' She looked at Donald.

'After the funeral, Janet and I went for a browse, not looking for anything in particular. At random I pulled the book from the shelf, and we looked at it, didn't we, Janet? I couldn't believe it. I thought straight away it looked an original copy....'

'... an original? You mean when it was first published?'

'Yes.'

'... I didn't know they printed books like that in the 1600s' Lucy smiled.

'It was Charles Dickens' first book, published in 1836.'

'There you go. It shows how little I know about literature.'

'Anyway, after I looked at the book some more, I realised it couldn't be an original. However, it's a compelling copy.'

'Did Godfrey try to pass it off as an original?' Janet asked.

Lucy hesitated. She had already lied to her friends and needed to be consistent. 'He did at first, but he could see I knew a bit about books, so he admitted it is a copy.'

'Oh, that's a shame, kiddo.'

'Not really. If it had been an original, I wouldn't have been able to afford it. Godfrey is an expert. That's what he's in business for, so he'd hardly be likely to let a valuable book slip through his fingers.'

'So, what did you do?'

'I bought it, anyway. Godfrey wanted £100, but I got him down to £25. So, I have a bargain. Here it is.' She opened her bag and passed it to Janet.'

Janet picked it up and looked at the faded signature. 'It sure looks convincing, doesn't it, Donald?' She passed it to him.

'I'm no expert, but it looks old. Look at the brown-coloured edges to the pages.'

'The forgers create that effect by dipping the pages in tea.'

'Lucy, I've told you I'm no fan of literature, but couldn't you have bought a more modern, smarter looking version of the book. It would cost you less than £25, surely. The edges of the pages and the covers are tatty, and phew, it smells a bit.' He sniffed the book and grimaced.

'Donald has a point, Lucy.'

'Yes, I suppose so.'

'Perhaps Godfrey is a better entrepreneur than you've given him credit for?' Donald pointed out. 'From what I've seen of him, he's an odious man devoid of sympathy or compassion for anybody.'

'Don't be too hard on him, Donald. The more I got to talk to him, the more I liked him.'

'What! I can't believe you're saying that! He didn't give a toss about that poor man, Jack Beecham, who slit his throat at his shop door. He was more concerned about the mess of blood fouling his pavement.'

'Well, you will be surprised to learn he was standing a few feet away from us in the honour guard for Joe Swales at the church.'

'I am surprised, Lucy. Why would he pay respects to a victim of a murderer and yet dismiss suicide on his doorstep? It makes little sense. I didn't see him, and I had a good look around at who was attending.'

'No, I didn't see him either, but he said he saw the three of us standing together.'

The following morning, as Lucy drove south back to London, she had the book on the passenger seat and, at various intervals, kept looking at it. She couldn't believe she now owned such a unique asset. Had she looked more closely inside the rear cover, she would have seen the indelible red ink stamp.

This book is the property of Doctor Godfrey Warlock, Purveyor of rare and unusual books.'

Her thoughts transferred to how she could make evidence disappear that was holding Dariusz and Vlad Krueger on remand pending a trial.

Lucy had set off early at 7:00. Over breakfast an hour later, Donald commented to Janet. 'I'm so surprised at Lucy. What is she thinking? How could she defend such an obnoxious immoral man as Godfrey Warlock?'

Nineteen

Godfrey smiled with a wide grin, letting his obnoxious breath be refreshed by the town's cool morning air. He'd raised the shop's blinds and opened the door. Standing on the threshold, he looked out at people passing by; some were in a hurry, some casually sauntered along. Others displayed frowns and concerned looks as if the weight of the world's troubles were causing them to stoop. 'Everyone is different, and I have a different book for everyone,' he thought. 'There I go again, I'm a genius! I only carelessly open my mind to create such literary masterpieces. I'll have to use that at some point to advertise my wares.' He smiled at the saying he'd created. *Everyone is different, and I have a different book for everyone.* 'He chuckled and repeated it aloud.

'That's extremely clever,' a man murmured to him, standing looking in the shop window. Godfrey hadn't noticed him but turned and addressed the well-dressed small, rotund, brown-faced man.

'Good morning sir, how can I help you?'

'Hello. Are you the proprietor?'

'Yes, I am. Doctor Godfrey Warlock at your service, sir. Are you looking for a book?'

'Not a particular book. I've read the reviews about your bookshop in the local newspaper. Also, my wife has commented that she would like to come and browse your bookshelves if that is permissible?'

'Everyone is welcome here,'

'Good! As I'm on my way to my surgery, I thought I'd stop and have a look for myself.'

'I take it you are a doctor, then?'

'Yes! Doctor Anwar Patel's my name. My surgery is The Ganges Practice, situated further along this street, where High Green ends, and Shoal Hill begins.'

'Ah! Yes, I've heard of your practice. I don't need to use such establishments as yours. I'm exceptionally fortunate in my existence here on earth; I enjoy such good health.'

'You are indeed fortunate, sir. I imagine that you are also fortunate in your line of work because your clients must be of a congenial disposition. Book reading, after all, is such a pleasurable pastime. Alas, my clients only come to see me when they are suffering ill health. Consequently, most people arrive at my door displaying miserable expressions before they even get around to telling me their tale of woe.' Anwar looked wistfully hypnotic before carrying on. 'I have a particularly upsetting case of a beautiful, middle-aged woman coming to see me this morning. Unfortunately, I can do nothing for her except make her last few months as comfortable as possible. Ah! Such burdens we impose on ourselves by deciding which career path to take when we are young. Enough of me, may I have a look at what you have in this interesting shop of yours?'

'Come in, Doctor Patel. You are welcome. Mind the step.' The doctor's eyes pinched together, aided by a heavy-lined frown, refocusing, trying to adapt to the gloom of the shop's mysterious ambience. He held the handrail as he stepped down to the lower level. Ambling down the lines of books, he looked ahead to the brighter reading section, where he noticed many people studying. Godfrey disturbed his concentration.

'What sort of books are you interested in?'

'Oh! Travel and medicine, of course.'

'Of course. Any particular branch of medicine?'

'Yes! As I hinted to you outside your shop, a significant part of my work these days is more and more involved in administering pain killers and narcotics to alleviate suffering….'

'I would have thought the health service provides you with books and literature on those matters?'

'Yes, they do, but most of them are prepared and published by the companies that sell the drugs. So, I always think we're only getting one aspect put forward. It would be refreshing to be able to read a book written impartially, especially on euthanasia…?'

'… you'll be interested to learn I have a wide-ranging choice on that topic.' They reached a section in the bookshop where Godfrey held out his hand. 'Here we are, there are lots for you to browse. You also mentioned travel. Do you get to travel much?'

'Not as much as I'd like. My parents brought me here from India when I was a boy. I was born in a town called Kanpur on the banks of the Ganges. At least it was a town when I left, but it's a sprawling city today. Hence, I called my practice after the sacred river that has such a special place in the psyche of Indian people. It's the most sacred of all Indian rivers, you know....'

'... and I understand where the remains of most Indian people end up....'

'... including the best Prime Minister that India has ever had....'

'... ah yes, Indira Gandhi. It's a misfortune she came to such a tragic end.'

'... and where I'd also like my remains to follow.'

'If that is your desire, in that, I wish you luck.' Godfrey leered. 'I understand the Ganges is so polluted these days with the cremated remains of human beings.'

'Yes, I would imagine it is.'

'I had the pleasure of visiting a town on the Ganges called Bhagalpur....'

'... yes, a charming old colonial town, where a British garrison was stationed, I believe? Were you there as part of the British Raj?'

Godfrey smiled. 'No, I don't really support any particular nationality. No, I was there in a private capacity. I remember watching a public cremation service that was taking place on the banks of the river on the upstream part of the town. Even before the poor woman's ashes had cooled from the raging fire, the local guru shovelled the ashes into the swirling current. I was just walking along the riverbank, amusing myself, admiring the scenery. Further downstream, children and young adults bathed in the very water with the dead woman's ashes. Your countrymen have some strange customs, don't they?'

'Indeed they do, Sahib.'

'Even further downstream, I stumbled into a mass of delirious people celebrating Kumbh Mela ....'

'...ah yes, Kumbh Mela. It's a very sacred pilgrimage ceremony for thousands of my compatriots who take a dip in the holy waters of the Ganges. They believe it washes away their sins ....'

'I wouldn't have thought the act of washing themselves in the polluted Ganges is very appropriate, do you ...?'

Anwar smiled.

'I watched people urinating and defecating in the water, crouching down in the river next to other people who were dowsing their bodies in the same water. Very odd, and it's no wonder there is so much disease and malady in India.'

'My people have carried out these customs for thousands of years, Sahib.'

'I read somewhere that the public river authority responsible for the river navigation must dredge a navigable channel to allow the fishing boats to get to the sea. Of course, their machines merely churn up mounds of sedimentary deposits of human ash that flows further out with the current. I've also read that out in the Ganges delta, where it flows into the Indian Ocean, a species of fish subsists upon these ashes. The grey, long-tailed grouper, I think it's called; these fish have evolved to feed and depend on what's left of human beings. What I feel is most peculiar about your fellow countrymen, doctor, is that these fish are now considered a delicacy in their everyday cuisine. It has a certain poetic symmetry about it, don't you think?' Anwar's robotic stare told Godfrey he had him spellbound. 'Consider, doctor, who exists for whom in your native land? Does the grouper depend upon dead people, or do living people depend upon the grouper? If the river authority didn't dredge the river, the fishing boats wouldn't sail to sea to fish for the grouper? The exploding population growth in your old country naturally transmits into an increased death rate. More people being cremated means more ash flowing down the Ganges, and the much-maligned grouper is thriving. In one of my books, I read where oceanographers have estimated the species has increased by over five hundred per cent in the past four years alone. It's mutually cannibalistic! I must admit it's a multi-faceted conundrum that I have yet to resolve.'

Anwar looked at Godfrey's leer, enthralled. 'Perhaps start from the beginning of life?'

'Which is...?'

'Birth, or in this instance, the prevention of birth. It's long overdue that some sort of compulsory sterilisation of women or mass contraception in India is put in place?'

'I can foresee that if a solution isn't found soon, mounds of human ash will accumulate in the Ganges delta resembling piles of salt on a Spanish salt lake.'

'Not a sight that tourists will wish to travel to see, is it?'

Godfrey shook his head. 'It's reminiscent of the fields surrounding the site of Treblinka, the Nazi extermination camp northeast of Warsaw. The Polish farmers still turn up human ash when they plough the fields. The human race is indeed a peculiar species.' Godfrey and Anwar stared at each other in silence.

'I'll leave you to browse then, doctor.'

Anwar peered at several books and read their forewords before pulling a particular book with Hindu religious symbols running down its spine. He sat in the reading room with the book; becoming engrossed, he forgot about the time and his surgery appointments. Godfrey sauntered to his side and sat down. 'I see you like that book, doctor.' His voice was calm and soothing.

'Yes! This is fascinating.' Anwar answered without looking up. 'Do you know it expounds different theories on how we treat people at the end of their lives?' Godfrey offered encouraging quips, exerting his psychological influence. 'The chapters offer opposing discussion regarding when and how much diamorphine to administer.'

'In conclusion, it suggests choices and suggestions. Do you know, Doctor Warlock, that the book recommends that most medical practitioners in today's National Health Service don't really understand diamorphine qualities at all? The author suggests we all waste so much public money in prolonging patients' lives merely to endure more suffering and more doses of strong opioid analgesics. This is fascinating.' He eventually looked across at Godfrey.

'Well, you are such a unique person with your practice here in our nice little town. You have it in your power to alleviate so much suffering. Although I have my own PhD, alas not in medicine, but in literature, of course ...' Anwar returned Godfrey's leering smile. '... but I do know that diamorphine is used in treating severe pain associated with surgical procedures, myocardial infarction and pain for the terminally ill....'

'... you are well informed.'

'... it's only what I know, doctor. I understand you also administer small doses for the relief of dyspnoea in acute pulmonary oedema.'

'... you are indeed exceedingly knowledgeable.'

'My dear doctor, you deal with such a lot of distress in your vocation; surely the time has come to dispense with such outdated methods?'

'Which are?'

'Administering such minimal doses of opioids.'

'It's what the drug manufacturers recommend.'

'... and why do they do that, doctor? Have you given it wider thought? They only recommend small doses, so the patient suffering excruciating pain recovers for a short time. Then after a few weeks, they need more morphine. The drug manufacturers are bloodsuckers, doctor. They are in business, are they not? More small doses mean more drugs, given in repeated doses ad infinitum. You are merely keeping these multinational conglomerates in business. They don't really care about the suffering of patients; they only exist to create money to pay their shareholders and raise the company's dividends each year.' Anwar looked over at his hypnotic gaze.

'I hadn't thought about it like that before.'

'Just think, doctor, how you could save the public purse millions of pounds by administering one large dose of diamorphine instead of several smaller doses. You'd be saving the health service and the country a great deal of money. Plus, more importantly, think of the perpetual suffering of your patients that you are not prolonging. They would be happier and free from pain. You would have extra appointment slots for more deserving patients and at the end of each day, you would have more free time. You'd be more contented, and your hard-working staff would operate in an increasingly enjoyable environment. *Voila*! Everyone's a winner!'

Anwar stared at the pages of the book before, in the silence, they heard the town clock striking ten. Anwar had been subconsciously counting the chimes and reacted when the last one ended. 'Oh, goodness gracious me, it's ten o'clock. I'm late for my appointment.'

'It's been a pleasure meeting you, doctor.' Anwar rose and replaced the book on the shelves, but he kept his fingers on the spine. 'Wouldn't you like to keep the book?' Godfrey's question sounded inviting but held a hint of menace.

'Could I? I can't remember the last time I was so enthralled by a book.' He pulled back the book and gripped it in his fist.

'Take it with you. You may decide to implement some of its recommendations? Why don't you come back here in a few days and let me know how you have progressed by giving out your new treatments? You told me you have a distressing woman waiting for you in your surgery now. Perhaps today may be a good time to start?'

'Yes! Yes! I'll go to my surgery now. Thank you, Doctor Warlock. I'll see you in a few days.' Godfrey followed Anwar up the step, through the bell-jangling open door, and watched him stroll purposefully towards Shoal Hill. He noticed the book clutched in his hand as he carefully crossed the pedestrian area, calling cheerfully to a passer-by who greeted him.

'Another satisfied customer,' Godfrey chuckled before returning into the gloom of his shop and laughing violently, in sync with the jangling bell above his closed door.

Anwar approached the automatic, glass-sided doors of his Ganges practice. A computer-generated jingle sounded in the receptionist's confined area, telling her that someone had entered the surgery. He passed the area where the waiting room was packed with anxious-looking patients. He turned to face them. 'I apologise for my lateness today...' His voice was drowned out by the receptionist.

'... doctor, thank goodness you've arrived. It's Susan Waitrose. She was your first patient scheduled for nine-thirty. She's been very agitated and in a lot of pain. I've given her a mild sedative, and she's lying on the couch in your consulting room. I didn't know what else to do. She was disrupting the other patients.'

'You've done well, Elaine, thank you. I'll go and see her now.'

'Poor thing, she's in so much pain....'

Anwar pushed his door open and saw the curtain closed around his consulting couch. He put the book on his desk before drawing aside the curtain.

'Hello, Susan. How are you? I can see you've been crying. I'm sorry, I am late.'

Anwar sat at his desk and called up Susan's records on his computer screen. Susan's whimpering disturbed his concentration, reading the long pages of endless documents. He turned and looked longingly at her. She saw him looking. 'I'm sorry, Doctor Patel, I'm in pain. During the night, I was hurting so much I kept passing out.'

'I'm sorry there isn't a bed available for you in the hospice, Susan; you need special treatment.' He looked back at her records. 'I notice you have no dependents or other family to care for you....'

'... I only have my cousin, Mildred. She lives down the south of the country. I haven't seen her in years.'

'It's obvious you need another dose of morphine....'

'... I don't want another dose of that stuff, doctor; it makes me feel sick for days.'

'Unfortunately, it's the only effective pain killer that's available to me....' He went and sat on the side of the couch and held her hand. He looked into her pained eyes and then back to Doctor Godfrey's book on his desk and thought of what he'd said to him. He reconciled that his words were in direct confrontation with the Hippocratic oath he'd taken when qualifying as a doctor. His mind was reciting the terms of the oldest binding document in history. In Greek culture, written by Hippocrates, it is still held sacred by physicians. '... *to treat the ill to the best of one's ability, to preserve life....*'

Susan gasping and clutching at her stomach disturbed his thoughts. 'I can't stand much more of this, doctor; can't you do something, please? Last year, I had to have my poodle, Jemima, put down. The vet told me she had an incurable tumour. I couldn't stand to see her suffer. Why isn't there such an arrangement for us?' She started sobbing. Anwar went to his desk, sat, held his hand on Godfrey's book before looking at the locked medicine cabinet on his wall. He reached for his key-ring and found a key. In a few minutes, he sat poised on the couch; Susan turned her face to the wall. Anwar lifted her gown, exposing her thigh. He looked at the syringe driver full of yellow coloured benzodiazepine. He'd thought about using diamorphine, but sometimes administering excessive doses caused agitation, sweating, and jerking. A thousand milligrams of the propriety drug of benzodiazepine known as benzo wouldn't cause any of those distressing symptoms. Susan would calmly and quickly go to sleep as the drug paralysed her heart muscles and immediately render her unconscious. Death would occur milliseconds later. He hesitated. Her whimpering subsided almost immediately he'd inserted the needle and pushed the fluid through the driver. He withdrew the syringe and held her hand. He felt her muscles relax. He felt the last pulse of blood flowing through her arteries and she was at peace.

He quickly disposed of the syringe and called his receptionist for help. She came dashing into his consulting room. 'Elaine, send for the paramedics straight away; Susan Waitrose has collapsed; she's unconscious.'

Twenty

'James, you remember I introduced you to my friend, Detective Sergeant Barnes from the Met?'

'Yes, gov, the blonde standing with us at the church....'

'... well, the blonde, as you call her, has gone back to London, but yesterday she went into *Godfrey's Bookshop*. He told her he knows of a woman arsonist who is currently reading in his shop.'

James' eyes widened. 'Exactly, and if you think as I do, it would be sensible to carry out a more in-depth investigation on Mrs Christine Follows. As we thought at her interview, she could be entirely innocent, but eight people have been murdered, for God's sake. There are going to be no stones unturned in this. We wouldn't be doing our jobs correctly if we didn't. She lives in Cannock, where the fire took place; Godfrey Warlock knows a woman arsonist who is frequenting his premises. There's too much of a coincidence at large here.'

'Where do you suggest I start, gov?'

Donald held out his hand and started counting on his fingers as if he were referencing bullet points on a page. 'She said she was watching birds. Was she honest in that? Start there. Visit the nature reserve. Do other bird watchers know her? Lucas said someone started the fire with petrol; does she own a vehicle? If she'd used petrol, she'd have transported it to the apartments. Find out more about her background. She said her husband left her. Who is he? Where does he live? Perhaps he could shed some light on her personality and past behaviour? I think that's enough to be going on with, don't you?' Donald stopped and walked back to his office, but turned, 'then there's the bookshop. Keep an eye out to see when she visits. Perhaps we could eavesdrop to see what she's reading...? How does Godfrey Warlock fit in with all this?' Donald resumed walking, reached his door, and came back to James' desk deep in thought.

'... on the last point, gov, it would be better for someone who Godfrey and Mrs Follows haven't met...?'

'Nicky!'

'That's what I thought. Although we did briefly go into the bookshop together. I doubt whether Godfrey will remember her.'

'Where is she?'

'She hasn't come in yet. We had a late night last evening.'

'We? Don't tell me; I have enough complications in police work now. From experience, can I suggest, James, you keep your private life separate from police work?' Donald walked back to his office, thinking of the problems his relationships with Janet and Lucy had caused him in the past.

'I'll get down to the nature reserve.' James called to him.

As James was leaving, Donald thrust his head out of his office door. 'James, Lucas has sent the videos and still photos from the fire scene. They're in the mailroom. Have a look and see if there's a photo of Christine Follows you can print off. Perhaps someone at the nature reserve can recognise her?'

James parked his car and looked at the shiny, enamelled signboard and plan of Mill Green Nature Reserve. He noticed a circular walk of three miles extended around the entire area. 'Ah, this would be a pleasant walk with Nicky one lunchtime,' James thought. He also noted where the hides were and set out in the direction of the nearest one. He'd only walked a few steps up to the wooden cabin when he heard someone telling him to be quiet.

'Shh! Don't you know not to climb wooden steps in hard shoes around here? If you come here again, wear soft trainers. We try our best not to disturb the birds as much as is necessary.' An elderly man challenged James as he walked away from the hide. James entered the dim timber structure. Through a narrow slit in the front, two men and a woman looked through binoculars towards an area of reeds and bullrushes at the water's edge. A second woman had a long telescope pointing to the open water.

James sidled up to one man and whispered. 'What can you see today?' Without averting his gaze through his eyepiece, he replied, 'Reed warblers. They only flew in from Scandinavia last week, dodging in and out at the water's edge. Fascinating! They're collecting nest material.'

'Ah! Good!' James answered, not wanting to cause too much disturbance to the tranquil scene. He crept next to the woman with the telescope. 'What's out in the open water today?' Before she could answer, the first man exhaled excitedly.

'Oh my God, there's a spoonbill. That's the first of the season.' The middle-aged telescope woman, wearing a tartan deer-stalker cap, momentarily looked to where the spoonbill was wading before turning to James.

'Oh, you're a new watcher, aren't you? Have you been made a member? I'm Jane Street, I'm the secretary of the Cannock Watchers.'

James shook his head. 'No, I'm not a member yet. What are you watching?'

'Oh, yes. It's absolutely captivating! There are two white-tipped cormorants perched on a piece of floating driftwood. It's incredible to see what they fetch out of the depths when they dive. Would you like to see?' She offered the telescope to James. He bent his back and tried to focus on the blurred images, pretended he'd seen them, and gave the telescope back to her.

'Oh, yes. They're beauties,' he quipped, trying to emulate her excitement.

'... but you haven't had to refocus the eyepiece? You must have similar vision defects to mine. My left eye has a retrograde point seven difference to my right eye.'

'... err! Ahem! Yes, same as me. That's a remarkable coincidence, isn't it? Anyway, I wonder if you could help me...?'

'... I'm always happy to help to inspire new members, especially someone as handsome as you.'

'... ahem! Yes! I'm a police officer...'

'... ooh!' She turned to the first man. 'Did you hear that, Eustace; we have a police officer wanting to join our club.' Eustace only sighed and didn't answer or deviate from looking through his binoculars.

James held out a photograph of Christine Follows. 'Do you know this woman? Is she a member of your club...?' Jane peered at the coloured picture.

'No, I've never seen this lady before. Is she a watcher?'

'That's what I'm trying to find out.' He turned to the two men, who shook their heads in annoyance. One man replied in a soft voice, 'Young man, it's the feathered variety of birds we come to look at here. We gave up ogling birds like this years ago.' His attempt at humour fell on deaf ears, except for Jane muttering and looking at James with raised eyes, expressing sarcasm.

'Yes, don't we know it? That's my husband.' She shook her head. 'I'm sorry we can't help you, young man. The woman in your photograph is certainly not a member of Cannock Watchers.' She held out her hand.

James shook her hand. 'I'm Detective Constable James Garbett...'

'... I'm pleased to meet you, James. Please come and see me again soon, so I can make you a member.'

'Shh!' The others issued in unison.

'Blast it! That spoonbill has flown off. We really must have a quieter atmosphere in here,' Jane's husband offered a stern rebuke to James as he turned to leave.

Back in his car, he reached for his notebook and wrote the results of his visit to the Cannock Watcher's hide. He also noticed Christine Follows' address. He'd written it when she was being interviewed at the police station. 'Here I come, Christine,' he muttered and decided to pay her a call.

He stopped the car outside twenty-one Fremantle Avenue. It was a townhouse in the middle of a row of Victorian cottages where the front door opened directly onto the pavement. James noted no parked cars in front of the houses, but he had parked on double yellow lines.

After tapping on the door a few times, he was about to leave. Looking up at the bedroom windows, he noticed a curtain being held aside and waved. He and Christine locked stares. He motioned for her to come down and open the front door.

'What do *you* want? I've nothing further to say to...'

'... Hello, Mrs Follows. Forgive me for disturbing you. I wanted to apologise for my brusque behaviour when we last met. My guvnor doesn't know I'm here. I felt I misjudged you and wanted to make amends.'

'Well, well. A police officer apologising. That's not something you hear every day, is it?' she sneered. James noted her continuing confident, arrogant attitude but renewed ingratiating himself with her.

'When we went to Cannock police station, we missed some more explosions at those blazing apartments....'

'... were there? I didn't really take much notice afterwards.'

'Eight people died there. It's so sad, isn't it?'

'Yes, incredibly sad. I have only taken a brief interest since. I've been so busy.'

'I'm sorry to take up your time today. What do you do for a living?'

'I sell cosmetics. It's only part-time....'

'... I'm always looking for some perfume for my Mom; perhaps you could help? I live by myself in a flat in the lower part of town, so

I don't see many people. It's nice to have a chat with you now,' James was immediately pleased with himself. Christine had softened her attitude and invited him in.

'Sit yourself down, and I'll fetch the catalogue that I sell from. What sort does your Mom like?'

'Ha-ha! Unfortunately, only the expensive type, Chanel and Estée Lauder.' James perused the pages and decided on some Chanel. 'How shall I pay you?'

'Give me your phone number and address, and I'll deliver it to your door. You can pay me then. It'll take a couple of weeks for my next order to arrive.'

'Sounds wonderful. You provide a wonderful service. It will save me trawling the shops.'

'I only do it for money to pay some bills.'

'Listen, I must level with you, Christine. When you told me your husband had left you... well, I'm single and lonely.'

'Whoa! Forget it! I'm not interested in any more men. I'm sorry if I gave you the wrong impression of me. Men only bring problems into my life.' James had lit her fire of resentment towards men. 'My damned ex, Terry, won't leave me alone. He only lives around the corner in Dewsbury Grove. He continually keeps a watch on me. That's why I wanted to be shut of him. He's a sex maniac! If he shows up again on my doorstep, I swear I'll stick a knife in his gut.'

'I see. I'm so sorry.' He looked out of the window and tried to continue a nonchalant conversation. 'Is that where you watch your birds, out the back?' He motioned to her rear window, looking over the bricked yard. She calmed a little before answering.

'Yes, a few, and at the nature reserve as I told you at the police station.' James noticed she was nervous and perspiring.

'It must be fascinating, watching birds, I mean. What type of birds do you watch at the reserve?'

'There aren't many special varieties at all around here. Cannock is a backwater for different bird species. Only sparrows, blackbirds and common starlings.'

'Oh, I see; what a shame. I would've thought you'd see those more common varieties in your back yard?'

'Yeah, a few.' Christine fidgeted and became impatient. 'I'm really busy...'

'... yes, of course. I'm sorry to have taken up your time.' James noticed several books on a shelf as he stood up.

'Snap. We have a common interest...'

'What?'

'... books! I see you're a reader. So am I, but the pickings in Cannock are pretty slim, aren't they...?'

'... have you tried *Godfrey's Bookshop* in High Green. He stocks a superb choice.'

'No, I haven't; thanks for the advice.' James moved into the hall. 'The town is so sprawling these days, isn't it? I don't know what I'd do without my car. Are you mobile?' he asked as he stood on the threshold, looking at his car.

'Thankfully, yes, but as you can see, there are yellow lines in front of the cottages. We can't park here. You want to watch out for that damned rude traffic warden. He'll give you a ticket; little Hitler, we call him. Still, you're a police officer; you could easily shrug off a ticket...'

'... I must follow the rules like everyone else. So where do you park then?'

Christine only wanted to get rid of James, who was getting on her nerves. She answered dismissively before closing the door, 'We have garages at the rear of the cottages. Goodbye!'

James sat back in the car, reached for his notebook, and wrote the results of his conversation with Christine. His instinct told him she is the arsonist. She had continually lied and tried to be evasive.

He slowly left Fremantle Avenue and turned into the next junction on the left. He saw a sign for Dewsbury Grove and parked the car. The small cul-de-sac, bedecked with smart, detached houses, exuded wealth. He walked down the driveway of number five and knocked on the front door.

'Hello,' he gestured to a small woman wearing an apron over a pleated skirt. 'Could you help me? I'm looking for Terry Follows. I understand he lives in Dewsbury Grove?'

'Hello. Yes, he does. Terry lives at number thirteen over the road. There he is now. He's mowing his lawn; can you see him?' Donald looked behind him as the woman pointed.

'Thank you, sorry to have disturbed you,' James offered and walked towards the rumbling noise of the petrol-driven lawnmower. The man cut the motor as he spotted James walk onto his driveway.' Can I help you?'

'Are you Terry Follows?'

'Yes, I am; who's asking?' James showed him his warrant card.
'You'd better come in.'

The man left his gardening gloves and boots in the porch and beckoned James to enter the hallway. 'Now, what brings Cannock police to my door?'

'Can we sit down and talk about your wife...?'

'... Christine! What's she been up to now? Come through to the kitchen.' They sat at the pinewood dining table.

'Well, we aren't aware she's done anything, but I'd like you to treat this conversation as confidential, please.'

'... well, that depends on what you have to say. If this involves Christine, shouldn't you be talking to her? I don't know if you're aware; we're separated.'

'Yes, I'm aware of that. I've spoken to Christine. I just wanted a quick chat with you regarding her background and what's she's like....'

'... Detective Constable, if you've spoken with her, you'll know she's an extremely arrogant, self-opinionated person and exceedingly difficult to get on with.'

'Is that why you're separated...'

'... that's none of your business, Constable.'

'No, of course, forgive me for asking....'

'... look, I'm a busy man; what's this about?'

'She's recently come to our attention regarding the possibility of being involved in a crime. I hasten to add, we haven't charged her with anything. That's why I'd like you to keep this conversation private between us. I'd like some information on her background, please, that's all.'

'Look, I'm separated from my wife and we lead individual lives now. I'll not give you any information that will get her into trouble. Despite that, we don't get on; I'm no grass. There's already enough grief between us, with a good many expensive solicitors' letters discussing divorce. So, I don't see how I can help you.'

'Okay, sir, I understand...' James got up to leave.

'Can I ask what you are investigating her for...?' James hesitated. '... because if it's anything to do with her fascination with fire, it's all a load of nonsense...'

'... fascination with fire?'

'Look, I know the police aren't stupid. You probably already know we've only lived in Cannock for nine months. We came here from

Doncaster, in Yorkshire, after the damned annoying Tyke police there harassed us. They suspected her of causing a fire at a bakery and café. I ask you, a bakery. They had a fire going all day and every day to bake bread and pizzas, so why they thought my Christine had anything to do with the premises burning to the ground was beyond us. We couldn't put up with their persecution any longer. That's why we left Yorkshire to come here and make a new start. I'm sure I'm only repeating what you'll already have checked up on. So, that's all I'm prepared to say, Constable. Sorry, I can't be of any more help. If you're married, I'm sure you'll understand.'

'I understand perfectly, Mr Follows. I'm sorry to have troubled you. Good day to you.'

James sat back in his car and completed his notes. His hand was almost trembling with the information he'd gleaned from the few interviews he'd carried out. The facts all pointed to Christine Follows being the arsonist who had murdered eight people. He needed to talk with Donald to see where next they should go with the case. He recognised having suspicions and confirmed facts was okay to a point. To secure a conviction, he needed proof.

Twenty-one

James had only left the police station five minutes before Nicky turned up for work.

'Sorry, I'm late, gov,' she gestured apologetically to Donald.

'Late night, was it?'

'Er! Ahem! No, I'm having trouble with my car; I couldn't get it to start this morning.' She didn't like lying, but her answer wasn't a complete untruth. She had been having trouble with her car. Donald only smiled, content that Nicky had more judgment than James and wouldn't divulge her private life.

'Where's James?' she asked, looking across at his empty desk. Donald came to her desk and explained what Lucy had learned and that James had gone to check up on Christine Follows.

'So, you'd like me to visit *Godfrey's Bookshop*?'

'Yes, but please be careful. We already know what a devious character Godfrey Warlock is. Ideally, it would be good to verify the link between Christine Follows and the bookshop. Even better would be to find out what she's studying in his reading room. Is Godfrey encouraging her or directly involved in a more tangible way? I suspect the latter isn't the case. It doesn't seem to be his style. He's more content to provide the bullets for other people to fire.'

'How do we know when she visits the bookshop?'

'We don't. It would mean putting a watch on Christine. I don't have the manpower or resources to devote to something like that at this stage, the Super would only class it as nefarious....'

'... manpower?'

'... Oh yes! I'm sorry, Nicky. In this enlightened age, I should say womanpower...'

'... how about the workforce?' Donald smiled. 'I'll have a stroll into High Green,' she added.

'There's no rush. As I said to James before he went out, Lucas has sent over the videos and still photographs from the apartment fire. Can you have a look through them? Maybe we can identify known felons we have on record?'

It was lunchtime before Nicky had assembled various still photographs of the crowd watching the apartment inferno. She pinned them to the incident board; Christine Follows was among them. As she walked through the door en route to High Green, James almost bumped into her. 'Oh, hello, Nicky,' he called, then in a whisper asked, 'are you alright after last evening?'

'Yes, I'm fine,' she returned in an equally soft voice.

'It's lunchtime. Do you fancy a sandwich in the town centre?' he asked in a normal voice.

'I'm on my way to pay *Godfrey's Bookshop* a visit. We could have a sandwich first?'

'Good, I'll fill you in on what I've discovered this morning.' They walked out together, leaving Donald smiling in his office, having heard their exchange and feeble attempt to suppress their murmured words.

They finished their lunch sitting in the indoor café, for a change. A brisk breeze was blowing across the town, and although the apartment fire had been a mile away, they were sure the smell of smouldering embers wafted through the town. They didn't want reminding of the tragedy.

'Please be careful in the bookshop, Nicky. We shouldn't underestimate Godfrey Warlock for a second.'

'Thanks for your concern, but I'll be okay.' They walked outside. They looked at each other and felt like giving each other a more tangible reminder of their romantic evening. James was about to give her a kiss on her cheek, but Nicky saw his forward lunge and ambled away. She felt awkward, standing close to the café's doorway, where other people were passing.

'See you later,' she waved, walking towards the bookshop. James sauntered back to the office to acquaint Donald with his morning's work.

Nicky looked upwards at the jangling bell as she opened the door. She paused to let her eyes get accustomed to the dimness and walk down the step without falling. At the far end of the shop, people read under bright lamps in contrast to the gloom. She sniffed the unique odour given off by old books. Hearing a shuffling noise, she turned to look back at the front window where Godfrey stood in silhouette.

From his black cardboard cut-out shadow, he murmured, 'What sort of book are you searching for, madam?'

Nicky had thought about what she would say to Godfrey. She relaxed a little when it seemed evident, he didn't remember her. 'Hello, I didn't see you standing there. Well, I don't think you could help me, but ever since I was a little girl, fireworks have fascinated me. I have a spare half an hour and wondered if I could learn how they're made. I realise it's a long shot...'

'... I have books on every subject under the sun. There is a section at the other end of my shop entitled Pyrotechnics. I'm certain you'll find what you want in there. You'll forgive me if I don't come with you; I'm rearranging my window display. Shout to me if you need help.'

'Thank you,' she uttered, thinking, window display? 'The shop window is empty, devoid of any single item; what needs rearranging?'

Nicky ambled down the shop, eyeing bookshelves standing from the floor to the ceiling full of books. There didn't seem to be space anywhere as she reached the section marked Pyrotechnics. Picking a book at random, she moved into the reading room, sat down, and opened the book. Reaching into her handbag, she opened her glasses case. Nicky perched her reading spectacles on the end of her nose, trying to look bookish. She wasn't gazing at the words or chemical symbols in the book; she was more interested in who was in the room. It would have been more than she could have hoped for had Christine Follows been there but took an interest in the four men and three women who sat reading with their backs to her. There was no conversation passing between any of them, and she realised how robotic and overtly studious they were. There were bookshelves at the far end of the room, and she walked down there to gaze back at the readers' faces. As she examined the books, she reached for her phone and pressed the camera icon. Turning, she quickly took several photographs of the seven people reading. They didn't look up at her or even knew she had photographed them.

'That will make for interesting research back at the office. Perhaps some of these people may be the subject of current or future police investigations.' She ambled back through the shop, replacing the fireworks book back on the shelf. Godfrey was in the shop window, so she called.

'Thank you, I couldn't see what I wanted. Perhaps I'll call another day?' She heard Godfrey shout, 'Goodbye, madam.' The bell jangled as she closed the door; she gasped. The shop window display was now full of bookshelves packed with books. She swore the window had been empty when she went into the shop and wondered how Godfrey had filled the shelves in so short a time?

A more tremendous shock caused her to question her own sanity when she opened the camera images back at her desk. In the readers' photos, standing at the far end of the room, Godfrey Warlock was smiling. His eyes were slits and almost luminous, reflecting the light from the reading lamps.

Twenty-two

'You've done a fantastic job of basic detective work today, James, using different circumstances and situations to get at the facts. It also shows me you understand what drives people, their wants and needs ...'

'... but, with no proof that links Christine Follows to the inferno.'

'Not yet, but you've shown where we can get it.'

'Where?'

'The transport needed to move petrol to the apartment block. You've established Christine has a vehicle that's garaged behind her house ...'

'... forgive my inexperience, gov, but don't we need a search warrant to search her garage?'

'Yes, of course we do. Unless ...'

'... we had a stroke of luck; perhaps someone may be looking for a house to rent or purchase and, on a casual stroll around the street, find the garages are open?'

James looked at Nicky in a questioning manner. 'Would that be legal, gov?'

'Without a warrant, it certainly wouldn't be legal, and our unethical methods would be open for all to see and criticise when the case comes to court. It could even lead to an acquittal. We'd be accused of perverting the course of justice and be demoted or dismissed from the force. So, I'm not suggesting for one second either of you even think about it.'

'Would the same apply to searching her car?' Nicky asked.

'Technically, yes, but cars are always being broken into.'

'You're confusing me, gov; what's legal or not?' James commented.

'If this case were occurring at the Met, my old gov, Inspector Tom Cropper, would know what to do. He always used to instil in me when there seemed to be a dead end, you have to make your own luck.' Donald paced the floor for a minute, looking at the photographs of the inferno and the gruesome pictures of body bags in the garage. 'I don't suppose you saw any properties for sale or rent down Fremantle Avenue or the adjoining streets, did you, James?'

'I don't know, gov. I wasn't looking for properties ...'

'... Nicky, get on your laptop and search for properties in that area.' Donald returned to his office, deep in thought.

Later that afternoon, he was still pre-occupied when he came into the principal office and bade his farewell for the day.

'Gov,' Nicky called, 'before you go, there's a cottage for rent here at number eleven Fremantle Avenue.'

'That's five doors away from Christine Follows.' James said with enthusiasm.

'Have a look, gov, it's being offered on a permanent rent of £580 per month by Nicholls and Son, Estate Agents, the Estate Agents over the road from here.'

'Is there a garage included ...?'

'... hang on a sec. Yes, there is. It says here there's a lockup garage at the rear of the house.'

'Okay, leave it with me. Thanks, Nicky. Bye, everybody.' Donald's first stop before going directly home was at Nicholls and Son.

He kissed Janet when he arrived home. 'Can we have a chat at dinner time, please, darling?'

'That sounds intriguing,' she responded, as she served the dinner. Donald sat opposite his attentive wife and hesitated before speaking.

'How would you like to help me with this apartment inferno case?'

'What? Become a police officer again?'

'No, not really. In an unofficial capacity.'

'I'm all ears.'

Donald explained the background of where the investigation had reached with Christine Follows. 'I'm at an impasse to find evidence against her. I'm curious what our friend Tom Cropper would do in this circumstance'

'Exactly what you are doing now. Finding alternative ways of getting to the truth.'

'I've made an appointment for you at eleven o'clock tomorrow morning with the Estate Agents. The property is number eleven Fremantle Avenue with a Mrs Evelyn Brown. The property is empty, so you won't be meeting the present occupiers.'

'It's been a few days since I've taken Zak out for a walk; it will make a pleasant change.'

'It's obviously the garage I'm more interested in, and particularly the one for Christine Follows at number twenty-one.'

Twenty-three

Since his boyhood, Michael Ridgeway had always had a fascination with movies of the old wild west in America. His particular interest was with bank robberies in the late nineteenth-century fledgling new towns. There was always lots of gunfire and villains escaping with saddlebags full of money riding off into the sunset. Still, somehow, they always seemed to get caught by the hero of the movie. 'How stupid can you get?' Even now he was an adult, he often called out aloud when watching the old movies. His mother watched the television with him, smiled, and thought it was romantic that her son still retained his youthful traits. He remonstrated with his mother as if she was the director of the movie. 'If only they hadn't made so much noise and thought about how they could leave the bank without making a great disturbance, they would have got clean away.'

His fascination with movies involving bank robberies extended to more sophisticated modern-day films. Educated thieves managed to steal the money but later fell foul of internal squabbling within the gang because of greed. 'That wouldn't have happened if the bank hold-up had been a one-man operation' he concluded. His favourite bank robbery movie was *Hell or High Water* depicting two brothers. One of them successfully robbed many banks by intelligent planning and stealth rather than brandishing guns and killing people. 'That's how I would rob a bank,' he fantasised.

Michael lived on a council housing estate four miles from Cannock, so he rarely ventured into town. On one occasion, he accompanied his mother to do some shopping; he left her browsing the market while he explored. His imagination soared at the town's several banks fronting onto the main street where vehicles nonchalantly parked outside. 'If they haven't been robbed before, they are ripe for the taking,' he thought. He extended his walk into the High Green pedestrian area, where he saw *Godfrey's Bookshop.*

Godfrey's perpetual enchantment with the human spirit guaranteed he was always looking for new converts and clients. To the uninitiated passer-by, his confident stance on the threshold of his shop presented the impression of an optimistic proprietor eager for new business. If anyone had looked closer, his leering smile gave away his actual emotion. Rather than hopeful, it was expectant. He waited with impatience for Michael to come by and look in his window.

'Hello, young man, can I help you?' Godfrey offered as Michael peered into the murky shop front.

'Oh, you made me jump; I didn't see you standing there.' He held his hand across his chest and smiled.

'I'm Godfrey Warlock, proprietor of this little shop.'

'I'm Michael Ridgeway.'

'Hello Michael, I can see you're investigating our little town. I don't think I've seen you walk by here before. Why don't you come in, look through my bookshop and take the weight off your feet? I have a reading room where you can relax if you wish?'

Michael accepted Godfrey's welcoming gesture and stepped inside. Usually, Godfrey warned newcomers about the step but decided to stay silent, consequently, Michael fell headlong into the gloomy shop, having missed the step down.

'Oh, I'm sorry, I should have warned you about the step. Are you alright?'

Michael was unhurt and only shaken but felt stupid at having been so clumsy. Lying on the carpeted floor, he looked up at the towering figure of the scheming proprietor. Immediately, as Godfrey had speculated, the inconsequential, relatively immature man from out of town felt dwarfed and overwhelmed by his presence. When he stood up, Michael felt subservient to whatever Godfrey would suggest.

'I have some excellent books down this row here that may interest you,' Godfrey hissed and led Michael further down the aisles of bookshelves.

'Oh, these look exciting,' he purred. 'What a coincidence; as it happens, I'm interested in bank robberies and how they're planned. It's uncanny; it's as if you knew just what I was looking for.'

'Simply call it intuition. When a new customer comes into my shop, I can sense what interests them. My friends tell me it is a knack I have of judging people and their characters.'

'In your business, I can imagine your talent serves you well.'

Godfrey's fawning smile caused Michael to swallow uncomfortably, analogous to a helpless fly that had inadvertently entered a spider's web. He looked across the extensive selection of titles that espoused robbing banks in fictional stories or as actual accounts of failed occurrences. The latter offered advice to banks and shopkeepers on how to improve their security to avoid such robberies.

Michael selected one such self-help guide to bank managers and retreated to the reading section to sit among other avid readers. He researched the ten most common security faults that existed in modern banks. Michael salivated and almost read aloud how security companies often entered a bank to test whether a bank's defence system could cope with a hold-up. He visualised holding the book, entering a bank, and crossing off the bullet points verifying whether a particular bank was secure. Sitting in Godfrey's reading room was inspirational. Michael formulated a concept whereby he could visit every bank in Cannock and adjoining towns and survey how each premise measured up. He'd create a priority list of which were deficient and the most vulnerable. In his deluded foresight, the bank that came bottom of his survey was the one he would rob and provide for himself and his mother a prosperous financial future.

Godfrey hovered close to Michael and could see he'd successfully nurtured a talented new convert. He intervened at the most favourable time. 'Ah! Young man, I can see you like that book....'

Michael jumped up excitedly, like an enthusiastic child examining the choice on a shop's sweet counter. 'Yes, Mr Warlock...'

'... Please call me Godfrey; we're friends now.'

'This book is exactly what I've been looking for. How much is it?'

'I'm so glad, Michael; I'm happy for you to borrow the book, providing you're not going to disappear and abscond with my assets. Take it away with you; I'd be pleased for you to return and let me know what you think of the book and if it has helped you. Please know that I'm always here to assist you further if you're unsure how to develop your ideas.'

Michael left the bookshop, eager to find his mother and show her his new book.

Twenty-four

Black clouds were passing over Cannock as Janet set off for her walk. She had her anorak in the bottom of Zak's pram in case the recent fine weather ended. 'What a lovely baby boy, what's his name?' Mrs Brown of Nicholls and Son asked as Janet pushed the pram.

'Zak,' she responded and pulled the hood down for her to get a better view.

'The only thing is, I wouldn't recommend leaving the pram out here on the pavement. It's likely to be gone when we come back out. There's a rear entrance to these cottages. Walk to the side and come up the rear alleyway, past the garages.'

Mrs Brown met Janet at the rear door of number eleven. 'I understand a garage is included in the rent. While we're outside, could I look at the garage first?'

'No problem. You've already passed the garages. Did you see the numbers on the up and over doors?' They trudged down the row of garages passing number twenty-one. Janet's interest was at once stirred when she saw the door was open and no vehicle was inside. She paused.

'It's this way, Mrs Lawrence, number eleven is further on.'

'Do you know what, Mrs Brown? I've changed my mind. The area is not what I had in mind. If you consider someone could have stolen my pram, I don't think I could feel safe here....'

'... don't you want to look inside the house?'

'There's no point. Thank you for your help. I'm sorry if I've wasted your time.'

'That's no problem. I hope you find what you're looking for. Why don't you call in at our shop? We have other properties for rent, in better areas of the town.'

'I may do that.' Mrs Brown went inside number eleven and locked the rear door from the inside, leaving Janet alone in the back alley. Janet peered closer at Christine Follows' garage. It was drizzling with slight rain, so Janet was pleased to take shelter and pushed the pram in the garage. The rear of the garage seemed cluttered with rubbish. However, under a wooden bench, she noted two gas bottle cylinders and various green coloured plastic gallon fuel containers. Janet reached for her phone and took several photographs. The second she'd replaced the phone in her pocket, the noise of a chattering diesel engine deluged the calm garage. It was Christine Follows returning her clapped-out rusty, twenty-year-old red Ford Fiesta to the garage. In her hurry, she almost knocked over Zak's pram. Janet called out in alarm. Christine slammed on the car's breaks and exhaled a vast sigh of relief. Her temporary empathy that Zak hadn't been harmed soon turned to annoyance. She bounded out of the car and challenged Janet, remonstrating with herself for having left her garage door open. She took her frustration out on Janet.

'Who the sodding hell are you? What are you doing in my garage? Get out before I call the police.' She pointed for Janet to leave.

'I'm so sorry. It started to rain. I've been looking at number eleven with the Estate Agent intending to rent...' Janet pointed to the house further down the alleyway. 'We may become neighbours. I wanted to shelter with my baby until the rain stops. Your garage was open....'

'... so, you decided to trespass. I don't care if you become my neighbour or not, so bugger off.'

Janet pushed the pram and manoeuvred her way around Christine's car, thankful to be away from the unpleasant woman, noting her car registration as she went. Thankfully, the rain had stopped. Janet smiled as she made her way towards the police station in Wolverhampton Road.

She took the lift to the first floor and entered the main office. She saw James first and went over to his desk when he called to her.

'Hello, Mrs Lawrence, how nice to see you.'

Nicky got up and went to the pram. 'How is Zak?' she asked and peered into the pram.

In his office taking a telephone call, Donald heard the commotion outside. He finished his call before going to greet Janet. Veronica also joined in admiring Zak. Janet lifted him out of the pram and passed him to Veronica to hold. Janet met Donald's enquiring look. She went inside his office and told him what had happened.

'Bloody woman, I'd have screwed her scrawny neck myself, had she harmed you or Zak.'

Janet then showed him the photographs on her mobile phone. His eyes lit up. 'You are amazing, Detective Sergeant Janet Lawrence;

you always manage to come up with the goods, don't you?' He reached over and kissed her on the cheek. Janet reached across Donald's desk for a pencil and a sheet of yellow sticky memo paper. She wrote down Christine Follows car registration number-Y369WRE.

'Check your phone; I'll send you these photos now.' Janet collected Zak and made her way back home. No sooner had she left the office, Donald sent the photos to the office wireless digital colour printer. Returning from the print room, he pinned some copies to the incident board and placed a copy on James and Nicky's desks.

'What's this?' James asked.

'Photographs of the interior of Christine Follows' garage.'

'How...?' He looked towards Nicky. Simultaneously they both mimed 'Janet' and looked back at Donald. He smiled at them and held his fingers against his lips. 'What did my old gov, Tom, tell me. When there's a dead end, you make your own luck.'

'Petrol cans and gas bottles, eh?' James exhaled, looking at the photos.

'Yes. Now, I'm going to send a copy of these photos to Lucas over at Fire HQ....'

'... Lucas?' Nicky questioned.

'I'm wondering if there's something left of the petrol cans that started the fire. Also, if there's anything remaining of the gas bottles that exploded?'

'Of course!' James exclaimed.

'Perhaps Lucas can come up with a match? However, even if there is a match it's still not conclusive proof. A combatant defence barrister could show in court it was circumstantial evidence. I suppose anybody could buy gas bottles and petrol cans like these from most garages and filling stations. However, the odds are tipping in our favour. If I were on a jury looking at this evidence, I'd be ready to convict Follows. Janet has told me Christine's vehicle is a wreck. Here's the registration number. Nicky, can you check on the police database and with the DVLA at Swansea? Is the car roadworthy with a valid MOT certificate and up-to-date insurance? Is she licenced to drive? I don't care on what pretext we can bring her in.'

'What shall I do, gov?'

'James, tomorrow, I want you to go to the Doncaster Police Headquarters in Yorkshire. Get every detail you can on the bakery fire on their patch. Find out what evidence they hold on Christine Follows.

More importantly, what prevented them from bringing a charge against her?'

Twenty-five

Back at the Metropolitan Police at New Scotland Yard, Lucy explained to her guvnor, Detective Chief Inspector Jules Beaumont of the Fraud Squad, what she had discovered in Manchester. Looking over the embankment at the turbulent River Thames, they shared a cup of coffee. She asked what had happened at the Met in the few days she'd been away. Jules passed her a spreadsheet containing details of all the cases the department was currently handling. 'This is up to and including yesterday. I presume you'll be carrying on with the Dexter fraud case and update it with the info you've gleaned from our Lancashire colleagues?'

'Of course, gov. Can I keep this spreadsheet? It's good to know what everyone else in the department is doing.' The Chief Inspector nodded.

Back at her desk, Lucy typed the spreadsheet's reference number into her computer and brought it up on her screen. There were forty-nine current cases. Using her mouse, she scrolled down to the prime suspects in a gangland murder case, Dariusz and Vlad Krueger. She typed in her personal fifteen-character security code to access the details of the case. There were over three hundred pages of evidence that described how the Krueger brothers were involved. Using the copy and paste facility, she sent the complete file to her personal email account. Once back at her flat, she could study the case privately and at her convenience on her own laptop computer.

There was one more task she demanded of the Met police mainframe computer. She was curious about how the original primary copy of Charles Dickens's first book came into Doctor Godfrey Warlock's possession. She wanted to check its provenance. She wasn't surprised to note the chequered history of previous owners. Its precarious existence started with Charles' pitiful family.

Charles Dickens and Catherine Hogarth married in 1836 when he was twenty-four and she twenty-one. Three months after their marriage he published *'The Posthumous Papers of the Pickwick*

Club'. It was only from the book's initial proceeds that he could afford to support the young socialite. From then until their divorce twenty years later, Catherine got pregnant at least a dozen times, had two miscarriages and gave birth to ten children. Nine survived infancy, eight reached adulthood, and all of them disappointed their father. He lamented, *'Having brought up the largest family ever known with the smallest disposition to do anything for themselves.'* Having bequeathed many first edition novels to his children, his eldest child, Charles, sold *'The Posthumous Papers of the Pickwick Club'* for a pittance to release himself from a gambling debt.

At various times down the years, the book is known to have belonged to the famous Tennyson family, followed by the Thackeray children. The renowned poet Alfred Lord Tennyson and the novelist William Makepeace Thackeray were close friends of the Dickens family. In 1907 it was understood to be part of King Edward VII's considerable library in the west tower at Windsor Castle. In that year, his granddaughter, Princess Victoria aged ten, the future, Princess Royal, Mary, and later Countess of Harwood, read the book. In 1954, in her memoirs, she recounted how she had read the book many times to her younger siblings.

The book turned up several years later in the possession of Sir Fenston Langtry in Sussex. It's conjecture that King Edward, on his death, bequeathed the book as a gift to Fenston's mother, the famous actress, Lillie Langtry; over many years she had been one of his several mistresses.

Upon his death, Sir Fenston Langtry's estate was eventually bestowed to The National Trust in 1987, by his son Euripides. At that time, the substantial library at Carlingborough House contained many first edition classics, of which *'The Posthumous Papers of the Pickwick Club'* was one such valuable asset.

Sotheby's, the legendary auction house, classed themselves as the premier destination for fine arts and luxury objects. They estimated the value of the signed book as over a million pounds should it ever be presented at one of its auction houses. Charles Dickens' authenticated signature alone had contributed two hundred thousand pounds to that valuation. Shortly after the much-published valuation, the book went missing from Carlingborough House. The Metropolitan Police concluded that an incredibly skilful professional theft had occurred. They assumed the book was already likely to be in the possession of some foreign entrepreneur and literary enthusiast. Many hypotheses were put forward as to whom was responsible. The most popular culprit afforded by the fashionable British press was the international thief, Lord Sir Jeremy Carrington Porter, since one of his infamous calling cards had been discovered on a silver platter in the house's drawing room. His card bore a black silhouette of an Indian elephant. However, when Sir Jeremy was found with his throat cut in his ornate Barbados mansion, the book wasn't recorded as one of his possessions.

Lucy noted that was the last entry of the book's known existence in the public domain.

How long it had been in Doctor Godfrey Warlock's possession and whether he had anything to do with the elaborate theft is speculation. Now the book was hers. Her pleasure had known no bounds, having discovered a bookmark when she had first thumbed through the book at Donald and Janet's house. The bookmark was a card showing a silhouetted elephant. She thought of all the famous and legendary owners who had handled and read the book before her. One fact was beyond doubt, not one of its earlier owners would cherish the book as much as she did. She thought of the future, and perhaps on her own death she would bequeath the book back to The National Trust. It would reclaim its rightful place in Carlingborough House's library and remain in England, where it was written.

On the main computer, she closed the search engine and signed off using her personal password.

Relaxing in her flat that evening, she opened the Krueger brothers' file and straight away could see that the evidence against them was compelling. From being in the Metropolitan police for fifteen years, she had become aware of their reputation in the East End of London. Many people who knew them saw them as Robin Hood type figures. Despite their obvious criminal dealings, they gave generously to worthy local causes and deserving needy children. Further investigations into these worthy causes and starving families showed they were mostly petty criminals and cronies of the Krueger family, who existed on the margins of decent society. To the Krueger brothers, these minions merely lived to serve other criminals higher in the pecking order and perpetuate a hierarchal criminal fraternity system. Dariusz and Vlad were, of course, at the pinnacle of this dubious ranked system. They built a continual protective network around themselves, beginning with local police officers, who, being 'on the take' who would turn their heads when they came across misdemeanours that connected crimes to the Krueger's. Their evil tentacles spread as far as Fleet Street, where reporters and editors of the national and local press, for individual rewards, would only print details of the brothers' philanthropy. Stories of seedier illegal dealings that everyday readers consider being crimes against society were conveniently left in the editor's wastepaper basket.

Dariusz and Vlad faced charges relating to a minion, Harry Stevens, a small-time fraudster, several tiers below them in their system, who had broken rank and wanted out. He knew too much information. The brothers wouldn't allow Harry to become a loose cannon and divulge sensitive information to anyone interested - for a price, of course. Despite setting two expensive contracts to known assassins, they bungled their attempts to cause Harry to disappear. Dariusz and Vlad were furious and were left with no recourse but to do the job themselves.

The brothers arranged a meeting with Harry. The venue needed to be in general society with many people around, so Harry wouldn't suspect any threat to his life. He thought the brothers were going to offer him a generous package to remain part of their system. Harry happily accepted an invitation to dine with them at the prestigious Ritz Hotel in Mayfair on a Saturday evening, knowing the restaurant would be full. What could happen to him, he mistakenly presumed? By the time the dessert course was about to be served, Dariusz and Vlad had plied Harry with a mixture of several glasses of expensive wine and vodka cocktails. He needed the toilet and was visibly unsteady on his feet as he walked to the gentlemen's restroom. Outside the room, a polite notice told patrons female staff regularly cleaned the toilets. 'Perverts,' Harry thought in his alcohol confused brain, not knowing that a female cleaner, Doris Sparkes, was herself using one of the cubicles. Her current water infection meant she hadn't time to cross the room to the ladies toilet to relieve herself. Who could have known a woman was in there? As soon as Harry sat down, his trousers around his ankles, Dariusz and Vlad entered and forced open the door to his cubicle. 'No, boys, please don't do it? Think of all the good times...?' Harry pleaded as he looked down the barrel of two Mauser IV pistols, fitted with Knight suppressors and silencers. Doris, sitting in the next cubicle, heard every word.

There was a crack in the separating screen, and peering through, she recognised the Krueger's. She could even describe the firearms they were using. Hearing no louder sound than the cracking of eggs, she saw blood spreading down Harry's white shirt as he slumped backwards with staring eyes. Holding a hand to her mouth to prevent her from crying out, she saw Dariusz reach into Harry's inside pocket and take his wallet. The brothers were petty criminals themselves. 'This will pay for the ridiculous prices they charge at this flea-infested joint,' she heard Dariusz say as he closed the cubicle door. 'Thanks for the meal, Harry,' Vlad uttered before they both left the restroom, laughing. Doris sat in the cubicle for the next thirty minutes for fear of anyone knowing she was there.

Doris was sequestered in a witness protection programme. Her whereabouts were known only to two dedicated officers.

Lucy thought hard about what she should do. First, she abhorred the thought of doing anything illegal and jeopardising her career. In her opinion, losing Harry Stevens was no loss to society. If the Krueger's hadn't accounted for him, he would eventually have seen the inside of a prison cell. Perhaps they'd saved the British taxpayer a great deal of money that would have been spent on keeping Harry in jail for many years. So, if she could bring about Dariusz and Vlad's acquittal, the pursuit of justice wouldn't be that much compromised, and she could keep the book. Two issues could bring that about:

1. Discredit the testimony of Doris Sparkes or
2. Produce reliable alibis for the Krueger brothers.

Twenty-six

James saw the bright chromium sign for The South Yorkshire Constabulary, Doncaster Police Headquarters, as he drove around Balby Square. He pressed the bell on the unmanned reception desk and waited. A young, dark-haired woman constable came from behind the counter by way of a glass door.

'Can I help you?' she smiled.

James introduced himself by showing his warrant card. 'I have an appointment with Detective Chief Inspector Miles Illingworth.' The woman reached for a phone, mumbled a brief conversation, and then lifted a hinged part of the counter.

'Come with me, please, Constable, and I'll escort you directly to Inspector Illingworth's office.'

'Ow do, Constable. Nah then, what brings tha' t' Yarkshar?'

'Hello, Inspector, I've come to talk to you about Christine Follows....'

'... Chuffin' 'eck mi duck... before we crack off, d' tha' fancy a mashin?'

'... pardon me, sir?'

'A mashin! A cup o' tae.'

'Oh, yes, please.'

The Inspector picked up his phone. 'Ey up lass, nah then, two mashins mi duck. Oh, it's thee, Gloria, can ya ask tha Betty, that's if she ain't got a face on, or not too mardy, to bring two mashins... what? Oh, aye, - please.'

While drinking a mug of strong tea, James explained what he wanted to talk about and what had happened in Cannock.

'That ain't addled is it, mi duck? Lads en lasses hereabout like a reyt mashin o' tae.'

'It's fine, thank you!' James exclaimed, wondering how he would understand the Inspector's heavy accent for more technical information, but his concerns were allayed.

On the phone, Inspector Illingworth asked for Sergeant Davies. 'Ey up, nah then, Jack, if ya doin' nowt, a copper from up t' road a bit is 'ere.'

'Hello, Constable, I'm Sergeant Jack Davies; I'm sorry I should have met you when you first arrived. Please come with me to the incident room.'

'Si' thi, mi duck.'

'Goodbye, Inspector, thank you for the cup of tea.' As James closed the door behind him, he heard the Inspector muttering, 'Ta'ra, bloody middlin' posh folk from da'n t' road a bit.'

Sergeant Davies opened a thick file marked 'Minister Road Bakery.' 'As you can see, Constable, we had a lot going on here. We assembled this paperwork over eighteen months into the bakery fire, and Mrs Christine Follows' involvement.'

'With that much evidence in your file, how come she wasn't indicted?'

'Most of the paperwork here relates to what the Director of Public Prosecutions classed as circumstantial evidence. We tried gathering more evidence, but Christine led a charmed life and wriggled out of our grasp. In the end, an ongoing investigation must have an end date. Purely on cost grounds, how long can you devote the time of full-time officers to a case that looked increasingly unlikely to get a conviction? I don't know about the cost of policing in Staffordshire, Constable, but here in Yorkshire we are extremely stretched. We had to close the file on Christine Follows. Afterwards, we still kept an eye on her movements, but as she'd been alerted, she decided to be a good girl and lie low. We all knew she was as guilty as hell. Proof to get a conviction for arson is another matter. You almost have to catch them in the act of striking a match. The next thing we knew, Terry and Christine Follows moved from their rented house and relocated south. Now you turn up, and you tell me she's on your patch. She must have been up to her old ways, or you wouldn't be here. Am I right, Constable?'

James smiled and nodded. 'Absolutely correct, Sergeant. She's our prime suspect in causing a fire at an apartment complex, resulting in the death of eight people....'

'... bloody hell! At least there were no fatalities here. That puts a different light on the matter, doesn't it? If she's guilty, she's a murderer. How can I help you, Constable?'

'Your advice, really. How would you suggest we get a conviction? Do you mind if I set my phone to record mode? I need to report back to my gov and don't want to forget anything.'

'No problem. I hope you'll be able to understand my Yorkshire accent.'

'At least you haven't said, *Ow do, Constable. Nah then, what brings tha' t'Yarkshar?'*

Sergeant Davies smiled. 'Inspector Illingworth is a character, isn't he? He's one of the old school, but an excellent copper and a better guvnor.' The sergeant checked James had primed his phone.

'Get concrete evidence! Were there fingerprints and possessions of hers left at the scene? Perhaps there are witnesses? People aren't always keen to come forward and give evidence to the police, especially if it means appearing in court. Too many crown witnesses and their families are intimidated and threatened these days. Check CCTV cameras. Does she have an alibi? I can tell you that Mrs Christine Follows has a chronic compulsion to start fires with a proclivity to create larger fires and causing more destruction. Until she's caught, she'll start other fires. Habitual recidivist was the description given to her by our criminal psychologist.'

James looked to the file. 'Is there anything in there that could help us?'

'I don't think so, Constable. Here she started small and built her way up. Her criminal ways started at primary school, and then she spent time at young offenders' institutions. At her secondary school, wastepaper baskets were set on fire. Then she progressed to fires in woodlands, harvest fields and on the moors. The bakery was her most profound. There were no fatalities, only destruction of property and several people's livelihoods ...'

'... she was practising here, but she's in the big league now.'

'Unfortunately for you and your community.'

He turned, switched off his phone and got up. 'Thank you for your help, Sergeant.'

'I hope you nail her quickly, Constable, before she commits more murders. She won't stop, you know. I'll si' thi'.'

'... er! Ahem! I'll si'thi' too.' James clumsily attempted his reply in a Yorkshire accent.

Sergeant Davies smiled. 'Good try.'

Twenty-seven

Michael Ridgeway visited seven banks in Cannock before he was able to complete his pro forma on their security. He concluded that five of them had sophisticated, coordinated systems that made them almost impregnable. Short of a team of commandos using explosives or having a tank to batter down the walls, his romantic notions of someone walking into them and demanding money seemed impossible. He discounted those five and devoted his thoughts to the two remaining ones that both fronted onto the main street. Up to an hour's free parking was allowed outside each bank. The National Barchester Bank was closest to the edge of town and had automatic, sliding, reinforced glass doors, controlled from inside the bank. The Assured Providential Building Society, adjoining the old snooker hall opposite Saint Luke's church, had two old-fashioned revolving doors.

Since he had become friends with Godfrey Warlock, Michael had lost interest in his job at Lichfield, a city ten miles from Cannock. He came to realise that operating a battery-powered fork-lift stacker in a furniture warehouse wasn't the most glamorous of careers. He knew his position in the firm would soon be filled by another equally muscular young man, more interested in the work than Michael ever would be. Godfrey assured him that his potential lay in more worthwhile ideals and encouraged him to devote his time to follow his dreams.

For several weeks, Michael had become a familiar sight in Cannock's town centre. People became curious about the lanky, fair-haired young man wandering around town, filling in his pro forma and tables with facts and figures. He kept himself to himself and, other than Godfrey, didn't get involved with anyone or make new friends. Meanwhile, his mother was getting more and more concerned about him. He had distanced himself from her. They didn't laugh and joke together anymore, and he had stopped eating the regular meals she prepared for him. Subsisting on dole money, he had no surplus cash to keep himself smart and buy new clothes. He became a regular customer of the town's several charity shops. He clothed himself in second-hand garments that very rarely fitted him correctly. He didn't mind; his sole concentration was on The Assured Providential Building Society, the bank he'd narrowed down as being the one he intended to rob. He gradually assumed the persona of a scruffy tramp, sitting on the public bench opposite the Providential. He had long ago given up shaving or attending to his personal hygiene. If the public toilets weren't open, he relieved himself in the church cemetery. His blonde, short goatee beard blended in with his dirty, dishevelled appearance.

Several mobile fast-food stalls set up in the pedestrian area, especially on market days. He knew which ones he could cadge leftover cheeseburgers and the dregs of the coffee urns. Eating them on his bench, he didn't care when excess tomato sauce or mayonnaise dripped onto his moustache and stayed there until the next morning. The patrolling police constables grew to accept him and rarely thought about moving him on from his bench. Michael acquired a waterproof sleeping bag left behind by a tramp who'd died in the cold, and he spent most of his nights on the bench watching the building society. To the police and everyone else, he was a rough sleeper. A tramp. A man with no ambition or future. His appearance belied his sharp, calculating mind. He knew when the armoured vans delivered cash to the bank. He understood the bank held more money on market days. A gradual conversation developed between him and personnel working at the bank who went into the premises in the morning and left in the late afternoons. They greeted him as Michael, and he got to know their names. One man who stayed aloof was the manager. Mr Miles Buffet who was a stereotypical, middle-aged, spectacled, stiff-upper-lipped Englishman who preferred not to engage with riffraff like Michael. He wasn't, nor ever would be, one of his bank's customers.

Michael saved a few pounds from his dole money. To put this to the best use to suit his goal, he needed a closer look inside the bank. He decided to open a deposit account. He still had his driving licence that he'd retrieved from his mother's house, along with a utility bill. He had proof of an address and identity to satisfy the cashier's requirements to create a new deposit account. When he entered the Providential, a bank employee, perpetually wandering around the open plan floor, offered help and guidance to direct customers to where their needs could be met. On the first occasion when Michael walked in, the bank official screwed his face up at the stench that wafted from Michael's clothes and was about to eject him back out onto the street. 'I'm here to open a new account,' Michael remonstrated loudly. Other bank officials looked towards the direction of the disturbance. The manager, Mr Buffet, eventually walked over and verified that Michael was a bona fide customer. He directed him into the queue for the next available cashier.

After that first deposit, Michael became a bank regular, albeit, on most of his visits, he only deposited his spare change of a few pence at a time. He availed himself of the plush benches in the waiting area and familiarised himself with the bank's layout. The staff were regularly on the lookout for him. To avoid serving him, some of the bank's team would excuse themselves for a visit to the toilet. The ones left at the counters always had their fresh air sprays handy for after he'd left.

Conversely, one person who was delighted with him regularly depositing his spare cash was his mother. Mrs Muriel Ridgeway thought it an encouraging sign her son was developing a more responsible attitude. She even put some of her own pension money into his account to, hopefully, inspire him further. The bank staff took pity that such a respectable woman should have such a down and out, worthless son. Their collective opinion was that she was wasting her money. Of course, neither his mother nor the bank staff knew of the actual reasons behind Michael's regular visits. Michael was, however, gradually assembling such a paltry positive rising amount at The Providential. He merely saw that he was lending the building society his money. At some future date, he would recoup it, together with thousands, hopefully, millions of pounds extra.

Friday was the day of the week he envisaged getting the most considerable amount of money from the bank. An armoured truck would visit the bank on a Thursday afternoon and, under armed guard, would place several long steel boxes in the bank's walk-in safe. The market traders usually wound down their stalls by 2:30pm and took their day's earnings to deposit at the bank, until the bank closed at 4:00pm. During these hours, four cashiers would be standing behind the counters. Most banks, including The Assured Providential Building Society, employed young female employees as cashiers. By experience, the banks' owners knew most customers preferred to be served by personable, attractive young women rather than dour, elderly men. Michael saw this to his advantage. He envisaged such young women would be more easily frightened by violent threats than elderly men, who he guessed would be tempted to defend themselves.

After buying new clothes at a charity shop, he'd amble into the bank, and join the queue as if prepared to make another deposit into his account. The bank staff were used to him, and no undue notice would be taken that anything was different from any other time he'd stood in the bank. He'd quietly demand that one of the cashiers fill the bag he gave her with what she held in her cash drawer. One of her colleagues would open the vault and fill the other bag he'd handed over to fill with wads of fifty-pound notes. He envisaged that some customers wouldn't even know what was happening, let alone other staff members going about their everyday business. There would be no fuss, and he'd simply walk out of the bank and amble down the street. He'd seen many movies where villains dashing about threatening everyone brought attention to themselves and were invariably apprehended. Michael's approach was the opposite. He would be gentle but firm and demanding. It would also be quick, not giving the staff time to call the police or other security guards.

Cannock's pedestrian area on a Friday afternoon swarmed with shoppers. He'd simply blend in with the crowd and even sit down in one of the outdoor cafes, order a coffee, and watch the aftermath of his daring plan. He foresaw police cars with flashing blue lights and screaming sirens screeching to a halt outside the bank. Michael smiled, knowing that the ordinarily unflappable manager, Miles Buffet, would become agitated, on the edge of a nervous breakdown and in fear of losing his job. Throughout the whole of Michael's plans, there was one minor item missing. He needed a weapon. He needed a gun to show the cashiers that he meant business and would not tolerate any nonsense. He never intended to shoot anybody; the firearm would just be a prop, a necessary piece of equipment like the two bags for carrying the money. He puzzled where to buy such a gun. It was only in large cities where sports shops sold guns and they were for sporting use only. Provincial towns like Cannock and Lichfield didn't even cater to such ideals. He turned to the only person he knew could help him, Godfrey Warlock.

The bell jangled on its coiled spring as he thrust open the door. Two strides and he cleared the step. He looked through the gloom where Godfrey stood talking to his clients in the brightly lit reading room. Godfrey briefly looked up when he heard the bell, but resumed chatting. Michael approached and stood meekly by his side, waiting for him to give him his attention. Godfrey sensed how anxious he seemed and deliberately extended his discourse on the merits, or otherwise, of what caused gas explosions in domestic properties. Michael hopped uncomfortably from foot to foot.

'You know where the toilets are, Michael.' Godfrey whispered to him. Michael visited the gents and returned to find Godfrey had left the reading room and stood impassively behind his counter.

'Now, Michael, my friend, how are you? You seem impatient.'

'I need your help, Godfrey.'

'That's what I'm here for, you know that.'

'My plan is ready, Mr Warlock, but there's something I need.'

'What is it you need?'

'A gun...!' Godfrey laughed.

'Have you only lately come around to thinking about that? I would have thought you'd have asked me weeks ago for that?'

'I'm sorry, I've sorted my plan out now....'

'... which bank?'

'The Assured Providential Building Society in the main street.'

'I applaud your choice, Michael. It's the least security conscious bank in the town. I wish you good luck.'

'The gun is only to be used as a threat. I don't think for a second that I'll need to use it.'

'Of course not, I'm sure you have everything worked out to the second.'

'Can you help me, please? I don't know where to buy a gun.'

'There's a sports shop in Stafford that sells shotguns, but I don't recommend you walk into the bank with one over your shoulder. It's a bit of a giveaway, isn't it?' Michael nodded.

'I have a couple of dear friends who will help. Give me a couple of days. Come back here...' Godfrey felt his goatee beard. '... say, in three days. That will give them time to send it to me. Be a good boy in the meantime. Behave and don't attract attention to yourself. It would be a pity now to jeopardise your plan.'

Michael left the bookshop with the sound of the doorbell jangling in his ears. He headed for the cheeseburger stall on the market. He was suddenly hungry and knew they would soon be cleaning out their saucepans.

Godfrey watched him walk away and picked up his telephone. 'Dariusz, my dear friend, my colleague. How are you today? I hope I haven't caught you at a bad time. I need your help.'

'Godfrey, can I ring you back? Give me five minutes.' Godfrey had indeed caught him at an inconvenient moment.

Dariusz turned to the two naked women who were engaged in erotic games with him. 'Give it a rest for a few minutes, my lovelies. Go and get yourselves another drink and bring one back for me.' He reached for his mobile phone and dialled Godfrey's number.

'How can I help, Godfrey?'

'Sorry I disturbed you, Dariusz; have you sent the girls on their way?'

'They'll keep! We hadn't long started; the day's got a long way to go.'

Godfrey explained what he wanted.

'As it happens, I've only yesterday had a shipment from The States of some new shooters. I have the very thing for your friend. It's the latest in small weapons, fitting into the palm of your hand. Even the feds are using it. They call it the Kurtz. It's a Colt 380. It's getting more popular as the calibre of choice for small pocket pistols but offers much less power than a 9mm Luger.'

'Whatever you say, Dariusz, guns aren't my speciality. I presume there'll be some bullets too?'

'I'll send one of the girls to put one in the post to you with a box of shells.'

'That's very amenable of you, my friend. It seems a shame for one of your companions to have to get dressed to carry out a small favour for me.'

'I'll send Amber. It'll give Georgie free rein for a change. She's always complaining that Amber gets more than she does.'

Twenty-eight

Nicky pressed search in the police database after typing in Y369WRE the registration number of Christine Follows' car. 'Here it is,' she murmured, 'a red Ford Fiesta, 1.1 cc petrol engine. First registered 3rd February 2000. The car had had six owners before Christine became the owner six months ago.'

She wrote the details in her notebook before pressing an icon entitled 'Current Taxation'.

'Oho! Here we go. The vehicle owner has completed a SWORN statement, declaring it is off the road and garaged.' She wrote more determinedly. 'So, she's currently driving it around, having paid no vehicle tax. That's the first, what's next?'

Another icon was labelled as Ins, an anachronism for insured status. Nicky pressed the icon and wasn't surprised to see the result. 'Vehicle currently uninsured. Number two!'

The third icon was for MOT status. Nicky had her pen poised, ready to write the result. As she presumed, the last time the car received a valid MOT certificate was nearly four years ago. 'Number three.'

'Now, does Christine have a driving licence?' Nicky searched the DVLA database at Swansea. The quest took a little longer than the previous searches. 'There is no record of a Mrs Christine Follows having a licence to drive any vehicle. Number four.'

Nicky paused and thought about Christine driving her car around Cannock with no tax, MOT or Insurance. 'They are all indictable offences. That's it, of course, I can search the police criminal files.' A more prolonged investigation of the entire country's criminal records revealed Mrs Christine Follows had been convicted two years ago at Doncaster Magistrates Court for driving with undue care and attention. She had also received convictions for driving without a licence, car tax, insurance, or a valid MOT. She was fined £750 and was disqualified from driving for three years. 'That seems ridiculous, Nicky thought, when she didn't own a driving licence, anyway. So, there're more offences, perhaps more severe. She's now driving around Cannock while disqualified.' Nicky knew this offence could carry a custodial sentence for transgression.

Nicky read further down the page to reveal more. Mrs Follows had been given three months to pay the fine. Upon defaulting, she served four months in Wakefield Women's open prison in reparation. Still, she was released for good behaviour after serving two months.

From working at Staffordshire County Headquarters, something resonated in Nicky's mind about the Open Prison in Wakefield. Another search of prison records showed that during the time Christine had been incarcerated in the short-term wing, a fire had gutted part of the recreation block. 'Well! Well! I bet the prison authorities were glad to see the back of her.'

Nicky spent the next hour and a half typing up the results of all her searches. The resulting document was a litany of continual criminal activity.

'She's a real bad girl, isn't she?' Nicky muttered. Had Donald been in his office, she would have presented her dossier to him at once. Unfortunately, he was at Staffordshire Police Headquarters in meetings with Superintendent Woodhouse, and likely to be there all day.

'Ah well, it can wait until tomorrow morning. James will be back from Doncaster. We can have a comprehensive meeting about Christine in the morning.'

Twenty-nine

Nicky's photographs taken at *Godfrey's Bookshop* showed a lot more than the enigmatic slit-eyed shop proprietor. Amongst the people studying in the reading room was David Shaw, the controller of the rail network on West Midland Railway. Godfrey Warlock had long ago ear-marked David as his brightest protégée. David, being aspirational and, possessing an inflated ego desiring broader fulfilment, made him an ideal candidate for Godfrey. He exerted influence and guidance for the former railways signalman, to help him achieve his ambitions. Being an avid reader in the bookshop, David gained encouragement and unlimited support.

After Nicky had left the bookshop, Godfrey went and sat with David and offered him a new book he had acquired. 'Read this, David; I think this is exactly what you've been looking for.'

David learned that radioactive nuclear waste always kept its radioactivity. Whereas compaction and cementation of the hazardous material reduce the radiation it emits, the opposite is true. As the volume is reduced, it increases radiation. If the waste is reduced to dust and allowed to disperse, widespread radioactivity will take place. David laughed as he read the last few sentences. Godfrey had moved away but turned as David's chuckle echoed around the reading room. 'I thought you might like that, David,' and laughed in unison with him. 'It reminds me of what used to be a lovely place near Pripyat in the north of Ukraine. You must have read about what happened there?' David's face was blank. 'I'll remind you. I'm sure you'll recall it when I say Chernobyl.'

'Oh, yes! I remember.'

'It was a miserable morning - the 26th April 1986. It was drizzly and cold. In those northern climes of The Soviet Union, the weather always seemed like that, even on a spring morning. Of course, it's now an independent country after the communists lost power in their dubious regime. People I was with, wrapped up like Eskimos, turned and pointed when they saw the mushroom cloud on the skyline. Then the blast knocked us all off our feet. It was such a pitiful sight to see my friends whom I'd just been talking to become skeletons, with only a few bits of radiated flesh hanging off their bones. It's still a radioactive ghost town today. Do you know there are parts of the site that will remain uninhabitable for the next one hundred thousand years? Just think, David, that's what Cannock would look like if such a disaster happened here.'

'It's like opening Pandora's box, isn't it...?' David suggested.

'... and we all know what happened when she did that, don't we?' Godfrey laughed again, but David was ignorant of the mythical consequences.

'I can see you haven't studied Greek mythology, have you, David?' He shook his head. 'Let me remind you. She unleashed sickness, death and countless unspecified evils upon the world....'

'... unspecified evils?' David asked.

'Of course. The moment Pandora succumbed to temptation and opened the box, no one knew what those evils were, but I can tell you....'

'... yes?' David replicated Godfrey's enthusiasm and was swept along by his mysterious teachings.

'... horrible things.' Godfrey shrieked in ecstasy. 'Greed, envy, hatred, pain, disease, hunger, war, poverty, unending warfare and death. All of human life's miseries.' David looked in wide-eyed wonder. 'Yes, my apprentice, my disciple, my neophyte, you have it within your power to create these things. What has humanity ever given you only constrain you to a sycophantic, subordinate role in the dust of human life's miserable existence on earth where everyone else walks upon you? Now you can rise above everyone and show the pampered infidels in control who you really are. Whatever you achieve in your life, David, remember, there is no terror in the bang, only in the anticipation of it.'

With his boosted self-esteem, David lowered his head into the book for more information, leaving Godfrey to add the finishing touches to two more of his students.

'There, I think you have everything you need, Brian and Belinda. My books have shown you the authentic way to live, spontaneously and as nature intended.'

As David received his latest tutorial in the bookshop, Janet had ventured into the town pushing Zak before her in his pram. By chance, she again met her neighbour, Barbara Williams.

144

'We must stop meeting like this, Janet,' she said.

'Exactly, Barbara, why don't you come around to my house for a coffee together? We can catch up with what's happening in the town.'

'Why don't we have coffee now? There's a new bistro opened in the pedestrian area by the covered bandstand.'

They sat together, enjoying the sunshine and watching Zak, happily gurgling and chewing on his plastic teething ring. Their attention was diverted when a signboard was placed on an easel in front of the bandstand. A collective murmur rippled around others seated outside.

'Oh, look, Janet, there's some sort of activity group going to perform on the bandstand. I can't read what it says; I've left my distance glasses at home.'

'Ooh, this seems intriguing; someone called Brian and Belinda.' Janet answered. 'Here they come now. He looks a bit of alright, doesn't he? He's a real handsome bloke.'

'Hey, steady on, *Mrs* Lawrence, it's us unattached women in the queue before you,' Barbara laughed.

Brian and Belinda strolled onto the paved performing area under the covered bandstand.

'Are they going to sing?' Barbara asked, 'or are they a conjuring act?'

'Ah! They're taking their clothes off; it looks like an acrobatic or gymnastic performance.' Janet took a slurp of coffee and nearly choked. 'Oh my God, Babs, she's taken her bikini top off!'

They turned when people, mostly men, behind them, started cheering.

'Oh, this is getting interesting, Janet, he's down to his swimming trunks.' The following action on stage caused Janet and Barbara, and everyone else in the audience, to stare wide-eyed in shock. Even Zak tried to peer around the hood of his pram to see what his mother was staring at.

Barbara edged closer to Janet and whispered. 'Bloody hell, Janet, he's done the full Monty; he's as naked as the day he was born!'

Janet returned her whisper, 'On his birthday, I don't think he had what he's got now!'

Barbara held her hand to her mouth. 'Oh my word, Janet, whatever next? Look at that ...!'

Janet beamed an enormous smile, '... and I know what you mean by *that*! It's huge....'

Barbara smiled and had difficulty stifling a loud cheer, '… I must get out more… Oh, Janet, he's gorgeous, and he's walking towards us….'

'Looks like it,' Janet tried to appear nonchalant as his muscled torso edged closer.

The lull in the audience soon turned into an uproar. Women were cheering and clapping as Brian walked around, brandishing his nakedness. Men's cheers soon joined them as Belinda joined her partner, and she too stripped off her bikini bottom. Hand in hand, they strolled around, shamelessly displaying their nudity.

Brian came and stood directly in front of Janet and Barbara with his legs wide apart. He flexed his biceps and pulled his shoulders forward, displaying his rippling chest muscles and a solid six-pack across his stomach. He smiled and tried to make eye contact with the two women, but their eyes never strayed above his navel. By now, the crowd had grown and extended into High Green and the adjoining open-air market. Belinda came over, smiled, and held Brian's hand. He turned and held her close before they kissed in a full body embrace. Amid loud cheering and applause, Barbara looked at Janet. 'That's one lucky woman.' Janet nodded.

'Oh, no, this is going too far,' Janet exclaimed, but she continued to stare.

'What's going on?' Barbara asked, before looking back at the naked couple. 'Ooh! I've never been to a pornographic show. Yes! Yes!' she shouted. The crowd picked up on her stark words and, in unison, they all called, 'Yes! Yes!' and clapped their hands in sync with their shouts. There were bright flashes as photographers took their opportunities of capturing images that would feature in tomorrow's national press.

Belinda and Brian were fondling each other. Within seconds Brian's obvious sexual arousal was covered by Police Constable Wilson's helmet. Two more officers draped blankets around Belinda and Brian as they were led away. 'Spoilsports! Shame! Leave them alone!' were the most audible words yelled above the general commotion.

After five minutes, the town square quietened down as passers-by went back to their shopping. Barbara turned to Janet. 'Well! What about that? What's happening around Cannock these days?'

'I can't believe it either. When Donald and I left London we looked forward to a quieter life. I can tell you, Barbara, London has nothing to compare with that....' They laughed and ordered another coffee.

'... and I know what you mean by *that*.' Barbara repeated Janet's earlier words while Constable Wilson was washing his helmet in the restroom at Cannock Police Station. Christine Follows received a knock on her front door. She peered through the glass spy hole before opening the door to her husband. 'What do you want? I've nothing to say to you, Terry. Leave me alone.'

'Oh! Very nice! Not a nice greeting for a husband, is it? What's happened to hello, darling, how are you?... and you look bloody awful. What have you done to yourself?'

'Piss off!' Christine tried to close the door, but Terry held his foot in the gap.

'I'm going. I only came to tell you that the police are onto you. They've been to my house asking questions about you.'

'Well! So what?'

'Before I go, please tell me you had nothing to do with that horrific fire at the Station apartment block...?'

'... as I said, piss off....'

'... but, Chrissie, eight people died. Seven pensioners and a baby.'

Christine kicked his foot from her door threshold and slammed the door. Terry walked disconsolately back to Dewsbury Grove.

Thirty

That evening the clock at the town's war memorial showed seven-thirty. It was a beautiful early summer dusk, with the clear sky streaked with long, pink altostratus clouds. The town centre buzzed with people strolling around the pedestrian square. Most of the excited chatter revolved around Brian and Belinda's lurid performance earlier in the day. Shops were still open as their neon lights glowed in the approaching twilight. *Godfrey's Bookshop* was no different. His shop window was edged with yellow, twinkling strip lights effusing a warm welcome. Godfrey stood expectantly in his doorway. He knew he was going to have a visitor.

A loud clattering noise and a screech of brakes destroyed the peaceful evening. A man standing looking in the bookshop window turned and saw a battered red Ford Fiesta car crossing the pedestrian area. It drew to a stop outside *Godfrey's Bookshop*. Godfrey Warlock opened his door as Christine walked towards him. They hugged each other briefly before he held her at arm's length and looked into her eyes. 'You have done well, my good and faithful servant. Your excellent work will stand you in good stead in the next world. Farewell for now, Christine. May your journey go smoothly.'

Christine got back in the car and revved the engine, causing the back wheels to spin and issue clouds of smoke. Letting go of the handbrake, the car accelerated the fifteen yards towards the war memorial in the middle of the pedestrian area. Godfrey walked into the paved area and watched her go. Several people dived aside or would have been struck. One man walking sedately with his wife saw the car was approaching but wasn't quick enough to avoid it. Instead, he violently pushed his wife aside milliseconds before the dented red bonnet hit him in the midriff. The car's forward motion carried him over the low concrete wall and pinned his fractured body to the base of the clock tower as the front of the Fiesta crumpled in the bed of salvias and petunias. The vehicle came to rest at a tilted angle. Passers-by gasped and shouted out. Many witnesses would later testify that they watched Christine Follows calmly get out of the car and empty two-gallon canisters of petrol over the entire length of the car's bodywork. People standing nearest to the car saw the flowing gasoline. Instincts of self-preservation came into play as they turned to run away. Several bemused people near the war memorial didn't realise what was happening and watched in curious fascination. Christine sat back in the driver's seat, turned behind her and opened the taps on three steel bottles of propane gas that were secured by the rear seats' safety belts. Packed around the gas bottles were buckets full of nails and screws. She smelled and heard the gas hissing from the pressurised containers and waited until the car's interior was filled with gas. Suppressing an urge to retch and vomit, she reached down; her hand hovered over the cigar lighter knob. She gazed into the rear-view mirror, smiled at her reflection, and depressed her forefinger.

Over two miles away, Donald and Janet were sitting at the dining table eating their evening meal. Zak dozed peacefully in his carrycot by their side. Janet told him what had happened in the town square. He already knew, having watched their conduct as Nicky and James charged them with indecent behaviour and conducted them to the station cells for the night to cool off.

'It was quite a performance, darling.'

'I can imagine. The pair stripped off again in the interview room when we weren't looking. Much to James' embarrassment, Nicky kept rewinding the video surveillance tape to get a second and third opinion.'

'I don't blame her....' They felt the thud hitting the soles of their feet through the floor. Then a millisecond afterwards felt the force of changing air pressure on their eardrums. Zak woke with a loud cry.

'Wha...!' Janet exclaimed.

'What now?' Donald questioned. 'That's an explosion.' Donald rushed outside and saw the orange ball of light coming from the direction of the town centre. From the kitchen, Donald's mobile rang. Janet picked it up and brought it out to him, then went back to tend to Zak. It was Lucas.

'Lucas, tell me! What's happened?'

'There's been an explosion in the town centre....'

'... where exactly?'

'As far as we can tell from eyewitness reports, near the war memorial, except that isn't there anymore. I'm on my way now.'

'Oh, my God, more carnage! I'll be there in five minutes.'

'Don't wait up for me, darling. I've a feeling this is going to be a long night!'

In the lower part of the town, James was relaxing after returning from Yorkshire. He heard and felt the blast and was soon at the scene.

At her home in Stafford, Nicky was doing some writing on her laptop. Across her screen appeared the latest news bulletin describing the explosion. She donned her coat and, within five minutes, was driving the eight miles to Cannock.

As the first element in the car's cigar lighter glowed orange, the gas ignited. Shattered into a thousand pieces, the cells and biological compounds that constituted Christine's head propelled through the gap where the windscreen had been, like a shower of red and white paint. The eruption of exploding gas instantly heated to 100,000 degrees centigrade. The Red Fiesta and everything in it disintegrated. Microscopic fragments scattered for a radius of twenty metres, smashing every pane of glass in every window within that circle. The air blast shattered windows in a radius of a further fifty metres. Fortunately, the buckets of nails had not been compacted into the explosive material and weren't propelled as far.

Explosives experts later estimated this had saved the lives of over fifty people. People within five metres of Christine's car suffered complete dismemberment and decapitation. The dominant force of the explosion rocketed skywards, creating a mushroom cloud like a miniature nuclear explosion. Most people living near the town centre suffered damage to their hearing. In the resulting three-foot deep crater where Christine's car had stood, fractured water mains propelled pressurised water twenty feet into the air. An area of up to two square miles was at once without electrical power or phone signals. Fortunately, the gas mains that supplied properties and shops surrounding the pedestrian area were confined to the square's periphery and remained intact. The resulting fire and burning petrol were soon extinguished as the mains water cascaded down. There was minimal combustible material within the pedestrian area. Outside, restaurant chairs and tables and a canvas-covered market stall were the only extraneous objects left burning. Thirteen people, including Christine Follows, perished. A further twenty people needed hospital treatment, of which three were critical.

Within ten minutes, a traffic jam of ambulances with wailing sirens congregated on the town's ring road, parking as close as they could to the damaged area. Lucas and his team of fire-fighters secured and cordoned off the area so they could begin trying to identify every scrap of wreckage to determine the source and cause of the explosion.

Within a further thirty minutes, the nation's news media converged on Cannock to gather information on the catastrophe. Neither the camera operators nor photographers recorded Godfrey Warlock quietly content, standing in the shadows within his bookshop's enforced gloom and dimness. He recited aloud so that only his readers could hear his words. 'When we die, we leave behind us all that we have and take with us all that we are.' Slight applause came from the reading room. He turned and smiled. 'Poor Christine, but for some people like our dear colleague, there are far worse things than death – take life, for instance.' He smiled at his captive readers. 'My beloved friends, the only certain thing about life is that we must all leave it.'

For the following five hours, Donald and the whole of personnel employed at Cannock Police Station supplied help and support to the injured and confused. Nicky and James walked around the damaged area, looking for clues to what had happened. James saw it first, a shiny piece of metal sticking in a bit of cedar-wood that had been part of a bench around the war memorial. With difficulty, he prised it from the wooden splinters. It was about two inches by four inches of what once was a white reflective car registration plate. Two embossed black letters were still visible together - W and R, followed by half a letter that could be an E or F. He showed it to Nicky.

'It looks like a vehicle registration plate.'

'So, do you think this belonged to a vehicle that was damaged in the explosion?'

'This is a pedestrian area, James. I can't think why any vehicle would be parked here in the evening. If it was, where's the rest of the vehicle?'

'Puzzling or what?' he questioned. 'Or, if this is all that's left of the vehicle, perhaps it was next to the explosion...?'

'... or, James, the source of the explosion?' She looked again at the fragment of the registration plate. 'My mind is doing somersaults, James....'

'... are you alright? Amongst all the dust and muck on your face, you look pale. We should have a rest in the office. I could do with a cup of tea.'

Slowly and deliberately, Nicky asked James a question. She held his arms.

'What?'

'Can you remember the registration plate number of Christine Follows' car…?'

'… oh, come on, Nicky, you're not suggesting…?'

'… I don't know what to think…?' Donald came walking over to them and asked what they were doing?

'Hi, gov. It's like those war zone films you see in the movies.'

'At least we still have a town left and can repair the damage. There are enough photographs of the war memorial to rebuild it with every name inscribed again.'

'Gov, look what James found embedded in a piece of a wooden bench.'

'Hmm! It looks what's left of a vehicle registration plate.'

'Exactly what James and I deduced.'

'What do you think the letters are?'

'… a W and R and something else, an E or F perhaps?'

'James and I have been thinking….'

'What? Of a vehicle this plate belongs to?'

'Gov, I've just asked James if he can remember the number of Christine Follows car?'

'… you don't think this is…?'

'Your wife wrote the number down for you after she'd visited Christine's house, and I've carried out internet searches on Christine's vehicle, as you asked me to.'

'… and…?'

'Gov, I've remembered her number was Y369WRE.'

James shone a torch on the ground and in the dust on the paving, with his finger, wrote, Y369WRE. Then held the fragment of the plate against it.

'Well, it fits, I suppose. The last letter could be an E?' Donald conceded.

'There's only one way to prove it, gov. Go to her house and check in her garage.'

'Not tonight, James, there's no power, anyway. We're all exhausted, and it'll keep until the morning. I'm so tired, I could sleep for a month. But somehow, I don't think I'll sleep a wink.'

Thirty-one

Doris Sparkes had only taken the job as a cleaner at The Ritz Hotel in Mayfair, Central London because she needed the money. She detested cleaning away the mess that wealthy people left behind in their rooms. She realised, in their pampered eyes she was the lowest of the working-class in London society. A servant that existed purely to satisfy their whims and needs. She had pride in herself and many times had resisted retaliating against the dismissive way affluent guests treated her. At a regular appraisal of her work, she unwisely confided to her supervisor exactly how she felt. After that, they confined her cleaning work to the gentlemen's toilets on the same floor as the premier restaurant where there was less conflict with the guests. She wished she had kept her views to herself because she disliked this work even more.

'Ugh! Doris, how can you do such disgusting work?' her flatmate, Dolores, whinged as she drank a glass of Prosecco while waiting for her nail varnish to dry. 'By basic definition, men are such vulgar animals. Their pee stinks, and in any bathroom they use they splash droplets around the floor. They can't help it. You always know when you're within fifty yards of a men's toilet, can't you? You only have to watch a stallion or a bull in the fields. When did you last see such an animal have a pee in one steady flow? Start, pee for a while, then finish. Never, that's when! They always splash a few drops here and there in the grass. Men are just the same.'

'Whatever you get up to in your spare time, Dolores Mainwaring, is no concern of mine. It's not a pursuit of mine, lusting after the willies of such creatures, or men, come to that. I do have to look after myself, you know. Some men at The Ritz, who enter the restroom....'

'... here get you, all la de dah now you're at The Ritz. It's a restroom now, is it? Most men I know simply call it the bog or the khazi.' Doris stared at her without commenting.

'As I said, some men think I'm a soft touch. Some think I must be a nymphomaniac working in there to get a view of what they fetch out of their trousers.'

'I suppose that could be classed as one of the perks of the job?'

'Dolores, whatever do you think of me? When I'm cleaning, I don't deliberately look in their direction… but I must admit, sometimes I do get a glance….'

'… and…?' Doris blushed and laughed.

'… I think a lot of men must be shy. They don't even want other men seeing what they've got. Some men hold their fingers around it, shielding it from view as they pee, but some others don't give a fig.'

'You can bet your wages the first sort only have little ones, and they're ashamed what other blokes might think? Whereas, what's with the ones who don't care?'

'Well, that's just why I'm making the point, Dolores… she looked furtively from side to side as if someone was eavesdropping on their conversation. Those sorts of blokes always have big ones.'

'… here, Doris, how do you know what differentiates a big one from a little one?'

Doris tapped the side of her nose. 'That's for me to know and you to wonder about. I haven't lived in a convent, you know.'

'Perhaps I should get a job in your posh restroom? These days, the closest I seem to get to one is in Saville Row's tailors measuring men's inside leg. Mind you, I do get some funny looks sometimes when I ask them what side they dress?'

'Side? Whatever do you mean, Dolores?'

'Bloody hell, Doris, where've you been for the past twenty years? Which leg do they hang their willy down, left, or right, of course!'

'Does it make a difference to how their trousers fit?'

'How the bleedin' hell do I know. It must do, I suppose. When I get a regular boyfriend, remind me to ask him.'

'When you get a proper boyfriend, and you're on intimate terms with him to ask that question, it's not likely to be hanging down at all, is it?' The following five minutes in their flat resounded with mutual hysterical laughter that reverberated down the street.

On the day that Harry Stevens used the men's restroom at The Ritz, Doris had been suffering a water infection for three days. She'd only been taking antibiotics for two days and still needed to pee a lot and usually at short notice.

'I ain't walking to the other side of the building, I'll use one of the men's cubicles,' she convinced herself, as the urge to pee became overwhelming. Enduring the pain of her urine stinging her flesh, she heard Harry enter the cubicle next to her and tried to keep quiet. That's more than Harry did because she heard him unbuckle his belt and let his trousers fall to the floor. The loud banging as Dariusz and Vlad forced Harry's cubicle door open had caused her to startle.

When she'd watched the Kreuger brothers commit murder, her whole life changed. When she'd eventually called the supervisor to report Harry's body, the hotel manager called the police. She was interviewed as a key eyewitness, the only observer of what had happened. Two weeks later, without even informing her flatmate, Dolores, she started a new life in the Metropolitan police's witness protection programme. With a new name, address, and telephone number, she was depressed. She missed her flatmate, she had no friends or family to socialise with; she wanted her old life back.

Lucy had thought about somehow discrediting Doris as a credible witness. A situation presented itself whereby she may be able to get access to her. On the department's calendar, Lucy saw the Mansion House was the venue for the annual Metropolitan Police Force dinner and dance. She knew the officers who ran the witness protection programme. One young, unattached officer, Sergeant Eric Chambers, had expressed affection for her in the past. She smiled, thinking now would be ideal for bringing her feminine guile to bear and gain his confidence.

The following day she departed from her usual lunchtime routine of walking to the bistro in Horse Guards Avenue, *La Vista*. Instead, she ambled into the staff restaurant on the top floor of New Scotland Yard. It was pleasant dining there, with fabulous views looking over the River Thames towards Waterloo Bridge. She knew Eric was a regular diner in the restaurant. It was a self-serve arrangement, so she joined the small queue and selected a light tomato salad and fruit dessert. Lucy had already seen Eric sitting by the far window that looks down onto The Embankment. He was sitting with three other male colleagues; they were busy chatting and laughing together; they didn't notice her as she sat at the next table to them. By the time she'd placed her lunch tray on the table and sat down, the men had stopped fraternising with each other and looked across to greet her. She had taken extra care with her appearance, making sure she looked the best she could. Lucy wore a deep blue coloured one-piece dress that hugged her curves, revealing a hint of her generous cleavage. The admiring glances she received were not confined to Eric's table. The whole restaurant dominated by male police officers stopped and turned. Lucy made a particular note to catch Eric's eye. She gave him a different smile from the perfunctory one she gave to everyone else. Eric's colleagues left the table. Usually, he would have joined them, but he hung back and leaned over towards her.

'Hello, Lucy. It's lovely to see you. It's been a while since you dined in here.'

'Hello, Eric. I thought I'd give it a try again. The last time I was in here, the bread and butter pudding gave me indigestion for a week.'

'Not anymore. The catering department has new chefs in here now. Didn't you read it in the Yard's magazine?'

'No, I didn't. I've been terribly busy lately. I must say this salad tastes delicious.' They were having the conversation from adjoining tables. Two high-ranking officers came and sat at Eric's table, so he asked Lucy if he could join her.

'Of course.' Lucy offered another irresistible smile.

'You haven't got a drink. What would you like? I'm having another cup of tea.'

'Oh, yes, please, Eric, make that two.'

They sat chatting together for the next hour. The dregs of their tea had long gone cold as the restaurant manager came and reminded them they were the last diners, and she would be closing in ten minutes.

'Oh, my! Look at the time!' Lucy exclaimed. 'Where's that hour gone?'

'It's been lovely catching up with you. I don't suppose you'd consider dining with me away from the Yard, would you?' Eric asked, nervously.

'That would be lovely. It's been a while since I've been on a date.'

'Would we be on a date?'

Lucy laughed. 'Well, not in the truest definition of the word, but who knows...?' She gave him a teasing, sultry gaze from under her eyelashes.

'... Ahem! Er! That's great. Do you have a favourite restaurant?'

She told him about the bistro, *La Vista,* 'But I know you live out of the City, near Brent Cross. We could dine closer to your home, if you like?'

'There's a pleasant restaurant near where I live called *Giacomo's*; I'll make a booking.'

They arranged to meet there at 7:30 the following evening. Lucy sat back at her office desk, satisfied that phase one of her strategy had gone according to plan.

Thirty-two

Donald, James, and Nicky met in the police station's main office the morning after the explosion. They were thankful that the police offices were tucked away from the town's main pedestrian area, only a couple of windows had been broken. Other neighbouring shops and offices had also been relatively untouched by the blast.

'I think we should have a meeting about Christine Follows,' Donald asserted.

James began by relating everything he had gleaned from Doncaster police headquarters, including replaying the recording he had made.

Nicky produced the file she had created. She pointed out all the offences Christine had been committing and the records of her criminal past.

'Okay, let's go after her before she causes any more misery.' Donald ordered as they all rose from the table and put on their coats.

'I don't think we'll find her….' Nicky added. 'I've thought about it overnight. I'm convinced she caused the explosion by driving her car into the war memorial.'

James looked at her and then at Donald. 'I'm of the same opinion, gov. I'm sure that the number plate is from her car.'

'You both may well be right, but we have a job to do. Let's go to Christine's house now!'

Donald parked the car outside number twenty-one Fremantle Avenue. 'Looks as if she's not up yet; all the curtains are closed…' Donald stepped out onto the pavement.

'… hey, you can't park here, you bloody arrogant motorist, can't you see the double yellow lines. You're breaking the law.' Donald turned to look at a traffic warden walking towards him from across the road, already writing in his notebook. James remembered what Christine had said about him. *'Little Hitler,'* we call him. James smiled, noting the black smudge moustache that resembled pictures and movies he'd seen of the wartime German dictator.

Donald held up his warrant card before the thick lenses of the traffic warden's glasses. The small, uniformed warden blinked and expressed his disappointment. 'Oh, so you're a bloody policeman. I've wasted a ticket now. I've already written your number on the official form. I'll miss my target now.'

Donald was calm and reasoned. 'I'd like you to give your name and warden's number to my sergeant here…' he gestured to Nicky as she stepped out of the car. 'I consider your tone and demeanour offensive and over-zealous. I could have been any ordinary motorist. They'd have received a parking violation for merely stopping at the kerbside. Your provocative conduct is not what the community expects from a public servant….'

'… but?'

'Report back to your supervisor, now! I'm suspending you from other duties for today. Further, I'd be failing in my duty if the circumstances of all your previous traffic violation bookings aren't investigated. I'd stake my pension most of them will prove unwarranted.'

'Name and number, please?' Nicky asked him, with her pen poised above her notebook. Donald turned from the blustering traffic warden and knocked on Christine Follows' door. He waited before hitting harder. James knocked on the neighbour's door as he heard the traffic warden answer Nicky's question - Damien Cross, number 7656.

A flustered woman answered James' repeated knocking at the door of number nineteen. 'Yes, what is it? You've woken my baby!' Donald showed her his warrant card.

'We are looking for your neighbour, Mrs Christine Follows….'

'… is that all you want? It'll take hours for Tyrone to get to sleep now. What with that bleedin' poxy explosion last evening, this is like purgatory….'

'… Christine Follows?' James reminded her with a questioning gesture.

'I haven't seen the bitch since yesterday afternoon. She went off roaring up the street in that decrepit old banger of hers. It ought to be condemned that damned car of hers should. Chucking dangerous fumes out all over the place, polluting the neighbourhood. I'm sure it's a direct cause of my Tyrone's cough….'

James didn't respond to the woman's statement. 'Thank you, madam,' he answered calmly, and she slammed the door. The loud noise caused the baby to squeal and howl. As the three police officers went to walk round to the back alley, they heard the woman shouting. 'Shut up ya gob, can't ya? Bleedin' kids. Hey Jack, get out of bed and do something about this bastard son of yours.'

Donald murmured to his junior officers as they turned the corner. 'That sounds like a nice family, doesn't it? Marital harmony, eh?'

They turned another corner and entered the alley. Straight away Donald saw the painted number twenty-one above a garage with no vehicle inside. James went and knocked on the rear door before calling for Christine. Apart from listening to some sparrows chirping on the broken plastic guttering and Tyrone whimpering, the alley and the house were quiet. Donald went into the garage and brought out a crowbar type tyre wrench.

'Mind your eyes,' he called to them as he smashed the glass in the rear door. He reached inside and turned the key left on the inside of the door.

'Phew!' James called as he stepped inside the kitchen. 'What's that smell? It didn't stink like this the last time I came here.'

'Christine?!' Donald shouted.

Nicky carefully pushed open the lounge door and peered inside. She heard Donald's boots echoing on the bare floor-boarded stairway. 'James, Nicky, come up here,' he called. They entered the first bedroom at the top of the stairs. Donald was sitting on the bed, avoiding the excrement-stained bedclothes, looking at the gas bottles that lined the room. 'Try the other rooms,' he asked them, as he held a handkerchief to his nose.

Nicky called from a smaller bedroom. 'Gov, James, there are buckets and packets of nails and screws in here.'

'… and look what's in the bathroom, apart from all the shit on the floor.'

'What?' Donald asked.

'Plastic fuel canisters, full of petrol.' James and Nicky didn't hear Donald respond. They carefully trod around the clutter on the floor and peered at Donald. He was holding two folded letters.

'Gov?' James called.

'Two letters here at her bedside, inside a book. One addressed to Terry and the other to Godfrey.'

'Terry's her estranged husband,' James confirmed. Donald opened the loosely folded single sheet of handwriting. He read aloud.

'Terry,

I'm sorry for the way things have turned out between us. I remember how in love we once were with each other. It seems like a dream now. Whatever the differences between us, I want to thank you for helping me with the problem I've always had, which eventually has come between us.

By the time you read this letter, I'll be out of your hair for good.
Christine'

Donald's sombre words carried on the mood of the letter. 'It seems both of you may be right. This is a suicide letter.'

'What does the other one say, gov?' Nicky asked. He passed her the letter. 'Here, you read it.'

Nicky opened the letter and read it to her colleagues.

'Dearest Godfrey,

Since I first met you, my life changed for the better. You showed me how to live and how to make the best of myself. I've suffered most of my life with an incurable phobia. You taught me that I hadn't inherited a horrible curse but an outstanding talent.

I'll take your wonderful smile with me, giving me the courage to enter your world.

Christine.'

'Bloody hell!' James commented. 'It sounds like a letter to a lover....'

'... yes, it does. It's only another tormented suicide letter, though, isn't it?' Donald picked up the book and examined it before exclaiming, 'Incredible! Look at the title of this book.' James and Nicky looked over...

'... gov...?'

'How To Create Fire And Explosions.'

Donald put the book down on the bed and left the bedroom. 'I need some air!' he called, as they heard his boots on the stairway, and he shouted back. 'Before you come out, James, check those gas bottles, one or more of them are leaking gas. If someone had been using the cooker in the kitchen, this place and adjoining houses would have exploded as well.'

James picked up the book and flicked through the pages of equations, chemical symbols and diagrams until he reached the last page. He gasped and showed it to Nicky.

'This book is the property of Doctor Godfrey Warlock, Purveyor of rare and unusual books.'

Thirty-three

Lucy and Eric were shown to their cosy seats in *Giacomo's*. When he'd made the reservation, Eric had asked for a secluded table in a romantic setting. The manager had obliged. Their table was in a raised section of the restaurant away from the main floor and surrounded by tropical plants and palm trees.

During the delicious meal, Lucy made sure their mundane conversation eventually included what cases they were working on at Scotland Yard. Slowly and surreptitiously she was gaining Eric's confidence. Lucy clarified the complicated investigations she was carrying out into various fraud cases. Eric explained that most of his work involved arranging new identities for people who gave evidence in murder trials.

Lucy falsely expressed her surprise, as if she didn't know.

'Don't you know about the witness protection programme at The Yard?'

'Not much. I know it goes on somewhere in Scotland Yard, but they have never involved me in it at all. It sounds mysterious and romantic somehow?'

Eric laughed. 'Mysterious and romantic? I've never described my work like that. Boring and complicated, maybe.'

'I suppose I'm thinking of the American movies where protected witnesses lead exciting lives?'

He looked around to make sure they were completely alone and lowered his voice. 'Of course, my work is completely confidential. If the villains on remand knew where the witnesses were, they'd be brown bread!'

'Brown bread?'

'Oh, I'm sorry, Lucy. I forgot you weren't born in the smoke, were you? Brown bread means dead. It's cockney rhyming slang.' Lucy made certain that Eric had drunk several glasses of wine. She could tell his earlier defensive attitude was slipping. He was trying to impress her with stories of how his department operated under the Scotland Yard bosses' radar.

'You wouldn't think that on this special mobile i-phone, I have the details of all the folks on the programme, would you?' He showed her a red coloured phone that he put on the lacy tablecloth next to his plate of half-eaten rump steak.

Lucy looked at the shiny red cover and at once wondered how she could get access to his phone. In her overall scheme, she had considered going as far as sleeping with Eric to obtain information about Doris Sparkes. Perhaps, now, she didn't need to go that far? She liked Eric. He was a pleasant companion, but having intercourse with him would be the last resort.

'Is that safe to be carrying all those details around with you?'

'We consider it's safe....'

'... we?'

'... my superior officers on the programme. We don't subscribe anymore to leaving papers containing such sensitive details lying around in cumbersome files. They can be easily pinched and copied.'

'Oh, I see. You are so clever.'

'... my phone is password protected, anyway. Who would get to know my secret password...?'

'Of course, it makes perfect sense. We in the Fraud Squad use a similar way of working.' She reached for her own silver-coloured i-phone and lowered her voice. 'We're encouraged to keep changing our pin code, but I can't do that. I keep forgetting them anyway, so I use my Dad's first name. The only thing is, it's so long. My Dad's name is Bartholomew.' Eric laughed.

'Same here. I'm hopeless with passwords. I simply use my police number.'

Lucy smiled and nodded. As Eric ate more rump steak and poured more wine, Lucy feigned receiving a text message. 'Forgive me while I reply to this. It's a text from my Mom. She'll only worry if I don't text back straight away.' Instead, she made a quick search on the police computer website for Detective Sergeant Eric Chambers. 'Here it is,' she thought. 'His police number is 789345.' She consigned it to memory and closed the phone. She wagered that, as with most men, he would need to use the men's toilet sooner rather than later. Between courses and waiting for the dessert to be brought to their table, he excused himself and went to the men's restroom. As Lucy had hoped, he left his phone on the tablecloth. Looking around to make sure he'd gone, she entered his police number and gained access to his personal information. She saw an app for the Witness Protection Scheme. She pressed the icon, typed in Doris Sparkes' name, and smiled as her alias, new address, and phone number appeared. Opening her own phone, she quickly took a photograph of Eric's screen. She closed his phone and slid it back to his side of the table seconds before he returned. As their desserts were put on the table, he reached for his phone.

'Phew, it's still here. I shouldn't leave my phone lying around, should I?' he sighed.

'I saw you'd left it, but I wouldn't have let anyone take it, would I, and anyway, you said you have it password protected.' Eric smiled and put it back in his pocket.

Lucy had what she wanted and wondered how to bring the evening to a close. She looked at the dessert she had chosen and knew how to let Eric down gently. They shared a cup of coffee before Lucy clutched her stomach. 'Ooh, Eric, I'm having tummy pains. I did wonder about those figs in the fruit salad; they seemed overripe to me. Please excuse me, I'll have to visit the ladies.' She spent some time in the restroom before feigning an unsteady walk back to the table.

'Are you alright, Lucy? You look unsteady….'

'… I'm so sorry, I've vomited. I think I'd better go home. I was so much looking forward to spending more time with you.'

'Oh, dear! I'm sorry, too.' He paid the bill, and once out of the pedestrian complex, he called a taxi for her.

'Goodnight, Eric,' Lucy called from the rear seat. 'We'll do this again, but without me being poorly next time.'

'Goodnight,' he called as he closed the door, waved, and the cab roared away.

Thirty-four

As the deepening dusk darkened the skies over central London, she held the book close to her chest once more. It was as if she needed to convince herself that what she was doing was worthwhile. Staring at the faded cover and Dickens' signature she was emboldened and banished any second thoughts to the shadows. She waited until after dark. Dressed in a dark brown overcoat and wearing a knitted bobble hat pulled down over her ears, she approached the apartment block. Sliding her index finger down the plastic-covered panel, Lucy searched the residents' list against individual buttons. She pressed the switch on the intercom at the entrance door to Dolores Mainwaring and Doris Sparkes' apartment number five. She waited for a reply.

'Yes, who's that?' Dolores' sharp voice crackled on the speaker. Lucy was about to answer, but Dolores spoke again. 'If you're that pervert from across the street again, I've told you I'm calling the police. So, bugger off and leave me alone.'

'Dolores. My name is Amy Bagshot…' Lucy gave a false name in case there would be any subsequent investigation by the Met police.

'… Amy Bagshot. I don't know anybody called Amy….'

'… Dolores, I'm here about your friend, Doris Sparkes.' Lucy felt the silence and Dolores' hesitancy.

'Doris! What about her?'

'Please let me in, and we can talk. I know you must be worried about her.'

'Why should I be worried about Doris?'

'Well, she's not here, is she…?'

Silence once again was overwhelming. Lucy heard the wailing wind blowing under the crack at the bottom of the apartment door. The click of the door opening straight away stopped the noise. Lucy looked around before going through. She ensured the self-closing mechanism secured the lock against the metal door jamb, and turned to see a sign for apartment number five on the first floor. Lucy raised her hand to knock on the door, but it opened slowly, and she saw the security chain. A pair of dark eyes peered through the narrow opening.

'Dolores?' Lucy heard the chain rattle, and the door opened.

'Come in.'

'Dolores, I'm Amy Bagshot…'

'… so you said. What do you know about Doris?'

'Can we sit down?'

'I suppose so!' Dolores was dressed in a cotton nightie with a heavy woollen dressing gown secured by a leather belt against her slight frame. She pointed to a chair; Dolores sat opposite and stared at Lucy.

'Don't you want to know where Doris is?'

'Maybe? Who are you, and what do you know about my friend?'

'Did Doris tell you anything before she went away?' Dolores stared sceptically.

Lucy realised how she was suspicious of anything and everyone. She was frightened.

'I know Doris worked at The Ritz. I know she saw something in the men's toilets there. That's why she's missing.' Dolores raised her eyes in acceptance that Lucy knew the truth.

'So, she did tell you!' Dolores held a handkerchief to her mouth, and tears flowed down her face.

'I told her she would get into trouble if she said anything to the police. Is she dead? Is that what you've come to tell me?'

'Doris isn't dead. As far as I know, she's okay. Like you, frightened, but safe. That's all that matters to you, isn't it?'

'I miss my friend. I wish she'd kept her mouth shut, and we'd still be sharing this flat.' Dolores suddenly got up and dashed towards the door. 'Get out of my flat now. How do I know you're not one of the friends of the man who was shot…?'

Lucy continued to sit in the chair. 'For reasons I can't tell you about, I want to help you and Doris. If you do as I say, she could be back with you soon, friends and living in this apartment together as you were before.'

Dolores slowly returned to her chair. 'What do I need to do?'

'I have on my phone Doris's new telephone number, address and the name she is now known by.' Lucy held up her phone.

'I don't understand.'

'Doris is being held by The Metropolitan Police under their witness protection programme. No one knows where she is or what her new name is, other than police officers running that programme.'

'How do you know?'

'Because I'm also a police officer.'

'I still don't understand why you're telling me this?'

'For private reasons, but just know this, if we can get Doris back with you, here in this flat, it helps me as well.'

'Do you know Doris?'

'I've never met her as I'd never met you before this evening.'

'She only saw what happened by accident. Then the police came and collected her early one morning before we were properly awake. That's the last I saw of her. I went to the local police station, and they told me they knew nothing about Doris and for me to stay out of it....'

'... Would you like to speak to Doris?'

'Yes, of course I would.'

'Okay, but here's what you have to do.' Dolores listened intently. 'There's every chance that the witness protection people are keeping guard on Doris for her own safety. That means they'll also be checking her mobile phone. So, any calls she receives, the officers will know who called her. Therefore, call her from a public phone box. Simply tell her to take a walk somewhere and call you from a public telephone, preferably where the protection guys can't see her. I know her new address is somewhere in rural Hertfordshire, so she's not too far away.'

'Okay, what then?'

'Encourage her not to bother giving evidence against the men who shot the man in the toilet. Tell her to come home and inform the Metropolitan Police from here, that she's changed her mind.'

'Do you think that will work?'

'Yes, I do. Doris is missing you and her old life and wished she'd never got mixed up in this. When she comes home, I'll be here and try to explain further why there'll be no comebacks on her. Lucy picked up a piece of paper from the coffee table and wrote down Doris's mobile phone number. I'll come with you to the phone box. Do you know if there's one close by?'

'There's one a few yards down the street. Doris and I have used it in the past when the mobile signals go down. Living around these crummy parts of London, that happens often.'

Lucy thought before speaking. 'On the other hand, the protection guys will see the public call box number on their computer screen, check-up and see it's from your street. They'll assume it's you. Let's go a bit further afield. There's Camden Town tube station down the street, isn't there. I travelled here on the underground and came out of that station. Let's take a ride further up the Northern line.'

'Okay! I'll get my coat.'

Lucy and Dolores sat on the tube train gazing at the map of the underground above their heads. Stations came and went. Lucy mused as they passed Brent Cross Station, thinking of the time she'd dined there with Eric a few nights before. 'The next station is Colindale. Let's get off here. I think that's far enough.'

Sheltering in a public call box from the slight drizzle, Lucy held the paper while Dolores read it and pressed Doris's number.

'Who's this…?' Dolores heard her friend's anxious voice.

'… Doris! Don't ask questions; ring me from a public telephone as soon as you can.' Lucy pressed the receiver lever and replaced the phone. Lucy knew the protection officers' automatic recording machine would have activated, and they were alerted to Doris's activity.

'We'll have to wait for Doris to go out to find a phone box. You have your mobile with you, don't you? Let's go and have a coffee in that café over there and wait for her to ring.'

Lucy looked out on the busy rain-swept streets of Colindale, starting to question what she was doing there and whether it was all worthwhile. Then she thought of Dickens' book, and any earlier doubts evaporated. Dolores answered Lucy's question about what she did for a living as they drank their coffee, but then her phone rang. Lucy moved closer to Dolores so she could eavesdrop on the conversation.

'Dolores, how did you get my number? It's supposed to be untraceable.'

'That doesn't matter for now, Doris. Are you're sure you haven't been followed, or anybody can overhear this conversation…?'

'… I'm in a call box at the end of a street. There isn't another person I can see within one hundred yards of me.…'

'… Doris. Come home, back to the flat.…'

'… but Dolores, I'm in hiding in a witness protection scheme so I can give evidence against the murder I saw.'

'I know that. I have a lady police officer with me. She gave me your number and says the guy that was shot was another crook, anyway. If you want your old life back, come home. Once you're back in the flat, you can tell the police you've changed your mind about giving evidence. Don't you think all this is unnecessary, giving up your entire life, because the police want to prosecute some guys...'

'... but, Dolores, there was a murder....'

'... so, there was a murder. Is it worth giving up your life for?'

'... I hadn't thought about it like that.'

'Well, think about it now.' Lucy smiled and nodded. 'The police lady is with me now, and she's nodding. Do you want a word with her?'

'Yes, put her on.'

'Hello, Doris. My name is Amy Bagshot. I work for the police but can't tell you where I'm based. What Dolores has told you is correct.'

'Why are you helping me, Amy?'

'Because I know the witness protection officers are only using you to help with their case....'

'... I see!'

'... It's your life, Doris, but think about it. You're only there in hiding because you're in danger. What will change after you've given evidence in court? You'll still be in danger, only more so? Friends of these guys will want revenge. You'll never be safe. Once your evidence puts these blokes in prison, the police officers will go back to their lives, leaving you high and dry. Where will you be, in a new town, with a new name, with no friends? You want to have a boyfriend and eventually settle down to married life, don't you?'

'I suppose so!'

'What will you tell him when he asks why you haven't got any family? You won't be able to tell him the truth, Doris. The whole of the rest of your life will be based upon what you decide to do now.'

'I hadn't thought of the consequences.'

'You'll have to find a new job and all the time having to look over your shoulder for as long as you live. Do you think it's worth it?'

'No, it's not worth it. Can you put Dolores on again, please?' Lucy handed the phone to her and listened.

'Dolores, you've convinced me. I'm coming back to the flat. I'm in Hertford now, so I can't return tonight. I'll come back in the morning.' Lucy beckoned to have the phone again.

'Doris, it's Amy again. You do know that the witness protection officers are keeping watch over you, don't you? They have cameras and microphones in every room of the flat you're living in. So tomorrow when you leave your flat, don't pack a suitcase or anything. Pick up a carrier bag, so they'll think you're only going out to do some shopping. Then they won't be alerted and follow you.'

'Okay. Thank you.' Lucy handed the phone back to Dolores.

'I'll see you tomorrow, Doris. I'll have a bottle of wine ready, and we can celebrate you being back home.'

Lucy parted company when Dolores left the underground train at Camden Town. Lucy remained seated for her brief journey into the city. 'Give me a ring when Doris comes back tomorrow, and I'll come and have a chat with her.'

The following morning, Doris put her personal items in a carrier bag and left her apartment without fuss or regret. After what Lucy had told her, she didn't feel comfortable, aware that the witness protection officers watched her every movement.

'Inspector, it's Detective Sergeant Eric Chambers here. I'm ringing to let you know about some unusual movements by Doris Sparkes. She hasn't been out of her apartment in a fortnight, but since last evening, she's been out twice. She took a carrier bag with her over an hour ago. We think she's gone shopping, but the local supermarket is only around the corner....'

'If she's not back in another hour, let me know.'

'Amy, it's Dolores here. Doris is back here at the flat. I told her you'd like a word with her. She's anxious and doesn't know what to do.'

'I'll be with you in half an hour.'

By the time Lucy had pressed the intercom to gain access to Doris and Dolores' apartment, Eric was showing two senior detectives around Doris's apartment. 'If she hasn't gone shopping, I have no idea where she's gone,' he replied to their questions. 'She had one phone call yesterday. Listen to this, a woman's voice.' '... *Doris, don't ask any questions. Ring me from a public call box as soon as you can.*'

'So, I assume that's where she went last evening. She was only out about thirty minutes.'

'It's obvious it's someone she knows. Whoever called her knew she was being monitored.' The senior detective turned to his colleague. 'Let's get back to the Yard. We need to talk to the superintendent.'

'Hello Doris, I'm Amy Bagshot. We spoke last evening. I'm glad you're back home.'

'Please tell me what's going on.'

'The man you saw get shot was Harry Stevens, a crook from the East End. His criminal record doesn't make for pleasant reading, having served several spells in prison totalling twenty years. He was fifty-two, so you see, he's been in and out of prison for most of his adult life. What I'm trying to explain is, his death is no loss to society.'

'... but I saw two men shoot him!'

'Yes, you did. Those two men are also hardened criminals from the East End who are currently under investigation for several other crimes. With or without your testimony, Doris, they will bring these men to justice. So, I consider losing your normal life too high a price to pay to help police officers solve a case for them. As I said to you on the phone, if you testify against them, your life will irrevocably change forever.'

'What shall I do now?'

'The person in charge of the witness protection programme is Superintendent Basil Spence. Here is his telephone number. Ring him now and ask for a personal interview.'

'What shall I tell him?'

'Inform him you've changed your mind about testifying. Tell him you're not sure exactly what you saw and were confused at the time due to the shock of the shooting. The superintendent will have no choice but to discharge you from the programme. You can resume your normal life again.'

Lucy returned to her apartment content in the knowledge that Doris Sparkes would be discredited as a credible witness. They would release the Krueger brothers from their imprisonment on remand. She had kept her side of the agreement she had with Godfrey Warlock. Now the First Edition Dickens was indeed hers.

The next day, Lucy once again went to the staff dining room at Scotland Yard. She'd been sitting eating for fifteen minutes when Eric came and sat next to her.

'How are you feeling now, Lucy? Better than the other evening, I hope?'

'I'm fine now. I'm sorry I spoilt the evening; I could see you were upset....'

'... yes, I was, and am still disappointed, but it's quite alright. Now I'm feeling down because a case I was supervising on the witness protection programme has gone pear-shaped.' He explained what had happened with Doris Sparkes. 'It's puzzling how someone became aware of where she was and how to get in touch with her.'

'Haven't you any idea?'

'We have our suspicions. It must be an inside job. Only a fellow officer could know any of those details about where Doris was. Every one of us, seven altogether on the scheme, are being interviewed over the next two weeks by a unit brought in from another force.'

'Best of luck, Eric. I'm sure all will be well.'

'I was going to ask if you'd like to come out with me for another dinner, but until this leak can be sorted out, I can't think of much else. I'm sorry, Lucy.'

'It can't be helped. Another time maybe?'

Lucy left the dining room, smiling. The self-satisfaction she felt that the matter was closed would prove to be premature.

Thirty-five

In the days following the Cannock town centre explosion, the district council engineers had been hard at work. Fractured electricity cables and water mains had been repaired. Paving stones, walls and flower beds in the pedestrian area had been systematically cleaned and restored to their former glory. Selected manufacturers were already designing the new town clock. Ecclesiastes Incorporated, the town's principal stonemasons, had been given a contract to manufacture and install a new war memorial. The Town Council had been awarded a grant to repair and replace every broken windowpane. People with damaged hearing had been given priority to attend hospital to receive treatment.

Further down towards the lower part of town, at Saint Luke's church, twelve funerals had taken place for the innocent victims. There was no such ceremony for Christine Follows. Her remains were as dust, swept away with all the other debris and deposited on the town's refuse dump. A further task for the stonemasons was to carve a memorial plaque inscribed with the deceased's names to be added at the base of the new war memorial. Christine Follows' name would not be on the list.

In the following days and weeks, Cannock lost another resident. Christine's husband, Terry. He couldn't face the stares and increasing abuse from townspeople who knew who he was. Since arriving from Doncaster, his brief tenure in the town had only lasted nine months. He tried to ensure his next place to live would be well removed from Cannock, and where nobody knew his history.

Many meetings were held at police headquarters discussing, through internal inquiries, whether the tragedy could have been avoided. Donald submitted all the evidence gathered on Christine in mitigation to prove that they could not have foreseen the tragedy. A less attended meeting was convened with Superintendent Woodhouse and the detectives from Cannock to discuss whether Doctor Godfrey Warlock was implicated or held indictable. His book, found on

Christine's bedside table entitled, *How to Create Fire and Explosions,* was presented at the meeting. He also opened Christine's suicide letter. The superintendent read the letter to the meeting.

'Since I first met you, my life changed for the better. You showed me how to live and how to make the best of myself. I've suffered most of my life with an incurable phobia. You taught me that I hadn't inherited a horrible curse but an outstanding talent. I'll take your wonderful smile with me, giving me the courage to enter your world.'

'Can anybody tell me what this means? It seems obvious to me he's encouraged this woman to create carnage and death.'

James spoke confidently. 'Could I point out the words of the police psychologist from Yorkshire? He considered her to be a habitual recidivist concerning her being an arsonist. So it seems the horrible curse she considered herself to have, was praised by Godfrey Warlock as an outstanding talent. How much more encouragement can a person receive than that?' The superintendent nodded and recognised James's excellent assessment.

Donald reminded everyone that this wasn't the only time they had connected Godfrey Warlock to a tragedy. He related the suicide of Jack Beecham outside his shop.

'Then there's the curiosity of Brian and Belinda Hazelhurst.' Nicky commented.

The superintendent turned to Donald. 'Remind me, Donald, I remember their names in one of your reports, but their misdemeanours escape me....'

'They danced and performed pornographic acts, naked in the town centre. When interviewed, they maintained Godfrey Warlock had encouraged them. We have charged them with committing lewd acts in public. Their case is being held at the magistrate's court tomorrow.'

'They'll behave themselves and be fully clothed, will they, Donald?' A collective laugh lifted the dour mood of the meeting.

'Well, if they don't, the sitting magistrate tomorrow is Miss Dando....'

'... not Susie Dando?'

'The very same.' Donald smiled.

'This Brian and Belinda won't know what's hit them. Three months ago, at Stafford Magistrates Court, she sentenced a man to one month in prison for running around Stafford Park wearing only his swimming trunks. In her opinion, he offended public decency.'

'When she looks at the photographs the press took of the pair performing lewd pornography before the public, including my wife, I may add, she'll lock them up and throw away the key,' Donald added. 'What we haven't included in the indictment submitted to the court is that they even stripped off here in this police station when being interviewed.'

Raising his eyebrows in a sarcastic gesture, the superintendent smiled. 'How awful for you, Donald.'

Superintendent Woodhouse sat back and looked towards Donald. 'I can see no actual fact that this Doctor Warlock has committed a crime, but I think it would prove useful if you brought him into the station for a chat. If nothing else, it seems he is a disruptive influence and needs reminding about being a good citizen. The town has suffered some alarming and life-changing events in the past few months. I hope for all our sakes nothing more eventful is going to occur.'

Thirty-six

In a committee room in New Scotland Yard's basement, Superintendent Basil Spence convened and chaired a Witness Protection Programme meeting. As well as Sergeant Eric Chambers, there were seven other officers present. All had their laptop computers in front of them on the table.

'In all my thirteen years heading this programme, I've never encountered a problem of the magnitude that we are confronted with in the Doris Sparkes' case. I won't beat about the bush; someone in this room has compromised the secrecy that our entire existence here at The Yard depends upon. There has been a major security leak. Unless this can be satisfactorily sorted out, I have to tell you all the Chief Commissioner has mentioned the possible closure of the unit.' The officers looked round at each other, wondering who could have jeopardised the entire department.

'Yesterday, Doris Sparkes telephoned me, on my personal mobile number, I might add, to request a meeting with me in my office. You can imagine my initial confusion and shock at receiving the call when, as far as I was aware, she was still sequestered in Hertford. How she obtained my private number is a mystery to me. Then what she told me came as a more tremendous shock. I understand the inspectors in this room had known for many hours before Miss Sparkes came to my office that she had gone missing from her apartment. A question to be answered later is, why wasn't I kept informed?'

One of the inspectors tried to explain. 'We were searching....'

'It doesn't matter. What does matter is what we all know, Doris Sparkes has changed her mind about giving evidence against the Krueger brothers! That means the cornerstone of the case against them has gone. The Director of Public Prosecutions is going to chew my balls off over this. I'm asking all of you; what happened? You all saw her in that apartment; she was content with our arrangements. Then...'

'... Excuse me for interrupting Super, but *then* she had a telephone call....' Eric stuttered.

'... yes, Sergeant Chambers, I've read the report. A woman... where is it in this pile of papers?' Displaying his annoyance and frustration, the superintendent erratically flipped through some pages. 'Here it is, and I quote, '*Doris, don't ask questions. Ring me from a public call box as soon as you can*'. *What* can we now deduce from this that the officers on duty that evening didn't?

1. The woman knew Doris.
2. Didn't any of you guess that it could be her flatmate Dolores Mainwaring?
3. She asked her to go to a public payphone. That means she knew Doris was being watched.
4. Why didn't any of you follow Doris?
5. When Doris left the flat the next morning, none of you thought of preventing her, following her, or reporting to my office.'

The officers looked down as their superior's sarcasm hung in the air like an unpleasant smell.

'This whole episode reeks of bloody incompetence! Now we come to where the leak could have occurred. You all have your laptops and mobile phones with you.' The officers appeared flustered by what the superintendent was going to suggest.

'Come on, come on, open your bloody laptops; we haven't got all day. The commissioner wants to see me straight after this meeting. I must tell him something constructive. The least consequence of this is that you can *all* expect some demotion to come out of this debacle. Note I said *you,* not me. The buck stops with every one of you. I've laboured too long in my career to have my rank and pension reduced.'

'Our laptops are open, gov.' Eric prompted meekly.

'I have new passwords here for each of you.' He passed out separate small business size cards for each officer. 'Change your passwords. Now!'

After completing their tasks, the officers looked expectantly towards the superintendent.

'Now, do the same with your mobile phones. I don't care what old passwords you used, your first girlfriend's name or the nickname for your dog. I'm assured by the information technology gurus at The

Yard, these codes are foolproof and impossible to commit to memory.'

While the officers reset their phones, the superintendent carried on. 'I want each of you to think of any occasion in the past three weeks you may have left your phone anywhere. Or told anybody details of your personal passwords? If you can think of any such occasion, I don't want to know about it at this stage. It's up to you to sort it out. Bring me solutions, not more problems.'

The officers looked at each other. Eric thought of the only occasion he could consider his phone was not in his possession, and that was when he'd dined with Lucy. He at once dismissed the absurd notion that it could implicate her in this.

'Now, we come to the department's files on The Met's mainframe computer system.' The superintendent typed into his own laptop and brought up the file on the murder of Harry Stevens. Everybody turned to gaze at the sizeable eighty-inch, high-definition screen monitor fixed to the wall.

'I'm drawing your attention to this file because this is the only place where a leak could have originated. There are several entries; I've counted thirty-two in total where officers have accessed this file. Your log-in codes are displayed in this list...' he pressed some keys on his laptop and brought up the list. 'Starting at number one, shout out and tell me if you recognise your code.' Various officers called out when the superintendent referred to each number. He marked off each one in turn before coming to number twenty-three, and the room went silent. 'Can nobody attest to the ownership of this access code?' They all shook their heads. The superintendent highlighted the code in a bold coloured font before progressing through the list.

'So, in conclusion. Every one of you has accessed this file at some stage, and none of you can own up to this particular code...?' Everyone answered 'no'. 'Okay, thank you very much. The meeting is closed.' The officers got up and left the room, leaving the superintendent typing on his laptop. He reached for his phone to talk to one of the information technology team. 'Bradley, it's Superintendent Spence here. I'm sending you a text containing an access code. Someone has accessed a current file. I don't know who this person is, and I need to know quickly. Please find out who this code is assigned to and get back to me. How long will it take you?'

'Less than five minutes,' Bradley answered, confidently.

'I'm in the basement now; I'll hang on.' He carried on typing for a further two minutes before his phone rang.

'Yes, Bradley.'

'Sir, this code belongs to Detective Sergeant Lucy Barnes of the Fraud Squad.'

'What?! Are you sure?'

'Absolutely certain, gov.'

Thirty-seven

In *Godfrey's Bookshop*, the telephone rang. 'Hello, my dear Dariusz, I'm delighted to hear from you, my boy. Didn't I tell you I'd arrange for you to be cleared? How is Vlad?'

Godfrey smirked as he answered the phone. 'Why don't the two of you come and visit me here in Cannock? I have a business proposition that I know will interest you.'

Earlier that morning, Lucy had telephoned Godfrey to inform him she had carried out her side of their bargain. 'The only witness against the Kreuger's has changed her mind. The brothers were released from remand yesterday.'

'You've done well, my dear. Enjoy the book, won't you, while you can?'

'What do mean, while I can?'

'Well, we're all transients, aren't we? My dear, please don't be so hostile. I only meant similar to someone owning a piece of land or property. We all only rent them while we're alive. After we've gone, the land or property will revert to someone else. So, it's your turn now to own Dickens' book. That's all I meant; I'm not going to take the book from you. You remember I did say from time to time you could help me with other matters. For now, you can rest and bask in my sincere approval for a job well done.'

Lucy replaced the phone and couldn't prevent a shudder from passing down her spine. A sobering realisation pierced her brain like a razor-sharp sword. As long as she was the owner of Dickens' book, she would never be free from Godfrey Warlock's grip.

'Is that you, Lucy?' Detective Chief Inspector Jules Beaumont of the Fraud Squad, asked on his telephone.

'How can I help you, Jules?'

'By clearing something up for me, I hope. Can you come to my office now, please?'

'Hello, gov.' She knocked on his door and walked straight in.

'Sit down, Lucy. I've had Superintendent Basil Spence call me.'

'He's in charge of The Witness Protection Scheme, isn't he?' Lucy gulped and tried to remain calm.

'Yes, he is. Do you remember a few weeks ago when you returned from Manchester, you asked me what had been going on at The Yard while you were away?'

'Yes, I remember, gov. You gave me a list of the current cases....'

'... and according to Superintendent Spence, you accessed details on one of the cases. The murder of Harry Stevens by the Krueger brothers.'

'Yes. I did. I remember now, the case looked interesting. Those guys have been evading justice for far too long, but it looks as if they're going down for this one. Why are you asking?'

'Because Superintendent Spence tells me he's had to release them....'

'... why?'

'... there's been a security leak on the Witness Protection Programme. The sole witness to the murder has been got at....'

'... What! While she's been under the protection of the programme?'

'Exactly! The witness changed her mind about giving evidence. The super is livid and getting his balls chewed off by the commissioner. Basil is looking for how and where the leak happened? He's incensed and suggests the culprit must be here at The Yard. He's checked every avenue and saw an access code against the Harry Steven file. It's your code, Lucy. Why did you look at the file?'

'Gov, let's get something straight here. Are you suggesting I'm a suspect in this supposed leak?'

'No, I'm not! I'm carrying out Basil's request by asking you first. He may wish to ask you himself. Why, Lucy?'

'Purely out of interest. The case looked interesting. As I said, in my career at The Met, I've seen Krueger's names several times, but they always seem to get away with their crimes.'

'... and it looks as if they are in the clear yet again.'

'Okay, Lucy. Thanks for coming in.' Standing outside her gov's office, Lucy exhaled a sigh of relief. 'I'm not comfortable with this,' she thought.

'Hello, Basil, Jules here, in Fraud. I've interviewed Sergeant Lucy Barnes. She accessed the file purely out of interest. She's got no contact with the case, as far as I'm aware. I'd stake my pension on her honesty and integrity. She's a career woman with no family and lives for her job. Wherever the leak has come from, it's not here in the Fraud Squad.'

As Superintendent Spence put the phone down, he called, 'Come in' to a knock on his door.

'Hi, gov, here's the report, recordings, videos on Doris Sparkes and all her movements while she was on the programme.' Eric put the information on his desk and turned to go. He stopped. 'Oh, by the way, gov, did you find out who accessed the Harry Stevens file?'

'Yes, I did. I've had a chat with Superintendent Jules Beaumont in the Fraud Squad. One of his sergeants, Lucy Barnes, accessed the file. He assures me she's on the level and unapproachable to be on the take. So, I'm still looking for the perpetrator. Keep looking yourself, Eric, whoever it is, has to be here at The Yard.'

'I sure will, gov.' Eric turned and left the office. Outside he stood against the wall in the corridor, deep in thought. A colleague passed him and offered his hello. Eric's thoughts went back to the meal he'd had with Lucy at Giacomo's restaurant. Eric never answered as he looked to the floor.

'It's not like Eric to be unsociable,' his colleague thought and went on his way. For the rest of the day, Eric involved himself with his work, but all the time only really thinking about Lucy.

'It seems too much of a coincidence; she has to be implicated,' he concluded, before thinking again. 'I'm overreacting. She had no way of knowing the password to my phone. I was only away for two minutes while I had a pee.' He made himself a cup of coffee and came around full circle again. 'She knew I worked on the witness protection programme; that's the only reason she came on a date with me. It's no good; I need to talk to her.'

He took a slurp of coffee, inhaled a huge breath, and reached for his phone. 'Hi, Lucy, it's me, Eric.'

'Hello, Eric. How are you?' After the conversation with her gov, she was on her guard, and she wasn't surprised that Eric had contacted her. She knew he wasn't stupid and would probably put two and two together. 'It's lovely to hear from you. I was going to ring you....'

'... were you?'

'Yes. I wanted to make it up to you after I was poorly when we went to Giacomo's....'

Her words took him by surprise and stole his thunder. All he could think about now was having another date with her. 'What do you suggest?'

'Make another reservation, and we'll take it from there.'

Eric couldn't believe his luck. The girl he had always fancied wanted a date with him at last. 'Okay, I'll ring Giacomo's. How about this evening?'

The speed at which he jumped at her suggestion surprised her, but she thought it best to quickly get it over. 'I'll see you there at 7:30.' She thought of the implications of his call. 'It could be he's on to me? I need to put him off the scent. Oh well, if it means going to bed with him, so be it.'

Eric sat back in his revolving office chair, pleased with himself. He'd made the restaurant reservation and thought about what he would discuss with her later. His phone ringing disturbed his reverie. 'Eric, it's superintendent Spence again. I have a job for you. It's been bothering me about how Doris's flatmate… what's her name…?'

'… Dolores Mainwaring.'

'That's it, Mainwaring. How did she get Doris's new phone number? Someone must have visited her. Pay them a visit. They may want nothing more to do with the police after what's gone on, but it's worth a try.'

Eric pressed the intercom at Doris's flat. 'Yes, what do you want?' He recognised her voice.

'Doris, it's me, Sergeant Eric Chambers from the Witness Protection Programme. Do you remember me?' Only hissing static came from the speaker.

'Doris, can I come in, please?'

'Eric, I've had enough of the police and all that's happened….'

'… I understand that, Doris. Actually, it's Dolores I want to speak to….'

'… Oh! I see! Well, she's not in; she's at work. Tonight's her late night, so I'm not expecting her back until the evening.'

'Perhaps I could see her at her workplace?'

'She'd be upset if I told you where she worked….'

'… only a couple of minutes chat with her. That's all, I promise.'

'Okay, she works at a Savile Row tailor, Bustard and Company….'

'… thanks, Doris. Look after yourself.'

Eric ambled down Savile Row. It was a street he'd never been to before, mainly because he would never be able to afford their inflated prices for clothes. The pavements were busy with elegantly clothed elderly men. He stepped into the kerb to let a group of men pass by and received a sharp retort from the horn of a Silver Cloud vintage

Rolls Royce. One of the men reached and pulled him back on the pavement. 'Watch what you're doing, old boy,' he called in a posh voice straight from Eton's school playing fields. 'I wouldn't like to think of the damage you'd have caused to that beautiful old banger had the old lady hit you.'

As Eric regained his footing, he saw Bustard's name in gold-coloured Old English style lettering above a shop directly opposite. He waited until two more expensive-looking cars went by and walked over. Peering through the window in between several stern-looking manikins attired in sporting tweeds, he saw a young woman. She held a tape measure around the waist of an elderly, grey-haired man smoking a cigar. He opened the door and needed to clear his throat at the overwhelming stench of the smoke billowing from the Cohiba.

Eric walked to the counter and saw the sign to press the bell for assistance. After pressing several times and waiting, still no one came. He looked at the woman who shrugged her shoulders and carried on measuring the cigar smoker. 'Bloody Hell, what sort of shop is this?'

The man called to him. 'Hey! Watch your language, old chap.' Eric saw a sign and started to laugh.

'That's alright, it says Modern men swear.' The young woman explained.

'No sir, there's an apostrophe missing; it should say Modern men's wear.' Eric laughed some more. Eric pressed the bell once more and a middle-aged moustachioed inconsequential-looking man appeared and offered to help. 'Yes, sir, welcome to Bustards. What are you looking for?' Eric held up his warrant card folder holding his sergeant's badge. 'I'm from the Metropolitan Police...'

The man being measured heard and spoke to the man standing behind the counter. 'Oh, I say, Nigel, old man, are you in trouble, old chap?' Eric stared at the man puffing bluish smoke before speaking to the shop assistant. 'I'm looking for Dolores Mainwaring.' Eric heard a faint 'Oh'.

She had been bending down looking into a low pinewood drawer holding men's corduroy trousers and turned to stare at Eric. 'Are you Dolores?' he asked. She appeared non-plussed and nodded, displaying a massive flush across her face and neck. Eric turned to the man behind the counter again. 'Can I have a quick word with the young lady, please?'

Nigel peered across to Dolores. 'This is all highly irregular, Dolores. You haven't finished measuring Sir Caspar yet....'

'… I can wait,' Eric interrupted. Sir Caspar puffed even more smoke from his cigar, looking from one man to the other before addressing Dolores.

Holding the cigar in his fingers and pulling it from between his brown stained lips, he uttered, 'My dear, you only have to check my details for my corduroys, get it over with, and you can see what this policeman wants with you.' She nodded and reached for her notebook. She held the metal edge of her tape measure under his crotch and let it drop to his ankles. He looked to the ceiling. Thirty inches, she wrote. While kneeling on the floor, she looked up at him expectantly. 'Left, as you know very well, my dear.' The implication wasn't lost on Eric, who thought it immoral that Dolores should have to record such details.

Sir Caspar approached the counter. 'Now, Nigel, I'm shortly going to my cottage in The Bahamas. Can you put up five pairs of Bermuda shorts in different colours for me? What? You know my size, of course. I'm entertaining The Sultan of Belize and his entourage of five Sultanas. A fresh pair of shorts for each Sultana, I thought, What? I really can't be bothered with entertaining Arabs these days; it's somewhat tiresome. It's only because he wants to buy several purebred stallions from my stud farm over there in the sunshine that I'm humouring the old colonial.'

Eric walked over to Dolores. 'Hello, I'm a police officer from the Metropolitan Police. I've had a word with your flatmate, Doris. She told me I could find you here. Can we have a chat about her, please?'

'Mr Bustard, this policeman wants a chat with me. Can I take my break now, please, instead of later?'

Nigel nodded as he served Sir Caspar. 'There's a nice café around the corner; let's go for a coffee,' she whispered to Eric.

'Goodbye, my dear,' Sir Caspar offered as they left the shop. Nigel Bustard only glowered at her.

'Two coffees, please,' Eric ordered from the short-skirted waitress who came to their table. Her nonchalant attitude was displayed by the massive bubble of chewing gum she blew and the dismissive way she slammed the receipt on the tawdry, stained, plastic-covered table. When she turned around, giant gaping holes from her black tights were all too apparent. 'I'm glad we didn't come to a cheap-skate place,' Eric smiled, sarcastically. Dolores didn't respond but continued to stare at him, wondering what he wanted from her.

'You may have guessed what I want to ask you…?'

'… no, I haven't.'

'It's about Doris!'

'She's back home now.'

'Did you know she was due to give evidence in a murder trial?'

'I may have done.'

'Who talked to you, Dolores? Who came to see you? We know it was you who phoned Doris from a public call box….'

'… if you know that, why are you giving me grief?'

'All I'm trying to find out is, who persuaded you to contact Doris and afterwards must have persuaded her to leave the Witness Protection Programme?'

'What does it matter now? Doris is at home and has her life back. The murder of a criminal is hardly worth losing all the life she's had up to now, is it?'

'Is that what this person told you…?'

'No, she only….' Eric coughed the mouthful of coffee he'd just taken onto the tiled floor.

'Hey, you. This is a respectable café. Don't create a mess on the floor!' the waitress called. Eric looked around at the decaying scraps of food in the corner that were probably weeks old.

'She? You said 'she'.'

'She said she was a police officer and what Doris was doing wasn't worth it. Look, I can't stay much longer. You saw what a horrible boss I've got. He's likely to give me the sack the second I step back into the shop for this….'

'… I'll come with you and explain.'

'I can look after myself, thank you.'

'Did this policewoman say where she was from?'

'No!'

'Did she give her name?'

'Amy Bagshot.'

'What did she look like?'

'You want your pound of flesh for the price of a fifty pence cup of coffee, don't you?'

'Do you call this coffee?'

Dolores smiled, 'It's wet and warm….'

'… and probably full of botulism microbes.'

Dolores pushed her cup away from her. 'I have to go.'

'What did Amy Bagshot look like?'

'I never got to see her properly. She always wore a large overcoat down to her knees and a large woollen bobble hat pulled over her ears.'

'Was she short, tall, plump?'

'Medium height, but as I said, she could be slim or fat for all I could tell under that large overcoat.'

'Colour of hair?'

'No more questions. I'm going back to work now. Thanks for the coffee.' Dolores got up, walked, and opened the door. As Eric felt the fresh air on his face, she called back, 'Blonde, I think,' and she was gone.

Eric placed a one-pound coin on the greasy table-top. Deep in thought, he turned it over and over until he saw the waitress holding out her hand for it. He had very little information to report back to the superintendent.

Thirty-eight

The waitress in Giacomo's was smartly dressed in a black dress with a spotless white starched apron pinned to the front. Eric smiled at her as she came to his table to take his order. 'My girlfriend still hasn't arrived yet. I'll have another glass of wine, please.' He looked at his watch; it was 19:50. Lucy was already twenty minutes late. He began to think she wouldn't show up. As the waitress brought the wine, he smiled again, contrasting her smart appearance and pleasant manner with that of the waitress in Camden Town's seedy café.

Then he heard the waitress's accented voice. 'Come this way, please.' Eric only then realised the waitress was Scottish. He hadn't noticed before, but immediately forgot about the waitress and concentrated on Lucy's beauty as he watched her climb the few steps to the secluded part of the restaurant.

Eric stood open mouthed as she approached the table. He was about to tell her how beautiful she looked, but she spoke first. 'I'm so sorry for being late, Eric. I caught a tube, and it stood still in the darkness for fifteen minutes at a red light, waiting for a slow train to pass by. I'd have rung you, but there was no signal underground, of course. I should have taken a taxi.'

The waitress came and took Lucy's coat to hang on the stand next to the door and asked what she wanted to drink. Lucy looked at what Eric was drinking. 'I'll have the same as my companion, please.' She sat down, and they stared at each other. A pregnant pause developed between them before they both spoke together. 'What shall we talk about?' she asked.

'Have you been busy?' he questioned. They laughed before he added, 'Sorry, you go first.'

'Yes! I've been extremely busy. Life at Scotland Yard these days is one round of crises after another. I didn't realise how short-staffed we are at The Met. I've been asked to participate in a recruitment film to bring in more diversity. Apparently, you, me and the stereotypical English middle-class person is not considered a priority.'

'Surely, any recruitment drive should concentrate on the qualities of the person, not segregate applicants before they even get selected for an interview?' Lucy nodded in agreement.

'Are you going to be filmed endorsing this narrow-minded policy then?'

'I'm not sure yet. I'll wait until I see the script.'

They reverted to staring at each other. Eric wanted to ask her many questions about what he knew about the Doris Sparkes saga but was unsure how to start. Lucy's guilty conscience clouded any regular topics of conversation. The waitress rescued the awkward silence by bringing the menus. Eric broke the ice by talking to the waitress. 'Whereabouts in Scotland do you come from?' Lucy kept her head down, studying the menu.

'Oh! I'm a Clyde girl. I come from a tiny village on the banks of The Clyde, west of Glasgow.'

'Dear Ol' Glasgy, eh? Goin' rund 'n rund?' Eric tried to lighten the atmosphere by making a joke about the popular drinking song.

'Only on a Saturday night.' The waitress laughed and turned to let them choose their meal, but Lucy called her back.

'A tomato and prawn salad for me, please,' Lucy asked.

'… and you, sir?'

'The rump steak for me, medium rare, please. Could you also bring a bottle of Chianti?'

Lucy decided to meet head-on the subject that was on both their minds. 'Have you sorted out the leak in your department?'

'Ahem!' Eric cleared his throat. 'No, we haven't. We can't pin it down to any internal officer. The gov's current thinking is that it's someone else.'

'Is that why he's been making enquiries about me? My gov called me in for a chat.'

'From our point of view, it looked suspicious. We all had to verify our access codes regarding the Harry Stevens murder file. Yours was the only code to access the file other than anybody in the department.'

'I thought the case looked interesting. I saw it on the list of current cases being investigated at The Yard.' Eric looked under his eyebrows at her. Lucy could see he was suspicious.

'You don't believe me, do you?'

'I don't know what to think, Lucy.' Earlier in the day she had come to a decision about her involvement in the case. She treasured her rank and position in The Metropolitan Police and wasn't going to jeopardise her vocation any further. By disclosing to Eric what she had done, she would compromise him. He would have a dilemma whether to divulge to his superiors what he knew about her. She wasn't going to put him in that position and decided to stay silent.

'In that case, I don't think I can stay a moment longer.' She stood. 'Goodnight, Eric,' she offered, purposefully.

'… but?' Eric was embarrassed as the waitress brought their food.

'Oh!' The waitress gasped, turned, and watched Lucy grab her coat and leave.

Thirty-nine

'My boys, it's so good to see you both. Welcome to Cannock; I'd have erected some bunting out to greet you. Still, the pathetic archaic town councillors here wouldn't have given their permission.' Godfrey's broad, sickly smile matched his obsequious gestures.

'Once we have our feet under the table in this little place, we can change all that nonsense. In a democracy who needs politicians, anyway?' Dariusz commented, as he looked down his hooked nose at the main street.

'I thought you said your bookshop was in the town centre, Godfrey?' Vlad asked. 'Don't tell me this is the main street; it resembles a back alley we know in Millwall.'

'My dear comrades, once your empire has expanded, this back alley, as you call it, will become as famous as Fremont Street in Las Vegas. I remember saying as much to your dear father back in Vilnius in the seventies before the Russians moved out. Today, look at Gediminas Avenue; it's a thriving cosmopolitan thoroughfare. Tycoons worldwide visit there, eager to impress your associates and invest in your financial empire. Why, only the other day I read a report in The Vilnius Times. It's a magnificent tribute to your esteemed family.' The brothers perked up their interest in his words. 'The report reckoned that the fundamental difference between Lithuania and the United Kingdom is that the state owns everything in the old motherland. In the UK, Krueger finance companies do.' The brothers merely nodded their acceptance of the facts.

Dariusz turned his gigantic nose towards Godfrey like a rudder on a cruise liner changing course. 'Yeah, but when the Russians moved out, the flea-bitten do-gooders let the European Union move in. They merely substituted one politburo for another.'

'The EU! Pah! Demigods and interlopers! The people will see sense and realise what drives their economy, people like you and Vlad. Sensible, good men who create an underworld economy based on drugs and intimidation. It's ideals such as yours that enhance society so that everyone respects and fears their neighbour. Because of those emotions, it teaches them self-resilience and how to defend themselves. Remember the bad old days when Lithuania's society was based on fairness and democracy. Still, your family fought to change all that.' Godfrey's sycophantic praise continued. 'By the way, didn't I assure you that the minor matter of Harry Stevens' homicide wouldn't detain you in Parkhurst any longer than necessary. I know you didn't like the cuisine in there.'

Vlad feigned vomit by sticking his fingers in his throat. 'Come on, bro, we got used to the grub, eventually; it was the unhygienic way they served it up to us that caused us a few sleepless nights. Can you credit their audacity, Godfrey? We had to eat with common criminals in a communal, stinking mess hall. You'd have thought they'd have recognised who we were and provided us with a formal dining room, wouldn't you? After all, what do we pay the police commissioners to keep them sweet for?' Godfrey tutted his disgust. 'Mind you, the governor did send down a bottle of vodka for us when he found out who we were.'

'I should think so too. I would've imagined he was honoured to have you as his guests.'

'Now, are you going to show us these premises you've got lined up?'

'Yes, I will. Let's take a walk.'

They passed the cleaning and restoration work in the pedestrian area on their way to the lower part of town. 'What's happened here, Godfrey?' Vlad asked.

'A few days ago, a cherished customer of mine ascended to glory here. The method she chose was entirely of her own volition. It was rather messy, though.' Vlad nodded as if he understood. He didn't; his blinking, screwed-up eyes revealed his confusion.

They reached an unloved Victorian, plastered building opposite the church wall.

'Is this it? Look at the bird shit stains and leaking, cracked iron gutters. This place ain't been lived in since Queen Victoria had her first period.' Dariusz scoffed and smirked at his brother, still trying to fathom what Godfrey had said earlier. Vlad's twitching, enflamed nostrils purged his jumbled thoughts as sure as a resident living near a sewage works inhales the fresh morning air.

'…and it stinks of piss …!' he added, with renewed confidence. ' … it reminds me of the back alley behind Hammersmith's Roxy flix after the Saturday matinée. It's nice to be reminded of home, though, ain't it, bro.'

Godfrey quickly interceded to allay their downbeat expressions. 'I know what you're both thinking; it looks small and dingy. It's only an old snooker hall now, and it's seen better days. You can change all that. Think of the flashing neon lights and revolving doors. It's easily extendible too. There's a small-time chemist on the left and a one-man bakery business to the right. Get your lads to apply some pressure; I know the current owners will see sense. They may even want to become customers of your casino?'

Dariusz looked over the red-brick church wall. 'That's a church opposite, isn't it? Won't the local diocese bigwigs object to a casino on their doorstep?'

'My dear boy, when have such apparent obstacles been a problem for your Uncle Godfrey?' He looked towards the church door, pointed threateningly, and murmured. 'Judging by the way some church members live, they need fire insurance. They think my domain is getting out of date by today's thinking, but it's not out of business. If my trusted mode of living doesn't exist, many preachers in there are obtaining the confidence of their parishioner's deluded souls under false pretences.' Dariusz looked towards Vlad, querying with each other what Godfrey meant? 'Never worry, my friends. Saint Luke's church won't present a problem.'

They pushed the shabby door open and entered. As the brothers strolled around the twelve empty snooker tables, they occasionally bounced balls against the worn-out side cushions and watched where they went. The disused snooker hall was dusty and neglected. It reeked of stale beer and withered décor that hadn't been refurbished in years. Dariusz, the elder brother by five years, tried to look through the cigarette smoke-stained windows out onto the pedestrian area and the imposing church tower but gave up and turned to Godfrey. 'There's something else we need help with.'

'Tell me how I can assist? Is there someone you know in trouble?'

'Not trouble as in the Met is after them. It's our half-brother Igorovitch Bild-Krueger. You must remember his father, our stepdad? The Polish peasants, still tied by apron strings to Russian influence, strung him up for crossing the border at Ramoniskiai and raping that woman in the farmhouse.'

'Yes! Nasty business! He only visited that farm because he was hungry. Rape is not a hanging offence, is it? He was miserable and unfortunate that the first farm he came to belonged to the chief of police.'

'The locals around Vilnius, where Igorovitch is living, won't let him forget it. Is it any wonder he's had to resort to violence to eke out a living? They tell him he and his father have brought disgrace upon the country. The old motherland is not what it was, so he wants to come to the UK and start a new life.'

'... and what better examples could he have of decent upright citizens than his half-brothers to set him on the right path to prosperity?' Godfrey eased his lithe frame onto the edge of a snooker table.

'Well...?'

'He needs someone to vouch for him so he can get UK citizenship. His situation needs someone to attest to his moral character. I don't suppose you have anyone in mind who could arrange that?'

Godfrey's smile, to most people, would appear as a leering smirk. To Dariusz and Vlad, it exuded confidence and happy times ahead. 'I do have someone in mind right now, boys; I know she will help us.' With a violent fling, he hurled the black snooker ball against a threadbare cushion. The ball flew four times around the table before dropping into a corner pocket. 'It's as certain as that,' referring to the sharp bang as the ball disappeared from the green baize. 'I'll leave you two boys to have a look around the beginnings of your new empire.'

Dariusz and Vlad sauntered around the building, trying to visualise where their personal inner sanctum offices would be. 'Is this crummy joint the best that Godfrey could find for us?' Vlad asked.

'That's what I was thinking, bruv. I'm sure there must be better located buildings than this. It's that church over there that concerns me. We'll always be getting grief from the so-called upper class of the town who prefer to blow their snot into a handkerchief.'

'I think we can do better for ourselves like we always have done in the past. It's our gut instinct that counts. That's what's kept us one step ahead of the law and people like Warlock that want to muscle in on our territory.'

As Godfrey walked back to High Green, his leering smile turned into a roaring laugh. People passing by and seated on benches turned to see where the disturbance came from. 'Human nature has so many facets,' he whispered. 'I can always guarantee the many different forms it takes will boggle my imagination. Greed being near the top of the sorry pile. They're like rats scurrying over a pile of horse shit. So, they think I'm redundant, do they?' A woman ambling past him carrying her shopping almost dropped her bags as he directed another laughing outburst in her direction. She flinched and recoiled at the sight of his blackened, spaced teeth and brown saliva dropping onto the paving.

Forty

David Shaw knew every junction and crossing of the rail network in every part of the West Midland Railway he controlled. A mile and a half before trains slowed into Cannock railway station on the up line to Rugeley, many points in the tracks created a junction into vast goods yards. The area of fifteen acres once formed marshalling yards for coal wagons from the defunct Mid Cannock Colliery. The goods yard now provided a convenient storage site for transient goods carriages being transported along the whole of the United Kingdom rail network. Many companies availed themselves of the cheap rates the West Midland Railway Company charged for storage. Among one of the many companies that rented space was British Nuclear Fuels. Their special, sealed, armoured railway wagons containing over a thousand tonnes of spent fuel from power stations, regularly spent up to three weeks at any given time parked less than a mile from Cannock town centre. The area's geography, with several inclines and depressions in the landscape, was ideal for the rail network goods yard. Trains entered the yard on a downward incline for safety reasons. It ensured any parked wagon could not roll back onto the main line. The lives and safety of passengers were the primary consideration. The two principal railway lines had been electrified. This hadn't been extended to the goods yard, so diesel locomotives were required to shunt the wagons into different parking areas.

With his immature mind, corrupted and poisoned by Godfrey's books and his incessant brainwashing, David was obsessed with creating a name for himself that would live on in the history books. He envisaged a future where children at school would be taught about the changes to everyday life he had created. Films and documentaries would be a regular part of viewing on domestic television for millions of people worldwide. Numerous books detailing his life story would bedeck every library and bookshop. He foresaw the future when historians would refer to this century as the defining moment in how the measurement of time changed, all because of him. For the past two thousand years, time had been measured with an AD suffix, anno Domini, in the year of our Lord. Before then, as BC, before Christ. After David had exacted his revenge upon society for labelling him as an underling, time would be known as AS, after Shaw.

When leaving his Controller's office and returning home, even his wife, Margaret, by now used to his ramblings, was severely worried about him. His customary routine consisted of being studiously immersed in his books while rambling on incoherently about generating sufficient heat and the ignition point to explode nuclear waste. He meticulously scanned weather forecasts to decide when the best prevailing wind would scatter dust and for how far. One evening, after he'd gone to bed, Margaret discovered a book he'd been reading entitled 'The Horrors and Aftermath of Hiroshima.' She scanned through the pages and photographs, revealing ghastly images of irradiated skeletons and living people with only half their flesh hanging on blackened bones. Flicking through different pages, Margaret noticed David had been inserting notes against the technical details of the atomic bomb that destroyed the Japanese city in 1945. To her mounting revulsion, she found he had been making comparisons. The population of Hiroshima had been 1.19 million, while the West Midlands has 2.9 million inhabitants. The World War II bomb produced the equivalent of 15 kilotons of TNT. The one thousand tonnes of spent nuclear fuel currently lying idle in Cannock's goods yards would produce over a hundred thousand tonnes of TNT when detonated. The spread of radiation in Japan extended for only three square miles. David predicted a Cannock bomb would extend complete obliteration to dust for over fifty square miles. With mounting concern, she read a note he had scribbled. *Most of England, Wales, parts of Scotland and the east coast of Ireland would remain irradiated for over a hundred years.* With a favourable prevailing wind, aided by a high-altitude jet-stream, the radiation would engulf Scandinavia and extend into eastern Europe.

Margaret closed the book and wondered why her husband seemed to be making the issue his major pastime. For weeks and months, David's hobby had become more than a passion; it was an obsession. On another evening, she found sketches detailing the marshalling yards at Cannock pinpointing the site of an explosion; she became seriously worried about his sanity and what was in his mind. 'Why, David?' she murmured aloud. 'What's driving you to think about such evil things?' Had she looked at his book's flyleaf, she would have read:

This book is the property of Doctor Godfrey Warlock, Purveyor of rare and unusual books.

Margaret only worked part-time at the local supermarket, so she had lots of free hours during the day to consider her life and marriage to David. Until they came to Cannock, they had enjoyed a happy cohabitation, full of love and laughter. They had been God-fearing Christians enjoying an occasional church service. Now he had become a shell of his former self. He only paid her the minimum of attention demanded by living with someone, relating to what they ate or what bills needed to be paid. She wanted no further part of the life that her husband now lived and decided the time had come to confront him.

That evening after dinner, David retreated to his books, leaving Margaret to clear away the dishes and do whatever she did with her evening. He didn't care anymore; his one aim was to create a unique place in history for himself. So, he was more than surprised when she came over to him, closed the book he was reading and told him they needed to talk.

'I don't want to create an argument between us, darling, but why don't you want to be married to me anymore…?'

'… I don't know what you mean.'

'I think you do. All you want to do when you come home from work is read your ridiculous books….'

'… how dare you call my books ridiculous?'

'Alright then, your books on horrible things, creating explosions and destruction….'

'… and a place in history for myself and you too, of course, darling. Future generations will revere you as my wife. In the future, your name will be synonymous with Mary Magdalen to Jesus. After many years have passed, the powers that be will decide to award you posthumous sainthood; all for being my wife, nurturing and supplying sustenance for me. The Pope will confirm your beatification; it has a certain ring to it, don't you think, Saint Margaret of…?'

Margaret's confusion manifested itself by her living room appearing to revolve. Her immediate siblings and family suffered from blood pressure problems and this symptom was how it started, they'd told her. She held her head in her hands before looking up in relief to find the spinning sensation had stopped. Her immediate concern increased a hundred times to see David's wild eyes and hear his ranting about their place in the annals of history.

'Stop!' she shouted. David shut up in complete surprise at her outburst.

'Darling, are you alright? Perhaps you're suffering from…?'

'There's nothing the matter with me other than being worried to death about you….'

'… me?'

'Yes! You! What's got into you? I can't recognise what I see before me now, in this room, you're nothing like the man I married.'

'I haven't changed!'

'Oh, yes you have! Please tell me that I haven't been imagining what you've been reading and what, I hope to God, you aren't thinking of creating….'

'Thank God, you've come round to see what I want is going to be the most important event in our life together. Have you read my books while I've been sleeping? Of course you have; I see that now. You mustn't concern yourself, my dear. I have everything in hand, and my plans are almost in place.' He approached her, but she moved backwards, hoping he wouldn't touch her. He grabbed her hand and held it to his face. 'My darling wife, we'll share such a momentous moment in history only shared by other such notable partnerships that have gone before us. Only nothing before will have the notoriety or impact that we will have. Think of Alexander the Great and Roxana; Kublah Khan and Chabi; Hitler and Eva Braun; President Kennedy and Jacqueline Bouvier; King Alphonso of Aragon and Lucretia Borgia. Alas, I'm not suggesting that you'll be aligned with the many noble feats Lucretia carried out. Think about it, darling, and be encouraged and thankful that our marriage was ordained on high. I'm going back to my reading now, content that you're now with me, and the glorious occasion we'll generate in our nation's history.'

Margaret sat back in her chair, realising reluctantly, that their marriage was beyond any hope of salvage; David had utterly lost his mind. She wondered about the best course of action to bring him some help. The Samaritans could talk to him, perhaps? She dismissed this; they would only suggest he's committed to an asylum for urgent mental therapy. I think I need to talk to our doctor, in the first instance. I'll make an appointment with Doctor Patel in the morning.

Forty-one

Lucy had made a cup of cocoa and retired to bed earlier in the evening than she usually managed to do. She'd experienced an incredibly tiresome day confined to her desk at Scotland Yard, completing the increasing workload of paperwork demanded by her rank. Aided by the soft glow from her bedside lamp, she purred as she read from *The Posthumous Papers of the Pickwick Club.* Her delight was almost orgasmic, touching the unique Victorian handmade paper and running her fingers across Charles Dickens' signature. She visualised Princess Mary, King George V's daughter, holding the same book, reading to her siblings around a roaring fireplace in Windsor Castle.

So, when a ring of her doorbell invaded her reveries and ruined her cosiness, she was displeased. A few months before, she'd improved her apartment's security by having an expert install an intercom and camera on the communal landing. She didn't have to physically go and open her door anymore to an uninvited caller. Merely pressing a button on a handheld remote control, she could speak to and see whoever stood there. Without looking, she reached over and pressed the button marked with an ear symbol. She didn't need to see who it was; she'd decided whoever it was could go away. Putting the remote control unit to her mouth to tell them that, her senses reeled in shock and confusion when she recognised the feeble voice. 'Hello, my dear.' She swallowed the excess saliva forming in the back of her mouth. In a panic, she pressed the camera icon. She almost threw the plastic remote control across the room, reacting in horror with what she saw.

'Yes, you're right, my dear. It's me! I know you can see me now.' Lucy couldn't speak.

'I've come a long way to have a chat with you. I know it's inconvenient and I'm disturbing your reading. But…' Lucy remained silent. She hadn't spoken, so she gambled Godfrey wouldn't really know she was at home.

'… What are you reading? *The Posthumous Papers of the Pickwick Club?*'

Lucy pushed the book from her lap. 'How does he know?' she gasped.

'Come on, Lucy, this is tiresome. I won't stay long. There's something I have to ask you.' Annoyingly, it dawned on her that she would, reluctantly, have to let him into her apartment. She looked again at the camera image and grimaced at the unpleasant sight of his crooked and blackened teeth grinning at her. She reached into her wardrobe and draped a long woollen dressing gown around her. She could easily have pressed another icon on the remote control that would have automatically opened the door. Instead, she preferred to open the latch herself and confront him face to face. Lucy partially opened the door and peered through the gap. The automatic security lighting that operated when anyone stood at her door illuminated Godfrey's lithe frame.

'That's better, my dear; I can see you now. You'd already gone to bed, had you? It is a tough old life at Scotland Yard, isn't it? Still, cheer up, your Uncle Godfrey is here....'

'... how did you know my address?' Lucy still held the door slightly ajar.

'You gave it to me, don't you remember?'

'Godfrey, apart from my personal friends and family, I don't give my private address to anyone else. So, I know I didn't give it to you.'

'Ah well, someone must have given it to me, but no matter. I'm here now and I must talk to you.'

'You've come one hundred miles from Cannock, solely to talk to me at my apartment, knowing there's a possibility that I wouldn't be at home? And, yes, it matters to me about who knows my address, so before I even consider letting you in, I want to know who told you.'

'Oh, Lucy! Tut! Tut! I can't understand why you are so cross. Aren't you pleased to see me?'

Lucy could see he wasn't going away. She saw a man from an upper apartment pass by behind Godfrey, looking concerned. A second later, he came back and asked. 'Are you okay, Miss? Is this man bothering you? I can call the police if you'd like?'

Lucy teased open the door a little more in order to speak with the man, at which Godfrey took his opportunity to step inside. 'No, it's quite alright, thank you.' The man nodded, smiled, and turned in the direction of the stairs. She closed the door and turned to Godfrey.

'What do you want? I've had a tedious day.' Lucy went and sat in an armchair and gestured for him to sit opposite. He sat and crossed his legs before leering at her with slanted eyes.

'Considering all we've been through together, my dear Lucy, I don't like your tone. I think you should consider your position and remember your place.' Having experienced it once before at his bookshop, Lucy recognised the familiar shudders travelling down her spine, reacting to Godfrey's implied threats. She looked under her eyelids at him.

'... but I don't want to cause you alarm or for us to get off on the wrong foot. I'd sooner we dance together in perfect timing and synchronisation.'

'Damn it!' Lucy thought. 'It's as if he knows what I'm thinking.' Godfrey's unsettling leer extended from ear to ear.

'Just to put your mind at rest how I obtained your address, my dear, I simply looked it up in the local register of electors. There's nothing sinister or suspicious in that, is there? Now then, as to why I'm here....'

'... would you like a cup of coffee? I need one.'

'That's very civil of you to ask, but I don't drink these derivatives of earth's cultivated plantations; they don't quench my thirst at all but, please, you carry on, my dear.' He watched her go into the kitchen. He raised his voice as he carried on talking.

'I've never got around to thanking you for the excellent outcome with the Krueger brothers, have I? I know it must have caused you some embarrassing moments at Scotland Yard. I hope your career prospects are as secure now as they were before I asked you to help me?'

'Godfrey, please tell me what you want. I'm drained and want an early night....'

'... oh, okay. I was thinking maybe, because you know I've travelled all this way this evening, you could let me stay the night. It's going to be in the early hours of tomorrow before I arrive back in that lovely provincial town of Cannock.'

'Absolutely not! For a start, there's only one bedroom in this apartment. Even if there wasn't, I wouldn't be inviting you to stay here, anyway.' Lucy raised her voice even higher, anxious that he knew exactly what the position was.

'Ooh! How bitter you sound, my dear Lucy. I would imagine in the past you haven't always been so dismissive to male company in this apartment.' Lucy gulped at his all-knowing knowledge of her life and business. She returned to the lounge with her steaming cup of coffee and looked at him, expectantly.

'Okay, you've made your point. I'll get to the reason I'm here. Oh, but before then, are you still pleased with your ownership of Charlie's book? He stared at her with an analytical gaze. 'Yes, I can see you are, and I know you'd like that status quo to continue, wouldn't you?'

'Is that a veiled threat?' Godfrey shrugged his shoulders. 'Because I have to tell you, I don't respond to threats. You've hinted before that by some method you may have in mind, you'd take back ownership of Dickens' book. I'm beginning to wonder whether being the owner of the book is worthwhile having to suffer your company and your threats?'

Godfrey stood, 'Before I go then, my dear, hand the book over and I'll take it back to my bookshop.'

Lucy stammered. 'Not so fast, I earned the book. We made an agreement, and I carried out what you asked...' Lucy put her coffee down and also stood.

'... and I told you that I may call upon you for further help as part of that agreement. That is why I'm here tonight but, as I said, hand the book over and I'll leave you in peace.'

Lucy hesitated. 'What is it you want from me? If it involves more delving into the records of Scotland Yard, I can't do it. You'll have to find someone else. I'll fetch the book now.'

'Not so fast! What I'm asking is not connected to any current case at The Metropolitan Police, so your concerns about your position as a detective sergeant will not be compromised.'

They both sat down. 'That's better. Perhaps now we can talk about why I'm here.' Lucy took a considerable slurp of coffee.

'It is connected to the Krueger brothers....' Lucy raised her eyebrows to the ceiling. '... I can see you're sceptical; however, it's regarding their step-brother Igorovitch Bild-Krueger.' Godfrey went on to explain what he wanted.

'How can I vouch for this man when I don't know the slightest detail about him? He could be an international terrorist for all I know, probably even on Interpol's list of the ten most wanted criminals?'

'I can supply you with all the pertinent facts to support his application to leave Lithuania for first, a work permit, secondly a visa, and afterwards citizenship. Igorovitch is a decent, ambitious man desirous of a better life.'

'So why do you want my help if he's totally honourable?'

'He and his family have had their difficulties with neighbouring States. Your signature as a serving detective sergeant with The Metropolitan Police will merely add certain respectability to his application. It will show he has friends here who will support him.'

'So, you only want my signature on documents to be submitted to the immigration department. My support will begin and end with my signing the papers.'

'That's all I'm asking, and you can retain ownership of the book.'

'How will you get the documents to me? I value my privacy here and don't want any more visitors about this.'

'Other than you revisiting Cannock, I can't....'

'I'll come to your Cannock bookshop if my friends and colleagues will welcome me again. Have the papers waiting for me so I can sign them and leave.'

Within a few seconds, Godfrey had left. He didn't say goodnight or even look towards Lucy. He rose stealthily from the chair, walked to the door and closed it silently behind him.

Forty-two

'Margaret Shaw to Doctor Patel, in consulting room six, please,' the surgery's loudspeaker delivered to people seated in the waiting room. People looked around to see who Margaret Shaw was because, for a brief moment, nobody stirred. Everyone else hoped they'd hear the next patient's name being called because Margaret wasn't present, and their turn would come sooner. Their hopes were dashed as Margaret, after reaching into her handbag for her spectacles, slowly gathered her bag and umbrella that she'd put on the floor. She needed her glasses to read which was consulting room six.

Ambling down the carpeted corridor, she squinted at the bright glare behind the silhouetted black figure six. She nervously knocked on the door and waited for the doctor to give his permission to enter. She didn't hear anything and knocked louder. 'Yes, come in.' She listened and thought the doctor sounded irritable, but he was only shouting louder, having called 'enter' at the first knock on his door. 'Perhaps my next patient is deaf?' he thought.

'Hello, doctor,' she offered and waited to be told to sit. When she did, she systematically put her bag and umbrella on the floor, then reached into her bag again for the case for her glasses.

Doctor Patel had been in Cannock's surgical practice for over twenty years; he had seen and experienced all sorts of people, their peculiarities and whims. His general assumption that slowness was associated with age and, or illness. Margaret seemed in her early thirties, so he couldn't attribute either category to her. He smiled and waited for her to explain why she wanted to see him.

Since he'd become one of Godfrey Warlock's converts, he was a regular reader at his bookshop. Many times, over the past few months, he'd walked into *Godfrey's Bookshop*. Sometimes he read different medical books that Godfrey had selected for him. Other times he merely chatted with him to relate how his patients' revised treatments were progressing. It wasn't only his wife who had commented on how more agreeable he was these days; his staff also were happier and more productive. Because of his new friendship with Godfrey Warlock, his life had changed for the better.

With Godfrey's help and encouragement, Anwar had become an expert at practising euthanasia. He saw himself as a force for good in society, removing older people from the population who might otherwise have become a burden to the health care system. The records of the patients' treatment at The Ganges Practice would never reveal the truth of how over two hundred and fifty patients had met their demise. Despite all of them receiving a terminal diagnosis for their condition, it wasn't lost on him that he derived pleasure from the knowledge that, as a doctor, he had the power of life or death. Killing them was the means through which he expressed his power. It never dawned on him that taking advantage of his patient's trust in him as a doctor made his illegal actions odious and abhorrent. He only saw himself as an angel of mercy who relieved his patients' suffering.

He brought up Margaret's records on his computer screen. 'Oh, I see you've only been here to my surgery once before. How can I help you today?'

She started to stammer, being nervous as to how to discuss her husband's condition. 'It's my husband, David....'

'Is your husband David Shaw?' Margaret nodded. Anwar's thought processes went into overtime. 'Where do I know that name from?' His heavily lined forehead betrayed his inner puzzlement. He put his thoughts to one side as Margaret tried to explain why she was there.

'I'm worried about him. I think he's lost his mind.'

'Is he working?'

Margaret nodded.

'What does he do for a living?'

'He's the chief controller for rail traffic with The West Midlands Railway company.'

Anwar didn't answer; he now realised who David Shaw was. He regularly sat by him in *Godfrey's Bookshop*. They were both trusted converts of Godfrey Warlock. They enjoyed the facilities of unlimited books and the opportunity to study them in his reading room.

'What makes you think he's lost his mind? That's quite a profound statement to make for a wife about her husband, Mrs Shaw.'

'I've thought long and hard about coming here today and realise the implications of what I'm saying.'

'Has he threatened you, or do you consider yourself to be in danger from him?'

'No, he hasn't. I don't feel in personal danger from him, but I've come to believe he's a danger to me, you, all of us and everyone in society.'

'I don't understand....'

'... neither do I really, but I think he needs investigating.'

'Mrs Shaw, I'm not sure I'm the right person you should be talking to you. Perhaps if you feel as you do, the police would be more appropriate?'

'... but I feel he's mentally ill, surely that's a medical matter?'

'Of course, but I'm not specialised in psychiatry. I have a friend and colleague, whom I could refer you to if you wish?'

'Yes, please. I'm frightened, doctor, if something is not done, I fear for the future.'

'Mrs Shaw, I can see you're very disturbed; what is it exactly that you suspect your husband will do?'

'It's more than a suspicion, doctor. I've seen his writings, his planning, and his calculations. He definitely has a plan in mind....'

'... for what?'

'To create a nuclear explosion that will wipe Cannock off the map and irradiate most of the United Kingdom for the next fifty years.'

A heavy silence descended between them. Anwar looked in incredulity at Margaret. In everyday conversation with anyone else outside of his medical practice, he would have laughed at what she'd suggested. Knowing how serious and level-headed she seemed, it wasn't appropriate to laugh, or suggest she is imagining such fearful things. However, he did question her own sanity and if she needed investigating rather than her husband.

'Okay, Mrs Shaw, I'll telephone my psychiatry friend now. His name is Doctor Jack Branding and perhaps he'll suggest an appointment time for you to visit him.' Margaret nodded as he accessed the number.

'Hello, Jack, it's Anwar here. I have a Mrs Margaret Shaw with me. She's a patient of mine, but I think she needs your expertise rather than mine from a discussion we've had. Okay!' Anwar wrote as he listened to Jack's response before closing his phone.

'Here we are, Mrs Shaw. He's given you an appointment slot at his consulting room at the hospital here in Cannock. Tomorrow at 3:30.'

After giving her thanks and leaving the medical practice, Anwar immediately redialled Jack Branding's number.

'Jack, It's Anwar again. Mrs Shaw has left now.' He explained why Margaret had come to him. 'So, I'd be grateful if you'd listen to her and get back to me with your assessment.'

Forty-three

Donald and his team at Cannock police station had been tying up loose ends from the various disturbing cases they had recently been involved with. James reminded his gov of the meeting they'd had with Superintendent Woodhouse. 'You said we need to have a chat with Godfrey Warlock, gov.'

'Yes, we do. Now we've cleared some paperwork, let's have him in here for a chat.'

'Shall I go to his bookshop and ask him to come in?'

'Yes, do that. See what Godfrey's reaction is. If he refuses, tell him we'll issue a subpoena, but if he's got any sense, he'll cooperate.'

James pushed open the shop door and peered into the gloom. 'Mr Warlock,' he called, but couldn't see anyone. James knew about the step down and felt for the nose of the step with his foot. Godfrey then appeared from behind his counter.

'Ah! It's Mr policeman again. How can I help you? I take it you're not seeking a book to read?'

'Not today, sir. Detective Inspector Lawrence has sent me here to ask if you wouldn't mind coming to the police station....'

'... to the police station? Oh dear, am I in trouble? I don't own a vehicle, so I know it can't be about a traffic violation...?' Godfrey was flippant with James.

'... Mr Warlock, I have to tell you that if you refuse, we....'

'... did I say anything about refusing to come with you?'

'Well, I wasn't thinking of you coming back with me now. More like agreeing a time at your convenience.'

'It's convenient for me now. I assume it's not convenient for you?'

'... Er! Um! No, that's quite alright. Let me clear it with the Inspector first....'

'... make up your mind, young man. I do have a business to run.' James rang Donald's number and turned away from Godfrey.

'Gov, it's James. Godfrey Warlock wants to come back with me to the station now. I thought I'd better clear it with you?'

'That's fine, James; stall him for five minutes to give me a chance to get my breath. Good work.' James turned back to Godfrey.

'That's perfectly agreeable with the Inspector, sir. We'll walk together then.'

'You'll have to wait a moment, I need to close my shop.' He turned to the people sitting in the reading room. 'Carry on the wonderful work, my friends. I'll be out for ten minutes.'

Donald called for Nicky. 'James is bringing Godfrey Warlock back with him now. I'll interview him with James. I'd like you to watch from the adjoining room.'

'I feel like Daniel entering the lion's den,' Godfrey quipped as James let him enter the police station first. 'It must have taken a great deal of courage for Daniel to have done that, mustn't it, young man?'

'Pardon me?' James half turned as they climbed the stairs from the reception area.

'He could have been set upon by the whole pride of seven lions and devoured at any moment, you know. Is that what you intend to do with me, devour me?'

James didn't respond and held the door open into the general office on the first floor.

Godfrey stepped confidently into the large office. His eyes became oblique fissures as he peered around the office. In the corner, Donald's secretary looked up, gasped and held a handkerchief to her nose and mouth.

Godfrey's eyes widened when he saw her. His spiky hair seemed to stand up more prominently, and he thrust out his goatee beard. His eyes resumed their piss holes in the snow appearance. He murmured in her direction as if greeting an old friend. 'Hello, Veronica, how are you keeping? It was such a shame about your husband, Adrian. He really didn't feel any pain, you know.'

Donald and Nicky were standing at her desk. They looked over and wondered how Veronica knew Godfrey. When he saw her starting to cry, Donald walked over to her. 'Are you okay? Come and have a sit down in my office for a while.'

'No, I'm quite alright, Inspector, thank you. I'll carry on with my work.' She looked nervously across at Godfrey. Donald followed her stare and whispered.

'I can see Godfrey Warlock is upsetting you. May I ask how you know him?'

'Tell him, Veronica, my dear.' Godfrey hissed. Donald turned in surprise at how he could have heard him speak so quietly to Veronica.

'How dare you come and show your face in here?' Veronica called across in a sobbing cry, peering around Donald's frame.

'It's your boss's fault; he's invited me here. Blame him for your distress, my dear.' Godfrey pointed his hooked finger at Donald in a theatrically camp manner, replicating the mannerisms of a homosexual.

Donald turned back to her. 'What's going on?'

'Tell him, for God's sake, if only to put everyone out of their misery, darling.' Godfrey looked impatiently to the ceiling and then to his fingernails as if they needed trimming. 'This is so tiresome,' he murmured.

'Don't you call me darling, you monster! You caused Adrian's accident. It was you who killed him.'

'I did no such thing. The former Inspector went into all that nonsense. How could I have been blamed for Adrian's pathetic driving abilities? He really shouldn't have been driving, you know, my dear.'

Donald, James, and Nicky looked on in confusion as Veronica stood and faced Godfrey.

'This man, Inspector, caused my husband's death. It was before you came here. There is a file on the incident in one of your filing cabinets. It was a Saturday morning; Adrian was taking me shopping in our car to the supermarket down the Avon Road.'

Godfrey looked to the ceiling. 'Here we go again,' he murmured and tutted. 'Do you mind if I take a seat, young man?' He turned to James, who offered him a chair. 'Not that I'm weary, I'm just bored at having to listen to this pathetic woman....'

'... whatever is going on, Mr Warlock, you'll keep a civil tongue in your head in this police station and not refer to my secretary in such a vile manner,' Donald hissed. In response, Godfrey flippantly waved his hand as if he were royalty, perfunctorily revolving his hand at public crowds. He caught Nicky's eye as he did so, expressing a sickly smirk.

Donald looked back at Veronica. 'Adrian was a good driver, Inspector. This man suddenly stepped off the kerb opposite the pizza parlour. He was holding several black crows. They perched on his head and shoulders; he was holding an entire flock of crows! He stood in front of our car and clapped his hands; the birds flew everywhere.

Some flew into the windscreen. Adrian slammed on the breaks and turned to avoid him. The offside wheel hit the opposite kerb, and the car turned over. Adrian hit his head on the steering wheel and was rendered unconscious. I was only shaken, but all I can remember is that man standing in the middle of the road laughing hysterically as people tried to get us out of the car. My husband died later, in the hospital. The doctor said the cause had been a heart attack....'

'... you know as well as I that Adrian had suffered previous heart attacks, my dear....'

'... don't you, my dear, me! You are a vile man...' She turned to Donald. 'Inspector, if I had a gun in my hand at this moment, I'd shoot him and you'd be arresting me, but I'd be glad. This ghoul of a pervert would be dead and gone....'

'... ooh! How provocative is that, Inspector? Who's not got a civil tongue in their head now?' Godfrey scoffed at Veronica. 'It will take more than a bullet to get rid of me, darling.'

Donald called to Nicky. 'Make Veronica some tea, please; stay with her for a little while before coming down to do as I asked.'

'Come with me please, Mr Warlock, to the interview room. You too, please, James.'

Donald and James faced Godfrey across the table. 'This interview is being recorded, Mr Warlock.'

'Continue with any procedures you little policemen must do in your job,' Godfrey responded, with derision.

'The incident just now with my secretary is another example of why we are having this conversation today. There has been an alarming number of incidents during the past few months that have had some connection with you and your bookshop.'

'Really? Give me an example...!'

'Do you remember Harry and Maria Bailey?' Godfrey shook his head and sarcastically raised his eyebrows. 'My colleague and I investigated the murder of his wife and his subsequent suicide. When searching their house, I found one of your books that he had been reading. The book advocated the vile actions he had carried out....'

'I can't see how that implicates me, Inspector?'

'Then, a day later, Jack Beecham strangled his wife in their bath. Of course, you know all about him, because later he came and cut his throat at the door of your bookshop. Again, I found out he also was reading another of your books that encouraged him.' Godfrey opened his mouth to speak. 'There's more! Then a most disturbing occurrence at Heath Hayes. A Mr Keith Newsome killed and dismembered his wife, Glenda, and fed what was left of her to his pigs. Again, one of your books was discovered. The book that Mr Newsome had been reading supported feeding human remains to pigs as they are carnivores. He later took his own life, but not before beheading one of my constables.' Godfrey appeared bored and gazed at the mirror on the wall as if knowing Nicky had taken her place in the adjoining room. Nicky shuddered to notice his eerie smirk looking directly at her as if the mirror was clear glass.

'You know all too well about a friend of yours, Christine Follows, who attempted to blow Cannock off the map, killing herself in the process. This was after the distressing fire at the apartment block opposite the railway station. Mrs Follows was the prime suspect for causing that fire.'

'That was tragic, wasn't it?' Godfrey's tone displayed no more emotion than commenting about the weather.

'There have been other troubling events in the town. The Reverend Spencer, again after reading one of your books, paraded around the town with a wooden cross, purporting to be Jesus Christ. A man interrupted a music concert professing to be Beethoven. I could carry on, Mr Warlock....'

'... before you do go on, I think I should point out the correct term for addressing me, Inspector. I am a doctor and not a Mr.' Godfrey's dismissive tactile arm displays were irritating Donald.

'I stand corrected... *doctor*. Can you see a pattern here, Doctor?' Donald sarcastically emphasised the word. 'Several deaths and suicides and disturbing events in my town. All have a connection to you and your bookshop. How many more can we expect to happen?'

'What proof do you have that I have had any influence on the occurrences, Inspector?' Godfrey looked quizzically at Donald's blank expression.

'From your silence, I have my answer, don't I, Inspector Lawrence? You don't! Therefore, I'm asking myself why you have invited me in here today? Do you intend to charge me with an offence? Again, from your continued silence, I don't imagine that you will? It's a complete waste of my time. I do have a bookshop to run, you know, and I left several of my readers in there when your constable came for me.'

Godfrey gawked at Donald and James before turning to the mirror again.

He stood and sauntered out of the room. He turned back to face them. 'It's all down to the complicated matter of human nature. None of you can help what drives you to take the actions you do. Some people react differently to others. Can I challenge you to own up to something, Inspector? When picking up a newspaper in an evening, sitting alongside that lovely wife of yours...? What is her name...? Janet... yes, Janet. Oh, before I forget, digressing, could I offer my congratulations to you both? I think little Zak is going to have a little sister quite soon.'

Donald stared and gasped. 'Oh, but of course, you don't know that yet. That will make an interesting conversation between you and Janet this evening. Now, where was I...?' James and Nicky could see Godfrey was goading their gov and hoped he wouldn't react. '... if, in a newspaper, you read that a young drug addict, in a blind narcotic-filled rage has murdered a beautiful young, innocent girl, what would you think? My reaction would be, the lunatic needs executing, but others may think differently. Some social workers would take pity on the young man and suggest a course of therapy for him. Others would no doubt shoot him themselves if they had the chance. How would you react, Inspector? You see, we are all different when we react to events. That is all that is happening here in our little town. People with different human emotions put their own interpretation on what they read or listen to.'

Donald had heard enough and stood.

'Are we finished then, Inspector? Well, I think that concludes our business for today, everyone. Your young female sergeant does look especially attractive today, doesn't she?' Godfrey turned to the mirror.

'See you later, everyone, and don't forget if you want a book to read, you know where I am.' He started through the door and turned again. '... but it hasn't been a total waste of time; I've had the pleasure of meeting up with Veronica again. Please give her my best regards when you return to your office.'

Silently he glided along the lino floor, down the stairs and out into the sunshine. The police officers looked down from the first floor window on his bald patches and flamboyant yellow bowtie protruding from his upturned collar. As if he knew he was being watched, he half turned and waved up at them.

Forty-four

'Donald, while you've been out, Superintendent Woodhouse rang. Could you get back to him, please? He suggested it's quite urgent.' Veronica met him as he returned to his office.

'How are you, Veronica? I had no idea you had a history with Godfrey Warlock?'

'There's no reason to think you should, Donald. Thank you for your support this morning.'

'That man is a nasty piece of work....'

'... My Adrian would still be here today if he hadn't done what he did. I'm trying to get on with life without my husband, you understand. Until this morning, I thought I was progressing quite well but seeing him standing before me was too much.'

'I thought you handled the matter brilliantly.'

'I hate that man, Inspector, for what he did to Adrian, my family and me.'

'Come and sit in my office for a moment, please, Veronica.' She closed the door behind her and sat opposite Donald.

'Perhaps you can tell me more about Godfrey Warlock. You know I've only been in post for six months.' She looked at him and then out of the window as if focussing on somewhere far away.

'What I do know is that before he arrived in town, Cannock used to be such a pleasant place to live and bring up a family. Now there's so much violence and mistrust and people don't seem so friendly anymore. Perhaps it's me and how I look upon life now I'm by myself. I'm a widow now and my outlook has changed. I know everyone has to lose someone they love; it's part of life and will never change... but... and there's a big but, Inspector...' She paused, wringing her hands as if in mental torture. 'When that someone is a man I have loved and spent most of my life with and he's been murdered, because that's what Godfrey Warlock did; he committed murder and got away with it. Well, there's no justice, and that's what I'd like to see, justice for my Adrian.'

'How long has Godfrey Warlock been in town?'

'Oh, about six months before you came. He's been here for over twelve months now. I lost Adrian a month after he opened his bookshop.'

'Was it always a bookshop?'

'Before *Godfrey's Bookshop,* the premises had been a Salvation Army charity shop, but the short-sighted town councillors decided to increase the rates for premises fronting onto the new pedestrian area. Someone had to pay for the work, and they opted for the premises that opened their doors onto the new facilities to be the ones to pay. Of course, charity shops are what their name suggests - charities. As you probably know, the Salvation Army shop is now in Station Street, where the rates are much less.' Donald nodded.

'The owner of the premises was the previous town's doctor who gave up his practice years ago. He wanted to retire down to Cornwall; he couldn't afford the rates either, so he put the shop up for sale at a reduced price. In no time at all, *Godfrey's Bookshop* seemed to start trading overnight.'

'Is there anything else you can tell me about the accident that caused your husband's death?'

'It wasn't an accident. As I said, Godfrey Warlock murdered my husband.'

'Did the police investigate the matter?'

'Your predecessor, you mean, Inspector Wainwright.'

'Yes, and this police force.'

'For a while they did, then they dropped the case.'

'Why? Other officers concluded that it was only an accident, I suppose?'

Veronica looked wistfully out of the window again before facing Donald. 'Can you keep to yourself what I'm now going to tell you, please?' Donald nodded with mounting interest.

'Let me tell you something about Inspector Wainwright. Jerry and his wife, Lilian, used to be good friends with Adrian and me. Adrian and Jerry went to the same grammar school here in town. He'd served his time in the force and was going to take early retirement, then he changed, somehow? Jerry became sullen, kept himself to himself and developed an uncaring attitude. He certainly wasn't as friendly towards either Adrian or me anymore. The staff here also noticed the change in him. Eventually, Superintendent Woodhouse hastened his early retirement, but, I'm jumping ahead.' She paused, swallowed and resumed. 'Very often, I'd come into his office to find him reading books and neglecting the everyday police work. At the end of one day, after he left the office, I tidied his desk and noticed the books he'd been studying. They were weird! Books on different types of death; how previous executions took place in medieval England; gruesome, horrible descriptions of how miscreants were hung, drawn, and quartered for no more crime than stealing a loaf of bread. Then I noticed that the books all had red ink stamps on their covers. The books all belonged to Godfrey Warlock. Inspector Jerry Wainwright had become one of *Godfrey's Bookshop's* first customers.'

Donald stood, went to his bookshelves and pulled down three books. He turned them over to their rear covers and showed them to Veronica. 'Like these?' They stared at the same red stamps showing the books were Godfrey Warlock's.

'Yes! Exactly the same! Where did you get those?'

'All taken from properties where murders and suicides have occurred. The cases we've been investigating these past two months.' Donald sat down again and stared at Veronica.

'That man is evil, Inspector. It seems to add up, somehow. Anything bad that happens in town seems to have a connection with him.' Donald placed the books back on his shelves as she resumed.

'It was only a few days later that Adrian died. Of course, I was distraught, but Jerry offered me no sympathy or understanding. I had come to firmly believe that Jerry was instrumental in all suspicions about Adrian's death being diverted from Godfrey Warlock when the station investigated the accident.'

'Where is Inspector Wainwright now? Perhaps I should have a chat with him about Godfrey Warlock?'

'He's dead! Two months after retiring, he took his own life. One morning, Lilian woke, came downstairs and found him naked, hanging above the stairs. He'd tied a piece of rope around the landing banister to a noose around his neck. Of course, at the inquest in Stafford, the coroner pronounced he'd committed suicide.'

'Ah! Another death with connections to *Godfrey's Bookshop.*'

Veronica got up to leave Donald's office.

'I see! Thank you for that, Veronica. Are you sure you're alright? Why don't you take the rest of the day off and have a break…?'

'No, thank you, Inspector, I'd sooner keep busy.'

'Veronica, when we're by ourselves, please call me Donald; my title sounds so formal.'

'Okay, Donald,' she smiled and returned to her desk. Donald called after her.

'Can you get Superintendent Woodhouse for me now? I'll see what he wants.'

'Donald, is there any chance you could come to my office for a private chat, please? I have a report on my desk from the County Coroner's Office. You need to see it before we can progress any investigation arising from it. Note I'm asking for a personal chat first, before coming to any other action.'

'When?'

'What are you doing right now?'

'Right now, Ernest, I'm trying to come down from the ceiling. We've had Godfrey Warlock in here for an interview. A nice steady drive to Stafford will calm me down. See you in fifty minutes.'

Donald enjoyed the drive from Cannock to the County town of Stafford. The route took him through the splendid scenery of Cannock Chase resplendent with mature oak trees that were over seven hundred years old. He pulled up against the security barrier barring the entrance into the police headquarters. At once, a uniformed officer challenged him to show his identity. The receptionist asked him to follow her to Superintendent Woodhouse's office. She knocked on the door and announced Inspector Lawrence's presence to her superior. He stood when he saw Donald walking towards him.

'Donald, it's lovely to see you. I have a pot of coffee for us to share. I've given my secretary instructions that we're not to be disturbed unless World War Three has broken out. I thought we'd be more comfortable in the armchairs in my private lounge.'

'I never knew this existed. The perks of the rank, eh? This is wonderful.'

'Make yourself comfortable. The report I want you to look at is on the coffee table. It concerns excess deaths in the Cannock Chase district.'

Superintendent Woodhouse poured two cups of coffee as Donald reached for the report and started reading. Donald read a few pages before commenting, 'Oh no, Ernest; Cannock - more unexplained deaths - more misery.' Ernest watched him and waited until he'd read the entire twenty-page report.

'Well?'

'This is most disturbing. I know Doctor Anwar Patel, personally. He delivered my son Zak when Janet couldn't make it to the maternity hospital in time. My son was born on his surgery couch. It's difficult to imagine him being involved in anything like this?'

'You know as well as I do, we have to put personal feelings to one side. The report mentions one hundred and thirty-five deaths above the normal trends for the period mentioned. The doctor concerned in each death and with his signature on death certificates is Anwar Patel. That many excess deaths can't be overlooked or considered a coincidence. The coroner has pointed out there's no current pandemic or flu outbreak that could account for these extra deaths.'

'Is there any indictable proof?'

'That's the difficulty that presents itself to us – there isn't. That's why I'd like us to keep this to ourselves for now.'

'… and? You must have a motive for bringing me here, other than to update me on this?'

'We're getting to know each other, Donald. Keep this under the radar but investigate the hell out of this. I know you have two outstanding officers in Sergeant Bains and Constable… Er!'

'… Constable James Garbett'

'Yes! Take them into your confidence over this. It's the sort of investigation that can be carried out in parallel with other cases you're all working on. Most importantly, we mustn't have a leak. Imagine what the press would make of this. They'd think it was their birthday and Christmas on one day. The dreaded words S*erial Killer* comes to mind. What we'd consider was a normal life would be over. Our careers and life would never be the same again. Remember Peter Sutcliffe from Yorkshire and Doctor Harold Shipman from Hyde in Greater Manchester. Police careers ruined; their private lives harassed by the press for years afterwards. We need to tread with the utmost caution.'

Donald's eyes glazed over with the implications for him and his young family.

'The County Coroner, Colin Matthews, also has the same views on confidentiality as me. This report is his own personal property. He's typed it himself on his home laptop. He couldn't risk submitting it to his secretary to prepare. These are only facts at this stage. However, they are troubling facts and inescapable statistics. I'll leave it with you how you go ahead. As all the deaths are on your patch and under your authority, obviously, you're the first person I've called on. Tell me now if you feel you've got too much on your plate, and I'll draft in another Inspector.' Donald shook his head.

'No, that's okay, Ernest. The fact that I know Anwar Patel personally gives me an advantage on where to start.'

'Where will you begin?'

'Every death is detailed here. Who they were; where they lived; age; cause of death. We can go through each case and flush out more details from their families without raising concern or suspicion.'

'Good man. Keep me informed.'

Forty-five

The clock above the hospital entrance showed 3:15. Margaret Shaw
sauntered across the footbridge that connected a public footpath in
Brunswick Road directly with the hospital's first floor, where doctors'
consulting rooms were found. The footbridge enabled ambulances to
pass underneath, unhindered, directly to the Accident and Emergency
Department. The psychiatry department was situated at the end of a
long corridor. A reception desk displayed four consultants were in
attendance, one of them was Doctor Jack Branding. Margaret took a
seat and waited for her appointment to appear on a screen, directing
her to the correct door. 'Hello, Mrs Shaw. Please take a seat. Doctor
Patel has referred you to me; how can I help?'

'Has Doctor Patel told you why I went to see him?'

'Yes, he briefly outlined the situation, but I'd like you to tell me in
your own words. It's your husband you've come about, I understand.'

'I'm going to come straight to the point, doctor. I've come to
believe my husband is a danger to me, you, all of us and everyone in
society.'

'That's a profoundly serious assertion you're making....'

'... I realise that.' Doctor Branding eyed her with a sideways
glance as if assessing her own mental state. Margaret was quick to
notice his distrustful look.

'Oh, don't worry about me, doctor, I'm fine. I have all my wits
about me. It's David, my husband....'

'... What's he done?'

'Nothing yet. It's what he's planning to do.' Margaret was raising
her voice.

'Tell me calmly and slowly, so I can form an opinion....'

'... To create a nuclear explosion that will wipe Cannock off the
map and irradiate most of the United Kingdom for the next fifty
years.' Margaret went quiet to let the statement sink in.

'… What…!' Jack looked astonished at her. He had a pen poised to make notes, but in his surprise, he dropped the biro and it rolled onto the sanitised tiled floor. Margaret bent down and picked it up.

Handing it back to him, she commented further. 'It takes some believing, doesn't it? I told you, I wasn't going to beat around the bush.'

'Mrs Shaw, Margaret. Do you have any proof of the assertion you're making?'

'My mind is clear. I have my wits about me; of course, I do. I knew you'd think I was the loony one coming here without evidence to back up what I'm saying. I want you to help David. He's not a criminal. He's been overworking….'

'… the proof, Margaret. Where's the proof?'

'Of course, silly me. It's here in this bag. David's book and his notes.' She reached into her bag that she'd placed on the floor. In a few seconds, Jack's desk was littered with personal items that she'd had to remove from her bag to get to the book. He prided himself on what an orderly and tidy person he is, so he eyed with distaste his once pristine desk now resembling a jumble sale. He saw packets of condoms and sanitary towels, a sealed pack of tissues, her comb full of loose hairs, used train tickets, and supermarket till receipts.

'Mrs Shaw, this is all…'

'… Here it is.' He took the dishevelled book from her. Loose notes were dangling from between the pages.

'If you turn to his notes, you'll understand.' Jack looked at his wristwatch.

'Margaret, it's the policy here that to fit as many patients as possible into my busy schedule, I only usually allow fifteen minutes maximum to each appointment.'

'I'll leave the book with you….' Jack sighed that he didn't have to study the lengthy book and David's scribbles at that moment.

'… thank you. Yes! I'll take the book away with me to study later. My appointments secretary has your mobile number. I'll get her to contact you….'

'… you aren't going to fob me off that easily, doctor. I can guarantee that you won't be inviting me for another routine appointment once you've read David's thoughts. You'll be ringing me directly.' Margaret gathered the loose items back into her bag and stood to leave. 'I'm going, doctor. I'll be expecting your call.'

Jack watched her stride purposefully across his consulting room and close the door behind her. He turned to the book but quickly put it to one side, mentally noting that he'd take it home later, together with all the other patients' files.

Forty-six

Later that evening, Donald looked wistfully at Janet. Zak was lying contentedly asleep in his pushchair. 'That was a wonderful dinner, darling.' He complimented her on his favourite chicken fajita cooked with authentic Italian herbs. 'You look exceptionally beautiful this evening, darling,' he commented, wanting to lead up to a more meaningful conversation. Janet had migrated to the kitchen sink, loading the dishwasher with the dirty cutlery and plates. She turned and smiled.

'I know you, Inspector Donald Lawrence. Don't think for a second I'm not pleased to receive such flattering remarks, but....'

'... but what...?'

'... I'm wearing my cleaning apron for a start, my hair is all over the place, my nipples are sore from your son biting me again and I'm washing dirty dishes. It's not what I'd call a romantic setting to receive flattering words from a lover.'

'Is that what I am, your lover?'

'Well, aren't you?' He dashed over to where she stood and grabbed her around her waist. 'Yes, I am your lover. Since when does a dirty apron and untidy hair, prevent us from making mad, passionate love? Sore nipples maybe, but I'll kiss them better.'

'... You are incorrigible, I'm glad to say, but I know you. What were you going on to say? I've come to understand there's a purpose behind such compliments....'

'In future then I'll whisk you off to bed without any foreplay. Then I know I'll receive the standard English housewife's words that comedians always say in their acts....'

'... what are you talking about?'

'All those sayings they use, like, where has all the passion gone? Why can't you be like foreign lovers, instead of wham, bam, thank you, ma'am? We watched one comedian from Liverpool. Don't you remember, he said that Italian women lie in bed looking to the heavens, after being chatted up and cry, *molto amore, sempre amore*?

French woman shriek, plus *d'amour, beaucoup d'amour.* 'Donald tried his utmost to practise an Italian and then a French accent. 'Whereas, because their husbands don't chat them up, English women look up and say, this ceiling needs painting.' With a louder voice, Donald replicated the scowl of a frustrated woman.

Janet only shook her head, before answering, 'What's got into you?' Donald paused before, without any further attempt at amusing her, answered.

'Nothing... only... are... you... pregnant again? That's all I wanted to ask you.'

Janet dropped the tea-towel she was holding and stared at him before she went to sit back at the dining room table. Donald joined her and looked across at her flushed cheeks.

'How did you know I've missed two periods?'

'I suppose a husband should know these things, but I didn't know.'

'Then why have you asked if I'm pregnant?'

'Because it's what Godfrey Warlock said to me yesterday when we interviewed him.'

'I'm at a loss to understand how a man like Godfrey Warlock would waste his time formulating any thoughts about me, let alone to know if I'm pregnant or not.'

'I can visualise a scenario such as this in some households where it would lead to accusations of a wife having an affair. Imagine a man being told by a stranger that he knows his wife is pregnant....'

'... are you suggesting...?'

'... you haven't let me finish. I know you and, more relevantly, I know Godfrey Warlock. I'd defy anyone to find a more odious man alive.'

'How does he know...?'

'... are you pregnant then?'

'Darling, as I said, I've missed two periods, but I'm not sure. I could be, but I haven't taken a pregnancy test or been to see the doctor. What exactly did Godfrey say to you?'

'Well, you can imagine how I felt. The office was full when Godfrey told me. He offered his congratulations to the both of us because Zak is going to have a sister.' She reached across the table and grasped Donald's hands.

'Oh darling, Godfrey Warlock is such a horrible man, but I hope he's correct.'

Donald smiled. 'So do I, darling. As early as tomorrow, either go to see Doctor Patel or get a pregnancy test.'

'I have our neighbour, Barbara Williams, calling tomorrow to have a coffee with me. Why don't you call in at the chemist and bring a pregnancy test kit home with you tomorrow?'

Donald and Janet enjoyed a blissful night together. He awoke early, flung the windows open, and inhaled the fresh country air. He compared the satisfaction of such a simple luxury to the toxic air he'd have breathed in central London.

He strolled across the town, swinging his briefcase, savouring the early morning sunshine. 'Good morning, everybody,' he called as he entered the police station's main reception area. He took his seat in his office, noticing that Veronica wasn't at her desk. She usually got in half an hour before Donald and had a cup of tea waiting for him. 'Perhaps she has the day off today? It was an upsetting episode for her yesterday.' He placed the coroner's file on excess deaths in one of his locked drawers. He wrote down an aide memoire to chat to Nicky and James about the extra deaths incidents. He then remembered Janet had asked him to call at the chemists for the pregnancy test kit. He looked at his watch. It was 9:15, the shops were open now, so he ambled across the pedestrian area to the town's leading chemist. It occurred to him how, in his younger days, he was so naïve and self-conscious. Asking a beautiful young shop assistant for a pregnancy test kit was something he couldn't have done without suffering acute embarrassment.

He sauntered back across the town square. The tranquil scene and peace he felt were instantly shattered. Three loud bangs he recognised as gunfire seemed to emanate from the High Green area. He turned and began jogging through the pedestrian area. Other people had heard the bangs and looked to see where the disturbance had come from. He saw Veronica walking towards him. She didn't see him jogging past her. Her robotic stare caused him to stop. He called after her, but she carried on. His anxious thoughts about who could have fired a gun turned into dread when he saw she held a smoking hand pistol in her left hand. Approaching her stealthily from behind, he reached forward and grabbed the gun. She turned and spoke nonchalantly and as calmly as if Donald had just walked past her office desk. 'Oh, good morning, Inspector, it's a beautiful morning, isn't it?' Donald put the gun in his pocket. His fingers touched the warm barrel as he led Veronica to a nearby bench and sat down with her.

'Veronica, what have you done? Why do you have a gun? The barrel feels warm, so it's been used....'

'... oh that! I've killed Godfrey Warlock.'

'What?! Do you realise what you're saying?'

'Yes, I do, Donald. You told me it's alright to call you by your name, didn't you?'

Donald questioned her state of mind. 'You've killed Godfrey....'

'... three bullets into his chest. I aimed to his left a little, so I know the bullets went straight through his heart. I did it for Adrian. I suppose you'll be arresting me now, Donald, but please don't concern yourself about me. I knew what I was doing.'

He reached for his mobile phone and dialled 999. 'Hello, it's Inspector Lawrence here. I'm in High Green, Cannock town centre. There's been a firearm incident; I need an ambulance asap.' Seated on the bench, he looked across at the bookshop and puzzled that it appeared as on any other day, peaceful and mysterious. He thought of all the readers that usually studied in the shop. He questioned that if Godfrey had been killed, surely they would have reacted and run out of the shop shouting for help? 'Perhaps the shop is empty,' he thought. Reaching for his phone, he pressed the first icon. 'James, where are you?'

'At my office desk, gov....'

'... Get round here *now*. I'm at High Green outside Godfrey's Bookshop with Veronica.'

Recognising the urgency in his gov's voice, Donald heard him panting as he dashed to the side of the bench within two minutes.

'What's happening?' He looked in confusion at Donald and Veronica..

'James! Veronica has shot Godfrey Warlock. She says she's fired three bullets straight into his chest. I've sent for the paramedics, but I'd like you to go and see what mess there is inside.' As James walked over to the shop, Donald spoke to Veronica.

'Where did you get the gun from?'

'The armaments cupboard. The times I've gaped at the cupboard and thought about doing what I've just done. Seeing him yesterday convinced me it was long overdue.' Donald looked around as an ambulance, flashing its blue lights and with a blaring siren, drove through the pedestrian area. Donald waved at two paramedics, who jumped out.

'I'm Inspector Lawrence. I've sent my colleague into the bookshop; there's been a shooting in there.'

'Okay, Inspector. We'll have a look.'

'Let's get you back to the station, Veronica. I need a formal statement from you....'

'... gov!' Donald looked towards the bookshop where James stood on the threshold. He beckoned him to come over. The paramedics rushed past James carrying a stretcher and two bags.

'Veronica, stay here, will you please? I won't be a moment.'

'I'm taking Veronica back to the station, James....'

'... but, gov!' James lowered his voice and moved closer to Donald. He whispered. 'Godfrey Warlock is in there speaking to his readers....'

'... what?! I don't understand!'

'I asked Godfrey about Veronica and he's admitted that she did come into the shop and fire the gun but only at the area behind the counter. He says he was in the reading room watching what she was doing. He said he even had a laugh about it with his friends in there.' As Donald stared incredulously at James, the paramedics pushed past them.

'Inspector, there's nothing untoward in there. We're busy enough; we don't appreciate being called out for nothing.'

'You have my apologies, boys. I've been misinformed. I'd be happy to discuss the matter with your supervisor if you need to account for your time.' The lead paramedic shook his hand, and they left the scene. Veronica watched them go and then looked back at the bookshop. Donald walked back to the bench.

'What's happening, Donald? Why aren't the paramedics taking his body away?'

'Because he's not dead. He's not even hurt. You must have been confused or something....'

'... whatever's going on? I shot him, Donald. He was as close to me as you are now. Three bullets straight into his chest.' Donald shook his head and tried to think of the outcome of what had happened.

'Come back to the station with me. At least you're not going to be charged with murder. Probably only discharging a firearm without a licence?'

'… But, Donald, I watched the bullets penetrate his chest. I saw the holes appear in his waistcoat.'

Donald turned back to James. 'Hang on here for five minutes. I'm taking Veronica back to the station. I'll be back soon.'

James sat on the bench for fifteen minutes, soaking up the sun waiting for Donald to return. From inside the shop, Godfrey watched and was about to confront him but stopped when Donald returned.

'Let's go in there and verify what happened.' James got up and walked with his gov.

Godfrey was down in the reading room when they entered the gloom. 'Veronica said she fired into Godfrey from about here as he stood on the other side of the counter.'

Godfrey watched from the reading room but didn't intervene as Donald walked around the counter. 'James, the gun was warm when I took it from Veronica, so she definitely fired it. There must be evidence here. Where did the bullets go?' Donald opened his phone and used the torch to shine the bright beam of light onto the wood panelling behind the counter. 'Here they are! See, three bullet holes, all within a two-inch radius. She said he was standing here and fired point-blank into his chest. It's where you'd expect the bullets to be had they passed through Godfrey's body.'

'Could the explanation be that she thought it was him, or perhaps she saw a reflection? It's always gloomy in here and it takes a minute for your eyes to adjust. If she came straight in and fired, I'd say she really couldn't be sure what she fired at?'

'You're probably right, James. However, Veronica is so definite that she fired straight into his chest and saw holes appear in his clothes.' James examined the bullet holes.

'We can't do anything else here and I'm not going to grant Godfrey the opportunity of him bringing a charge against Veronica. She's suffered enough because of this man. Let's go! I have another matter that I want to chat with you and Nicky about.'

Walking back through the main office, they noticed Veronica worked at her desk as if nothing had happened. Donald decided not to disturb her and considered work was her best therapy now. With the coroner's report under his arm, he called James and Nicky to go with him to an interview room.

'Would both of you read this coroner's report? I'll be back in five minutes. I'd like your opinion, please?'

'Well?' Donald asked as he re-entered the room and sat down.

Nicky spoke first. 'One hundred and thirty-five excess deaths seem overwhelming, gov. How can we investigate all these cases?'

'We can't! Yet! We must first decide if crimes have been committed. As the coroner has pointed out, there's no proof of that. I suggest each of us take a name at random and investigate. I must emphasise complete confidentiality about this matter. That's why we're down here away from prying eyes and keen ears in the main office. Whenever we are having a conversation about these cases, this is where we'll talk. Superintendent Woodhouse has confided in me and given this file in secrecy. Imagine having a serial killer loose on our patch on top of everything else we're dealing with! Our lives would never be the same again.' Donald pulled two sheets of paper from the file and gave one to each of them. 'Use your mobile phones. Photograph these details. I don't want any loose sheets of paper lying about for anyone else to see. I know your phones are password-protected, so it will maintain confidentiality.'

'How much priority shall we give to this, gov?' James asked.

'Only when you have a spare hour or so. In a normal day's work, other more pressing cases must come first. Remember each one of these addresses has suffered a bereavement, so we need to show sympathy and respect.'

Later that afternoon, as Donald walked home, he reflected upon yet another eventful day. Janet welcomed him home with another delicious meal. Afterwards, they shared a happy time playing with Zak. Donald watched her happiness and appreciated how lucky he was to have such joy in contrast to the misery he saw every day in his work. He suddenly thought about the pregnancy testing kit in the pocket of his suit coat, wondered why Janet hadn't requested it and told her he'd been to the chemist.

'Oh, yes. I forgot all about that. I don't think it's essential, but I'll take it into the bathroom later.'

'Not necessary? Why?'

'Because I think I am pregnant. I should have started my third period today and you know me, you can set your clock by my menstrual cycle....'

'... and?'

'... I've missed again, and I feel different.'

'So, Godfrey may be right?'

'Seems like it.'

'I know this is a wonderful thing for us to celebrate and be happy about, darling. However, I'm getting perturbed about how much of my working day is involved with Godfrey Warlock in one way or another. It's almost as if he has a controlling influence on everybody he's involved with,' Donald went on to explain the disturbing event with Veronica.

'That's so unlike Veronica; she wouldn't hurt a fly.'

'It's Godfrey and his damned bookshop; he infects everybody with evil thoughts and deeds.'

Forty-seven

The psychiatrist, Doctor Jack Branding, had had a few days to read David Shaw's book. He'd put it on his study desk and forgotten all about it. It was only when his landline phone rang and he went into his study to take the call, he remembered the book. He thumbed through the untidy pages while speaking into his phone. The writing at once grabbed his attention, so much so that he made excuses to whomever he was talking to, ended the call, and investigated the book further.

He concluded that Margaret Shaw hadn't exaggerated her claims. The more he read, the more he understood her concerns. He reached for his mobile phone and rang her number.

'Mrs Shaw, it's Doctor Branding here. Can I come and talk to you, please?'

'I knew you'd ring me. David's out at the moment, so now would be a good time.'

Sitting down with her at her dining room table, he opened the book and the loose notes. 'You told me before that your husband is the controller of rail traffic for The West Midland Railway Company.' Margaret nodded. 'That is the fact that disturbs me about this. Ordinarily, you could look at a book and someone's sketches and idle doodling about what they've read. However, David's organised thoughts go way beyond that.'

'I knew I didn't imagine all of this.'

'You were right to seek help. I have several patients with certain conditions who, if they started to tell me they intended to set off a nuclear explosion, I would simply attribute their delusions to their condition and the medication they were taking. Your husband's ambitions are real and planned. In his position with the railway company, he has the capability to bring this about. I'm no expert at explosives or nuclear fission, but all the ingredients seem to be there. Waste nuclear fuel being stored at the railway sidings. His comprehensive research on how the waste is infinitely more radioactive spread over a large area and his ability to control the rail traffic. The only thing missing is how he'd create an explosion large enough to detonate nuclear fuel. The book details several ideas on how to do that. Something has to be done about this before he tries to carry out his plan.'

'What do you suggest?'

'Taking all this to the authorities….'

'… who?'

'In the first instance, I'd suggest the police here in Cannock. After that, it would be up to them. There must be some sort of civil defence department at a county or regional level that deals with this sort of thing. From what we read in the press and see on television these days, this case classifies as a major terrorism threat. Perhaps this is a matter for police officers at national level to get involved with. The new Inspector at the Cannock police station, I understand, came from Scotland Yard. I'm sure he'll know what to do.'

'Doctor, if I turned up at the police station with all this, I'm pretty certain they'll dismiss me as a disturbed woman with delusions. I suspect you thought that yourself when you first met me? It would be far better if you presented this to them.'

'I think you're right. There's no time like the present….'

'… David is due back in about half an hour….'

'We'll go now!'

Doctor Branding had theorised with Margaret Shaw that the only thing missing from her husband's plan was how to create an explosion. As his wife accompanied the doctor to the police station, David was piecing together the scheme's final elements.

Over the past months, a planning application had been submitted to the local council in East Staffordshire for a new hard rock quarry. The council had allowed the proposal and the mining company was busy setting up the new venture. The only viable method to extract hard igneous rocks was by using explosives to shatter the insitu strata, enabling heavy-duty machines to dig away at the resulting rubble. The favoured explosive was Semtex-H. It was stable at average temperatures and could easily be transported without fear of self-ignition, as was the risk with nitro-glycerine. The Semtex-H was scheduled to be transported by rail from the manufacturing factory in Cornwall to the new quarry site in East Staffordshire. The route would take the train through the English shire counties, to Birmingham and then on to Derby.

233

It was sheer coincidence that explosives would be travelling by rail so close to Cannock. David didn't consider that aspect for a second. He saw it was providence and a higher all-seeing authority had ordained it. It would be a simple matter for him to divert the train from the Birmingham-Derby route to travel via Cannock. The ultimate piece of his plan was coming into place.

'We must see Inspector Lawrence as a matter of urgency,' Doctor Branding explained to Cannock police station's officious receptionist.

'I'm sorry, the inspector is busy and can't see people without an appointment....'

'... you don't understand the importance of....'

'Everybody who comes here has important business, sir....'

'We'll wait!'

'I'm afraid I can't allow that, sir. For security reasons, you understand. We can't have people coming in here and having free rein to wander around the building. I can't continually keep a watch over you; I have my work to do and we are short-staffed. As you can see, the main doors into the inner offices have security codes, but what's stopping you from barging through when someone else is coming through the door? No, I can't allow it. Give me your number and I'll see that Inspector Lawrence gets it and we'll contact you for an appointment.'

'For God's sake, woman, this is an emergency. I'm Doctor Branding from the psychiatric department at Cannock Hospital. There could be a nuclear explosion!' The receptionist stared blankly at him before speaking into the telephone and microphone wrapped around her head. 'Giles, could you come to reception, please? I have a security issue.'

Within a few seconds, a tall, burly police sergeant came through the security door. 'What's the problem, Jean?'

She pointed to Doctor Branding. 'These people are from the psychiatric department at Cannock Hospital. He says there's going to be a nuclear explosion.'

The sergeant gazed at the doctor and Margaret and assumed a conciliatory tone. 'Now come on, let's be reasonable. We're busy at this police station and we can't afford to waste our time on such ridiculous matters. Why don't you move on and go back to the hospital? I'm sure that....'

'… Sergeant, you don't understand! I'm a doctor and I have proof here that a man living here in Cannock plans to detonate a nuclear explosion.' He brandished the book before him.

The sergeant's tone of voice changed. 'Now look here, I've explained once and I'm not going to repeat myself. If you don't move on, I'll have to arrest you for wasting police time. Now come on, be reasonable people and go.' He moved to the door and held it open for them.

'We're not going, sergeant, until we see Inspector Lawrence. You'll have to arrest us if that's the only way we can see him.' The sergeant raised his eyes to the ceiling and muttered.

'There's never a dull moment these days.'

'Here's my card; please take it to the inspector.'

'Come with me, please.' The sergeant pressed the door's security code and ushered them through. He spoke into his collar radio. 'Stuart, I could do with some help here. I'm taking a couple of jokers downstairs into room twenty-six. They reckon there's going to be a nuclear bomb exploding over the town. Bring some charge sheets with you.'

'You're arresting us? That's preposterous!' the doctor shouted.'

'You're being so stupid!' Margaret screamed.

Their raised voices travelled up the stairs and permeated into the general office where Sergeant Stuart Wright sat near James and Nicky.

'What's going on?' James asked as Donald came out of his office, also enquiring what the commotion was about. Stuart, holding some charge sheets was going through the door; he turned and explained. 'The station sergeant has asked me to help him in reception. There's a couple of clowns who reckon a nuclear bomb is about to explode over the town. I'm taking some charge sheets down. More folks wasting our time.'

'Oh! Is that all?' Donald sarcastically dismissed the sergeant's words and returned to his office to study more details of the coroner's report on excess deaths.

Doctor Branding wasn't going to be fobbed off lightly; he started shouting more loudly.

'I demand to see Inspector Lawrence. Inspector, I know you're in there somewhere. I'm Doctor Branding from Cannock Hospital. I must speak to you.'

'Stop that! Be quiet, can't you?' the station sergeant shouted equally loudly.

'Inspector Lawrence!' Margaret joined in the shouting.

'Bloody hell!' Donald muttered as he took a slurp of coffee that Veronica had placed on his desk.

'It doesn't look as if they're going away, Donald.' Her voice echoed the resignation he felt.

'I'd better go and see what they want, or none of us will get any peace.' Donald ambled down the stairs to where the station sergeant and Sergeant Wright took Margaret and Doctor Branding down to the basement. 'Hang on, Giles, Stuart. Take them to an interview room and I'll have a chat with them.'

'Are you Inspector Lawrence?'

'Yes, I am, and you're creating one hell of a disturbance in my police station.'

Jack Branding held his hand towards Donald. 'I'm Doctor Branding from Cannock Hospital and this is…'

'… Hang on! Let's take a seat in the interview room where we can all calm down.'

Donald ushered them into the room and turned to Giles. 'Stay outside the door, just in case they cut up rough, will you please, sergeant?

Jack overheard. 'You'll be having no trouble from us, Inspector. We only want you to hear what we have to say.' They sat down as the station sergeant stood guard on the door, keeping his ears receptive to the slightest disturbance.

For the next thirty minutes, the station sergeant didn't hear any more raised voices. His legs started aching. He was getting bored standing outside the door, watching other officers going about their everyday business. Then the door opened, and he stood aside.

'I'm sorry you've had to stand there, Giles. Everything's okay now. Go about your normal business, and thank you.'

Donald stood with Doctor Branding and Margaret. 'I can see now why you considered the matter so urgent. Thank you for bringing this to my attention. As I said to you in there, this isn't my area of expertise, but I'll get in touch straight away with my superiors at County headquarters. I'll keep the book and the notes if I may?' He held the book aloft.

'No problem, Inspector. If David misses it, I'll have to say he's lost it somewhere,' Margaret said as they started to leave. They all turned when they heard Jean, the officious receptionist, answer a telephone enquiry in a facetious, almost unfriendly voice. 'Yes! Cannock police station. How may I help you? Be quick, because we're extremely busy.'

As Donald climbed the stairs back to his office, he reminded himself at some point when they were all less busy, he would get a new receptionist who promoted a friendlier, helpful face to the public rather than an organisation that viewed each enquiry as if it was a burden and they shouldn't be contacting the police station.

As Donald walked through the general office, Nicky and James discussed the two sheets of paper Donald had given them. 'Two different deaths with one common factor, their doctor was Anwar Patel. I'm suggesting two heads are better than one, Nicky. What do you think if we go together to each property? We can each have our own opinion on what we find.' Nicky nodded.

After walking down a long asphalted driveway, they rang the bell of a smart, sprawling bungalow in the south of the town. A middle-aged woman answered. 'Yes...!' Donald explained who they were. '... and why are you here?'

'We understand you've recently suffered a bereavement...?'

'... my father, Bill Weatherall. He was eighty-five; he died a month ago. Why should the police be asking about him?'

'It's purely routine, madam. It's the policy of police departments these days to check that....'

'... please come in. I don't want to discuss my late father on the doorstep. There are too many prying eyes and ears.' She motioned with her head to the bungalow next door. 'Sit yourselves down. Would you like a cup of tea; I'm about to have one.'

'That sounds wonderful. Yes, please. Milk and one sugar in each, please,' Nicky asked as James looked through the floor to ceiling window that looked out over the rear garden.

'You have a lovely garden, Mrs... Er!'

'Jane Jones. William - Bill was my father. We've lived together for the past ten years since my husband died,' she called from the kitchen. In less than two minutes, they sat drinking their tea.

'Had your father been ill?' Nicky asked.

'Yes, he had. For the past seven years; he had been receiving treatment for prostate cancer.'

'... and Doctor Anwar Patel was his doctor?'

'Yes! Wonderful Doctor Patel. He'd done such a good job of looking after Dad; his prostate problem had cleared up. That's what's so upsetting; he'd got over the worst. He took all that chemotherapy and those drugs. He was looking forward to his last years with no serious problems other than what comes to us all through age.' She smiled. 'Dad used to make the best of the situation. My Dad was bald. He joked that was the worst bit about the chemo, that it made his hair fall out.' She reached for her handkerchief and held it to her nose. 'I'm sorry, it's still so raw. I miss him so much.' Nicky looked at James, sad to be causing Mrs Jones this upset.

'If he was doing so well, how did your father die?'

'I'll never forget. It was only another ordinary day. Dad had been out in the garden, pruning the roses. I was watching him from the kitchen window. He looked so well, fit, and happy. Then Doctor Patel called. He said he was passing and just wanted to see how Dad was doing. I knocked on the window and called him in. Dad sat where you are now.' She motioned her head to James. 'I went upstairs to change the beds; after a couple of minutes I heard the doctor call. When I came down, my dear father had passed away. The doc said he'd had a massive heart attack. When I look back at it now, it was as if the doctor was the grim reaper. You know the mythical devil's associate who comes to collect souls when someone passes away. Up until the doctor called, he'd been fit and well.'

'Did you ask Doctor Patel if he'd seen the signs beforehand? I understand when someone has a heart attack, there are warning signs, like pains in the joints, sweating and rapid pulse with a flushed face? Was he showing any of those signs before you went upstairs?'

'No! Not any of those things. As I said, only a few minutes before, he'd been in the garden. At least the doctor told me Dad went peacefully with no pain or distress. The doc called for an ambulance and he left before it arrived. He'd given me a written certificate describing how he'd passed away. I sat there looking at Dad, still in his gardening clothes. Only minutes earlier he'd been waving to me from the garden. There was no change in his expression; his face wasn't contorted as if he'd been in pain. He still had some colour in his cheeks. It was as if he'd nodded off for a quick nap.'

As Donald drove to the next property, Nicky wrote in her notebook Jane Jones' account of how her father, Bill Weatherall, had passed away.

'Who's the next one?' James asked as he pulled up outside a block of flats.

'Patrick Holloway, a sixty-three-year-old college lecturer. He'd been on sick leave for three months receiving regular drugs for kidney problems. For the last month of his life he'd begun to receive kidney dialysis at Cannock hospital. His doctor was Anwar Patel.'

James and Nicky learned from his widow, Mary, that Patrick had visited the hospital to receive his usual dialysis dose. 'He even walked there; he was so fit and well,' Mary explained.

'He'd been gone a bit longer than usual when I received a phone call from the hospital telling me Patrick had passed away. I was not to be unduly alarmed at how he'd died because Doctor Patel had been with him when it happened.'

As they drove away, Nicky muttered as she wrote in her notebook. 'Both deaths occurred to relatively fit and healthy men. Both men died in the presence of Doctor Patel. I wonder how many more of the one hundred and thirty-three other cases will have a similar outcome?'

James parked the car, and they walked through the town centre back to the police station. They found they could hardly move. The pedestrian area had been taken over by Hells Angels on motorcycles. In front of every shop, all around the war memorial railings, greasy oil-spilling bikes and scramblers were parked. Men of all ages clad in dark leather coats sat around, drinking beer. Nicky and James looked towards High Green, where Godfrey was outside his shop, talking and laughing with the men. The noise from the engines being revved was deafening. The town square resembled a jumble sale with scattered litter and leftover food wrappers being blown about. Empty beer cans rolled around the sloping paved area. More disturbing and disgusting, they had to navigate around piles of human defecation left in the corners of the paved areas. The damp patches and smells of urine wafted across the town. Entering the office, they asked what was going on? Donald poked his head out of his office. 'You may well ask! It's Godfrey Warlock again. Apparently, he's organised a convention of Hell's Angel's motorcyclists to converge upon Cannock. There's no aspect of life in this town where he doesn't have a malign influence.'

'Doesn't this sort of gathering have to be licensed?' Nicky asked.

'Yes, it does. I've enquired at the council house and lo and behold, a licence was issued three weeks ago to Doctor Godfrey Warlock. His tentacles even extend to the town council now.'

Forty-eight

Dariusz and Vlad Krueger congratulated themselves on their recent good fortune. 'It's been a wonderful month, bruv,' Vlad patted his elder brother on the back. 'That was a good move of yours getting rid of that hoodlum, Vic Magwicj from Shoreditch. We control all his pimps and prostitutes now and that gambling joint behind Saint Martins Church. It's a pity our boy, Freddie, made such a mess of poor old Vic, though. It must have been a sorry sight for his widow to find his head on her pillow....'

'Ha! ha! ha!' Dariusz laughed and pursed his lips in a self-complimentary mode. 'Normally that bitch would have been happy to see his head there; shame there wasn't anything else, eh?'

'Think of the surprise she must have had when she felt down the bed for his bits?' Vlad echoed his brother's laughter.

'Inspirational, that's what it was, bruv, and do you know what gave me the idea?'

'You're gonna tell me, aren't you?'

'Our Sissie's little girl, Miranda.'

'As usual, the workings of your mind baffle me, dear bruv.'

'Oranges and lemons, of course!' Vlad looked more confused than ever.

'The nursery rhyme song, 'Oranges and Lemons.'

'You've lost me on this one.'

'Miranda was singing as she played with her dollies. You don't listen to the little things in life, bruv; that's always been your trouble.'

Darius started singing in his deep bass baritone range.

'Oranges and lemons say the bells of Saint Clément's.

You owe me five farthings, say the bells of Saint Martin's. The bastard owed us, didn't he! And the gambling joint is behind Saint Martin's church.'

Vlad nodded, trying to follow his reasoning.

'When will you pay me, say the bells at Old Bailey?

240

When I grow rich, say the bells at Shoreditch. That's where Vic lived, wasn't it? That back alley behind Shoreditch market?'

'Yeah!' Vlad's eyes lit up.

'When will that be? Say the bells of Stepney.
I do not know, says the great bell at Bow.
Here comes a candle to light you to bed, and here comes a chopper to chop off your head.'

Dariusz carried on even though he couldn't hear himself for Vlad's childish laughter.

'Chip chop chip chop, the last man is dead.'

'... and you got Freddie to chop off Vic's head. That's brilliant, bruv. 'ere, we're going to his funeral, aren't we?'

'Of course we are! We need to pay our respects to his grieving family, so they can see who their new Godfathers are.'

'Where's his send-off being held?'

'At Shoreditch Church, of course. It adds to the nursery rhyme, doesn't it? And guess what song I've asked the bell ringers to play? Well, I've not asked. As it happens, the Captain of the bell tower is one of ours.'

'How about 'Happiness', that Ken Dodd song?'

'You've no finesse or imagination, bruv. *Oranges and lemons,* of course.'

They stood at Vic's graveside in their black leathers and obscure black sunglasses. Their glum faces suggested to anyone watching the ceremony that they were the chief mourners. Their imposing presence seemed to dwarf Vic's family stooped in grief. Dariusz lifted his head and swallowed his smile as Oranges and Lemons cheerfully rang out across the environs of Shoreditch. Trying to enforce their physical presence on Vic's colleagues who'd managed his illegal empire, they didn't see a willowy figure, also dressed in black, chatting at the rear of the ceremony.

'You must feel very bitter at his passing,' Godfrey suggested to Vic's former right-hand man, Barry Goldstraw. 'I'm sure you have your own ideas about who was responsible.'

'Aye, we know alright,' Barry whispered menacingly in his Scottish accent. Together with Godfrey, they both lifted their heads and gazed across the throng of mourners at Dariusz and Vlad. 'What goes around, comes around. Mark my words, it won't be too long before my Elspeth will be getting this funeral suit out of the wardrobe again.' His hot, threatening breath caused his huge opaque glasses to steam up.

'They've become too controlling and a little too big for their boots, haven't they?' Godfrey muttered out of the side of his mouth as Vic's coffin was lowered into the ground.

'It's time for a change, my friend. Thanks for your help. If only I knew where their headquarters were?'

Although they couldn't see each other's eyes, Godfrey exchanged stares with Barry. 'It beggar's belief that you don't eat much in Spitalfields these days. You must be blind!'

Barry smiled and at once knew to what Godfrey referred. He took a step forward to join the queue to scatter earth on the coffin but turned to shake his hand. However, Godfrey had gone.

Barry Goldstraw had been incarcerated in Pentonville for twelve of the thirty-one years of his troubled life. As an uncontrollable teenager in the East End of London, he'd knifed a rival gang boss in a back alley. The police suggested a new Jack the Ripper had been unleashed in Whitechapel. The Metropolitan police officers considered the murder scene as one of the most gruesome they had investigated. Body parts, trails of intestines and the man's severed head were scattered over several streets and alleyways. Since his release from prison, he'd been a good boy and gathered around him a new regime to rival that of the Krueger brothers.

Ever since Harry Stevens' demise at The Ritz Hotel in Mayfair, Barry owed the Krueger brothers some payback. Harry had been one of his associates and most trusted colleague when a more ruthless approach was needed to enforce their empire. Now his boss and mentor, Vic Magwicj, had met the same fate.

After throwing a fistful of soil onto Vic's coffin, Barry turned and shook hands with Dariusz and Vlad. Their heads remained unmoved. The darkened glasses concealed the quick movements of their eyes, appraising each other as colleagues from both sides looked on as the momentous meeting of the two rival criminal realms. Godfrey's witty advice had revitalised Barry's sharp mind, and he was able to visualise their headquarters. 'You think you're safe from any harm, don't you? I know where you hang out!' he thought as he stared at Dariusz.

Dariusz returned similar feelings as their black leather gloved hands clasped together. 'You look like another upstart to me, like your late friend, Vic.' He sneered at the unsightly scar that ran from the corner of Barry's mouth to his left ear, the trophy he'd earned from the man he'd served twelve years in Pentonville for.

The Krueger brothers knew they had nothing to fear. An army of faithful underlings formed tiers of protection through which an optimistic intruder could never pass. Their impenetrable lair lay at the rear of an attractive public house called 'The Blind Beggar' in Spitalfields. No one ever suspected that the fashionable pub and restaurant concealed the entrance to Dariusz and Vlad's headquarters. Even detectives from the Fraud Squad at New Scotland Yard had dined there with their families, completely ignorant that two of their most infamous antagonists lounged within a few yards of where they ate.

As the brothers examined deeds of new properties transferred to their extensive asset portfolio, they took mouthfuls of pizza delivered from the pub's kitchen. The fast food was a favoured delicacy of theirs, carrying on their parents' passion from Lithuania's old country. A diner eating pizza was classed as the aristocracy. Typical peasants' food was cheap vegetables usually fed to cattle, or tripe stew and dumplings made from pigs' eyes.

Loyalty was skin deep where criminal regimes were concerned. There was a price for everything, and every item had its value. Commitment to previous respected employers earned even less regard when enormous sums of cash, tied in bundles of fifty-pound notes, changed hands. Barry's associate made a reservation at The Blind Beggar for his boss and his wife, Elspeth, to dine and celebrate their wedding anniversary. Most of their earlier anniversaries had been celebrated apart. He ate in Pentonville's unhygienic mess and she in the company of her secret lover. Elspeth eyed her husband suspiciously when she'd only recently heard that her lover had died. He'd been found floating face down in the polluted waters of Shoreditch's overflow channel that discharged into the Thames. Barry was more interested in the pub's layout than anything the company of his unfaithful wife could offer. Her presence was only for show to deter the Krueger brothers' minions' suspicions, whom he knew were watching.

It wasn't until he left the pub that he noticed the one item that formulated the start of a plan of how he would bring about the brothers' downfall. An innocuous notice pinned to a stout timber column propping up the entrance porch's tiled roof, held an advertisement. The restaurant wanted a kitchen assistant to carry meals from the kitchen out into the main pub, preferably an attractive young woman. Barry's sickly smile extended as far as his colossal scar allowed his face to stretch. He knew precisely who the successful applicant for such an important job would be.

Deirdre Patterson was the wayward daughter of one of his associates. At twenty years of age, her shapely figure and flirtatious persona had already been unceremoniously sculptured into the adult world by Barry's callous hands and voracious sexual appetite. Deirdre had merely become one of his many mistresses to which he applied the drug Rohypnol before bedding them. The drug is a potent tranquillizer, sometimes used as an anaesthetic before surgery in countries in South America. In the western world, it had become known as a date-rape drug.

The paltry sum of ten pounds per hour wages she was offered to begin work at The Blind Beggar didn't even cater sufficiently for her habit of smoking hashish. The tips from admiring customers only partly covered her burgeoning alcoholism from drinking malt whiskey. By undoing more of the buttons on her blouse and flashing more cleavage to appreciative male diners, she considered three bottles a week of Tennessee bourbon a luxury. The manager of the restaurant didn't mind her flirtatious behaviour one jot. Since she'd started at the pub, his till receipts had nearly doubled.

Dierdre's performance and conduct were going ahead precisely as Barry had planned and paid her to do. Behind her skittish exterior, she owned a sharp mind and was able to progress to the next stage of her lover's plan. Barry and six of his henchmen had made reservations and sat eating in the restaurant. Barry waited until the last of strangers left their tables, and he watched Deirdre. She had been watching Bruno, the chef, preparing unique pizza dishes, and they were ready to be taken through the door into the rear of the pub. She surmised the meals were for the Krueger brothers. Barry had given Deirdre copious amounts of Rohypnol. As Bruno placed the meals on the brothers' trays, she waited until his back was turned and poured the transparent, tasteless liquid over the food. Diedre walked into the restaurant and looked back to see Bruno carry the trays through the door. She looked at her watch. The drug's efficacy would assume maximum effect in ten minutes. Barry also counted down the time before looking around to see where the Krueger's guards were. Two were sitting outside under the porch, smoking their cigarettes. Three more were seated at the bar drinking beer. Barry assumed there would be more on the other side of the rear door. He waited until ten minutes had elapsed and gave the signal.

Two men went outside. Using their silenced handguns, they efficiently shot the guards through the forehead. With cigarettes still sticking from their mouths, their bodies were pulled out of sight behind the porch. The 'open' sign was turned to display 'closed', and Barry's men locked the door. The three men seated at the bar heard the door being locked and only had time to half turn before they too received 19mm bullets to the back of their necks. Barry quickly dealt with Bruno, the chef, with one blow to the side of his head with his pistol. A wound opened where his right ear used to be. They dragged the three other bodies behind the bar to lie with Bruno in a tangled heap.

Barry and his six thugs regrouped outside the door that led into the Krueger's quarters. They all held their pistols in front of them and rushed through when Barry flung the door open. Three men guarding another internal door had no time to react, and they too received bullets penetrating their brains. There was now only a thin wooden interior door separating the Krueger brothers from Barry. He instructed two men to re-enter the restaurant, join Dierdre, turn off the lights, and stand guard if anyone came. One other was to wait outside the door that remained closed. Barry carefully turned the handle and gently pulled open the door. Pointing his pistol before him, he peered around the door jamb. The first thing he noticed in the brightly lit room was the dining table holding two half-eaten pizzas and an unopened bottle of white wine. He heard someone moaning and looked to the floor. Dariusz and Vlad lay slumped on the carpet. Barry, emboldened by what he saw, rushed into the room followed by his other men. 'Check there's no other way out, boys. Let's get these two pieces of shit onto the settee. I'm sure they'll be more comfortable there.'

Dariusz and Vlad were conscious but had no control over their limbs or speech. Their wild eyes darted from side to side, revealing the terror they felt in their helpless situation. Barry turned to his remaining two men. 'Leave me with them, boys. I have a personal score to settle. I'll shout if I need help.' Nonchalantly, he reached for the corkscrew, opened the bottle of Riesling, poured himself a glass and sat opposite the brothers in an armchair. Using the date rape drug before with girlfriends, he knew what the brothers could and couldn't do. He was in complete control, and they were helpless.

Barry started speaking, and Dariusz' eyes focussed on him. 'I meant to ask you; did you enjoy that meal at The Ritz? No? Yes? Oh, of course, you can't answer, can you? Never mind. Whatever. It must have been bloody expensive. Did you know that Harry Stevens was a good friend of mine? So, you can imagine how I felt when I learned you two prize pieces of stale turd-roll left him in a heap on the toilet floor. What I can't understand is how you squirmed out of the Met's clutches over that killing, but you know you're not going to escape this, don't you?' Vlad uttered a few moans.

Barry turned to him. 'Hello Vladimir, do you want to go first then, is that what you're asking me?' Barry pulled a razor-sharp surgical scalpel from his back pocket. He pulled the plastic protective cover from the blade. The bright ceiling lights reflected from the stainless steel blade as Barry drew it across Vlad's right cheek. Vlad moaned again. 'I'm so sorry. Is that a closer shave than you're used to?' Barry watched the bright red blood run down his neck and start soaking into his yellow and green striped tee-shirt. 'Do you know I've created a charming touch to send you back to your motherland, Vlad? You should be grateful that your rotten, stinking body will be draped in your patriotic colours. Your national flag is red, yellow, and green stripes, isn't it?'

'You both know that Vic Magwicj was also a good friend of mine ...' Barry took another slurp of wine. '... but Dariusz can pay for his murder, while you Vladimir Krueger... Oh, I'm sick of you hanging about.' Barry reached forward, dug the scalpel blade under his right ear, and slowly drew it across his neck. He didn't stop until the blade touched his left ear. He felt Vlad's oesophagus and trachea offer brief resistance as they divided into two pieces. His larynx also showed brief defiance but was powerless to prevent the surgical scalpel from slicing through. Barry's face and chest were sprayed with Vlad's blood as he slumped forward. His last breath gurgled through his trachea, deluged with blood.

'Look what I've done to your younger brother, Dariusz. My mother always told me I haven't got much patience. I get bored, you see, and I've got a special date with your lovely waitress, Deirdre, this evening. I don't want to keep her waiting, and I can't expect to get my leg over, dressed like this, now can I?'

Barry held the blood-stained blade in front of Dariusz's eyes. 'I'll not keep you long. In case you're wondering how I found you, we have our mutual friend, Godfrey Warlock, to thank. I don't think you saw him at Vic's funeral, did you?' Barry looked into his eyes. He pushed the scalpel's point into his neck and drew it first to the left and then to the right causing two parallel cuts that sprayed blood over Barry's face and clothes. He watched Dariusz' eyes cease looking terrified. They stopped moving and stared straight ahead, but Barry knew they couldn't see anything anymore. As he left the room, he gazed back at the brothers sitting side by side on their blood-drenched settee. 'Bloody foreigners,' he muttered.

Forty-nine

A mist hung over Spitalfields as the police car pulled up in The Blind Beggar's car park.

'It's the Krueger brothers. It's no loss, is it! They haven't escaped justice for long,' Sergeant Eric Chambers commented to his Inspector.

'Is this really justice, Eric? It's an execution! Bloody hell, it's hot in here; those electric fires are turned up to maximum.'

'I had no idea we'd find the Kruegers here when I had that phone tip-off.' Eric held a handkerchief over his nose and mouth as he peered at Dariusz and Vlad's partly decomposing bodies. He waved away some blue-bottle flies that were buzzing around the congealed blood. 'I think whoever did this wanted their bodies to rot away quicker than normal. Phew, it stinks in here, open the windows, gov.'

'Do you know who rang you?'

'Nah! Some woman's voice yelling into the phone, get your arses down to The Blind Beggar in Spitalfields. You'll be pleased with what you find,' she said.

'Are we pleased?'

'We have to be, Inspector. A couple of months ago they were due to stand trial for Harry Steven's murder and got away with it. Look at them now! I, for one, am not sorry. They caused too much suffering and folks going missing without a trace from the East End for there to be any sympathy for them.' The police officers stood aside as white-coated scene of crime officers flooded the room. 'There's the probable murder weapon, boys.' Eric pointed to the scalpel stuck to the blood-soaked carpet.

'I wonder how many bodies form part of concrete flyovers because of the Krueger's.'

'I guess society will never know until they're demolished in sixty or seventy years?' Eric scoffed.

'We've done all we can here; let's get back to The Yard and type up the report. We can close the Krueger's file for good then.'

Seated back at his desk, Eric looked at the time. 'Hmm, it's almost lunchtime. I wonder if Lucy's about?' He rang her number. 'Lucy, I'm glad I caught you. What are you doing for lunch?'

'I was just going around the corner for a salad at the bistro, *La Vista,* in Horse Guard's Avenue. Why?'

'I wondered if you'd like some company…?'

'… Eric, the last time we ate together you made it quite plain that you didn't trust me.'

'… Well, I have some news for you that will perk your ears up.'

'Okay! I'm going now, so I'll see you there in say… five minutes.'

'I'm on my way.'

'Two salads and two glasses of Chianti, please,' Eric asked the waitress. Eric and Lucy had arrived at *La Vista* at the same time.

'How are you? Are you busy?' Lucy asked quickly, to ease the tension between them.

'I'm fine! Before this morning, things have been quieter than normal just lately.'

'But…?'

'… It's all changed now.'

'What's happened to change your routine, then?'

'The Krueger brothers….'

'… look, Eric, I haven't come here to have my lunch ruined listening to you going on about them. I said all I had to….'

'… they're brown bread!' Lucy was stunned and opened her mouth to speak but stopped.

'I thought that would pull you up a bit.' Lucy's immediate thoughts were how it would affect the situation of keeping Godfrey Warlock's book. She looked to the ceiling before taking a massive gulp of wine.

'Don't you want to know how, why, when?'

'I can see you're dying to tell me.'

'I had an anonymous tip-off telling me to get down to The Blind Beggar at Spitalfields. Both were sitting there on their expensive upholstered settee, ruined with their own blood. Both with their throats cut.'

'Any idea who's done it?'

'None at all. The SOCO boys are still there as we speak. They may come up with something, but I doubt it.'

'It doesn't sound as if you're going to try too hard to find out?'

'Whoever it was has done us a favour, and you!' Eric looked accusingly at her. Lucy eyed him with suspicion.

'Come on; level with me, Lucy. Everybody at The Yard knows you accessed their file on the hard drive, and everybody has their own ideas why. What everybody doesn't know, because I've kept it to myself, are the other facts....'

'... other facts?' Lucy nervously took another drink of wine before twisting her fork into her salad, but suddenly not feeling hungry.

'Does the name Amy Bagshot mean anything to you?' Lucy swallowed.

'Never heard of her....'

'Doris Sparkes' flatmate, Dolores, told me a blonde-haired young woman named Amy Bagshot organised Doris's release from the Witness Protection Programme. She couldn't tell me much more about her because she always wore a large coat. Oh yes, there was one other fact, Amy told her she was a police officer ...'

'Why are you telling me this, Eric?' He carried on as if Lucy hadn't spoken.

'... I keep asking myself, why did Amy want to see The Krueger brothers released? More pertinently, how did Amy know that Doris Sparkes was the only witness against them? The only way that could happen was if Amy had access to the Krueger's criminal files on Scotland Yard's computer hard drive.' Eric could see how uncomfortable Lucy was becoming.

'Then the most astounding fact of this whole saga is how she knew where Doris was, sequestered with a new identity and telephone number? That information was confined to three mobile phone numbers, mine, my immediate Inspector, and Superintendent Basil Spence. I think back to the conversation we had when dining in Giacomo's. Do you remember, Lucy?'

'No! It's been a while....'

'... I'll remind you. It was about the passwords we use on our personal mobile phones. I remember I had drunk more wine than I usually do and needed the gents. This was after I'd told you my password was my police number. It doesn't take a brain surgeon to figure out how easy it was to find this number on Scotland Yard files. I left my phone on the table for how long, Lucy?' She looked blankly at him.

'You were a fast worker. I was only gone for two minutes.' Eric stopped talking, and they stared at each other. Lucy was unsure how to go ahead. She knew Eric had deduced that she had committed several crimes in bringing about the Krueger's release. As Lucy gazed at him, she understood he held her entire future at Scotland Yard in his hands. She opened her mouth to plead with him. Eric reached over and put his finger to her lips and then to his own and issued, 'Shh!' He grimaced.

'I don't really want to know why; except to say, I'm disappointed! You obviously used me when we ate in the staff restaurant and you knew I'd ask you out to dinner. We both know the rest.' A heavy silence enveloped the secluded table in *La Vista*.

'I'm sorry....'

'Shh! I don't want, or need, to know. I have to tell you, I really fancied you – still fancy you! That's why I'm talking to you now in this manner and not arresting you.'

'I don't understand?'

Eric stood and opened his coat. Lucy gasped and held her hand to her face. 'Yes, I'm wired to record our conversation. The Super and my Inspector *suspect* it could be you who brought about the Krueger's charges being dropped. I emphasise the word suspect, because without me telling them what I know, that's all it will ever be, only their suspicions. They suggested I wear this wire to either eliminate you or get evidence incriminating you.'

'So, why have you stopped me talking?'

'Because I don't want you to implicate yourself.' Lucy's mouth gaped open. Eric smiled and sat down again. 'Anyway, relax, I haven't turned the wire on. So, there's no recording being made.'

'Why?'

'Because you've asked that question, it's obvious that you don't feel the same about me as I do you, but never mind.'

'Eh?' Lucy's guilt was tempered with a growing realisation of Eric's deep feelings for her.

'The Krueger brothers are dead. For whatever reason, they were able to wriggle out of previous charges so none of it matters anymore. For your information, my Inspector has closed their file for now. Officially we're actively seeking their killers, but we have far more critical cases we're working on. We haven't touched our salads; shall we?' he motioned to their plates.

For the following ten minutes, they ate and drank in silence. Lucy was the last to finish. As she pushed away her empty plate, she noticed he'd already finished and was watching her.

'Shall we walk back to The Yard?'

Lucy nodded, but hesitated to get up. 'Eric, I, er ...!'

'… You don't have to say anything.'

'… but I do! I'm sorry I've let you down….'

He shrugged his shoulders, 'That's life! That's the way the cookie crumbles, some American cop said somewhere?'

'It doesn't have to be.'

'What are you saying?'

'I'm not sure, but I'd like to make it up to you. I'd also like to try to explain how and why things went the way they did.'

'You don't have to….'

'I know! How about we eat at Giacomo's again, only this time there'll be no false motives or pre-judged hidden agenda, other than…?' Eric's wide-eyed stare betrayed his surprise.

'… enjoying each other's company.' Eric stared at her in surprise and hope.

'Um! Er! You don't realise how much I'd like that.'

'Perhaps I do? I'd like that too.' Eric couldn't know, but Lucy had been swept off her feet. She hadn't really looked closely at him before for any reason other than he was a fall guy. She now saw a handsome, capable, intelligent, loyal man, whom she suspected was in love with her. Why else would he have done what he'd done? He reached across and briefly held her hand and grinned.

'I'll arrange a table. When?'

'As soon as you like.'

'Tomorrow evening. I'll come and pick you up. I don't want you travelling across London on buses or trains and in taxis.'

They both walked jauntily back to Scotland Yard and felt reluctant to part company when they went to their separate offices. He reported to his Inspector. 'No joy, gov. Detective Sergeant Lucy Barnes is completely in the clear.'

Lucy was met with a sealed letter on her desk. She ran her paperknife through the heavily gummed seal, noticing the postmark was Staffordshire. It was from Godfrey Warlock.

Godfrey's Bookshop
High Green
Cannock
Staffordshire.
WS11 1SS

My dear Lucy,
I hope you are keeping well and still enjoying 'The Posthumous Papers of the Pickwick Club'?
Igorovitch Bild-Krueger's immigration papers are here for you to sign and add your comments. So, as soon as convenient for you, I'll look forward to your visit.
I know you'll have heard by now about the unfortunate demise of the Krueger brothers. I know my intervention will have saved you some embarrassment with The Metropolitan Police, your employers.
Your friend
Doctor Godfrey Warlock

Lucy read the letter before folding it and concealing it in her briefcase. 'What does he mean, his *intervention in the death of the Krueger brothers?*' she thought. She picked up her phone to ring Donald and Janet to see if it would be convenient for her to stay with them again.

Fifty

The day after Lucy opened her mail in Scotland Yard, Godfrey opened a parcel in his bookshop. He smiled. 'I knew Dariusz had no intention of helping me to get a gun,' he thought. Then murmured, 'It shows what an excellent judge of character I am by putting my trust in Barry Goldstraw.' Godfrey had requested the favour at Vic Magwicj's funeral.

He looked at the long-barrelled black gun and laughed, envisaging Michael Ridgeway brandishing the firearm in The Assured Providential Building Society. 'What a tangled web he'll be creating. That's his business, stupid boy,' he muttered.

Lucy smelled the coffee brewing and Zak crying as she stood at Donald and Janet's door. In her one hand, she clutched her overnight suitcase, in the other the first edition Charles Dickens novel. Lucy waited, acknowledging the silence and then saw why, as Janet opened the door to her. Zak suckled her breast as she held him. 'Come in, Lucy. I knew it was you by looking at the camera monitor. I wouldn't have let anyone else in while I'm in this state.' They kissed. 'Give me a moment, please, and I'll give Zak a bottle upstairs in the nursery. There's fresh coffee in the pot in the kitchen; make yourself at home.' Lucy took off her coat and started to pour two cups of coffee.

Donald had taken the morning off. He had a meeting with Superintendent Woodhouse at Stafford at 14:00. Coming out of the bathroom, he too smelled the fresh coffee and sauntered down to the kitchen wearing only his boxer shorts. He hadn't heard Lucy arrive. 'Ooh, that coffee smells wonderful, darling!' He didn't look towards the kitchen but searched for the morning paper. 'A cup for me please, darling, and then I'll....'

'... Here you are, Donald,' Lucy purred, having watched him come into the room half-naked.

'... what? Lucy! I didn't know you'd arrived!'

'... I can see that, but I'm not complaining,' she grinned, before laughing.

'But! But!' he stammered as he took the cup of coffee from her and sat down at the table. 'Oh, excuse my manners. I'm sorry! I'm so pleased to see you.' He went to her and kissed both her cheeks just as Janet entered the kitchen.

'It's like the old days, isn't it?' Janet guffawed. 'There's always one of us in an uncompromising situation!' Janet laughed, before adding, 'For God's sake, Donald, go and get some clothes on.'

'Yes, of course. I smelled the coffee. I didn't know Lucy had arrived.' By attempting to excuse himself, Donald revealed his awkwardness and left to go and dress.

'I believe you!' Janet laughed again. She took Donald's place at the table and looked at Lucy as they drank their coffee.

'What brings you to Cannock again, although as far as we're concerned there doesn't have to be a reason, you know you're always welcome.'

'Thanks, Janet. I have unfinished business with Godfrey Warlock....'

Donald re-entered the kitchen, '... not him again. There isn't a day goes by that I don't hear his name being mentioned.' He sat down with Lucy and Janet as he pulled a light sweater over his head.

Donald sensed a tension in the air with Lucy but stayed silent and wondered what their conversations would reveal. His feelings were proven correct when Lucy started to speak.

'Er! Um! I feel I owe you two an explanation, but I'd also like your advice.'

'Wow! This sounds serious, kiddo. Would you like to be more comfortable sitting in the lounge?'

'No, thanks, Janet. I'm fine here if you are...?'

'... It looks like we'll need more coffee.' Janet went to refill the percolator.

'It's all about Godfrey Warlock...'

'... before you start, I have to tell you how disappointed I felt when you were last here. With all the mayhem and misery that man brings to the town, we couldn't understand why you were defending him. Lauding his qualities even!'

'I know, I'm sorry about that. I regret what I said. Even as I left and drove back to London, I felt terrible about that.'

'Why did...?'

'... Because I'd come under Godfrey's influence.'

'Was it to do with that book?' Janet asked, 'you were really excited about it, weren't you?'

'Yes, it's all about the book. I'm still excited about it, Janet. It **is** a genuine first edition of Charles Dickens and valued at over a million pounds. Dickens' signature alone is worth two hundred thousand.'

'Wow! You've made yourself rich for the rest of your life.'

Lucy reached into her handbag and placed the book on the table. 'There it is, the source of all this trouble in my life.'

'It seems unreal that it's worth such a huge amount?'

'I'm rich and corrupt! However, I can't keep it, Janet. Its ownership comes with too many conditions from Godfrey Warlock.' Donald smiled and nodded his agreement.

'Before I explain more about the book, can I tell you some personal news?'

'Wow! Kiddo, have you met your ideal man at last? Who is he?' Janet's flippancy didn't prevent Lucy from giving Donald a quick look, knowing in her soul that Donald is her ideal man.

'Yes! Maybe? I think I have. I hope so. We hardly know each other, and yet I've mistreated him.' Donald felt his emotions rising, thinking of all they had meant to each other in the past.

'Detective Sergeant Eric Chambers. He's a stalwart of the Fraud Squad at Scotland Yard. I can't remember you two ever having met him when you worked at The Met.' Donald looked at Janet, and they shook their heads.

'I'm so pleased for you....' Janet reached forward and grasped Lucy's arm affectionately.

'... It's because of Eric that I'm here, really.' She went on to explain all her criminal actions regarding the case of the Krueger brothers. At various points, both Donald and Janet were gasping in surprise and shaking their heads.

'Why did you do all these things, Lucy? You've been skating on thin ice. You could have lost everything you've ever worked for,' Donald admonished her.

'It's all about Godfrey's book. He's made it plain that my possession of the book depends upon me carrying out tasks for him. Getting the Krueger brothers released was the first. I'm here today to carry out another for him....'

'... What!'

'That's what he thinks, anyway. He has some papers requiring my signature, giving a stepbrother of the Kruegers, currently living in

Lithuania, commendation for him to obtain British citizenship. I've never met the man and know nothing about him, of course.'

'… and the book, Lucy? What are you going to do?'

'Give it back to him! I want my life back. I don't want to keep looking over my shoulder, or shudder in fright every time my doorbell rings.' She explained about the time Godfrey came to her apartment. She blew her nose and cleared her head.

'I think about my life and what I've achieved….'

'… you've accomplished so much….'

'… in my career, Donald, yes! In my private life, it's zilch! I think that's why I felt as I did about the book. It's a wonderful feeling to hold such a unique piece of history. But assets are only skin deep. By supporting me, Eric has made me realise how worthless it is to own something valued at over a million pounds. None of it matters, does it? It's not what's important in life. I envy you two. You've both shown me that human feelings and love for someone else are important and treasured ways to live our lives. I'll feel a great satisfaction today when I say goodbye to Godfrey Warlock, and to show him he has no further control over my life.'

'You have our support, Lucy,' Donald reached across and gave her a kiss on her cheek. Lucy felt for her handkerchief and brought it to her nose again. 'You're doing the right thing; you'll be able to breathe more easily afterwards. When are you going to his bookshop?'

'As soon as possible….'

'We'll have some lunch first. I've already prepared a salmon salad. Can you help me get it from the fridge, please, Donald?'

Lucy stood, 'No, I'll help. I want to make myself useful. You've made me so welcome, and I know I've no better friends.'.

As they sat eating their lunch, Janet smiled before she spoke. '… and we have some special personal news, don't we, darling?' She reached and held Donald's hand. Lucy looked from one to the other.

'I'm pregnant again!'

Lucy swallowed before offering her congratulations.

'It's wonderful news,' Donald added, '… according to Godfrey Warlock, Zak is going to have a sister….' He shook his head in frustration. 'That damned man has to get involved in everybody's life.'

'Relax, darling! Other than in your work, he has no personal influence over our lives. If we are incredibly lucky to be expecting a daughter, that's nothing to do with him at all.'

After lunch, Lucy visited the bathroom and refreshed her appearance. She grabbed the book and prepared to go to High Green. 'Do you want company? I'll come and hold your hand if you want?'

'Thanks, Janet. I must do this myself. I have my phone if I need help. Wish me luck.'

Fifty-one

'Hello, Michael, it's good to see you looking so well. I have something for you.' Godfrey reached behind his counter and passed a parcel to him. Michael eagerly unwrapped it and grinned. 'A gun!' he wheezed. He grasped it and swung it around his forefinger, replicating gunfighters in wild west movies, before blowing imaginary smoke from the end of the barrel.

'I can see you like that,' Godfrey enthused. 'I have some bullets here also, but I hope you won't need to use them.' He could see that Michael wasn't listening. He'd reached for his handkerchief and was polishing the long barrel and spinning the revolving chamber.

'Anyway, young Michael. There's your gun. Let me know when you decide to put your plan into operation, will you, please…?'

The shop door opened, and the jangling bell disturbed their conversation. 'Put it away, Michael, quickly! We don't want other people knowing about this, do we?' Godfrey urged him, with a hoarse whisper. Godfrey noticed Lucy walk into the shop and offered more words to Michael, but they were for Lucy's benefit.

'Thank you, Mr Ridgeway. I'm pleased to have been able to help.' He offered his scrawny hooked hand for Michael to shake. 'Good day to you!' He turned to Lucy as they listened to the doorbell jangling as Michael left the shop.

Godfrey raised his voice into a cheerful tone. 'Welcome to *Godfrey's Bookshop* again, my dear. It's so good to see you. Thank you for coming from London; I trust Inspector Lawrence and his charming wife are in good health? But you'll know that Mrs Lawrence is expecting again. They're certainly no slouches where the bedroom is concerned, are they?'

'Do you really expect me to comment on such an offensive remark?'

'Oh! Do you find it offensive? My informants tell me that you used to be engaged to Inspector Lawrence, so I would imagine your feelings are tinged with jealousy and regret?'

'Doctor Warlock, I'm not here to discuss anything other than the business we have to conclude, so I'm coming straight to the point....'

'What's the rush? I intended to show you the full extent of my bookshop today, giving you a guided tour with my remarkable protégés studying in my reading room....'

'... another time maybe....'

'... I have another first edition Dickens to show you.'

Lucy grinned and spoke clearly. 'I'm not interested!' Godfrey's face dropped.

'Not interested? What nonsense! Have you forgotten who you're talking to? I'm your Uncle Godfrey, the one person in your life who looks after you. Who do you think has brought about the demise of Dariusz and Vlad to keep the wolves at Scotland Yard from hanging you out to dry?'

'Where my career at Scotland Yard is concerned, I'll look after myself.'

'Ah, well! As you wish, my dear. Let's get down to our business, shall we? Here is the form from the Immigration Office for you to sign. Igorovitch Bild-Krueger will be extremely grateful to you when he becomes a citizen of this fair land.'

Lucy picked up the form and glanced at the three-page dossier. Godfrey held a pen for her to use. Lucy smiled directly at him when she held the papers between her two hands and slowly and deliberately ripped the pages into several pieces. She then placed the scraps of paper on his counter. Godfrey looked down at the fragments before screwing his face into a fierce rage. 'Do you know what you are doing...?'

'... Mr Igorovitch Bild-Krueger can join his infamous half-brothers for all I care. I don't know the man and could never support such fraudulent use of my signature.'

'You'll come to regret this!'

'The only regret I have is coming into this shop in the first place....'

Godfrey howled in frustrated rage. '... Then you'll have no regret in giving me my book back...?'

Lucy held the book in her hand. '... this? Your beloved book! Here it is. I no longer wish to have it in my possession. It makes me feel dirty.' She threw it on the counter. They both watched the book slide across the polished surface before coming to rest.

'Wow! I never realised how good that would feel. You have no hold over me anymore! Oh yes! Before I forget, don't ever come to my apartment again. I won't let you across my threshold, anyway. It took me three days to fumigate and disinfect my flat after you left, including maggots that had burrowed into my carpets....'

'... you've underestimated my power, Lucy. Don't think you've seen the last of me.' Lucy gulped in temporary fear as she watched his pupils flare with a hint of red. 'I can see you're changing your mind already, my dear.'

'I wasn't going to let your threats get the better of me, Godfrey; I think I've done well up until now. But do you know what, I'm going to fail in trying to hold myself together, so I'll lower my standards and just tell you to ...*piss off*!' She hesitated before issuing the last two syllables for maximum effect. Lucy didn't make eye contact with him as she turned away, displaying a huge smirk.

Godfrey watched her open the door and slam it behind her. The tremendous force with which she yanked the door caused the recoiling spring to sever, and the brass bell fell to the floor with a dull clang. As she cheerfully whisked herself through the town centre, Godfrey howled and issued expletives in seven languages as he picked up the book and threw it down the whole length of the shop. It landed in the reading room, where a couple of his students bent down to pick up several pages that had come loose from the binding. 'Leave it on the floor; it's only trash,' Godfrey bellowed before calming down a little.

Lucy felt like a new person. Reborn with a unique viewpoint on how to conduct the rest of her life. Her royal blue dress flowed around her shapely legs in the slight breeze that also caused her long blonde hair to sway seductively across her cleavage.

A loud wolf-whistle caused her to turn her head. In the past, she would have told the whistler what she had just said to Godfrey. Instead, she smiled and offered her thanks to a handsome young man who had walked past her. She felt good and looked forward to her future with optimism.

In *Godfrey's Bookshop,* the studious readers occupying the reading room knew when to keep their heads down. This occasion was the worst rage they had seen coming from his twisted scowling face. Godfrey sat down on a stool at his counter. He didn't care who heard him. 'These pathetic little people think they can overcome me and what I stand for. They are simply tadpoles in a foul-smelling putrid pond. What does it matter that one insignificant pollywog wriggles in the mire and escapes from the piss-soaked effluent and my influence? The water is already full of other brain-dead tadpoles and new frogspawn that I can nurture.'

Fifty-two

Superintendent Woodhouse held a meeting with the County Emergency Planning Officer, Major Martin James. He asked him a pertinent question. 'Major, this David Shaw from Cannock. Does he present a credible terrorist threat?'

'Ernest, yes, he does. Look at the facts. He has the means to access the stored nuclear fuel at the rail sidings, one mile from Cannock town centre. He only needs to get his hands around explosive material, and we have the potential for a major incident. the most powerful explosion this country has ever seen. He could deliver the explosive material into the static sidings at full force aboard a speeding train. I've studied his notes, and it's obvious to me he's aware of the outcome that most of the country will be irradiated for forty years or more. Every part of this nation will be a nuclear wasteland, polluted with radiation twenty times more concentrated than the Hiroshima residents suffered in 1945. It's because of this threat, we need to move this from County level. I've given you a conclusion of my fuller comments that I've placed in the file.'

'Who should we pass this to?'

'Straight to the Commander of the Anti-Terrorism Unit at New Scotland Yard. Preferably today! What causes me great concern is how easy it is to obtain explosives. They're prevalent in many aspects of society. I'm thinking of demolition companies, mines and quarries, construction projects in particular. These are very carefully regulated and responsible organisations, but... and where terrorism is concerned, those considerations don't apply anymore. Money talks, and it only needs one person to be paid to look the other way while a robbery occurs. This David Shaw is unique in that he has the means to easily transport the explosives. After this meeting, I'll pass this to the Metropolitan Police. Still, I'll also examine the sources of all explosives and how much could become available.'

Commander Sir Isaac Jacques read with mounting alarm the file that the head of Staffordshire's Emergency Planning Department had sent him. He immediately contacted all his colleagues in the Anti-Terror Unit for an urgent meeting. His large office on the top floor of the MI6 annexe at Scotland Yard bustled with eager young officers discussing the cases they are currently dealing with. He called the meeting to order, and they sat around the large oval table, focussing on him as he stood by a projector screen. Ike, as his colleagues call him, held a remote control that connected wirelessly to his laptop. After taking a drink of coffee, he brought the first image on the screen.

This situation in Staffordshire demands our urgent attention. One by one, he showed the pages of David Shaw's notes on how to detonate a nuclear explosion, followed by Godfrey Warlock's book. He left a photograph on the screen of the sealed containers in the railway's sidings holding spent nuclear fuel. 'I don't need to tell you the implications, not only for this tiny backwater of the Midlands but the entire country. If this maniac isn't stopped, this has the potential to put any other terrorist situation we've dealt with in the past look like a child's tea-party.'

'How do we know this isn't the doodles of a crank?' asked a young officer sitting at the far end of the oval table from the screen. Most officers seated at the table turned to see who had asked the question.

'We don't, young Francis! I know you are a recent addition to our unit, but because we don't know, we can't afford to take the risk.' The commander put a rhetorical question to the meeting, 'And why can't we afford to take the risk?...anybody?'

'There are no second chances here, gov. There's no comeback, is there? We'd all be finished if...?'

'Exactly, Sergeant Blewit! Fortunately, most terrorist incidents have been confined to some religious maniac brandishing swords and knives up till now. Unfortunately, they killed and maimed people, but such incidents are localised. This has the potential to become world-wide news and send parts of the United Kingdom into a radioactive wasteland for thousands of years.'

'Can anybody identify the one item in this maniac's plan that makes this such a credible scheme and not some Sunday afternoon day-dreaming fantasy of a frustrated nobody?'

'He has the opportunity and the means to create the explosion.'

'Well done, Constable Davies. Yes, he does! He's the controller of rail traffic for the whole of the West Midlands Railway. The only missing piece of this fantastic jigsaw is, does the freak have sufficient explosives to cause the nuclear stockpile to dispatch us to kingdom come? We have to assume this maniac is actively working on this as we speak, so time is of the essence. He must be stopped -NOW! We don't pussy-foot about! If he has to be taken down, that is the last consideration. The buck stops with me, so I'll take any flak that may come our way afterwards. You have my full authority to stop this fanatic by any means at your disposal.' The commander noticed the change in the demeanour of his officers. His harsh words had galvanised their full attention.

'I understand the Staffordshire Emergency Department is currently looking at potential sources for explosive material. However, I'm not taking any chances. These provincial guys, no matter how well-intentioned, don't deal with terrorists on a regular basis. We do! It's what we're all here for. So, lads and lasses, get to it. I'm now putting a photograph of David Shaw on the screen. If you get within ten yards of him, you know what to do. I've also passed details of this investigation onto GCHQ, the government communications centre at Cheltenham. You all know it is a highly sophisticated cryptography and intelligence agency that helps us out at times like this. They have specialised equipment that utilises satellite technology to feed Shaw's image into their computers, compare cameras around the country at various public locations, and instantly respond. If this man shows his face, we'll know about it.'

The commander started delegating tasks. 'Jasper and your team, I'm assigning you to identify any and every source of explosive material he could possibly use. Where is it located and stored? What construction or other demolition jobs are currently operating that require deliveries of volatiles? How are such deliveries made?' Inspector Jasper Conrad and three other officers left the room. The commander turned to an older, grey-haired, uniformed man.

'Inspector Joseph, you and your men find this David Shaw and bring him in for questioning. Use the local police if you need to. I'll contact our county and local colleagues to inform them what's going on.'

'Sergeant Williamson!' the commander called to a dark-haired man chatting to Inspector Joseph. 'Phillip, I want you and your men to stand guard over this stockpile of spent nuclear fuel. What the hell it's doing sitting around only a mile from a town centre is beyond me but keep anyone and everyone away from it; then arrange to have it taken somewhere else! Somewhere more remote, somewhere away from the public gaze and where it could be considered being potentially neutralised.'

The first call that went out from Scotland Yard was made by Inspector Joseph. He telephoned the West Midlands Railway headquarters to ask to speak with David Shaw. He wasn't surprised to find he wasn't in his office and had been absent for the previous three days.

Scotland Yard's comprehensive mainframe computer system became besieged with Inspector Conrad and his officers searching for explosive materials' sources and locations.

Sergeant Williamson and three other men were already driving the police Range Rover through north London to get onto the M1 motorway near Brent Cross. Their eta at the Cannock railway sidings was in one hour thirty minutes.

Earlier that morning, David, and Godfrey Warlock had a last conversation at the bookshop. Having been thanked for all his help, Godfrey sent David on his way with a few final words of encouragement. 'I'm immensely proud of you, my boy. May our Lord speed you on your way, and I hope all goes well with your plan.'

By the time Sergeant Williamson and his men would be standing guard at Cannock's railway sidings, David Shaw, at last, almost had explosives in his control. Days before, he'd monitored the shipment of Semtex-H being transported by rail from the manufacturing factory in Cornwall, en-route to the new quarry site in East Staffordshire. The itinerary was scheduled to take the train through the English shire counties to Birmingham and then on to Derby. Standing in the control office at New Street Station in Birmingham, David awaited the four-carriage diesel engine freight train. He watched the computer-generated display on a large screen showing where every rail movement took place in the Midlands. He planned to board the train. In his official capacity, boarding trains to check on the train's operating efficiency was an everyday occurrence and wouldn't attract undue attention. After the train had left Birmingham New Street, he intended to overpower the driver and take control of the train himself. He knew where the junction was in the rail network that diverted trains to the east or the north. He had the capacity on his mobile phone to switch and alter points. As he approached the junction, it would be a simple task to change the points and divert northwards towards Cannock.

In his earlier career at Crewe he had regularly driven diesel locomotives, shunting wagons and empty passenger carriages into the myriad of siding and freight yards at the vast complex. Driving a diesel locomotive at high speed would be a novel experience for him. Years before, in Crewe's rail sidings, he wasn't allowed to go above ten miles per hour. He would relish opening the throttle to its maximum. Watching the speedometer hopefully exceeding one hundred miles an hour, guiding the train to impact the wagons containing nuclear fuel.

'These are the five sources of explosive material, Inspector,' Constable Gillian Tobin pointed out to Jasper Conrad on her computer screen. 'Three relate to current mining and quarrying operations, and the other two to demolition companies. John Wilson is looking into the demolition companies. Leonard and I are looking into the quarry companies.'

'Good work!' Jasper enthused as he looked at a map to see where each explosive source was in relation to Cannock. The sources were spread across the whole of the United Kingdom. He scratched his head and wondered where David Shaw was going to get his volatiles.

'Gov', John Wilson called. 'Two demolition companies currently have explosives. One, located in Chichester, was used yesterday by blowing up a disused factory chimney. The Chief Executive of the other demolition company in Felixstowe says he has his dynamite under lock and key, right next to his office for use tomorrow on a disused power station's derelict cooling towers.'

'So that leaves the mining and quarrying businesses. Did you hear that, Gillian and Leonard? It's down to you! The only volatiles he can use must be connected to these firms. Who are they? Where are they found?'

Leonard passed two sheets of paper to the commander. 'Gov, I've eliminated one. South Shields Opencast Coal Company no longer use explosives. A recent planning appeal by the local council stopped them. All their stock was resold back to the manufacturers.'

Gillian immediately followed her colleague. 'Another company Hadrian's Blasting Incorporated, near Edinburgh, went bust six months ago. Their entire stock was resold by the liquidators to the producers in Stockholm, Sweden.'

'Well done, guys. By my mathematics, that only leaves one more. It must be that one. Or else we're back to square one, up the creek without a paddle. Well, guys?'

He didn't get a reply; Isaac eased off pressuring them when he could see how hard they were concentrating on their computer screens.

'My throat feels like the bottom of a Nagasaki's flip-flop. Is there any tea anywhere?' No-one replied. He turned to go to the kitchen but stopped when Inspector Joseph called to him.

'Gov, still no sighting of David Shaw. I've contacted the local police at Cannock, who are searching for him. They've checked his home, without any luck. His wife hasn't seen him for three days.' Isaac nodded and carried on, but was stopped again.

'Bingo!' Constable Gillian Tobin called. The commander returned to look at her computer screen. 'Semtex-H is manufactured at Cornish Demolition supplies, near Camborne, Cornwall. They currently have a shipment of seven tonnes being transported by rail to a new hard-rock quarrying venture near Cromford in Derbyshire. It's in transit as we speak….'

'…. Derbyshire is only twenty miles from Cannock,' he confirmed by running his figure over his map. 'It wouldn't take a rocket scientist to….'

'Gov.' Inspector Conrad called. 'Gov, there's a call for you on line one. It's GCHQ; they say it's urgent!'

'Commander Jacques, it's Robinson Bewes here at GCHQ. That David Shaw fellow you're looking for….'

'… tell me!'

'Cameras at New Street Railway station in Birmingham have picked him up standing on a platform there. It looks to us as if he's waiting to board a train.'

'Good man! Thank you very much! Isaac turned back to Inspector Conrad. The bastard is standing on a platform at New Street Station. Why do you stand on a platform if you're not going to board a train? Now, this second, find out what trains are due. Where's he going? We have to know!'

He called back to Constable Tobin, 'Gillian, what's the train's route carrying that Semtex-H. Can you find out now! I have a horrible feeling about this.' Everyone who wasn't actively engaged in other things came to stare at the computer screens where Gillian and Leonard sat.

Leonard called out. 'Gov, I was already on the Western Train Company's website. There's a separate webpage for freight. That train left Truro seven hours ago, en route for Derby, via Birmingham New Street....'

'... That's it, folks. The maniac, David Shaw, is waiting to board the train carrying the Semtex. What's the train's eta at Birmingham, Leonard?'

'The train is scheduled to arrive at Birmingham New Street at 13:45....'

Commander Jacques looked anxiously at his watch. 'Bloody hell, that's in only twelve minutes....'

'... hang on, gov. The train is running thirty minutes late. It was held up at Gloucester Central Station for repairs to a blocked hydraulic pump.'

'Pity it didn't stop it altogether!' He looked at his watch again. 'By my reckoning, that gives us forty-two minutes before David Shaw gets his hands on some Semtex.'

'What's he going to do, folks? Get your brains working! What would you do?'

Constable Tobin spoke. 'Gov, here's what I think. David Shaw is waiting at New Street Station. He knows that Semtex is coming on that train. He's the Controller of Trains at West Midlands Railway. No one will give him a second glance when he boards the train. He needs the train at Cannock to detonate the nuclear fuel with the Semtex, but the train's going to Derby...' She hesitated.

'... yes, carry on, Gillian.'

'... it's only my guess, gov, but if I was in David's shoes... I don't know?'

'Carry on...!'

'He's going to disable the driver and take over. It's not beyond the realms of clear thinking that he can drive a train. Then somehow, he's going to divert the train's route from Derby to Cannock. My guess also is that he'll drive the train at high speed into the nuclear fuel wagons to create the nuclear explosion, committing suicide in the process....'

'... and murdering thousands of people in the process too!' Inspector Joseph added.

'Well done, Gillian. If I were allowed, I'd kiss you, but these days you'd have me up in the disciplinary court for sexual harassment.'

'No, I wouldn't, gov!'

'Oh, alright, then.' Isaac bent down and kissed her cheek.

'How do we stop him, folks? The clock is ticking!'

Leonard broke the tension in the room. 'Gov! Look! I've got the rail network of tracks here on my screen... hang on a sec; I'll enlarge it for a better view.'

Everybody stared at the screen. 'Leonard put it onto the big screen out at the front of the room.'

Leonard pressed a few icons before everybody turned to stare where David Shaw's image had been leering at everybody. Commander Jacques turned to Leonard.

'Why were you looking at this...?'

'... David Shaw wants the train in Cannock, but it's going to Derby. Where's the junction in the tracks that he will have to take to put him on the Cannock route?'

'Good thinking!' Everybody stared at the screen. Isaac gazed anxiously at his watch. 'Only thirty-seven minutes left, folks.'

'There's several options, gov,' Inspector Joseph commented. Nobody had taken any notice of Gillian, who sat at her workstation pressing keys on her computer keyboard. While the others were examining different options for where the train would turn off its scheduled route, she studied the rail network around Cannock. She noticed the rail sidings where the nuclear fuel was stored was accessed by a junction in the tracks a mile before Cannock Station. She pointed back along the Birmingham to Cannock route. She noticed another insignificant intersection in the tracks three miles before Cannock near Essington village. The disused junction gave access to a seventy-one-acre site where coal mines used to be sited. It was now wasteland used by fly-tippers and courting couples in an evening. Colliery waste used to be tipped in high triangular mounds that had since been levelled and spread around the site, consequently the soil was of inferior quality, capable of only growing hawthorn trees and gorse bushes. Gillian thought aloud. 'This is where the train needs diverting,' she muttered.

She looked across to where a garbled conversation was going on between several officers. 'Gov!' she called. Commander Jacques didn't hear her for the hubbub, so she pressed a few more keys causing the map they were arguing over to disappear and be replaced by the map of the tracks around Cannock.

'What the f...?!' Inspector Joseph called. Gillian got up and walked over to stand before the screen.

'What, Gillian? I can see you have a suggestion.' She explained her ideas about diverting the train near Cannock.

'So, there's no need to prevent the train's diversion in the Birmingham area?' The Commander concluded.

'Exactly! Gov, how do we stop the train anyway? The Birmingham area is highly populated. Think of the danger if the Semtex exploded by stopping the train or derailing it there. No, we let it run on towards Cannock. David Shaw will think he's home and dry. He won't be expecting the train to suddenly turn into this wasteland area, where it can explode without harming anyone except himself.'

'You are brilliant, Gillian, the only question is how do we divert... wait a sec... where's Sergeant Williamson got to. He left an hour and a half ago.' The commander pressed the Sergeant's icon on his phone. 'Phillip, where are you?' Sergeant Williamson recognised the urgency in his gov's voice.

'Just arrived in Staffordshire at a place called Bassett's Pole, about six or seven miles from Cannock.'

'Good man. Phil, forget about going to the rail siding where the nuclear fuel is. Here's what I want you to do.' The commander explained the details of Gillian's plan. She tugged at his arm, so he stopped talking. '... hang on a sec, Phil.' He turned to Gillian.

'Gov, tell him I'll send an image of my computer screen to his phone. I've marked exactly where the location of the junction in the tracks is for Phil to see.' The commander turned back to Sergeant Williamson.

'Did you hear that, Phil...? Good man. That set of points has to be turned to make sure the train diverts into a disused colliery site. We expect the train to be going at high speed, so if it doesn't derail at the junction, it will plough into the wasteland and explode. So, once you've changed the points stay well out of the way...' Leonard interrupted Isaac.

'Gov, sorry to interrupt you. There's good news and bad news. The fair bit is I've got the West Midlands Railway Company's active traffic management system on screen. We can see where every train is currently running. The nasty bit is David Shaw's train has left New Street Station en route for Derby.'

'... Phil... the train has left Birmingham New Street Station, so you haven't got too long before it arrives there. Get to it! Phil, make sure the points are changed and locked in position so that any boffin in the rail networks control office can't change it by computer. Keep me informed what's happening, sergeant.'

The commander turned to Leonard. 'Bring up the primary screen, please, Leonard.'

Everyone went to watch the screen. The computer-controlled board looked like a map similar to London's underground network but with different coloured icons moving each way, like flies crawling on a draughts board. Sergeant Joseph pointed out the train carrying the Semtex-H and David Shaw. They held their breath as they watched the train turn off at the first junction taking it near Aston, then Walsall, and onwards towards Cannock. It obviously wasn't going to Derby as scheduled.

Commander Jacques commented, 'We can only assume that David Shaw has overpowered the driver and is now in control.' He stared at the screen, knowing time was running short.

Sergeant Williamson re-accessed his phone and tuned in to his mail inbox. He saw Gillian's message and opened it. 'Here it is signposted, the village of Essington. It's the next turn on the left, sergeant.' A constable sitting in the rear seats commented as he held his phone. 'It looks as if the turning into this area of scrubland is five hundred yards on the right after the junction.' Sergeant Williams pressed harder on the accelerator pedal, knowing they had extraordinarily little time. 'Turn here, Phil.' Ahead of them a tree trunk was lying horizontally, barring the way into the site. Phil accelerated even harder.

'Hang on, everybody!' He crashed through the eight-inch diameter wooden pole, splintering it into several pieces and crumpling part of the Range Rover's bonnet. 'The railway line is about a hundred yards to the right, Phil.' He swung the car's steering wheel. They could see the main railway line up ahead by the overhead electric gantries and hanging cable trails. The four men got out. Phil opened the boot and reached for the car's hydraulic jack and tyre lever. They all ran towards where they estimated the disused points were. 'Here they are!' a constable shouted out. 'They're all rusted up; this is going to be difficult, sergeant.' They tried kicking the section of the two rails that needed to move to the right preventing a train from carrying on towards Cannock. It wouldn't move.

'Pass that hydraulic jack,' another constable yelled. He lay down in the sharp angular limestone gravel and tried to make a place for the jack to act as a fulcrum. 'We need a concrete block or some bricks,' he bellowed. The others searched frantically in the grass, scrub and waste litter lying along the embankment.

'Here!' Phil shouted. 'Here are two concrete blocks.' The constable placed one block between the base of the jack and the one rail. The other he placed at the head of the jack and, using the tyre lever, moved the hydraulic joint up and down. They watched the shiny piston extend and close the gap onto the other railway line. It needed more pressure now to move the toggle. Three men used their powerful arms to move the lever up and down.

In Scotland yard's Terrorist Unit, Commander Jacques and his officers were perspiring from severe anxiety. They'd watched the train travel through Aston and Walsall. Inside a few minutes, it would be arriving at the site of the disused colliery. Within a few brief moments, the United Kingdom could suffer a catastrophic nuclear explosion. Such a blast would render a significant part of the country uninhabitable for thousands of years. The suffering of thousands of hideous deaths and unimaginable radiation burns to the citizens that survived would haunt human thinking for years to come. ''Oh my God!' he uttered. He turned to see some of his colleagues openly whispering in prayer. Others stared fixedly at the screen.

They could have breathed a little more easily had they known Phil's car jack was gradually moving the railway line inch by inch. Phil suddenly stopped and looked up. 'What's that?' he gasped. They felt the rumbling and vibrations going into their bones as they lay on the railway lines working the jack. The train was approaching! 'I can't see or hear it yet, gov,' a junior constable shrieked, as he looked down the track. 'We've got a few more minutes yet.'

'Come on! Let's finish it!' Phil shouted.

Seated in the 05:30 diesel train cab from Truro, Cornwall, David Shaw pulled the dead man's handle closer to his body. The train's speed picked up a little from the regulation forty miles an hour on that part of the track. He heard and sensed the wheels' rhythmic sound going over joints in the tracks, increasing in tempo. His evil grin poked out from under the train driver's greasy hat that he'd taken from the original driver's head after he'd hit him with a crowbar. Already he sensed his evil plan was nearing completion. He visualised the headlines in the world's press. David Shaw, 'The Man who changed the world'– 'The United Kingdom, a Nuclear Wilderness'– 'Terrorism on an unimaginable scale'–'David Shaw, who was he?' His broad grin turned into an evil laugh.

In *Godfrey's Bookshop,* Doctor Godfrey Warlock held his hands to his cheeks. He emulated David's evil laugh, like a naughty giggling child who had just cruelly tied a firework around a cat's tail, waiting expectantly for the bang.

People in Cannock's town centre went about their regular everyday business, oblivious to what was happening a few miles away. Godfrey Warlock speculated whether anybody would want to know if they were on the cusp of being instantly vapourised. Such an illogical thought never crossed James's mind. He and Nicky enjoyed a cup of coffee sitting in the sunshine, watching market traders shouting, advertising their wares.

At the former Essington Colliery site, the points had been almost entirely changed. 'It's coming! I can see it! the bloody train's almost here!' The junior constable screamed to his colleagues. Lying on the railway tracks, they still struggled with the car jack lever. The constable looked down to his friends in horror as the train bore closer and faster.

David Shaw laughed louder as he pulled the dead man's handle round to its maximum position. There was a delay in the transmission mechanism receiving the added electrical pulse to increase the wheels' rotation to a dizzying eighty miles an hour. David estimated by the time it would take to travel the three miles to the nuclear fuel sidings, the train would be travelling at over one hundred miles an hour.

David's mind visualised his forthcoming posthumous elevation to international recognition. His eyes were focussed upon the track ahead, so he never saw the changed points. Phil and his men managed to pull themselves off the track seconds before the train wheels thundered to within a few feet of their prostrate bodies. They rolled down the embankment, ensnaring themselves in gorse bushes and nettle beds and disturbing a wasps' nest before they reached the bottom. Lying against a metal railing fence, with angry wasps buzzing around their faces, they curled into a foetal position and held their hands over their heads.

The momentum of the swinging train as it turned the corner flung David to the left. His head hit the floor of the cab in shocked bewilderment, and he joined the dead driver lying on the floor. Releasing the dead man's handle, it automatically swung back to the stop position and the train momentarily ceased to accelerate. David heard a sharp whistling noise coming from the diesel motor as fuel drained from the straining engine's cylinder igniters. With blood running down his face, he tried to stand and, in that unique moment, a look of puzzlement crossed his face as he saw the fast-approaching end of the tracks.

In the Terrorism Unit in Scotland Yard, Commander Jacques and his team watched in suspended animation as the train's icon veered sharply to the right.

David's confusion lasted only a few seconds. That's all the time it took for the front of the diesel engine to hit the turned-up rails. The twisted metal rested against several layers of large blocks of reinforced concrete weighing over two hundred tonnes. With the crumbling cab coming to an instant halt, the remaining four carriages catapulted into the air. They landed on top of the splintered remains of what was left of the cab. The Semtex-H was held in suspended crates in the third carriage. It wouldn't have mattered if it had been in the first or the last carriage. The entire train immediately disappeared in a huge fireball. Tempered metal parts, cast iron wheels, glass windows and doors, seven hundred gallons of diesel fuel, the pathetic human being, David Shaw, and the innocent driver instantaneously disintegrated. The whole jumbled mess was reduced to fragments no larger than three inches in length. Like confetti being flung at a wedding, the bits and pieces rose within the orange mushroom cloud of smoke and debris rising one hundred feet into the sky. Within the next few seconds, the orange flames turned to yellow, then to white, as temperatures within the expanding Semtex's confines rose to over ten thousand degrees centigrade. Anything combustible instantly incinerated, including the remains of David Shaw.

Phil and his colleagues, lying in the lee of the railway embankment, had their eardrums instantly pierced from the air blast, before being showered by falling hot cinders and splinters. He puzzled at the wonderment of the natural world as he saw hundreds of dead wasps lying around him and his colleagues. 'They must have been susceptible to the changing air pressure caused by the blast,' he assumed. He saw the junior constable speaking, but couldn't hear him. He gestured that he couldn't hear what he was saying, before all the officers realised they too had been deafened. They quickly doused bits of smouldering ash that had landed on their clothes and the surrounding grass. Phil reached into his pocket for his phone. He breathed a sigh of relief when he found it undamaged. He crawled to the top of the embankment, switched the phone to video record mode and captured the images of the aftermath of the explosion.

275

On the large screen in Scotland Yard, the icon depicting David Shaw's train blipped and vanished from the screen, accompanied by wild cheering and applause. Commander Jacques went over to Gillian and Leonard. Hugging them both, he told them their work had been invaluable in the successful outcome. 'Excellent teamwork,' he enthused.

Sitting expectantly behind his counter in the bookshop, Godfrey Warlock heard and felt the shuddering vibrations in the ground from the blast from over four miles away. He looked up, expecting the roof and the rest of his bookshop to disappear, to be whisked away in the nuclear explosion. When the vibrations ceased, and Godfrey could still see his readers and the books standing undisturbed on his shelves, he puzzled over what was happening. He rushed to the front door, flung it open and expected to see nothing but a wilderness of blackened dust. Stumbling into the pedestrian area, he almost bumped into a woman sitting on the bench opposite her young son, both eating a giant cheeseburger. He looked down the pedestrian area at the town centre. Everything was as it always had been. Dejectedly, his shoulders slumped, he returned to his bookshop, muttering, 'You've let me down badly, David.'

From their seat in the market area café, James commented to Nicky that he thought an earthquake had just happened. 'Did the earth move for you then?' Nicky joked. James smiled and nodded, knowing that she alluded to their romantic date on the previous evening rather than the tremors they'd felt under their feet.

At the disused Essington Colliery site, most of the disintegrated debris had eventually fallen back to earth. A colossal crater now existed where the diesel train from Truro had come to its last resting place. The last of the remaining flames and black and grey smoke drifted off to the east in the prevailing gathering winds. Peace and quiet quickly returned to the site of the former coal mine. A skylark dared to soar back up into the air and send out its sweet call. As if the bird had given the all-clear, a buck rabbit's nose twitched as it ventured to the entrance of its burrow. He smelled the acrid fumes still hanging in the air and returned to his does suckling their young.

Seated in his office, Donald received a telephone call from Superintendent Woodhouse in Stafford explaining what had happened. 'I heard the explosion. Thank goodness it's all over.' Donald thanked him for letting him know the situation. He returned to the dossier on Anwar Patel and the excess deaths in Cannock.

In the Lawrence household, only Zak was temporarily disturbed into slight whimpers as the floor vibrated. Even in her slumbering state, Janet was maternally tuned to listen for any disturbance from her son. She reached forward and replaced the plastic dummy back into his mouth before they both reverted to their former pleasant dreams.

In her salubrious detached house on the Hawkes Green housing estate, Margaret Shaw stood at the kitchen sink washing the dishes. She instinctively knew she was now a widow when she felt the thud of the explosion through her shoes. Tears came to her eyes as Margaret remembered the kind and loving man David had once been. 'I just don't understand. What caused you to change?' she whispered, as she gazed at David's photograph hanging on the living room wall.

Fifty-three

The newspapers' sensational, lurid headlines came and went as quickly as the publishers' rising and falling sales. Events such as the explosion and the destruction of the train at the former Essington colliery site were good for their editions' circulation. So, when a typical peaceful ambience returned to the town and surrounding area, news editors returned to their more usual journalistic tactics of creating headlines. Much to Donald's mounting chagrin, one local newspaper even decided to publish an exposé on *Godfrey's Bookshop.* The gushing comments made by the young reporter who'd become one of Godfrey's converts espoused the shop's qualities. The ambitious journalist even suggested the shop had become the town's major tourist asset, attracting readers from every corner of the United Kingdom.

Relaxing at home, reading the editorial with disgust, Donald didn't realise the newspaper article's implication. It would later prove to be the foundation of how he could bring about Godfrey Warlock's downfall.

The newspaper editors needn't have worried about falling sales. Michael Ridgeway would solve their anxieties. He had everything he needed to put into effect how he would bring about changes to his life to make him and his mother rich. Holding and cherishing Godfrey's gun brought added confidence to his ambition to rob the Assured Providential Building Society in Cannock's town centre.

He chose a morning when the weather was benign. There was no wind or rain, and the temperatures were average, with a mackerel sky keeping the worst of the sun's heat at bay. He dressed in the smartest clothes he had bought from the local charity shops. A side pocket of his new pin-striped suit held the gun. He slid his deposit book into the inside breast pocket. He carried two large canvas bags, both folded inside a smaller plastic carrier bag.

'Ooh, our Michael, you do look smart, son. I'm so glad you've turned the corner, and you're making something of yourself,' his swooning mother gushed. Of course, Michael hadn't taken her into his confidence. She was ignorant of his outrageous plans for the coming day as she bade him goodbye. 'See you later, Michael,' she called as she proudly watched him walk down the avenue from their home.

Michael sat on the bench opposite the building society for an hour, choosing his moment to enter. He'd watched the usual morning's delivery of cash by their security company's armoured van. He salivated that the bank's tills would be oozing in money. Michael estimated there were only a few customers in the bank. Friday was a busy day, so he knew the bank wouldn't ever be entirely empty. As he rose from the bench, he heard a voice calling; it was Doctor Patel. They had become on speaking terms after they'd met a few times in the bookshop's reading room. 'Hello, Michael,' he called as he went into the bank through the revolving door, marked entry. Michael ambled across the paved area and followed Anwar Patel. Once inside, he looked around and reassessed his plan. He knew the two young female cashiers standing behind the counters as Jane and Loretta. Joe, the usual male assistant who was employed to meet and greet the customers, stood having a cup of coffee in the corner. He glanced at the side offices where other advisors sat talking to customers. Apart from Anwar Patel standing waiting to be served, only one other elderly woman was queuing. Michael moved behind her and waited his turn. He reached inside the plastic bag and pulled out the two large canvas bags. He felt calm and confident and returned Loretta's smile as she looked across.

The queue at once disappeared as Anwar and the elderly woman were called to the counter. He was next in line to be served. Nervously, he looked behind him as an elderly, grey-haired man came and stood behind him, then he heard Loretta's voice call, 'Next, please.' He approached the counter and handed over his deposit book. Loretta opened it, looked at Michael, and asked, 'How much would you like to deposit today, Mr Ridgeway?'

'Whatever you have in your till, whatever amount Jane has in her till and what the security guys delivered half an hour ago,' Michael said, calmly and without fuss. Loretta stared at the black barrel of the gun that Michael pointed at her. 'Don't do anything silly, darling, like raising the alarm or calling for your soppy manager. I don't want to use this thing, but I will if you force me to.' He saw Jane look across. '… and that goes for you too, darling.' Michael handed the two large bags across the counter. 'Fill these with the cash you have in your tills first and then go to the safe….'

'… only the manager can open the safe,' Loretta answered quietly. She stared at the gun and wondered if she dared press the alarm button under her counter. Her eyes moved to glance at the red button.

'… and don't even think about it. I saw you look at the alarm button. Call the manager over!'

Loretta hesitated, still transfixed by the gun. '*Now!*' Michael raised his voice, causing Anwar Patel, standing at Jane's counter, to look across at Jane. Sweating and looking terrified, she filled one of the bags with money from her till.

'Mr Buffet!' Loretta called, 'Mr Buffet, could you help me please?'

The building society manager, Miles Buffet, was enjoying a cup of tea in his office. He heard the cashier's calls, 'Oh! Damn it! That's my elevenses ruined,' he grumbled, and without looking around, he ambled to where Loretta stood behind the counter.

Anwar whispered in a hoarse voice, 'Michael, what are you doing? You can't do this….'

'Keep out of it, Doctor Patel.' Michael watched the manager sidle up to Loretta.

'What's the prob…?' he stared wide-eyed at Michael's gun.

'Open the safe, Mr Buffet. Do as you're told, and nobody will get hurt. Fill the other bag, please. Do it now and do it quietly and forget about raising any alarm. My gun is loaded with 19mm calibre bullets. I understand they make such a mess of human flesh. They expand inside a human body, you see, so in no time at all, half your lung will go AWOL.' Miles Buffet nodded and took the bag. Michael watched him turn the two dials on the safe door to the required combination.

Anwar called again. 'Michael, don't be a fool; you can't get away….'

'… shut it, Anwar! Or you'll go the way of these poor sods behind the counter.'

Loretta, helping Jane fill the other bag, could see he and Anwar were acquainted. 'Mr Ridgeway, please do as your friend asks before this goes any further. Nobody needs to get hurt,' she pleaded, quietly. Michael could see his plan was coming to fruition. He eyed the large bundles of notes that the manager stuffed into his bag. The other bag was almost full.

'... that's it! That's all there is in our tills,' Jane muttered. Michael could see the beads of sweat resting on her forehead. She lifted the bag over the counter to him.

'That's a good girl, Jane. I can see you're frightened, but there's no need to be. Move away from the counter now, like a good girl. Go and sit in the corner; you too, Loretta, out of harm's way.' He motioned with the barrel of the gun.

Behind Michael, the other man standing in the queue had edged backwards, quietly trying to leave the bank. Michael turned and called him. 'Hey, you! Come here!' For a second, as Michael looked away, Loretta thought she could lunge forward and press the alarm, but he turned back. The sheepish looking man came towards the counter. Using the gun barrel, Michael motioned for him to go behind the counter and stand with the two girls.

'Sit on the floor, all of you, *now!*' He watched them sit huddled together.

The manager had filled the bag with money and offered it to Michael. 'Bring it around here,' Michael called. Mr Buffet placed it by Michael's feet. 'Now go and sit with your girls.'

Anwar Patel had stood idly by and watched Michael receive the bags of money. He decided to intervene. 'Michael, I'm not going to let you do this. Our mutual friend, Godfrey Warlock, would be appalled....'

'... You'll keep your trap shut and do as you're told....'

'... I'm not letting you do....' Michael slung the bags over his shoulders while still holding the gun. He grabbed the lapels of Anwar's coat and spun him around before prodding the barrel of the gun in his back. 'You're coming with me as insurance.'

Michael called over the counter. 'Stay exactly where you are for the next ten minutes, or this man will get it. Do you understand? Don't even think of moving those pretty arms of yours, girls, to reach for the alarm button. If I hear one iota of the siren, this man gets his comeuppance.' He saw them all nodding. 'I can see you all understand me. Stay like you are and nobody will come to any harm.'

Michael prodded Anwar to start walking. 'Slowly and gently, Doctor Patel, we don't want to attract attention, do we? That's it, nice and easy!' They walked the entire length of the bank and approached the exit revolving door. 'Speak to the nice man, please,' Michael prodded his back again as they neared the bank assistant standing in the corner, who hadn't a clue what was going on. To him, it was just another dull Friday morning in the building society.

'Thank you,' Anwar gestured as the bank assistant smiled. Michael offered his smile before they exited through the revolving door. Michael heaved a sigh of relief, realising his scheme had worked. 'All that planning, I've actually done it,' he thought with mounting optimism. 'Now, I've only to get away. Time for part two of my plan!'

'Carry on walking; easy does it, doctor, we're going over to the church....'

'... but... but...'

'... I know, but I can't help it. I know a church isn't top of your list for a place to visit, but I've no alternative.' They ambled slowly over the roadway looking both ways to avoid any traffic and entered through the church's lych-gate. 'Slowly, doctor, we're only visitors to the church like all these other lovely people.' Michael prodded him in the back with the gun, 'Don't underestimate me, Anwar. I won't hesitate to send you to meet Allah if I have to.' They sauntered up the pathway that led to the southern doorway.

The second that Michael had gone through the bank's revolving doors, Miles Buffet had crept forward and reached for the alarm button. He pressed it and a loud, screeching siren wailed out across the town centre. Michael and Anwar looked back and joined with everybody else as they stared towards the building society, before calmly entering the church's nave.

Once inside, Michael peered down the aisle to see the vicar standing at the altar rail, giving out pieces of bread to kneeling parishioners. At the same time, the verger offered a glass of wine. Michael had entered the church during the regular morning Eucharist service, but nobody noticed him. He edged backwards to the door that led to the tower. Once through the door, he prodded Anwar to start climbing the spiral stone staircase. The one hundred and fifteen wedge-shaped, sandstone steps were well worn in the middle.

As part of his forward planning, Michael had sat on the bench outside the building society, looking up at the church tower. 'Of course,' he realised one drizzly morning as he sat in his dishevelled clothes, 'that's the perfect escape route. I can hold out in the tower until the fuss dies down.' A week before he entered the building society with his gun, he'd brought two carrier bags full of food and drink into the tower. He'd secreted them in a dusty, unused cupboard that held old brass hand-bells.

'What are we doing here?' Anwar pleaded with him, 'I have to get to my surgery; I have patients waiting to be treated.'

'Shut up, doc! It's your own fault; you shouldn't have intervened.'

'You can't get away with this, you know!'

'Can't I?' Michael asked, and laughed as they sat on a wooden bench looking at the 'Queen' bell hanging from a large wooden yolk. 'What's this then?' He showed the two bags full of money to Anwar; 'I think I've already got away with it, don't you?'

'What's that...?' Anwar asked. They cocked their heads before going outside on top of the tower and looked out over the town. Michael smiled as they saw two police cars, their sirens blaring and blue lights flashing, roar to a sudden stop outside the building society. A small crowd had gathered, peering curiously into the bank. They waved away the foul-smelling blue smoke that came from the police cars' brakes as they'd skidded to a halt. Crouching behind the castellated battlements, Michael and Anwar saw five police officers rush into the bank. 'Fancy a can of beer?' Michael asked. Anwar shook his head and looked to the floor.

'Of course, you lot don't drink alcohol, do you? What's it like being a Muslim?' Anwar didn't answer and began to think about how he could evade Michael's clutches. He saw that he'd put the gun in his coat pocket.

'Hello, Inspector, you're too late!' Miles Buffet called to Donald as he strolled through the bank. James, Nicky and two other armed, uniformed constables followed.

'How many were there?' James asked.

'Only one man!' Loretta interrupted.

'One solitary man has robbed your building society... wow!....'

'He was armed with a gun.' Miles added, quickly.

'Did he fire it?' Nicky asked.

'Fortunately, no, because we did what he asked,' Jane shouted.

'There's no need to shout, Jane. I think you're a little over-wrought, why don't....'

'... Of course I'm upset, Mr Buffet. The man threatened me with a gun.'

'Did you recognise the man...?' Donald asked.

'Yes, of course, we did!' Miles stressed, 'it's that damned tramp who's been sitting outside on the bench for months. He's been watching us, planning all this, hasn't he?'

'Has he actually been in the bank before today?'

'Every week; Michael comes in here to make a deposit. It's usually only a few pence at a time, but….'

'It sounds like he's been sizing you up in preparation for today?' James suggested, 'do you know his name?'

'I can do better than that,' Loretta butted in, 'here's his deposit book. He gave it to me and asked me to deposit all the money we have in the tills and the vault into his book.' She passed it to James. He read aloud.

'Listen here, gov. Michael Ridgeway, 15 Hawthorn Crescent, Chasetown. I see what you mean, Miss. There's only twenty-one pounds, fifteen pence balance in the book.'

'If you study it further, twenty pounds of that was put in by his mother.'

'James, you and Nicky get to his home now. Take Constable Walker with you in case he's there; he may still be armed with the gun. Find out everything you can.'

'Do you think he's stupid enough to go back home after this?' Nicky asked. The manager answered.

'Inspector, I would think he's quite likely to do that. He was very calm and unruffled. He didn't raise his voice, so much so the bank floor officer stood by the doorway throughout the whole of the robbery and didn't realise anything was amiss. When he walked out, he didn't rush; Michael gave the appearance that he'd visited the bank as normal and afterwards going for a stroll around the town.' James, Nicky and Constable Walker dashed out of the bank.

'Oho! Three of them are leaving,' Michael whispered, as he watched from the tower. He stared at Anwar. 'You've gone quiet, doc!' Michael brought the gun back out of his pocket.

'… in case you're thinking of doing anything stupid.'

'How long are you going to keep me here?'

'As long as it takes, old son. As long as it takes. Now, shut up and make yourself comfortable.'

Back in the bank, cups of tea were being passed around. 'You haven't told the inspector about his accomplice, Mr Buffet' Jane offered.

'I didn't see an accomplice,' the manager countered.

'You were busy unlocking the vault, sir.' Loretta voiced sarcastically. 'I'm not sure if Doctor Patel was his accomplice, but they were talking together for quite a while as the robbery was taking place.'

'Doctor Anwar Patel from the Ganges practice in High Green?' Donald asked, in surprise.

'Yes, the doctor! He's our family doctor, I think he was only using the bank as he normally did, but he certainly knew Michael.'

'Do you know how much this Michael Ridgeway got away with?'

'Not yet!' The bank manager was abrupt in his answer. Donald recognised his current embarrassment and the grief he imagined he was going to get from his superiors.

'Can you describe Michael Ridgeway?'

The bank official who had been standing by the door came forward. 'Mr Buffet?'

'Not now, Joe. Can't you see I'm busy?' The manager's dismissive gesture displayed the low esteem in which he held this employee.

Joe persisted. 'But, Mr Buffet…'

'Joe, you must be busy. If you aren't, I can soon find you something to do, like sweeping the floors, for instance.' The manager's icy stare was sufficient to make any other employee slink away. Joe held his ground and stared back.

'Haven't you gone yet…?'

'… I'm going! But if you think the head office would be pleased if they knew one of their chartered accountants was employed sweeping floors, then so be it. I'll make sure I put the task on my CV.' He turned to go.

'Joe! Come back! I'm sorry. This is a bad business for everyone.'

'Then it's even more important at a time like this, that you showed a little respect for your staff and a lot more leadership….'

'… That's enough…! You are being impertinent.'

'Inspector, if my manager won't listen to me, perhaps you will…?' He turned to Donald. 'All I was going to point out is something that must be clear to a blind man and his dog. I bet Michael Ridgeway knew all about it.'

'What's that, Joe?' Donald smiled.

'That!' Joe pointed to the corner of the room. 'The camera!'

Everybody turned to see where Joe had pointed. Jane and Loretta sniggered. Miles Buffet's face turned red.

'It seems to me, Mr Buffet, you should listen more to your staff,' Donald added, to the manager's mounting embarrassment.

'Um! Er! Of course, I was aware of that. I hadn't got around to it yet.'

'Yes, of course you were.' Donald added, with a smirk.

'So, you'd know if it is working and has a rewind facility to examine any recording?'

'Um! Er! I'll have to check on that.' Joe came forward again.

'Yes, it does, Inspector. The digital tapes are automatically discharged and reset every evening. It's motion-activated and there are three situated around the bank. This one is especially positioned to record everything that happens at the counters. They have 4G capability and full sound rewind from the integral microphones, but I'm sure Mr Buffet would have told you that.'

The manager tried to disguise his acute embarrassment by asking Joe to show Donald where to access the recording in the utility room, where the mainframe computer was situated.

'There's no need, Inspector!' Joe walked to the other side of the counter. 'Can I access your monitor, please, Loretta?' He spoke aloud as he expertly used the keyboard. 'The camera uses the well known YCC365 Plus technology. The code for this camera is 556G. Let's see! Here we are. See, Inspector!' He rewound the images until Michael Ridgeway stood directly in front of the camera in the act of pointing the gun straight at Loretta.

'Fantastic, Joe. You certainly know how to operate this aspect of your security system.' He half-turned to Miles Buffet, 'you must be very proud that you have such capable staff, sir.' The manager stayed silent.

'Would you like a printout of this, Inspector?' Joe asked. Donald nodded and Joe pressed the printer icon. 'Be a dear and pop into office number three, please, Jane, to get the photo.' Joe turned back to Donald. 'The printer in office number three is the only one currently working.' Miles Buffet's embarrassment increased further each time Joe spoke.

Jane returned with the printout. 'Thanks for the photo. Are the other cameras working, Joe?' Donald called.

'All of them!'

'You say they simply walked out of the bank?' Donald asked the crimson faced manager.

'Yes! As calmly as if they were walking along the prom at a seaside resort in the sunshine.'

'I'm wondering if a camera facing the doorway would give an indication where Michael and the doctor went after leaving the bank?'

'Bring up the image from that camera, please, Joe?' the manager asked, eager to be able to revert to exercising his authority.

'Here we are,' Joe muttered, 'have a look!' Everybody stared at the images of Michael and Anwar walking through the revolving door. 'They seem to be walking straight over the road,' Joe added.

The manager raised his voice at Joe. '... and look at what that camera also showed, you imbecile, Joe! You stood there like a shop manikin and let the robbers walk straight past you.'

'That's not fair, Mr Buffet,' Loretta butted in, 'Anybody standing all the way down by the door, including Joe, wouldn't have known what was going on!'

'Speak when you're spoken to, Loretta.' Miles chastised her.

'Oh! Pardon me for breathing, I'm sure!' Loretta scoffed. Donald looked in exasperation at the building society manager, clearly out of his depth in the responsible position he held.

'Well, Joe? What do you have to say for yourself? I'm sure when Head Office holds an inquiry into all this, they'll be extremely interested to hear what you have to tell them. That will make a delightful addition to your CV.' Joe was not to be outdone.

'Sir, I'm sure you're aware that the cameras have been continuing to record our conversations over the past thirty minutes. Head office, I'm sure, will review everything that has happened today.' The manager stared towards the camera and swallowed hard. '... and there's something that has really puzzled me since I learned the bank had been robbed. With respect, sir, can I ask why you didn't raise the alarm earlier?'

'... but, Joe, the robber always held a gun on us,' Jane added.

'Thank you, Jane. Joe obviously doesn't know what it feels like to have a gun pointed at him, does he?'

'I understand that, sir. It must have been very frightening.' The manager nodded.

'Mr Buffet did press the alarm button as soon as Michael Ridgeway left the bank,' Jane added again. The manager nodded with increased vigour.

'Very commendable,' Joe pursed his lips, 'but why, oh why, didn't you raise the alarm earlier, sir?'

'You heard what Jane said....'

'Yes, but she doesn't know what I know, and I assume you do too, sir?'

'What's that...?' Mr Buffet gasped in frustration.

'We both attended the company seminar in Cheltenham three months ago....'

'… and?'

'Item three on the agenda that day…' the manager looked blank. Donald listened with interest.

'On your mobile phone, sir, you and only you in the bank, has an icon installed to be able to raise the alarm remotely, without anyone knowing. As we all do, I assume you keep your mobile in your pocket. You only had to put your hand in your pocket and press the stop/start circular button twice to raise the alarm. You could have done that the second you realised the bank was being robbed. You've already mentioned bringing my conduct to the attention of our Head Office. I assume you'll be raising this issue with them too, but then again, they'll know. They will only have to listen and watch the camera's recording of all of this.' The manager held his head in his hands; he had forgotten all about the facility he had on his phone. He walked back to his office.

Donald's ringing phone disturbed his presence with the bank staff. He turned away to answer his phone. 'Yes!'

'Gov, James here! Nicky and I have spoken to Michael Ridgeway's mother. She is distraught! Michael left her house this morning as usual. She has absolutely no knowledge of what Michael was going to do. We believe her, gov, she's a genuine lady.'

'Okay, James, thanks. Get back to the office; we have to find where Michael and Anwar have gone.'

'Inspector?' Joe called, 'there's one more thing I should mention that I'm sure you already know about. This is especially relevant to what you just said on your phone.'

'Go on!'

'There's another camera you can access.'

'Is there? Where?'

'Come with me, please. It's not the building society's camera, you understand. It belongs to the town council. Miles Buffet watched Joe lead the inspector down the bank past his glass-sided office. He slumped in his chair, holding his head in his hands. Once outside the bank, Joe pointed to the tall pole standing next to the bandstand. 'There, Inspector. On top of that pole, there's a camera. It must record everything that goes on in the town centre. You may be able to see where Michael Ridgeway went after he left the bank?'

'Well, thank you, Joe. I've never noticed that before. You've been extremely helpful. I hope your superiors at Head Office recognise how valuable you are to their organisation. I'm going back to my office now, please give my regards to your manager.'

Returning to the bank, Joe knocked on Miles Buffet's door and walked in. 'The Inspector has gone now, sir; he asked me to give you his regards.'

Miles lifted his head and looked daggers at Joe. Knowing cameras could pick up his conversation, he mimed. 'Piss off!'

'Yes, I will, thank you, sir.' Joe smiled and closed the door.

Fifty-four

Donald walked up the steps into Cannock police station ten minutes before James and Nicky returned from Michael Ridgeway's home. Donald heard their cheerful chatter as they walked into the office. He was pinning a photograph of Michael Ridgeway on the notice board. They came and stood beside him. 'This is Michael Ridgeway, pointing a gun at the building society cashier. This was taken from the security camera.'

'Oh, that's Michael Ridgeway, is it? I'm sure I've seen him somewhere before!' Nicky exclaimed.

'Probably around the town centre. The building society's cashiers told me he's been sitting on benches in the town centre like a tramp for the last six months.'

'Isn't this Michael Ridgeway?' James asked, as he pointed to the photograph Nicky had taken in Godfrey's Bookshop.

'Yes, it is! That's where I saw him, sitting in the bookshop.'

'… bloody hell! Look who he's sitting with in your photo,' Donald pointed out, 'there's Michael Ridgeway, Doctor Anwar Patel, and David Shaw.'

'It's like a school for criminals, gov,' James quipped, in jest.

'That's exactly what it is. Godfrey Warlock's protégés, all being schooled in how to commit vile, sensational crimes. It's like Godfrey is exacting some ghastly revenge upon society and mankind.'

'Gov, look at all the other people sitting in the photograph. We don't know them. Should we anticipate all these others are going to commit crimes as well?'

'It's something we have to consider, but I hope you're wrong, Nicky.'

Donald started to walk back to his office but turned. 'James, Nicky, I have to speak with Superintendent Woodhouse in a couple of minutes. I was going to come with you, but can the two of you go without me?'

'Go where, gov?'

'Oh, yes! Over to the council house. There's a camera on a tall pole in the middle of the town by the bandstand. Check it out and get a copy of the recording if you can. Looking at its orientation, it must have picked up the direction Michael Ridgeway and Doctor Patel went when they left the building society. Can you go now, please? The sooner we find out, the sooner we can track them down, and the stolen money.'

James and Nicky showed their warrant cards and identification at the town council's heptagonal-shaped reception building. After explaining what they wanted, the young receptionist rang a number, and a face appeared on her computer monitor. It was a video call, and she explained what the two police officers wanted. 'Send them to room 233, Louise,' the man asked.

James and Nicky explained to the Camera Utility Officer which images they needed to examine from the bandstand camera. 'You can have a copy of the whole film if you wish. Give me your email address, and I'll send it over.'

'Brilliant!' said Nicky, and they left. Back at their desks, they had the luxury of watching the video in comfort. Donald came into the office and watched the video with them.

'Here they come!' James exclaimed. 'They're out of the building society's revolving doors.'

'… and see the gun he's holding in Doctor Patel's back. This proves he's no accomplice to the robbery,' Nicky added.

'They're walking across the road. That's as far as the building society's cameras have shown,' Donald said, 'but where are they going now?'

'Bloody hell!' James exclaimed, 'the nerve of the man. They're going under the church lych-gate as if they're on a Sunday afternoon stroll.'

'… and other people are passing them by, oblivious to who they are.' Nicky added.

'Look where they've gone; straight into the church. They're in the church. The last place anybody would think of looking for them,' Donald guffawed, 'you've got to hand it to the lad; he's planned the robbery and his getaway really well.'

'Perhaps going into the church is another smokescreen, gov? There's another door on the north side of the church into the cemetery. They could have simply walked straight through the church and out to a waiting car on the other side.'

'That's certainly possible, Nicky. There's only one sure way to find out; let's pay Saint Luke's a visit. Who's the incumbent vicar?'

'I don't know, gov. It'll say on the notice board by the southern lych-gate.' Nicky prompted.

'Here it is, the Reverend John Taylor,' Donald read from the notice board before the three of them walked up the path where they'd stood in the honour guard for Constable Joe Swales' coffin a few weeks before.

They lifted the wrought-iron, circular handle and entered the church. Soft organ music was gently playing one of Chopin's nocturnes. They felt the unique stillness and calm that can only be experienced in a church. Although it was dry outside and their shoes weren't dirty, they felt obliged to wipe their feet on the coconut matting inside the door. Donald looked towards the altar and saw a priest clad from neck to foot in a white surplice. The sunshine filtering through the stained glass windows highlighted the starched, clean white gown. After exchanging greetings, Donald held a photograph of Michael Ridgeway before the Reverend John Taylor. 'Have you seen this man? We know from camera footage that he came into the church this morning.'

The vicar studied the photograph before shaking his head, 'I've never seen him before, sorry!' Donald lowered the photo, but stopped. 'Oh, wait a minute, yes, I think I have! Let me have another look. Hmm! This man in the photo is smartly dressed, but he looks like a scruffy tramp who regularly sits on the bench outside the church wall by the building society.'

'Yes, that's him....'

'... oh dear! Is that a gun he's holding?'

'He robbed the Assured Providential Building Society this morning and got away with two bags full of money. He was also holding a hostage, Doctor Patel....'

'... Doctor Patel from High Green? He's my doctor.'

'... and mine! Anyway, please keep a lookout for them.'

'Inspector, if they did come into the church, you do know there's another way out. They could have passed straight through...?'

'... excuse me for interrupting, Reverend.' They turned to see an elderly woman wearing an apron. She was flushed, panting, and her semi-circular spectacles were steamed up.

'Yes, Florence, what's the matter? You seem anxious.'

'Reverend, you know I always come and clean the bell ringers' room on a Friday morning after Thursday night's campanology session....'

'... yes, Florence.'

'Well, I've finished now, but before I go, I thought I'd better come and let you know there's somebody up at the top of the tower, outside, I mean. I can hear them talking. I know you don't like anybody being up there as it's dangerous....'

'... What!? No, I don't! It's over seventy feet high ...'

'Well, I know that because you told me before, so that's why I'm telling you....'

'... How long have they been there?'

'Oh, I don't know. I heard them when I first started cleaning over an hour ago....'

'... and you've only just decided to come and let me know?'

'I did come down about half an hour ago, but I saw you praying at the altar and I didn't want to disturb you....'

The Reverend Taylor looked expectantly towards Donald.

'... yes, it could be!' Donald turned back to James and Nicky, who examined relics and artefacts of the town's mining history displayed on a table.

'James, Nicky. The cleaning lady over there has said there's someone up in the tower....'

'... do you think?'

'It's a distinct possibility. If it is Michael Ridgeway, don't forget he's armed.'

'Shall I go and have a look...?'

'I'll come with you, James.'

They gently opened the arched wooden door that led to the stone spiral staircase. They looked up at the underside of the wedge-shaped steps. They started climbing, holding on to the handrail, a thick braided rope hanging from the outside wall. Donald estimated they had risen through four complete revolutions and had passed two small windows before they came to another arched wooden door. James gently pressed the handle and peered around the door's black-stained jamb.

'It looks as if this is where the bells are,' he whispered. Donald followed. They looked upon a series of six different sized bells, all hanging from wooden yolks and the ropes attached to them. Donald put his hand to his lips, indicating that James kept silent as he prised open another smaller door.

They eased their heads through to see more rising sandstone spiral steps. Donald eased his head sideways, 'Listen,' he prompted. They heard Michael talking.

'Stop your moaning, doc; I've only got some bacon and mustard sandwiches. Can I help it if your lot don't eat bacon because of your religion? I didn't know I would have company, did I? You'll have to go hungry; it's no skin off my nose. That's all my Mom made for me, bless her cotton socks. I can't wait to get back home and show her how much the building society has let me have.'

'I've told you; I have patients to see....'

'... and I've told you; you aren't going anywhere, so shut your trap and make yourself comfortable. We've a long night ahead of us.'

Donald turned to James. 'That's Michael Ridgway, alright!' Donald murmured, 'and it's obvious he's still holding Doctor Patel. Did you hear what he said? He's prepared to spend the night up there.'

'What shall we do, gov?' They carefully closed the door and looked out of the window over the town centre.

'Let's quietly go back down.' They re-entered the church to see Nicky talking to the vicar.

'Reverend! The bank robber, Michael Ridgeway, is up in your tower, and from what I heard him say, they will be spending the night there. I say *they* because he's holding Doctor Patel as a hostage. He's armed and dangerous, so here's what I want you to do. Clear the church of everybody. Then I'm going to put police officers at every vantage point around the church grounds. Nobody is to come onto church premises.' The vicar nodded. Donald reached for his phone. 'Superintendent, Donald here. I have a developing situation here and need more men, preferably armed.' He went on to explain to his superior what was happening.

'At this moment, Michael Ridgeway is unaware that anyone knows he's in the church tower. That gives us the advantage to get everything in place before we confront him.'

Back at his office, Donald telephoned Janet. He explained what was happening and not to expect him back home for the night. 'Please be careful, darling,' she whispered.

Fifty-five

As dusk approached, Michael and Anwar were snuggled under some old dustsheets that they'd found in the bell tower cupboards. They were unaware that twenty police officers, drafted in from the county constabulary stood guard at every access point around the church grounds. Blue and white striped plastic tape surrounded the cemetery and every gate and pathway, informing anyone who cared to look, that it is the site of a current police investigation. Superintendent Woodhouse had joined Donald and his officers standing under the overhanging flat roof outside the Assured Providential Building Society. From there, they had an excellent view of the church tower. They had rigged floodlights at each side of the church grounds, ready to illuminate the square, castellated stone pillar. Donald commanded the operation and had a megaphone prepared to talk to Michael. What was not apparent to anyone other than police officers were the armed riot-squad officers positioned on the roofs of nearby buildings overlooking the church tower. The nearest facility to the church was the post office across Market Street. Armed with a high powered 38 calibre rifle with a telescopic sight, Sergeant Albert Cross had a perfect view of anyone standing on the top of the tower. The post office building roof was slightly lower than the tower summit, meaning his rifle's trajectory would point upward.

Donald had ordered the town centre and nearby streets to be sealed off from the general public. Carrying out such an operation meant the media immediately became aware that something was occurring. As Donald prepared to give the signal to illuminate the tower, two burly police sergeants struggled to keep back harassing press reporters and photographers, eager to get a story. The town centre was quiet. Even pigeons seemed to sense that something momentous was about to happen and were content to keep to their usual rooftop roosts.

Godfrey Warlock had known long before what was happening. Michael had discussed the details of his plan with him weeks before. Godfrey crept stealthily through the town, positioned himself inside the bandstand where no one could see him, and awaited the impending confrontation. He smiled and licked his lips while pressing his crooked hands together, causing the brittle joints to crack.

The weather was benign and peaceful. A full moon sneaked along the pre-ordained heavenly trajectory and positioned itself, illuminating the centre of the town. Had anybody been standing near the church, seeing the clear sky, they would have been puzzled why rainwater was flowing from the mouths of the four grotesque gargoyles. It wasn't rainwater. Michael and Anwar had urinated onto the lead flashing that covered the tower's flat area. The steaming liquid channelled itself to the mediaeval carved stone figures. Michael, in particular, was desperate to relieve himself having consumed four litre cans of beer.

Godfrey Warlock, crouching in the moon's shadow from the ornate, pagoda-shaped bandstand's roof, smiled then grinned. 'That's my Michael bringing everything down to basics.' His face crumpled into a silent laugh, thinking of his protégés pissing onto the rooftop of a house of God. 'That seems a very apt thing to do,' he concluded, continuing his difficulty at not laughing aloud and giving himself away.

Another half an hour had elapsed while police put the final preparations in place. Anwar managed to doze in the tower even though Michael's loud snoring had previously kept him awake. He'd thought about how he could escape. but noticed that Michael always held a firm grip on his gun.

James and Nicky stood anxiously by Donald as he gave the signal to switch on the floodlights. Sergeant Cross and his armed colleagues trained their rifle sights on the tower's summit. The church and its tower had been illuminated many times before, for national celebrations and public festivities. The last occasion was when a new bell had been installed, but now the lights weren't coloured, or twinkling a rhythmic changing pattern; they were harsh, bright, white lights, penetrating every crevice in the centuries old stonework. Donald switched his megaphone to maximum volume and squeezed the trigger.

'Michael Ridgeway, can you hear me?' Donald's echoing voice clogged his hearing, as if he was speaking into a biscuit tin; to everyone else in the town centre, it sounded like a stark thunderclap announcing the start of World War Three! In the tower, Michael's serene dream of sharing an ice-cream cornet with his mother on

Blackpool's promenade instantly evaporated, and he jumped up. Seeing his head appear between the stone castellations, Sergeant Cross's first instinct was to fire his gun. His rigorous training had honed his reactions to fire at images suddenly appearing like tin animals moving across a shooting range at a fairground. He held his finger off the trigger.

He whispered into his lapel speaker connected to his armed colleague's radios, 'Be ready, but hold your fire until we get an instruction.'

Looking out into the night sky from the tower, Michael blinked. All he could see was the glaring floodlights blotting out anything else. 'What's happening?' he called.

'The police have you covered, Michael. Give yourself up!' Anwar whispered to him.

'Like hell, I will....'

'... Michael Ridgeway, we can see you. This is Inspector Lawrence of the Cannock Police. Come down, and we can talk about this sensibly. The town is sealed off. We have the church surrounded by armed officers. You can't escape....'

'... fuck off!' Michael bellowed out into the cooling night air.

In the bandstand, Godfrey's face lit up again. 'Good answer, Michael!'

Donald ignored his response. 'Michael, we know you have Doctor Patel with you. Send him down now. He has nothing to do with this. He has a family, a wife and daughters, think....'

'... he's staying here with me.' Michael yelled.

'You're leaving us no alternative, Michael. This has to end, *now*! Armed officers will come and drag you down from there....'

Michael peered out between two castellations and fired the gun towards the beam of one floodlight. He'd never fired a real gun before and was pleasantly surprised how easy it was. Anwar held his hands over his ears and screwed up his face. If he hadn't been taking Michael seriously before, he did now. He was trembling with fear.

On the ground, police officers, including Donald and his colleagues, instinctively ducked. Although the bullet hadn't gone anywhere near them, they now knew how dangerous Michael Ridgeway was.

While crouching on the ground, he turned to the superintendent. 'It looks as if this is going to take a while. Michael's not going to make it easy. I have an idea that might bring this to a peaceful end. James,

Nicky, go back to Michael's home in Chasetown and bring his mother here. Explain the situation to her; perhaps she can entice him down?' James and Nicky nodded and left.

'Good thinking, Donald. A peaceful end to this is what we all want.' Superintendent Woodhouse purred his approval of Donald's actions.

Fifty-six

For the following two hours, the standoff continued. Donald kept looking at his watch, wondering how long James and Nicky were going to be? From time to time, he kept provoking Michael, reminding him that he would never live to enjoy the money he had stolen. 'Why don't you give yourself up before anybody gets hurt?' Michael had ceased to answer back; he sat on the tower's leaded floor next to Anwar. With nothing happening, the police officers were getting tired and bored. The floodlights had been burning at full power for over two hours. One of them suddenly fused and fizzled out with a loud 'phut'. Part of the tower was suddenly in shadow. Anwar could see that Michael was getting tired too. He bided his time and tried to stay alert until he could see the right moment for him to slip through the door and escape.

Donald was in turmoil. This operation was his responsibility and there seemed no way it would end other than in tragedy. He tried again to bring some sense to Michael.

'We're not going away, Michael. No matter how long you think you can stay up there, we'll still be here. I know you had some food and drink with you, but that can't last forever. We'll starve you out if necessary. This is futile and senseless...' A constable passed a mug of hot tea to Donald. 'As it happens, Michael, I'm having a cup of tea right now; would you like one?'

Michael suddenly felt he'd had enough of Donald's constant chattering and griping; he leapt to his feet and stood between two castellations. '... Why can't you shut your cakehole, so we can all have some peace?' Sergeant Cross's index finger again pinched onto the trigger of his rifle. He could take a shot with a clear sight of Michael Ridgeway's head. He spoke again into his lapel speaker. 'Inspector Lawrence, this is Sergeant Cross on the roof of the post office. I have a clear sight of the target. Give me a sign, and this can all be over in a second.'

'No, wait!' Donald called. While Michael and Donald engaged in more bantering back and forward, Anwar saw his opportunity. He carefully slid across the floor and silently pushed the door open with his feet. Once he'd eased himself through, he stood and started towards the spiral staircase. Michael heard the door creak and looked around.

'You rotten swine!' Michael called after Anwar, and bounded through the door after him. Michael slid around the circular outer stone wall until he had him in his sight five steps below. He fired the gun twice into Anwar's back. He gazed in morbid fascination as the doctor's expensive, pin-striped suit became flooded with dark patches. Anwar teetered forward, managing to stumble down four more steps until he came to rest by one of the narrow windows. Michael suddenly saw the previous dark patches become bright crimson as the stark, illuminating floodlights pierced through the gloom into the circular staircase. Michael's perversion came to the fore as he watched Anwar tumbling forward, and he smiled. He heard his head crack on a stone step further down. Michael followed, watching Anwar's body, slide, slide, and somersault down the circular flight of stairs until it came to rest at the next window. Another floodlight through the second window revealed his staring eyes gazing unseeing towards the bright glare. He was dead.

In the bandstand, Godfrey stifled a regurgitating titter. 'Well, Michael, you're for the high jump now, aren't you?'

Out in the town centre, everybody heard the gunfire. Donald was still connected to Sergeant Cross's radio. 'Did you hear that, Inspector? I told you I could have stopped it all five seconds ago!'

'Stay alert, Sergeant!' Donald hissed into the speaker. He looked at the Superintendent, who Donald could see thought his Sergeant had been correct. He opened his mouth to speak, but turned when James called.

'Oh! Thank goodness you're back....'

'Gov, this is Michael's mother, Mrs Muriel Ridgeway. I'm sorry we've been so long. Mrs Ridgeway had gone to bed. She wears a hearing aid and turns it off when she goes to bed. We had to break in her rear door.'

'Mrs Ridgeway, I'm Inspector Donald Lawrence, we'd like your help. Your son, Michael, has....'

'Your officers have explained on the way here what Michael's done. I can't believe it; he's such a good boy.'

'I have a megaphone here. Can you talk to Michael and coax him to give himself up?' he passed it to her, 'squeeze the trigger here and speak into the mouthpiece.'

Mrs Ridgeway cleared her throat, 'Hmm! Ugh!' Michael had climbed back up to the tower and immediately knew it was his mother. She always cleared her voice like that before speaking. He looked out between the castellations and listened.

'Michael, this is your mother. The police have got me out of bed to come here and ask you to give yourself up. Please, son, before you get hurt. There are policemen down here with rifles. Please come home. I can make you your usual mug of cocoa before I tuck you safely in bed like I always do….'

'Mother!' Michael hollered, 'I'm sorry, I wanted to surprise you. I only wanted to treat you to a holiday in Blackpool, like we did when I was a lad. We used to have such lovely times with dad, didn't we?'

'It doesn't matter about that now, son, please come down so all these people can go home to their beds and….'

'… and where will I go, Mom? I won't be coming home with you– ever again. I can't spend the rest of my days in some stinking jail.' Michael's yells went hoarse with emotion.

'Michael, please…'

'… Mom, I've killed a man!' he screamed.

'Oh! Michael, you've been a silly…' Everyone looked up when they saw a movement in the tower. It was Michael. A police officer in charge of one of the floodlights focussed the beam to highlight him like a spotlight picking out the leading actor on a theatre stage.

'Michael, what are you doing…?' Holding her breath, she watched her son climb on top of the battlements. He stood between two castellations, looking up into the sky and raised the gun to his temple. Michael knew he still had three bullets left in the revolving chamber. He only needed one. Everyone looked upwards at the unfolding drama.

'Oh, my God!' Donald muttered.

'May the saints preserve us,' the Superintendent whispered.

Nicky and James were holding hands, and she gasped, 'Is he going to jump?'

In the bandstand, Godfrey giggled and clasped his hands together like a child asking a parent for more sweeties, 'Jump, Michael, jump,' he called.

Michael squeezed the trigger and didn't need to jump. Parts of his brain, highlighted in the floodlight, flew away from him into the night air. The rest of his body slumped like a stack of bricks falling from a bricklayer's hod, and plummeted the seventy feet to land in the cemetery below. Everybody heard and felt the sickening crunch of most of Michael's bones cracking and splintering as he hit the ground.

Mrs Ridgeway turned, and Donald held her as he felt her go limp. James saw her collapse and helped by easing her into a sitting position on the floor. As James and Nicky attended to her, Donald muttered into his speaker. 'Show's over, folks; Sergeant Cross, you and your men can stand down. Officers in charge of the floodlights, can one of you shine it on the ground where the suspect fell, please?'

Superintendent Woodhouse looked to Donald. 'I'm off; send your full report when you can please, Donald.'

'Okay, Ernest… what's that?'

They turned towards the church tower. 'For God's sake, somebody is laughing.'

'Laughing? It sounds as if someone is having hysterics.'

'In these unpleasant circumstances, there's no call for that, can't you shut him or her up, Donald?'

'It's him! I recognise that hideous laugh, Ernest. Come with me and I'll introduce you to Godfrey Warlock.'

Donald and Ernest walked up the church path as James and Nicky watched their elongated shadows cast weird shapes and silhouettes across the cemetery. Nicky held her hand on Muriel Ridgeway's shoulders. 'When you're ready, I'll run you back home.'

'What the bloody hell do you think you're doing here? How did you get through the police cordon? No matter, I'm arresting you for trespassing onto a police incident.'

'Oh! You petty little policeman. Come and have a laugh. It's providence really. There! Look!' He pointed at Michael's broken body slumped across a gravestone. Michael's face and limbs were distorted with bloodied bones poking through the withered flesh. Some of his intestines hung over an upright marble headstone, dripping blood and faeces onto the horizontal concrete slab. Donald twisted his face in revulsion at the colossal, blackened hole in the side of Michael's head. The 19mm calibre dum-dum bullet had expanded inside his skull and blown his head apart. Godfrey started laughing again.

'Inspector Lawrence, you either shut that man up, or I will forget my rank and bring him down.'

'Shut it, Warlock! Why does it seem appropriate that you're here? Wherever there is chaos and misery, you show your face....'

... but, Inspector, look! It's not poor Michael Ridgway I'm laughing at, can't you read?' Donald and Ernest's eyes followed him as he walked away towards High Green. They turned back to the gravestone, puzzling at what Godfrey referred to?

They read the indented inscription carved into the granite slab.

'That man needs putting away. Who can interpret anything funny in that? Goodnight, Donald.'

Donald watched the superintendent leave before looking at the gravestone again, 'It does have a certain irony to it, though?'

Precious Gold, 1923-1990
Rich in name; Rich in God's blessings
that she knew one day would fall upon her.

Fifty-seven

A few weeks later, Donald strolled out of his office and made himself a cup of tea. 'I'd have done that for you, Donald,' Veronica scolded him, playfully.

'I know; thank you, anyway. I wanted to stretch my legs.' He stood and looked at everyone working and realised how much extra work everybody had contributed over the past few months. He frowned at the common link in almost every case they had been involved in; Godfrey Warlock. James looked across and caught his eye.

'Are you alright, gov? You seem miles away.' Donald walked over and sat between James and Nicky's desks, drinking his tea.

'I don't know what I'd have done without you two.'

'What do you mean, gov?' Nicky queried.

'All these multitudes of different cases, and most of them involving Godfrey Warlock. I can't believe we've had nearly a week now of quiet, dealing with nothing more serious than burglaries and traffic violations. Do you think he's gone away?'

'No, gov, he's still in his bookshop. I saw his slanted eyes staring out at me when I passed his shop yesterday as I was coming from the surgery.'

'Have you managed to tie up loose ends over Doctor Patel's cases?'

'Not all of them. How far do we go with these now, gov? Now Anwar is dead, do we let sleeping dogs lie? I can't help thinking what good will it do anybody? His patients are dead....'

'... I know. Perhaps it's best to let their families grieve in peace and not cause them more anguish? I'm currently discussing aspects of the case with Superintendent Woodhouse.'

'It seems to me that Michael Ridgeway did us all a favour,' Nicky added.

'Did Godfrey acknowledge you yesterday, James?'

'No, he simply gave me one of those piercing stares. It's as though he's waiting to pounce.'

'I know what you mean.'

'It feels to me like the proverbial lull before the storm,' James added.

'Don't underestimate him, please,' Veronica added from across the office.

Donald looked at her, paused, and looked to the floor. 'I don't, Veronica. We've all been on the receiving end of his evil and pernicious activities. I think it's time we had a change, don't you? I'm sick of having our lives controlled by him. From this moment on, I'm going to be proactive and not reactive. Watch this space, folks.' He strolled back into his office, where he finished his tea while looking through his phone's address book. After pressing the icon for his former guvnor, Inspector Tom Cropper, he sat back and waited.

'I can't believe it; is that you, Donald? I heard the phone ring and looked at the photo I've got stored for you. I'm delighted to hear from you.'

'It's good to hear you too, Tom. It's been too long since we were together.'

'How's Janet? And of course, you're a father now.'

'Both mother and baby are doing fine as the standard hospital statement goes, but Zak is eight months old now.'

'Is this a social call, or can I help? Not as it matters, I'm always glad to hear from you.'

'Tom, I need your help, please. You always had a down to earth common-sense way of looking at things when we worked together. I could do with some advice, please. There's a unique problem here on my patch in Cannock that, quite frankly, has got me puzzled. I don't know how to resolve it.'

'Donald, I've been retired two years now, and you wouldn't believe how much I miss police work. I'd be glad to help.'

'Why don't you come and stay with us for a few days, a week if you like. I know when we worked together in Staffordshire on The Crucified Abbot case, you loved it up here. I know Janet will be delighted to see you.'

'When?'

'Tomorrow?'

'Ha-ha! I'm on my way!'

Janet and Tom welcomed Tom into their home. 'This is Zak Lawrence, eh? You have a wonderful family, Donald.'

'... and another on the way,' Janet added with a laugh.

'You've both come a long way since you went on that walk down the Thames beaches on the Mudlarks case, haven't you?'

'Pardon the pun, but so much water has run under the bridge since then.'

While eating their evening meal together, Donald explained the multiple cases he'd had to deal with since getting the Inspector promotion.

'It must seem to you like a poisoned chalice?'

'Yes, it does at times. Life was certainly simpler and more enjoyable when I was a Sergeant with less responsibility. As I said to you, if Godfrey Warlock was out of my hair....'

'... That's the nature of promotion up the ranks. I know you'll come to deal with it as easily as you ever dealt with anything at The Yard when you were a constable.'

'I'll never have your common-sense way of assessing problems, Tom. Our old gov, Jack Croaker, depended upon you so much.'

'What's this Doctor Godfrey Warlock like?'

'Why don't you come into the office with me in the morning. I'll introduce you to my staff. After coffee, we'll pay *Godfrey'sBookshop* a visit, and I'd welcome your opinion of the man.'

'Good morning everybody, I'd like to introduce you all to my old friend, Inspector Tom Cropper....'

'... now retired!' Tom interrupted with a laugh.

'Everything I know is down to Tom. He's the best friend and mentor anyone could have....'

'... be careful, Donald, if my halo slips any further, you'll see my bald patches.'

'Gov, in the office the other day, you said you thought it was time for a change in how we dealt with Godfrey Warlock and something about being proactive and not reactive. Is this what you meant, bringing Inspector Cropper in, I mean?'

'Yes, I did, but Tom is here in an unofficial capacity as an advisor and friend....'

'As Donald knows, when we worked together, we used to come up against stumbling blocks, that for a while seemed insurmountable, didn't we, Donald...?'

'Yes, and then somehow you'd come up with a brilliant solution and then everything was alright again.'

'I think it's best to take things back to basics and analyse what the problems are and what to do next. The trouble with us coppers, I include me because I'm still a copper at heart, we are decent people and play by the rules. The trouble is villains don't, so they always have an advantage. I'm not recommending we ever break those rules but pick your moment and go around them. Make your own luck. Anyway, that's the mantra that used to get me out of right pickles at times. Sorry for the lecture, everybody.' Tom turned when Veronica handed him a cup of coffee.

'Shall we have a walk around to the bookshop, Tom?'

'I'm eager to meet this Godfrey Warlock.' Veronica heard Donald and Tom talking as she sat outside Donald's office. She waited for them to pass her and commented to Tom.

'The man you're going to meet is pure evil, Inspector Cropper....'

'... I told Tom what happened to your husband.'

'I tried my best to do away with him myself, but....'

'... He knows that also, Veronica.'

'I'm sorry for your loss; I'll be pleased to help if I can?'

'This is a nice little town, Donald; I can see why you like it here,' Tom enthused as they ambled around the large open plan square. He peered at the quaint, half-timbered buildings, including the pagoda bandstand and Saint Luke's church. Further along the paved area, he looked over a low red-brick wall. 'This is unusual to see in the middle of town.' He referred to the pristine bowling green next to High Green. They watched two elderly men stooping over the black bowls they delivered to see which one was next to the smaller white Jack.

'It's a pity the pleasant view isn't extended any further though,' Donald screwed his face in anxiety. Tom looked across to see why Donald's comments had turned downbeat. He was looking towards *Godfrey's Bookshop,* where Godfrey was standing on his doorstep watching them.

'Is that the infamous bookshop?'

'Yes, and Godfrey Warlock himself keeping an eye on us. Can you see him?'

'Yes! He presents an ominous aura; I can sense that before I've even meet him.'

'Let's do that now; he seems to be waiting for us to go over.'

'Good morning, Inspector. How are you keeping and how's that lovely wife and son of yours? I haven't seen you for a couple of weeks...'

Donald wasn't going to extend the pleasantries that Godfrey offered. 'That's because things have quietened down a little since

Michael Ridgeway tumbled from the church tower. And I know you're only too aware, as I am, that I only ever visit you when there is trouble involving yourself. So that's why I haven't been here lately…'

'So, what brings you to my bookshop this fine morning? I can't see any trouble, can you…?' Godfrey motioned towards Tom, who he realised was studying him carefully.

'This is my friend, Tom.' Tom's only acknowledgement of Godfrey was a slight nod of his head.

'… another police colleague, I presume, come to examine my renowned bookshop, no doubt?'

Tom baulked at Godfrey's obsequious sickly leer and looked towards the shop window.

'Are you looking for any particular book, Tom? I have all sorts inside on every subject you could name.'

'Nothing in particular.' Tom didn't want to get involved or listen to his facetious ramblings.

'A man of few words, I see. Well, this curious world of ours caters for anyone, and everyone is different, but you are welcome to step inside. You too, Inspector; forgive me if I'm wrong, but this is the first time you've paid me a social visit…?

'This isn't a social visit, Warlock, and never could be. Why would I want to come and spend time at this school for criminals?' Donald had already reacted adversely to Godfrey's sarcasm. He noticed Tom's reproachful look. 'I'm sorry, Tom. Godfrey may have a short memory, but I don't. The last time we were in each other's company, he…' Donald pointed to Godfrey, 'he was doubled up in laughter at a poor, deluded man who'd committed suicide at the church tower….'

'… ah! Yes, inadequate Michael. He was really gullible….'

'Let's have a look inside, Donald.' Tom gently tugged Donald's coat sleeve, eager to avoid seeing Donald get more and more wound up by Godfrey.

'Mind the step,' Godfrey shouted, as he continued to stand on the pavement, calling to a passer-by. Tom and Donald ambled along the avenue of bookshelves.

'It is gloomy in here,' Tom spoke quietly, 'I can understand how Veronica thought she may have shot Godfrey. What's down there?' he motioned to the brighter lit reading room.

'That's where all of Godfrey's so-called students are studying.'

'Hmm! Let's have a look.'

The reading room was full of young and old, reading books. Tom whispered, 'Do you know these folks?'

'Not by name. I may have seen a few of them about the town. I hope this is all I'll ever see. Godfrey's readers usually progress to committing the crimes that I've had to deal with ever since I came to Cannock.'

'What's that on the far wall?' That looks interesting. They walked past the readers, who didn't even look up. 'It's a notice board, full of newspaper clippings.'

'Yes, and every item is reporting a crime committed by Godfrey's former students.'

'You have had a busy time. Wow! Some are gruesome! Do you know what this reminds me of?' Donald looked back at the notice board, wondering what Tom meant.

'Our own incident boards we used to have in Scotland Yard. I noticed you've kept up the same method with the notice board in your office.'

'It keeps our minds focussed on what we're dealing with, doesn't it?'

'Except there's one major difference it seems to me, Donald?'

Tom felt his skin tingle, paused, and looked back down the room. He saw Godfrey standing at the far end, watching them. Donald turned and locked icy stares with him.

Turning back to the notice board, Tom continued. 'This notice board glorifies violence. All the evil acts carried out by whom you say were his students. It's a celebration of past victories, to encourage these poor sods sitting here currently under his influence and control. When we consider what you're going to do about Godfrey, we have to think about where all these people come from.'

Donald looked back at the people, some of whom returned his stare.

'There's even a newspaper article here, lauding *Godfrey's Bookshop* as some sort of tourist attraction....'

'... yes, I was fuming when I read that in the local newspaper. You asked me earlier if I recognised anybody here. The bloke that wrote the article is sitting in the third row back there.' Tom was still concentrating on the notice board, overflowing with photographs, articles and reports.

'Donald, what this also reminds me of is a trophy cabinet. Other people awarded cups and shields for achieving excellence at sports or education degrees would display them on their sideboard at home. This notice board stands for Godfrey's trophy cabinet. He's proud of all this misery and chaos brought about by people he's nurtured. What we're looking at here is his downfall, Donald.'

'Forgive me, Tom, I don't see how?'

'Don't you see, he's hung himself by his own petard!' Donald looked as confused as ever.

'In Shakespeare's play, Hamlet! It's a phrase he wrote in the play. In today's parlance, it means a bomber has blown himself up by his own bomb. Godfrey's source of strength is also his weakness. Where does he get his readers and converts? – by publicity!' Tom paused before carrying on. 'Godfrey's immensely proud of all this, and what does it say in the Bible, in the book of James 4:6…?' Donald looked in deference at Tom's grasp of bringing complicated issues down to simple ways of dealing with problems.

'… pride comes before a fall. Or the actual words are, *pride goeth before destruction and a haughty spirit before a fall.*'

Donald's frown disappeared from his forehead. 'I can see you understand me now.'

'We can also use the publicity. Two can play at that game.' Donald nodded.

'Good day, Mr Warlock,' Tom offered, as they walked back through the shop. Donald didn't even acknowledge him. Godfrey gazed after them, feeling diminished and insecure. For once, he had met someone who didn't succumb to his influence and, for the first time during his occupation of the town, felt threatened, sensing his time in Cannock was coming to an end.

Walking through the town, Tom saw the open-air pavement restaurant where adults and children were sitting. 'Let's stop and have a coffee; it's a beautiful day.'

Waiting for their coffee to be served, Tom smiled at Donald. 'It's wonderful to see the success you're making of your life and how you're putting into practice what you learnt at Scotland Yard….'

'… if there's any success, it's down to you, Tom, and our old gov, Jack Croaker. Frankly, I don't share your optimism. This Godfrey Warlock is…'

'… he's an evil man, perhaps the most formidable opponent I or any of us have faced before. And it's a perfectly natural reaction what I see with you and him. You let him get to you; you allow him under your skin. Try to ignore his ramblings. Every syllable that comes from his mouth… ah, here's the coffee… is designed to intimidate, cajole, and influence. It's as though his mission is to hypnotise everyone into his way of looking at life and how the world functions.'

'I'm not the only one around here that thinks he's the devil. Satan himself has positioned himself amongst us here in this town, causing mayhem and destruction….'

'… you know how I feel about things like that; remember back to Ben Strange at The Crucified Abbot. There's no such phenomenon as the devil. Human beings invent such fictitious creatures to berate, punish and condemn themselves. Godfrey Warlock is homing in on that human emotion and using it for his own purposes.'

'I respect what you're saying, Tom, but many won't agree with that, especially Veronica, my secretary.'

'Look around you, Donald. Happy people enjoying life and being alive. A more contented future beckons you. Godfrey Warlock is the antithesis of everything good in this world. *Godfrey's Bookshop* and his books are destined for a massive bonfire.'

Fifty-eight

A week after Tom had returned home, he held a video call with Donald. After exchanging pleasantries, he explained he'd carried out what they'd previously agreed.

'You'll recall, Donald, I told you I have three good journalist friends in Fleet Street. They've prepared a coordinated article based on the information you provided. It will appear in each of tomorrow's editions. I'm going to send it to you, so you can have a first glance before they publish the newspapers. I'm sure this will bring about closure regarding Godfrey Warlock and his bookshop.'

Donald's fingers tapped out a musical rhythm on his desk, waiting for Tom's email to arrive. A loud ping came from his laptop speakers. Sitting outside, Veronica heard the noise. 'You have an email, Donald,' she called.

'Thanks, Veronica, I'm on it.' His face broke into a massive grin as he read Tom's message.

Hi Donald, my journalist friends have prepared the following editorial article.

The publication appears in 'Daily Echoes,' 'The Morning Telegraph,' and 'The Eclipse.'

Between them, they have the largest circulation in the country. Everyone will become aware of Godfrey Warlock and what he stands for.

Best of luck, Donald.
Cheers, Tom.'

Daily Echoes:
The Morning Telegraph:
The Eclipse.

Cannock is a small town in the West Midlands. It's famed for its proud mining heritage. The people are hardworking, cheery folk who don't ask much out of life except to be happy and content with their lot. So, when a new enterprise appeared in the town by the name of *Godfrey's Bookshop*, they were enticed by the educational and recreational facilities the proprietor, Doctor Godfrey Warlock, provided.

This is the sign that hangs above the bookshop

Doctor Godfrey Warlock,

Purveyor of rare and

unusual books

That was eighteen months ago. Since then, the crime rate in the town has quadrupled. Unexplained deaths and suicides have soared. A major terrorist incident was averted at the last second that had the potential to lay ruin to whole swathes of the Midlands into a nuclear disaster zone with mass radiation. The local building society has suffered its first robbery in its long, proud history. An arsonist set fire to an apartment block, killing eight people before blowing herself up at the town's war memorial. A disturbing incident occurred when a man fed his dissected wife to his pigs. Another normally peaceful man strangled his wife and then committed suicide on the steps of the bookshop. The latter incident gives everyone a clue why such a charming little town has suddenly attracted every hideous crime and unpleasant incident known to man.

Doctor Godfrey Warlock.

In the reading room in the rear of his bookshop, he houses his students, his converts. These ordinary people who naively entered his shop for nothing more normal than to seek an exciting book to read, are brainwashed and coerced into a life of crime. Hideous perversions of human nature are encouraged by **Godfrey Warlock,** to wreak havoc upon the local society. He's also very smart in that, until now, he's evaded being charged by the police for committing a punishable offence.

The authorities in the town and adjoining districts urge people to rebel against this man and all he stands for. Evil only triumphs when good people stand by and do nothing. This is your opportunity to drive this cancer from within your midst, not by taking the law into your own hands, but by shunning and ostracising him. Cease any patronage of *Godfrey's Bookshop.* You'll only bring misery and ruin to yourselves and your family.

Fifty-nine

Nicky rushed up the steps and dashed into the Cannock police station. She wasn't late for work; she wanted to tell everybody about the headlines and the articles in the newspapers she'd seen on the newsagents' pavement clapper boards in Stafford. She brandished a copy of 'The Morning Telegraph' to show everybody.

Her enthusiasm became tempered. The surprise she felt showed on her face when she saw everybody in the offices were reading their own morning newspaper. 'Oh, I see everyone has already seen this,' she uttered and sat down, deflated.

'Yes!' They heard Donald shout from within his office before he appeared in the doorway. 'Everyone tune in to Sky News live on your phones, now!'

James quickly opened his phone and watched as Cannock town centre appeared on the international news bulletin. The reporter replicated the newspaper articles but showed a live video clip of *Godfrey's Bookshop*. James and Donald gasped in unison when they saw the vast, angry crowd gathered in High Green.

'James, Nicky, Sergeant and anyone else in the office, come with me now to High Green.'

They dashed around the corner and immediately heard the din of the crowd. 'Lynch him,' 'Hang him,' were some more audible comments that Donald heard as they reached the bookshop. The crowd had pelted the front of the shop with rotting fruit and vegetables. A large crack stretched across two of the shop front's panelled glass windows. The sign hanging by chains from above the shop had been torn down and trampled into pieces on the ornate paving stones. A crowd of about fifty or more people stretched across the pedestrian area as far back as the bowling green wall. They shouted abuse and threats. Donald, Nicky, and James realised anything they tried wouldn't appease the angry mob; they were only interested in seeing Godfrey Warlock swinging from a hangman's noose. It wasn't only Sky Television that covered the unfolding drama; every television station and company from across the country were in High Green. Nicky also noticed two American news agencies setting up their cameras and tripods, NBC and Reuters.

In Milton Keynes, Inspector Tom Cropper smiled triumphantly as he poured himself a cup of tea. He was pleased and satisfied that he'd been able to help his friend and former colleague.

Janet fed Zak solid food on a spoon from her seat at the kitchen table. She didn't mind about the ensuing mess dropping on the table and the floor; the events in High Green fascinated her. 'Oh, look, Zak, there's your daddy on television,' she called and grinned.

In Brent Cross, London, Lucy and Eric watched morning television snuggled together in comfort from their double bed. She smiled contentedly, knowing she'd found something in life far more valuable and worthwhile than Godfrey's book could ever have given her.

On television, Janet watched her husband and James brave the objects thrown towards the shop front and enter the bookshop. Donald nearly tripped over the brass bell that lay on the floor.

'What?! I don't believe it!' Donald gasped. 'This bookshop used to be so murky and dim, now it's bright and airy. The same windows are still here, so what's changed?'

'What's happened to that damned step? Where's everybody gone?' James called as he went down to the reading room, finding it empty. He kicked out at the notices and newspaper articles that used to be on the notice-board. They were now strewn untidily around the floor. The noise of his boots kicking the floor echoed around the barren room.

The bookshop was an empty shell. The long, gloomy room that had bulged with bookshelves full of books from floor to ceiling now was a bare, dusty, open area. The only item of furniture that Donald recognised from his previous visits was the wooden counter that Godfrey used to stand behind. He winced when he recalled how Godfrey Warlock used to intimidate people as soon as they entered his shop. He poked his forefinger into the black bullet holes from Veronica's gun, garishly prominent in the whitewashed blank wall behind the counter. Donald's astonishment turned into curiosity as he noticed a brown envelope resting on the back of the counter. He picked it up and read it was addressed to him. He screwed up his eyes, trying to decipher the scrawling handwriting.

To, Detective Inspector Donald Lawrence.

Hello Donald, by the time you read this letter, I will have left and gone to pastures new. I enjoyed my time in your little town. I lasted longer than I usually do in most places. I put that down to your naivety and your trusting nature. You ought to wise up and realise that human nature's depravities only need a little encouragement to thrive. I know I'll always be in demand and can find somewhere to be able to practise my skills, developed over centuries of humanoid existence.

Godfrey Warlock.

Postscript.
There was only your son, Zak, who realised who I really am. If only you and your wife had listened to him?

If you enjoyed Godfrey's Bookshop,
the author's riveting novel,
'Mudlarks', exploring Donald and
Janet Lawrence's first case at New
Scotland Yard will captivate you.
The novel is published by New
Generation Publishing.

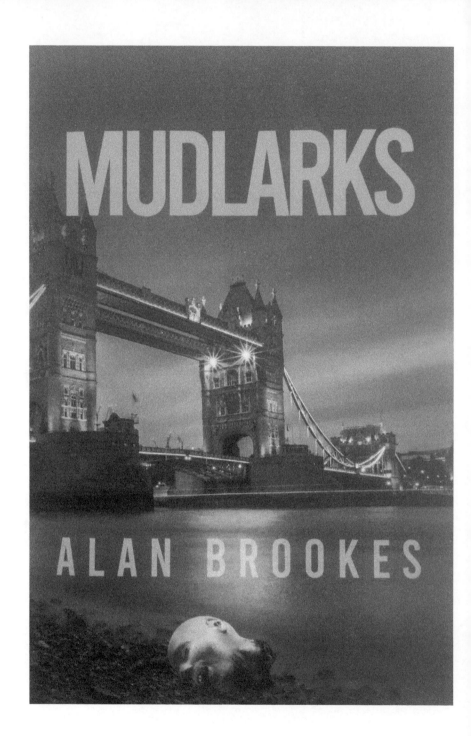

Published Reviews of the author's previous novel, 'The Crucified Abbott'

'The diverse titles of Alan's novels, alone, give an insight to his unique creativity.'

Nan Winter, Publishing executive at Authorhouse.

'This book benefits hugely from the author's sympathetic portrayal of his leading character and his expert knowledge of the landscape and environment of Cannock Chase.'

Brian Culdrose, Editor at Associated Press.

What a thrilling ride of suspense! The author has done an excellent job with this story. As soon as I started to read this book, I was hooked. I've found this book to be compulsive, exciting, sexy, full of suspense and a thoroughly enjoyable read. I really struggled to put this down. Several days were spent in a state of fatigue after nights reading well beyond normal sleeping hours where I would have literally propped my eyelids open with matchsticks if it had helped me keep awake so I could read on. That's how addictive I found this book.

He really knows how to tell a story and keep his audience engaged. I am not going to spoil this by saying anything about the plot, but in parts, it actually took my breath away, and I couldn't continue reading some paragraphs until I had settled down.

You couldn't guess what would happen next. The twists and turns were brilliant, and I'm sorry now that I have finished the book; this is because it was so good that I don't think I could find another book that was as good as this one and one which captivated me so much. You will have to buy it and read it, as I assure you, you will not be disappointed.

Janice Parker, Reader on Amazon.

ALAN BROOKES

Where forbidden desires return to haunt you

THE CRUCIFIED ABBOTT

Behind the ruins of the old priory at the summit of Brereton Hill, close by the village of Upper Slaughter and enclosed by two oak plantations grows the Abbot Ibáñez yew tree. This living relic is not so much a landmark, but is more than well known by all who live nearby, as a spooky feature embedded in the Triassic Sandstone of Cannock Chase. Here turtle doves nest on the primeval branches looking down at the myriads of foxgloves and the vivid yellow kingcups. The tree indeed holds some gruesome features, like the iron nails that crucified the Abbot. Still, few villagers will search for them in the shadows beneath those dark thickets where the sun seldom peeps through the trees. On their honeymoon, Detective Sergeant Donald Lawrence and his wife, Janet, from Scotland Yard in London, stay at *The Crucified Abbot* and become involved in pagan rituals that are still performed around the old yew tree. They witness a murder and are compelled to investigate. Their private and professional lives are compromised and become entangled with local villagers and the murderer. Whether the detectives live or die will depend upon them overcoming the evil that surrounds the ancient hotel.

About the Author

Alan was born in Chase Terrace, a coal-mining village in Cannock Chase, Staffordshire, in the English Midlands. He continued his father and grandfather's occupational legacy, working underground in the local coal mine before qualifying as a chartered land and mining surveyor.

Alan became a senior lecturer and a Master of Philosophy at Birmingham University. Before becoming an author, he achieved esteemed Chief Examiner posts with several United Kingdom examination boards and BTec, the United Kingdom's Business and Technology Education Council.

Apart from writing, his passion is playing the euphonium on the unique English brass band scene. From humble beginnings as a boy in a colliery band, Alan has performed in various musical ensembles across Europe, in France, Spain, Belgium, Holland, Italy, Cyprus, Malta and Germany.

Alan has written and published eight non-fiction books on the history of Cannock Chase in Staffordshire.

'Godfrey's Bookshop' is his fifth published fictional novel.

After living at a watermill in the Loire Valley in France, Alan now shares his time between his homes in Cannock, Staffordshire, and San Miguel de Salinas, a scenic coastal village on southern Spain's Costa Blanca.

Publications by Alan Brookes

Technical and professional
1991 **The Calibration of Electronic Surveying Instruments**
Published by The University of Birmingham
1993 **Electronic Creep in Theodolites**
Published by The Institution of Civil Engineering

Autobiographical
2001 **Arising from Coal Dust** Published by The Merault Press
2006 **The History of the Cannock Chase Colliery Brass Band**
Published by The Merault Press

Biographical
2005 **The Life of Doctor John Pooley** Published by The Merault Press
2007 **The Few of Cannock Chase (Chase Terrace)** Published by The Merault Press
2008 **The Few of Cannock Chase (Chasetown)** Published by The Merault Press
2009 **The Few of Cannock Chase (Burntwood)** Published by The Merault Press

Historical novels
2003 **Tales of Cannock Chase** Published by The Merault Press
2004 **Black Nuggets of Cannock Chase** Published by The Merault Press

Fictional novels

2016 **Bellesauvage** Published by Authorhouse

2019 **The Bellesauvage Redemption** Published by Authorhouse

2020 **Mudlarks** Published by New Generation

2021 **The Crucified Abbot** Published by New Generation

2022 **Godfrey's Bookshop** Published by New Generation

Sleeve notes

For a reader of modern literature, a new bookshop in town presents an exhilarating prospect.

To browse and find a book that you find fascinating is a worthwhile pastime for a bibliophile.

There are as many book subjects as there are readers, different books for different people.

Human nature's depravities only need a little encouragement to thrive. So, when the owner of a new, spooky bookshop caters for, and encourages, people's immoralities, chaos and mayhem ensue.

Detective Inspector Donald Lawrence, late of Scotland Yard, has been appointed the new Chief of Police at Cannock, Staffordshire, in the Midlands of England.

Following a short, quiet baptism into the post, his work becomes deluged with multiple murders, suicides, major terrorist incidents, a deranged arsonist, a bank robbery and troubling cases of indecent exposure, beheadings and a man feeding his wife's body to his pigs. Mass murders on an industrial scale prompt the inevitable conclusion that a serial killer can be added to Inspector Lawrence's phenomenal caseload.

These crimes are all perpetrated by ordinary people, hitherto regular, respectable members of society. Their lives change when they enter *Godfrey's Bookshop.*

Doctor Godfrey Warlock, the bookshop's proprietor, presents a mysterious figure who exists on humanity's edge. Who is he? Where did he come from?

Inspector Lawrence's former guvnor suggests Godfrey is an evil man, the most formidable opponent any police force have faced before.

Discover how Inspector Lawrence and his inexperienced team battles against a daunting foe, possessing inconceivable talents to bring about the end of everyday life in the United Kingdom, Doctor Warlock is always one step ahead of the law.

Lightning Source UK Ltd.
Milton Keynes UK
UKHW041829150622
404493UK00002B/43